COURT OF LIES AND DECEIT

COURT OF LIES AND DECEIT

MARION BLACKWOOD

SCARLETT PRESS

SIMON & SCHUSTER

London New York Amsterdam/Antwerp Sydney/Melbourne Toronto New Delhi

Originally published in 2025 by Marion Blackwood
First published in Great Britain in 2026 by Scarlett Press,
an imprint of Simon & Schuster UK Ltd

1 3 5 7 9 10 8 6 4 2

Simon & Schuster UK Ltd
7th Floor, 199 Bishopsgate,
London EC2M 3TY

www.simonandschuster.co.uk
www.simonandschuster.com.au
www.simonandschuster.co.in

Simon & Schuster Australia, Sydney
Simon & Schuster India, New Delhi

The authorised representative in the EEA is Simon & Schuster Netherlands BV, Herculesplein 96, 3584 AA Utrecht, Netherlands. info@simonandschuster.nl

A CIP catalogue record for this book is available from the British Library.

PB ISBN 978-1-3985-6124-3

Printed and Bound in the UK using 100% Renewable
Electricity at CPI Group (UK) Ltd

MIX
Paper | Supporting responsible forestry
FSC® C013604

For everyone who desperately wants
to have the freedom to choose their own fate

I

Pain crackles through my body like a lightning bolt. I cry out, but it only makes me cough blood onto the smooth surface beneath me. My mind spins. I'm lying on my stomach on what feels like a wooden table. Blinking hard, I try to push myself up, but my arms are so weak, they tremble with exhaustion. And my legs don't move at all. Another bolt of panic shoots through me.

"Careful!" Draven snaps from somewhere close to me. His voice is a vicious growl, brimming with threats and violence. "If you hurt her more, I will rip your fucking arms off."

"I'm sorry," a man stammers. "But I had to remove the shard quickly."

Blinking repeatedly, I try to get my eyes to focus on the room around me. But it's incredibly difficult because there is a sharp coldness in my back where the shard used to be. It's so intensely cold that it feels like it's burning me from the inside. And worst of all, I can feel it slowly spreading.

I gasp out a breath, and blood trickles down from the corner of my mouth where I'm lying with my cheek pressed to the cool wooden table. My hands are resting on either side of my head. I squeeze my fingers into fists and use every ounce of willpower I possess to force my eyes into focus.

My vision is still foggy, as if there is mist floating at the edges of it, and the room around me sways slightly, but I finally manage to take in my surroundings.

I'm in a room lit by bright faelights. The wall that I can see is completely covered by dark wooden bookcases. Vials and bottles in all shapes and colors line the shelves, and various blades and tools gleam next to them. I appear to be lying on a table in the middle of the room, and there is a man standing next to me. But because he is bent over my back, I can't see his face.

Pain shoots through me again. But just like last time, I can only feel it in my upper body. A wave of terror rises up inside me, threatening to drown me in its dark depths.

Then a pair of beautiful golden eyes appears right in front of me.

"Selena," Draven says.

And his voice is so heartbreakingly tender that tears well up in my eyes.

Agony floods his face. Crouched down next to the table beside me, he reaches out and gently strokes my cheek. His soft fingers carefully remove a few strands of my hair that had gotten stuck in the half-dried blood on my chin. Draven swallows hard and then rests his hand very lightly on my cheek.

"You're going to be okay," he promises. "Everything is going to be okay."

But given the fear in his eyes, I don't know who he is trying to reassure most. Me or himself.

I open my mouth to respond, but only a whimper makes it out. That burning coldness in my back is making it hard to concentrate on anything else.

"Oh no," the man who is bent over me suddenly says. The dread in his voice makes my hair stand on end.

For a moment, terror flashes across Draven's face as well before he manages to hide it. With a mask of confidence on his features, he leans forward and kisses my forehead before resolutely declaring, "You're going to be okay."

Then he stands up and turns to face the man who was bent over me. He has also straightened, and now that he isn't standing so close, I can see that he is a dragon shifter. His brown hair is disheveled, and his green eyes are nervous as he meets Draven's gaze.

"What is it?" another voice demands from somewhere behind me. It takes me a second to realize that it's Draven's best friend, Galen. "She will walk again, right?"

A hollow pit opens up in my stomach, and panic washes over me like a cold wave when the stranger doesn't immediately reply. Instead, his green eyes flit nervously between Draven and where I'm assuming that Galen is standing on the other side of the table.

"Her spine was severed," he finally replies, very carefully.

Which sounds an awful lot like a *no*.

That gaping pit inside me widens, threatening to swallow me whole.

"But that's not your biggest problem," the man continues before anyone can reply. His worried eyes settle on Draven. "The shard that struck her was ice fire from the Silver Clan."

All blood drains from Draven's face.

The sight of it rips the air from my lungs and sends a whip of fear through my chest.

"What does that mean?" someone else demands from the corner of the room.

Tilting my chin up slightly, I find two people standing there who I missed on my first inspection of the room. Alistair's orange-and-green eyes are locked on the stranger as he waits for him to answer his question. But Isera's gaze is locked on me. Her long black hair is windswept, but her silver-and-blue eyes are as cool and steady as ice as she watches me. There is an expression on her face that I can't read.

That burning coldness in my back creeps slowly outward. I gasp as the searing pain makes my head spin yet again.

"The ice flames the Silver Clan possesses can freeze a person completely," another voice replies from the same direction Galen's voice came from. It's Lyra, the usually so cheerful soldier from the Black Dragon Clan. Though right now, her voice is grim. "Basically turning the whole body into ice."

Memories flash before my eyes of the battle I witnessed on the mountainside outside the Ice Palace. Images of how Bane's and Jessina's ice flames encased the dragons from the Purple Clan, and how their bodies fell through the sky and shattered like glass on the stones below.

Dread washes through me. I try to swallow it down, but everything in my mouth tastes of blood and iron.

"And that shard made of those ice flames penetrated her body," the stranger picks up. "Which means that their magic is already inside her." His green eyes are filled with sympathy as he glances down at me. "It's going to turn her body into ice from the inside." He looks up at the others around the room. "It's slower than being fully encased by ice flames, which means instant death, but no less certain."

I suddenly can't breathe. I feel like someone just punched me in the gut and then ripped my lungs out.

That cold and unreadable expression remains on Isera's features as she drags her gaze up to the stranger. "She's going to die?"

"Yes."

A sob is wrenched from deep within my soul.

The room erupts into chaos.

Draven whips around and launches himself at Isera. Grabbing her by the collar of her silver tunic, he slams her up against the bookshelves so hard the glass bottles rattle behind her.

"Do something!" he growls in her face. "You have ice magic too."

"I can't," she replies.

His fist tightens in her shirt. "I was going to leave you. I was going to get Selena and my clan the hell out of there, and I was going to leave you collared and trapped inside that fucking Ice Palace." He stabs his free hand in my direction. "But *she* forced my hand. She forced me to buy her time that we really didn't have, just so that she could get the two of you out. So that she could save you." A muscle flickers in his jaw as he grinds out, "You owe her."

That unreadable mask on Isera's face slips for a second. Genuine shock pulses across Isera's and Alistair's features as both of them flick a glance at me.

I try to tell them to stop fighting, but I only manage to cough more blood onto the table.

"Don't you think I would help her if I could?" Isera snaps as she once more locks eyes with Draven. Now that her impassive mask has shattered, that world-ending fury that has filled her eyes these last few weeks has returned to her face. "If it was my ice, I could've just flicked my wrist and made it disappear. But it's not *my* ice. It's theirs. Which means I can't just make it disappear. All I can do is move it."

"Then move it! Move it out of her body!"

Isera's eyes begin to glow as she channels her magic and raises a hand.

But before she can do anything, the stranger screams, "Don't!"

Draven releases Isera's collar and whirls around to face him. The stranger swallows and takes a half step back when Draven's burning eyes lock on him.

Clearing his throat, he quickly elaborates. "Moving it won't remove it. I've already told you. The magic is already inside her body, which means it will continue to spread. So if you move the ice, all it will do is make it spread faster."

Isera's eyes stop glowing as she immediately cuts off the flow of her magic.

For a few moments, the room is eerily silent. The stunned quiet is so damning that it vibrates between the walls like death knells.

"Then what do we do?" Alistair at last asks, shattering the tense silence. His eyes are surprisingly desperate as he glances between me and the stranger. "There must be something you can do."

"I'm just a doctor," he replies with a helpless shrug. "For this, you need a healer. Someone with actual healing magic. Then they could both fix her spine and remove the ice."

Determination flashes across Draven's face. "Rin. Rin will do it."

"Rin Tanaka hates you," Galen points out softly.

"*Everyone* hates me," Draven growls back. "But they do as I say anyway."

The doctor scrambles back as Draven suddenly starts toward me. Alistair lurches into motion as well, and the scuff of boots behind my back tells me that Galen and Lyra are moving too.

"Let's go," Draven orders with a jerk of his chin. "We're getting out of this shithole village right now and—"

"Ryat." Isera's voice cracks through the room like the strike of a whip. "Stop and think for a moment."

Draven whirls back around to face her. She is still standing by the bookshelf he shoved her up against earlier, but she has now brushed her silver tunic down properly again. Her arms are crossed over her chest as she holds Draven's gaze.

"If you—" Draven begins, fury lacing his voice.

But Isera cuts him off. "Rin Tanaka is in the Ice Palace."

He jerks back slightly, as if he had completely forgotten that.

"Along with all the other clan leaders," Isera continues, her voice hard. "We escaped during that ridiculous allegiance ceremony where you were all supposed to renew your oaths of loyalty. Remember?" Her gaze is unwavering as she stares him down. "To get to Tanaka, you would need to fight your way back in through the entire might of the Silver Dragon Clan, along with all seven other clans."

"Then that is exactly what I will do!"

"And how long will that take? Huh? Can you win a war against the entire world in a matter of hours?"

"She's right," Galen interjects before Draven can reply. I still can't see him, but his voice is soft and gentle. As if he is trying to calm down a feral beast. But there is a hint of sadness in it too. "You know better than anyone how destructive their ice flames are. Selena will be long dead before we can win a battle against the Silver Clan alone. And with all other clans there too, we would never be able to break through and convince Rin to help us before the ice flames have spread through Selena's entire body."

Draven looks like someone just ripped his heart out. His mouth works up and down, but no sound makes it out. As if he wants to argue but knows that it is hopeless. The sight of it makes me want to wrap my arms around him and never let go. But I can't even push myself up from the table.

"There is another option," Lyra suddenly says into the ringing silence.

Everyone snaps their gaze toward her. I wish I could turn my head to look at her too, but the freezing, searing pain in my back is making it difficult to even cling on to consciousness.

The dragon shifter doctor finally seems to notice that, because he snatches a vial from one of the shelves and hurries toward me. A faint pop sounds as he pulls out the stopper.

"This will help with the pain," he whispers as he brings it to my lips. Helping me tilt my head, he pours the reddish-brown liquid into my mouth.

I swallow, wincing at the bitter taste.

Draven, who was watching the doctor like a hawk, at last shifts his attention back to Lyra and demands, "What other option?"

"Yes, what other option?" Galen cuts in. "The Orange Clan is the only one who has healing magic, so there . . ." He trails off, and he sounds completely stunned as he finally blurts out, "Wait. Don't tell me you're about to suggest what I think you're about to suggest."

Glass bottles clink as the doctor hurries over to another shelf and rifles through it. It makes Draven focus on him again, a fact that surprises the doctor enough that he almost jumps when he turns back around and finds Draven's sharp eyes on him.

Holding up a small green bottle, he explains, "This is like . . . liquid food. But twenty times stronger. It will give her body a burst of energy to help it heal the damage from the shard faster." His gaze darts to me. "So that she will be able to talk without coughing up blood."

"Then give it to her," Draven snaps. "Fast." His eyes, so full of pain, linger on me for a moment longer before he turns back to Galen and Lyra. "Stop speaking in riddles and just spit it out."

"Remember that skirmish outside the Unseelie Court five years ago?" Lyra begins. But she doesn't wait for them to reply; she simply continues speaking in a hurried voice. "After they dragged their people back in through the wards, I watched a woman heal them right there on the grass. Watched her heal serious wounds that are beyond the capabilities of a normal doctor."

Draven goes unnaturally still. "What are you saying?"

"I'm saying that there is a fae with healing magic in the Unseelie Court."

Shocked silence descends on the brightly lit room for a few seconds. The doctor ignores them all as he instead gently tilts my head again and brings the bottle to my lips before pouring pale green liquid into my mouth. I swallow it quickly, coughing again when a few drops hit my windpipe instead. But at least this potion tastes much better than the last did.

The sound of my coughing shatters the stunned silence, and Draven lurches into motion. Closing the final distance to the table, he very carefully moves my body and then picks me up without touching the wound in my back.

"Then we're going to the Unseelie Court," he declares.

His incredible scent of night mist and embers envelops me as he cradles me in his arms. My heart almost shatters at the way he is holding me. Like I'm the most precious thing in this world.

Leaning down, he brushes his lips over my forehead in a soft kiss and once more promises, "You're going to be okay."

Now that Draven is holding me, I can finally see Galen and Lyra for the first time since falling off Draven's back earlier. Lyra looks cautiously hopeful, her orange eyes lingering on my face for a moment before she looks back up at Draven. Next to her, Galen is watching me with violet eyes that are filled with worry. He drags a hand through his blond hair as he shifts his gaze back up to Draven.

“The Unseelie King has never let a dragon shifter through his wards,” Galen says carefully.

Draven’s expression darkens like an oncoming thunderstorm. “He will now. Or I will burn down this whole fucking world around his head.”

2

By the time we reach the forest that marks the edge of the Unseelie Court, I'm shivering from the ice that has spread through more than half of my body, and delirious from the painkiller potion Isera has been feeding me while we've been flying across the continent on Galen's back. My head is spinning from the strong potion, and I'm shivering so violently I'm shaking, but at least my body has managed to heal enough of the damage that I can now speak without coughing up blood. My chattering teeth still make that somewhat difficult, though.

Three loud thuds sound as Draven, Lyra, and Galen land hard on the grasslands before the forest. Black smoke explodes across the ground as Draven shifts into a half-shift. He shoots out of the smoke a moment later and flies up to where Isera and I are seated. Since I can barely manage to stay upright, she had to hold me in place while we were flying.

Pulling her arms back from where she has kept them around my body, she lets Draven pick me up and fly me down to the ground instead. Then she slides off Galen's back while Alistair does the same from Lyra's back.

My body shakes in Draven's arms as he flies us down. He presses me more firmly against his chest, as if he can share his own warmth with me. I let him think that it works and try my best to stop shivering so much. But the truth is that nothing any of them has done is working.

I'm so cold that I have lost feeling in most of my body. I know Draven's chest is pressed against the side of my body because I can see it. But I can't feel it. I can't feel anything except the bursts of searing pain that sometimes make it through the drugged haze of the painkiller potion, and the devastating coldness that is creeping closer to my heart with every passing minute.

"You're going to be okay," Draven repeats yet again as he sets me down so that I'm sitting on the grass with my back braced against a fallen tree. "Just hold on a little longer."

I manage a nod.

For a moment, he only holds my gaze with those agony-filled eyes of his. As if he doesn't want to leave me alone even for a second. But then he finally tears his gaze from mine and stands up. Sprinting back toward where Galen and Lyra are waiting, he shifts back into a dragon.

Wings boom through the night as the three of them take to the air. Alistair and Isera stagger sideways and have to brace themselves on the fallen log as the blasts of wind their wings create slam down over us. Climbing over the dark tree trunk, they sit down on either side of me.

After the hours Isera has spent holding me on Galen's back, she must already know that sharing body heat doesn't work. But she still sits down so close that her body is pressed against my side. To my surprise, Alistair does the same on my other side.

But before I can say anything, fire roars through the air above us.

I gasp as it barrels toward the trees ahead. My heart thuds in my chest. The moment those flames catch, the whole forest is going to be incinerated.

But right before the dragon fire can wash over the woods, the flames slam into an invisible wall.

Instinctively, I duck my head to protect myself. But the fire doesn't bounce back toward us. Instead, it washes out along the sides of the curving barrier.

My head is spinning, so I have to blink hard and squint before I can concentrate properly. It's only then that I realize the air in front of the forest is rippling and shimmering slightly. Kind of like a thick and clear liquid moving against glass.

"Is it just me or is the air shimmering?" I find myself saying.

"Yes, the air is shimmering," Isera replies. "I suspect it's the wards they mentioned."

"Oh good." I giggle. I'm not even sure why. It wasn't particularly funny. But I suddenly want to burst out laughing for some reason. I'm not sure if it's because I'm dying or high on painkillers.

Alistair and Isera glance at me as if they are wondering the same thing, but neither of them says anything.

Winds beat down over the grasslands as Draven, Lyra, and Galen hover at the edge of the forest. Opening their jaws, they breathe massive torrents of fire straight at the transparent barrier. The orange and yellow flames crash against it and wash out over the rippling surface. The three dragons simply torch it again.

The flames light up the night over and over again as they continue their onslaught.

Around us, the rest of the grasslands are silent and still. The bright moon shines down from a clear sky to illuminate the landscape in the brief moments between the waves of fire.

The trees on the other side of the barrier are strong and healthy and covered in bright green leaves, despite the fact that it's winter. As if those magical wards that both Nysara and Galen mentioned somehow keep out everything else. Even the seasons. I watch them, wondering what the Unseelie Court is like.

"How are you holding up?" Alistair suddenly asks.

This time, I do laugh out loud. Raising my eyebrows, I turn to meet his gaze. "See? It's not such a stupid question after all."

He winces, and embarrassment flits across his face as he remembers our conversation back in the Ice Palace. The first time I snuck down to see them, I asked Alistair that very same question. His answer had been a bit snippy, but given that it *had* been a stupid question, I hadn't minded. Now, it appears as though he understands why I asked it.

Clearing his throat, he drags a hand through his curly blond hair and then gives me a small nod. I'm not sure if it's the painkiller potion making me hallucinate, but I swear I can almost see the hint of a smile tug at his lips at my playful jab.

Above us, fire roars through the night in endless torrents. Isera discreetly wipes her temple where a bead of sweat trickled down. I watch her, my teeth still chattering and my body almost entirely numb from the cold, wishing that I could feel the heat of those flames too. She tugs at the collar of her tunic as another wave of fire crashes into the barrier before us.

Both she and Alistair are still wearing those silver garments the Icehearts made them wear in the castle. Though I suppose we're lucky that they were allowed to even wear these fancy tunics and pants rather than the underwear-like garments they were forced to wear earlier. But still. I can tell that they would much rather be wearing their own clothes.

"What happened to your clothes?"

Once again, the words are out of my mouth before I even know what I'm doing. That painkiller potion sure has loosened my tongue.

Alistair's expression darkens. "They burned them. The first day we woke up, Jessina and Bane cut our clothes off our bodies and burned them in front of us. Then they tossed us those ridiculous silver undergarments and told us to wear those or nothing at all."

My heart squeezes. "I'm sorry."

"Yeah. Me too."

Dark clouds start gathering in the sky above us. Storm winds rush through the night, making the clouds spin and ripple violently, as Draven gathers his magic. A bolt of lightning splits the air. It cracks into the transparent barrier ahead, but the wards merely ripple, as if it had no effect at all.

Draven lets out a deafening roar. I wince, clenching my chattering teeth. My body keeps shaking from the intense cold that now feels like a permanent part of my soul.

Without a word, Alistair and Isera shift closer to me. Even though it does nothing to chase the coldness away, I still appreciate the gesture.

"Is it true?" Alistair eventually asks.

Dragon fire and lightning and winds crash against the wards before us, turning the night into a raging storm of flames and white lightning.

Turning my head with some difficulty, I meet Alistair's gaze. "Is what true?"

"That Draven planned to make you leave without us and that you forced him to buy you time to get us out."

I turn my head back so that I'm watching the dark forest before us instead. "Yes."

For a moment, only the roaring of fire and zaps of lightning from above break the silence.

Then Alistair asks, "Why?"

"I promised that I would get you out."

"That's not reason enough. You wasted several minutes you didn't have getting us out, which caused the Icehearts to catch up, which led to the fight, which in turn is why you're dying right now."

I lick my numb lips, trying to figure out how to contradict him. But the truth is that he is right. If we had left straightaway instead of spending several minutes sneaking Isera and Alistair out of the ballroom and then going by foot to the Black Dragon Clan's barracks instead of simply flying there, we would have been able to leave before they figured out where we were.

"I would have left you," Isera suddenly says from my other side. Her voice is calm. Simply stating a fact. "If it had been me, I would have left you without looking back."

Alistair flicks a glance at her before returning his attention to me and lifting his toned shoulders in a shrug. "Me too."

I laugh. It comes out sounding weirdly genuine. Because for some reason, I really can't find it in myself to be offended.

"So why didn't *you*?" Alistair presses.

And once again, those damn drugs make me answer before I even know what I'm saying. "Because you're the first friends I ever made. The only friends I've ever had."

Alistair jerks back, his mouth dropping open as he stares at me with wide eyes. Even Isera blinks in what looks like stunned shock.

"Why are you—" I begin, but pain suddenly spikes through the back of my skull.

I suck in a sharp breath between my teeth, and the forest sways before me. That searing coldness burns through the back of my head.

And a sudden realization pulses through my whole soul. As clear as day and as natural as the rising sun.

I am going to die.

There is no way that Draven is going to be able to break through the wards around the Unseelie Court before the ice has frozen my body. This was a desperate hope. A stupid hope. I knew it the moment they suggested it back in that small nameless village. No matter what we do, I will never reach a healer in time.

A steady sort of resignation settles inside me. Because at least this is better than Draven and all of them dying while trying to fight their way back into the Ice Palace.

"What is it?" Isera demands, her sharp gaze assessing me.

With great effort, I force my eyes to focus through the searing pain at the back of my skull. Unclenching my jaw, I drag in a deep breath. "Nothing. I just have a little headache."

She and Alistair exchange a glance.

Then both of them are on their feet.

"No, don't—" I begin protesting as they no doubt get ready to signal to Draven.

But before I can even finish the sentence, there is movement inside the forest.

My stomach lurches as a tall man walks out of the shadows and comes to a halt right inside the barrier.

Dragon fire glints in the spiky black crown he wears on his head.

The Unseelie King has come.

3

The Unseelie King arches a dark eyebrow at the storm of fire and lightning that is crashing against his wards. Alistair and Isera notice him a second after me, and they whip around to stare at him. Up above, Draven and the others must have spotted him too, because all three of them stop their assault on the wards and instead speed down toward the ground.

From where I'm sitting against the fallen tree, I study the Unseelie King, who is still standing there right inside his wards looking faintly amused. And what I find surprises me. I'm not sure why, but I had imagined the ruler of the wicked Unseelie Court to look harsh and rugged. But it's the exact opposite.

My head spins from the drugs and my teeth continue chattering as I stare at the fae man on the other side of the transparent barrier.

He is not handsome in that masculine way that Draven is. Instead, he is beautiful. He's tall and his body is made up of lean muscles, which makes me think that he is both fast and lethal, but his facial features are more sharp and narrow and delicate. Almost to the point of looking a little feminine. That impression is heightened by the fact that he has long dark blue hair that cascades down to his ribs like a smooth waterfall. His eyes, which are a breathtaking mix of black and silver, look like slivers of the night sky.

The spiky black crown on his head gleams in the silver light from the moon, and his elegant garments made of black and dark blue fabric with touches of silver are perfectly tailored to his lean, muscular body.

He's gorgeous, but even through the wards, I can almost feel the ruthlessness radiating from his entire being. This man might be beautiful, but he is also incredibly dangerous. Like a venomous snake. Beautiful to look at but best viewed from a distance.

Black smoke explodes across the grass as Draven, Lyra, and Galen land hard on the ground and shift out of their dragon forms. When it clears, Galen and Lyra are in their human forms while Draven is in a half-shift. His massive black wings are spread wide in a show of power as he stalks toward the barrier. Lyra and Galen trail to an awkward halt halfway between it and us, as if they don't know if Draven wants their help or not. Draven doesn't even appear to notice, because his gaze is fixed on the fae man on the other side of the transparent barrier.

A slow smirk curls the Unseelie King's lips as he spreads his arms wide in a mocking gesture. "I thought you would have learned by now, Shadow of Death. Despite all your power, all your fire and your storm magic, you cannot breach these wards." He lets his arms drop again and then gives Draven a sharp look. "So why have you brought war to my court at this time of night?"

"I'm not here for war," Draven replies as he comes to a halt right outside the barrier. "I'm here for your healer."

"If you think that I would ever surrender Haldia to you, you have grown even more delusional since our last skirmish."

"I don't want to take her. I want her to save someone."

"Who?"

Draven turns to look at me. I try to keep my shivering to a minimum, but it's useless. My body shakes violently, and that searing, burning pain that is now creeping up the back of my skull is making black spots dance at the edges of my vision. Pure dread pulses in Draven's eyes as he watches me, but he wipes it off his features before turning back to the Unseelie King.

My heart jerks as those sharp black-and-silver eyes slide to me. The Unseelie King watches me in silence for a moment before returning his gaze to Draven.

"Ice flames," is all the king says.

"Yes," Draven confirms. "She needs a healer, or she's going to die."

"So take her to the Orange Dragon Clan. They have healing magic, don't they?"

"I can't."

A spark of interest suddenly gleams in the Unseelie King's eyes. "So it *is* true. You have betrayed the Icehearts."

Surprise pulses through me. How could he know that? It has only been hours since we escaped from the Ice Palace. Even though Nysara, his spy in Frostfell, witnessed the fight and helped glamour us so that we could escape, there is no way that she should have been able to get word all the way to the Unseelie Court this fast.

"We don't have time for this!" Draven snaps. "She's dying! So get your healer out here and save her, or I will—"

"Or you'll do what, exactly?" the Unseelie King cuts off, his voice as sharp as a blade.

Dark storm clouds gather around Draven, and lightning crackles around his powerful body as he growls, "You don't want to play this fucking game with me right now, Orion. Just get your fucking healer out here."

"*Or what?*" the Unseelie King, Orion, repeats. His black-and-silver eyes are merciless as he stares Draven down. "These wards have stood for thousands of years. You cannot breach them."

Lightning cracks against the barrier, but just like before, it only makes it ripple slightly before it grows still again.

Orion flashes Draven a cold smile. "You overstep, Shadow of Death. This is my court, Haldia is my healer, and these are my wards. If you wanted something, you should have begged me for it. Now you get to stand there and watch her die while I go back to bed."

Before Draven can so much as open his mouth, the Unseelie King spins on his heel. His long dark blue hair flutters in the air when he turns and starts back toward the trees.

"Orion!" Draven snaps.

But the Unseelie King just keeps walking.

"Orion Nightbane!" Draven yells, his voice echoing through the silent night like a thunderclap. "Don't you fucking dare!"

Bolts of white lightning crash into the wards as Draven throws the full extent of his storm magic at the barrier. But just like before, all it does is ripple.

"Get your healer out here right now," Draven continues bellowing. "Or I swear to God I will destroy everything you have ever touched. I will kill everyone you have ever met. I will burn your entire court to ashes and salt the fucking earth so that nothing will ever grow here again."

But the Unseelie King simply continues walking.

"ORION!" Panic bleeds into Draven's voice now. He casts a look at me over his shoulder, and the sheer terror in his eyes makes my stomach drop. Whirling back toward the wards, he slams his fist against the barrier. "Orion, please!"

That finally makes the Unseelie King pause. Turning slowly, he faces Draven again and arches an eyebrow.

Draven doesn't even try to hide the dread and desperation in his voice as he repeats, "Please, Orion. Save her."

Starlight glints in Orion Nightbane's eyes, but the smile on his beautiful face is vicious and full of challenge. "You call that begging?" He gives Draven a taunting once-over. "Pathetic."

Then he turns back around and starts walking again.

Draven casts another panicked look back at me.

Then he drops to his knees in front of the barrier and spreads his arms wide. "Orion, please, I'm begging you."

The sight of Draven on his knees, pleading for my life, makes a blast of fury shoot through me. After everything he has been through these past two hundred years, he should never have to bow to anyone else ever again. He shouldn't have to humiliate himself like this. Especially not for my sake.

"Don't—" I begin to protest.

But the word barely makes it out of my mouth before it's cut off by a gasp as a burst of pain spikes through my skull. It's so intense that my vision blacks out for a second. When my eyesight returns, the world around me sways. I blink hard, my body shaking uncontrollably and my teeth chattering so loudly that my skull rattles.

Once the world around me comes back into focus, I find the Unseelie King sauntering back toward the barrier where Draven is kneeling. But his black-and-silver eyes are fixed on me.

"We've dealt with ice flame wounds before," he says. "And given the state of her, she has about half an hour left to live. It would take me three minutes to get her to Haldia."

Sliding his gaze back to Draven, he raises his eyebrows expectantly while leaving that half-spoken offer hanging there in the air between them.

"Please, I'm begging you," Draven repeats, his arms still spread wide in surrender. "Name your price. I'll do anything. You want me to grovel at your feet? Done. Just please, save her."

My heart aches at the sight of Draven like that, and I squeeze my eyes shut for a moment as a wave of guilt crashes into me. He's begging for my life with everything he has, and all I can do is sit here uselessly. I should be the one begging the Unseelie King for my life. I should be the only one taking on that humiliation and shame. But with my spine severed and the ice flames rendering my body weak and numb, I can't even manage to crawl up to his feet and kneel there myself.

Rage burns through me. And I decide, right there in the grass under the impassive night sky outside the Unseelie Court, that if I survive this, I am going to make sure that Draven never has to sacrifice himself ever again. Never has to submit to someone else's whims ever again. I will take on the pain, I will take on the debt, I will take on whatever fate requires of me. Next time, I will be the one protecting him.

A few strides away, Galen and Lyra stare at Draven, looking completely stunned. Next to me, Isera only watches Orion Nightbane through narrowed eyes, while Alistair's gaze flits across the grasslands around us.

"Well, well, well." A wicked smile spreads across Orion's face. "The Shadow of Death begging on his knees. Now I almost wish I had brought my entire court out here with me to witness this."

Draven clenches his jaw but says nothing.

The Unseelie King flicks a glance in my direction. "Who is she to you?"

"Just tell me what you want," Draven grinds out through gritted teeth.

"Answer my question, and I might consider it."

Draven turns slightly to look at me over his shoulder, and when his golden eyes meet mine, I can see the desperation in them that I can already hear in his voice. "She's my mate."

Galen and Lyra whip their heads back to stare at him, their eyes wide and jaws dropping. Next to me, Alistair jerks back and flicks his gaze between me and Draven. And even Isera's silver-and-blue eyes widen in surprise.

Interest sparks in Orion's eyes. "A cross-species bond? Interesting. Very interesting."

Draven turns back to him. "I answered your question. Now, are you going to save her or not?"

Silence descends over the darkened grasslands and the gloomy woods behind the Unseelie King as he considers for an uncomfortably long time. My heart pounds in my chest. Or it might be my head that's pounding. It's getting difficult to tell because I can barely hear anything over the loud chattering of my teeth.

"I can allow Haldia to save her," Orion says at last, his sharp eyes lingering on me for a moment before he fixes them on Draven again. "If you do something for me."

"Name it," Draven replies immediately.

"I want you to kill someone for me."

"Who?"

"An Unseelie fae here in my court with a silver tongue and too much ambition." He raises a finger, stopping Draven's reply before he can even open his mouth. "But I wasn't done. I want you to kill this man *publicly*. So that everyone knows that it was you who killed him."

"You mean so that *you* don't take the heat for the assassination."

Orion doesn't confirm or deny it. Only flashes Draven a sharp smile. "Well, do we have a deal? My healer will remove the ice flames from your mate's body, and in return—"

"And fix her spine."

The Unseelie King arches an eyebrow in silent question.

"Her spine was severed when the ice flames struck."

His black-and-silver eyes slide to me for a second. "I see." Then he returns his gaze to Draven. "Fine. My healer will remove the ice flames from your mate's body *and* fix her spine. And in return, you will assassinate a member of my court in a manner which makes it clear that it was you who did it, and you will not disclose my involvement in the matter at any time. Now or in the future. That is the deal. Do you accept?"

Draven doesn't even hesitate for a second. "Yes."

"You won't be able to shift in here."

"I don't care."

Without waiting for Orion to answer, Draven gets to his feet and runs back to where I'm still sitting. Isera and Alistair move aside as he crouches down next to me and lifts me up from the ground.

"You're going to be okay," he promises yet again as he holds me tightly to his chest and straightens.

Turning around, he shifts into his fully human form and starts back toward the barrier. Isera marches along next to him. Across the grass, Lyra and Galen lurch into motion and hurry to his side as well. Only Alistair remains standing by the fallen tree.

Indecision flashes across his face as he once more flicks his gaze over the open grasslands around us. And for a moment, it looks like he's just going to take off across the fields and disappear into the great world beyond. But then he grinds his teeth and blows out a forceful breath.

Moonlight casts pale highlights in his curly blond hair as he jogs to catch up with the rest of us.

On the other side of the barrier, Orion Nightbane whispers words under his breath that are too soft for us to hear. Then a sly smile spreads across his lips as he draws his arms through the air in a show of inviting us into his realm.

Worry pulses through my frozen chest. I have no idea what kind of powers the Unseelie fae have. What if Orion can just strike us down the moment we step inside? Or what if he only pretended to open the wards for us and we will die the moment we try to walk through?

That sly smile remains on his lips as we reach the barrier, as if he can read the worry on my face. But he does nothing to help assure us that we will survive stepping inside. His eyes gleam with challenge as he keeps his arm out in that gesture of invitation.

"Welcome to the Unseelie Court."

4

To my relief, we are not incinerated the moment we step through the barrier. Instead, the wards simply vibrate a little around us. Then we're through. I try to blow out a long breath of relief, but it's getting increasingly difficult to breathe, so I only manage a small sigh.

Orion shoots us an amused look, as if he could read the trepidation on our faces when we walked through, but he doesn't comment on it. Once we are all inside his court, he spins on his heel and starts deeper into the woods.

"Follow me," he says without even turning to look at us.

Isera glares at his back in annoyance while Alistair shoots him a scowl. On my other side, Lyra and Galen exchange a look before they both glance at Draven. But Draven only starts after the Unseelie King without another word.

The fog at the corners of my vision is getting worse, and I blink hard several times to keep my eyes in focus as Draven carries me deeper into the forest. My body is still shaking violently from the searing cold inside me, and I clamp my teeth together to stop them from chattering too loudly. A stab of pain shoots through my skull again. I flinch, and my vision blacks out for a couple of seconds.

When I can once more see again, I find Draven's desperate eyes locked on mine.

"You need to make it through this," he says.

"Yeah, I'm—" My lungs seem to spasm for a moment, and I have to cough and clear my throat before I manage a weak smile. "Yeah, I'm trying to."

"No, you *need* to make it through this." His eyes are dead serious and full of both command and pleading as he holds my gaze. "Do you understand?"

The intensity of his stare steals what little air I have left in my lungs, so I only manage a nod.

All around us, the forest is humming with the soft tunes of nocturnal insects. Leaves rustle faintly above us as a gentle breeze sweeps through the trees. I watch the way the silver light from the moon plays over the impossibly fresh green leaves, wondering yet again what kind of magic can make them grow like this when the rest of the world is in the clutches of winter.

Up ahead, Orion is striding toward something rectangular that glitters slightly a short distance away. The rest of our companions are following a few steps behind Draven, so right now, we have a few moments of privacy.

But a few moments are not enough for what I want to say. For what I want to ask. But they're all we have, so I draw in a soft breath and meet Draven's gaze. I don't even know where to start. Or how to adequately summarize what it is that I actually want to ask.

In the end, what makes it out of my mouth is simply, "You begged for me."

Draven tears his gaze from that glittering shape up ahead and looks down to meet my eyes. His expression softens. And my heart aches, because he seems to be able to read the full question embedded in that one statement.

"I've already told you." He gives me a soft smile. "There is nothing I wouldn't do for you. I would crawl and grovel. I would slaughter entire nations." His golden eyes sear through my very soul as he holds my gaze. "So you had better fight with everything you have to make it through this.

Because if you die, I will rip my own heart out and then claw my way out of Azaroth's fiery realm and break the barriers between our afterlives so that I can follow you in death into Mabona's evergreen garden. I will never let you go. You are mine. In this life and every life after it."

My heart stops. And then beats twice as hard to make up for it. I can barely breathe as I stare up into his eyes while his words echo through my very soul. Warmth floods my chest like a wave of bright sunlight. Because I can tell, without a shadow of a doubt, that he means every word of that.

His arms tighten around me, and a hint of challenge glints in his eyes as he holds my gaze and flashes me a small smile. "So fight with everything you have to stay here with me, because I would hate to have to add *Destroyer of the Afterlife* to the already ridiculously long list of titles people have given me."

A surprised laugh rips from my lungs, which immediately makes me cough and wince again, but my frozen chest is somehow still full of sparkling warmth as I smile back up at Draven. "It really is ridiculously long, isn't it?"

Amusement gleams in his eyes as he leans down and brushes his lips against my forehead in a soft kiss. But before he can say anything, we reach that strange glittering rectangle that Orion has stopped next to. Frowning, I stare at it.

It looks like a doorway. But the glittering blue door frame isn't connected to anything. It's just standing there alone on the grass. I stare in confusion at the scenery visible inside the glimmering frame. All around us there are only darkened trees. But through the strange doorway, I can see a city.

"You have portal magic," Isera says as she and the others catch up with us. It sounds like half question, half accusation.

The Unseelie King slides his gaze to her and gives her a smile that looks vaguely threatening. "No. But one of my people does."

"Save this fucking conversation for when Selena isn't dying in my arms," Draven snaps.

Isera, seemingly unruffled by both Orion's threatening smile and Draven's harsh words, just shrugs as if conceding the point. The Unseelie King, on the other hand, watches Draven as if he's debating whether to make an issue of his rudeness or not. But in the end, he says nothing and simply walks through the portal.

Draven hurries through it a moment later, as if he was worried that Orion might close it before we could get through.

A slight tingling sensation ripples through me as we move through the glittering blue doorway, but it disappears the moment we step out on the other side.

I suck in a gasp at the view that is now visible before us.

Gone is the darkened forest. Instead, a sprawling city with rushing waterfalls and flowing rivers meets us below the small hill we're standing on. I gape at it, completely stunned.

Once again, my preconceived notions about the Unseelie Court turn out to be entirely false. From what we know of the Unseelie Court, they are supposed to be our dark counterpart. So I had been expecting a city hewn from dark rock, maybe even underground, with crude dwellings and harsh monuments.

But instead, I stare at the most beautiful city I have ever seen.

Grand rock formations frame one side of the city, and rippling waterfalls tumble down over the edges and into a massive pool that glitters in the starlight. The water from that pool then flows right through the city in several sparkling rivers that the fae have directed perfectly between buildings and streets by creating canals made of stone. On the other side of the large city, those rivers tumble down another cliffside before joining the grand river beneath that flows out through the fields and grasslands below.

My heart patters against my ribs as I stare at the incredible architecture before me. All the houses are made of pale stone, making the city look bright and clean, while the red tiles that cover all the roofs add a splash of color.

There is a grand arena in the middle of the city. It looks like the arena we fought inside during the Atonement Trials, except ten times as large and oval instead of round. The massive amphitheater looks to be the beating heart of the city.

Next to the glittering lake, with the cliff formations as a protective barrier behind, rises a beautiful castle made of shining white stone. It stuns me how similar it is to our Golden Palace in the Seelie Court. However, while ours gleams golden in the light, this one shimmers in silver instead.

It's breathtaking. The entire city is a work of art. And it's not at all what I was expecting to find in the infamous Unseelie Court.

"Wow," Lyra says from right next to us.

I blink, tearing my gaze from the stunning view and sliding it back to the six people around me instead. Except there are seven people here now.

Lyra and Alistair are standing side by side, gaping at the city below in much the same way that I was doing. Isera, on the other hand, doesn't appear to be very interested in the view. Instead, she watches Orion like a hawk as he speaks quietly to another fae man. The stranger nods and waves his hand, which makes the glittering portal sink into the ground. Then he closes his eyes and begins moving his hands again, as if summoning another portal.

"This is probably a trap," Galen whispers as he comes to stand next to Draven.

Draven glances over at him. "You know how it works. Unseelie fae *always* keep the bargains they make."

"I know. But they always try to trick people into more than they think they bargained for. Which means that this guy we're supposed to assassinate is probably going to be incredibly difficult to kill."

"Yeah, I think so too."

However, before either of them can say anything else, another portal shoots up from the ground. Through it, buildings and a stone street are visible.

"Well then," the Unseelie King says, that vaguely threatening smile once again on his lips. "Let's go see my healer."

5

The second portal takes us to a street close to the castle. Since it's the middle of the night, the buildings around us are dark and silent. But the entire street is still flooded with light. Glowing white faelight gems have been set atop swirling lampposts all along the street, illuminating the pale stone houses and lush trees that line it. I stare at them, my delirious mind trying to figure out why we never had lampposts like these in the Seelie Court.

A door is shoved open to my left. I turn my head toward it, which makes my vision swim. Once it has cleared again, I find a fae woman with curly brown hair rushing out the door and toward us.

"Your Majesty," she says, and hurriedly drops into a curtsy. "Please forgive me. If I had known you were coming, I would have—"

"It's fine, Haldia," Orion interrupts with a wave of his hand. "Are you in the middle of something?"

"No, no, not at all." She casts an uncertain glance at the rest of us. "What can I—" Her sentence is cut off abruptly by a small gasp when her gaze lands on Draven, Lyra, and Galen. Shock pulses across her features as she snaps her gaze back to her king, and she works her mouth up and down a few times. In the end, all that makes it out is a confused, "Your Majesty?"

Orion flicks a hand in my direction. "The silver-haired fae—"

"Selena," Draven cuts in.

The Unseelie King gives him a slow and bone-chillingly cold smile before he echoes, "Selena." Then he turns back to his healer. "Has been struck by ice fire from the Silver Dragon Clan. I want you to save her, and also fix her spine, which has apparently been severed."

"Of course." She turns to Draven and holds out her arms. "Give her to me."

Draven's arms tighten around me for a moment, as if he is reluctant to let me go. But then he carefully places me in Haldia's arms.

To my surprise, the healer doesn't even stagger from the sudden weight. She must be a lot stronger than she looks.

The moment that I'm safely in Haldia's arms, Draven whirls toward Orion. Haldia gasps, and almost drops me, when Draven suddenly grabs the Unseelie King by the collar of his shirt and yanks him closer.

"If she dies, so does your city," Draven growls in his face.

I suck in a sharp breath as a vision explodes before my eyes. The beautiful city is no longer visible around me. And neither are my companions. Instead, all I can see is myself. And Tommen and Jeb.

I'm lying on the floor. Blood coats my forearm, staining the shredded fabric of the sheer robe I'm wearing and turning it red instead of white. The short silk nightgown has slid up around my waist, which reveals a vicious stab wound in my thigh. Blood wells up from it and trickles down over my skin. My eyes are sliding in and out of focus, and my chest barely rises with ragged breaths. A few steps away, Tommen and Jeb are crouching in attack positions.

It makes no sense. Because instead of looking up from the floor, I'm looking down at myself from a position by the door. But the vision is so vivid, so *real*, that it makes fear crawl across my skin like tiny spiders.

Then the vision disappears, as if yanked away by a ruthless hand.

I gasp. My head spins and my heart pounds in my chest. Blinking, I try to focus on the world around me again.

Draven has released Orion's collar and staggered several steps back, and his face is ashen as he stares at the Unseelie King.

Orion locks merciless eyes on Draven. "If you ever put your hands on me again, I will *make sure* she dies."

Rage flashes across Draven's face, but I don't have time to see what he does, because Haldia abruptly turns around and hurries into her house. Threats and harsh voices are cut off as she closes the door behind us.

Her house is cozy. Full of books and plush armchairs and soft fabric. Several potted plants line the windowsills.

I drag in a deep breath, which sends a spike of pain through my chest, and try to get my mind to focus properly again.

"What was that?" I press out between bursts of pain.

"What was what?" Haldia asks as she carries me into another room.

"I saw . . . myself. Dying."

"Ah." She gently sets me down on the sturdy table in the middle of the room. "The king has nightmare powers."

I frown. "What?"

She rounds the table so that she is standing by my head instead. My shirt has slid up my stomach, and I try to reach up to pull it down again, but I find that I can no longer lift my arms. Panic crackles through my body. Swallowing, I try to force the dread down.

"Though I suppose it's not really nightmares as such," Haldia says while she lifts her hands and holds them to the sides of my head. "King Orion can pull bad memories from people's heads and make them relive them. He can show them to the person who carries the memory, but also to whoever else he wants, so I assume the memory you just saw belongs to someone else."

My heart jerks as I finally understand the vision. Draven. I was looking at myself through Draven's eyes when he broke the door down to save me from getting killed by Tommen and Jeb during the Atonement Trials.

A slight prickling sensation begins inside my head. I grit my teeth.

"Oh dear," Haldia says. Her blue-and-purple eyes meet mine as she tilts her chin and looks down at me from where she is still standing by my head. Her hands remain hovering close to my temples. "You have a lot of repressed emotions and memories in your head, girl."

I glance away, suddenly embarrassed. Of course I have a lot of repressed stuff in my head. I have spent my entire life swallowing down my real emotions so that I wouldn't upset the people around me. I couldn't show any anger or sadness or frustration or any other uncomfortable emotion since it might set off my parents and make them argue again.

Even with strangers, I couldn't let them see any of my negative feelings, since that would only make them dislike me even more than they already did. Sharing my grief or venting my anger would just make them see me as a drain on their energy. As a burden. As an undesirable person who brought negativity into other people's lives.

So contented but not-too-strong happiness is all I have ever been able to show others.

Everything else, all the rage and the fury and the sorrow and jealousy and all the negative emotions I have been drowning in all my life, has been locked up tight inside my chest. Buried underneath a thick lid. Never to be let out.

"But that is not my job to fix," Haldia continues. "The ice fire and your severed spine are."

I return my gaze to her face. To my surprise, she looks almost a little sad. Her words were straight, almost a little hard, but the expression on her face tells me that she sympathizes with me more than she's trying to let on.

"I'm going to put you to sleep now," she suddenly declares.

I panic. "Wait, I—"

But before I can even finish the sentence, my eyes start to droop as a wave of exhaustion crashes over me. And within a few heartbeats I've slipped into dark oblivion.

6

The room that comes back into focus around me when I open my eyes is not the same one. Gone are the rows of books and the sturdy table. Instead, I'm lying on a soft double bed covered in white sheets in what looks like some kind of bedroom. The walls have been painted in a pale green color, and there is a gleaming faelight lamp on the bedside table that casts a warm glow over the room. Given the position of the sun outside the window, I must have been unconscious for several hours.

For a moment, panic floods my body. Because I have no idea where I am or how I ended up here.

Then I see him.

Draven.

The panic inside me drains away the moment my gaze lands on his powerful body. I blink, clearing the last of the fog from my vision as I study him.

He is sitting on a chair next to the bed. His elbows are braced on his knees and his face is buried in his hands. Tension seems to pulse from his entire body like shock waves, and his black hair is disheveled, as if he has repeatedly run his hands through it.

I frown, trying to figure out why he looks so worried.

Then my confused mind finally catches up with the events of the past days. The battle. The shard of ice fire. The searing coldness that burned through my body, freezing me all the way into my very soul. My severed spine. The deal with the Unseelie King. The healer.

Dread and hope and confusion crash inside my chest like a violent storm. I barely dare to breathe. To hope.

Then I brace myself.

I move my foot.

And my foot *moves*.

A gasp rips from my lungs, and I jerk upright in bed, pulling my legs up to my chest. No lingering pain remains from the burning ice inside me. No coldness. Nothing. Instead, warmth fills my whole soul.

Draven snaps his head up.

His golden eyes are wide and haunted when they meet mine.

For a second, it's as if the moment is suspended in time. Then his gaze darts over my whole body, as if checking to make sure that I'm here. That I'm okay. That I'm alive.

And then relief, so intense that it snatches the breath from my lungs, washes over his face.

Lurching up from the chair, he slides his hands along my cheeks and into my hair and kisses me so desperately that it makes my heart skip several beats. I drag in an unsteady breath when he breaks the kiss. But he doesn't draw back. Instead, he keeps his hands in my hair and rests his forehead against mine.

"Don't you ever do something like that to me again," he whispers against my lips. "Do you hear me?"

My heart pounds in my chest, and several conflicting emotions tug at my soul.

This can't just be because of the mate bond. Can it?

The sheer terror in his eyes when I was dying. The desperation in his voice when he was bargaining with the Unseelie King. The relief on his face when I woke up. That heart-wrenching kiss. It has to be real. These kinds of emotions can't just have been forced upon him by the mate bond. Right?

Another memory pulses through my mind. A memory of a darkened forest. Of Draven carrying me toward a glittering portal. And of the words he spoke to me there under the silent trees.

There is nothing I wouldn't do for you. I would crawl and grovel. I would slaughter entire nations. So you had better fight with everything you have to make it through this. Because if you die, I will rip my own heart out and then claw my way out of Azaroth's fiery realm and break the barriers between our afterlives so that I can follow you in death into Mabona's evergreen garden. I will never let you go. You are mine. In this life and every life after it.

My heart aches at the memory of it.

Goddess above, this has to be real. Please, let this be real. Because if it's not, I don't know how I'm going to survive being near him.

Dragging in a shuddering breath, I once more curse the universe for making us fated mates. If we weren't mates, I could have chosen him on my own. But now I will never know. Now I will spend the rest of my life wondering how much of his and my feelings are our own and how much has been forced onto us by someone else.

Draven takes his forehead from mine and pulls back enough to lock eyes with me. Pure command pulses in those beautiful eyes of his as he slides his hands out of my hair and instead takes my chin in a firm grip.

"I said," he begins, his voice dripping with authority, "don't you ever do something like that to me again. Understood?"

My heart jerks, and a rush of giddy relief and gratitude washes over me. An absolutely ridiculous grin spreads across my mouth. But I can't help it.

Because Draven isn't treating me like I'm made of glass. Even though I almost died yesterday, he doesn't look at me like I'm weak. He isn't touching me like he's handling a fragile glass figurine that might break at any second.

Instead, he is treating me like he always has. As if I'm strong and powerful.

It makes me want to kiss him again.

But he's clearly waiting for me to acknowledge his order, so instead, I flash him a sly smile and reply, "Yes, sir."

Light flickers in his eyes like golden sparkles. While trying, and failing, to suppress a smile, he slides his thumb over my bottom lip. "Such a little troublemaker."

I press a hand to my chest in a show of exaggerated shock. "*I'm* the troublemaker? Did you forget the part where you're the legendary Red Hand and a member of not one but two rebellions? Talk about being an overachiever in the troublemaking department."

"Well, technically, I was never actually a part of the human—"

The door is pulled open.

"Draven," Lyra says as she strides into the room. "The Unseelie King just sent word that our presence has been requested for dinner, but since . . ."

She trails off. Blinking, she comes to a halt on the floor halfway between the door and the bed. Her orange eyes dart between Draven and me for a moment. Then her face lights up.

"Guys!" she yells, a grin spreading across her lips. "Selena is up!"

Something clatters from outside the door. It's followed by the sounds of scraping chairs and thudding feet.

While Lyra moves farther into the room and plops down on the empty side of the bed, Galen hurries across the threshold. Relief washes over his features when he sees me sitting up with my knees bent, but his eyes quickly shift to Draven. As if he was more worried about what it would do to Draven if I died rather than my death in itself. Given that he barely knows me, I can't say that I'm particularly offended by that.

Galen, however, seems to catch himself anyway. Clearing his throat, he tears his gaze from Draven and meets my eyes instead. "Glad you're okay."

I give him a small smile. "Yeah, me too."

Before he can say anything else, Alistair strolls into the bedroom.

Taking up position by the desk opposite the bed, he leans back against the edge of the table and crosses his arms.

"Damn, Soulstealer," he says, sounding strangely impressed. "If I had known you were this hard to kill, I would never have picked a fight with you during the trials all those months ago."

A surprised laugh escapes my chest.

Alistair looks like he is trying very hard not to smile, which stuns me. I have never seen him like this before. Never heard him tease and joke like this.

However, before I can say anything, Isera saunters into the room as well. But she doesn't move farther in like the others. She simply leans back against the wall right inside the door while her cool gaze slides over my body.

"You look like shit," she announces.

Another unexpected laugh rips from my lungs. On the mattress next to me, Lyra chuckles as well, while Alistair just rolls his eyes.

I snort. "Thanks."

She's right, though. I do look like shit. In fact, all of us do. My white shirt is covered in dirt and blood. Not to mention that I can feel the large hole in the back where the ice shard ripped through the fabric. Isera's and Alistair's silver tunics and thin pants are equally rumpled and splattered with blood. Only our three dragon shifters look relatively presentable in their black dragon scale armor.

We're going to have to figure out a way to acquire some new clothes for me, Isera, and Alistair. Especially the two of them, since their fancy silver garments are very conspicuous.

Draven turns back to Lyra. "What were you saying about Orion?"

"Oh. Right." She gives her head a quick shake as if to clear it. It makes her wavy brown hair ripple around her. "He's requesting our presence at dinner tonight."

"You mean *demanding* our presence."

By the wall, Isera scoffs. But when we all turn to look at her, she just looks back at us in silence instead of elaborating.

"Anyway," Lyra picks up. "I'm assuming it's to remind us of our bargain."

And just like that, the warm and light feeling inside me evaporates in a heartbeat.

Right. The bargain. The bargain they made and the price we now have to pay. An assassination. A nameless Unseelie fae's life in exchange for mine.

"As if we would forget," Draven huffs, and shakes his head in annoyance.

"Well then," Lyra says, and slaps her thighs before jumping up from the bed. "Let's go get ready to meet the Unseelie King."

"We've already met him," Alistair points out from where he is still leaning against the edge of the desk.

"Officially."

"What's the difference between *officially* meeting someone and just meeting someone?"

"Paperwork," she replies without hesitation. "There are lots of forms we have to fill out."

Alistair draws back and blinks at her in surprise. "Seriously?"

"Yes." Strolling over to him, she loops her arm through his and starts leading him to the door. "Come on, we have an entire stack of them to get through."

Alistair glances back at us, looking bewildered, but just staggers along with her as they cross the threshold.

The moment they disappear out the door, both Draven and Galen burst out laughing. Light dances in their eyes as they exchange a look.

"I can't believe he fell for that," Draven says, still chuckling.

"Me neither." Galen grins and shakes his head. "I'm telling you, she's gonna eat that guy up and swallow him whole. Remember that time when—" He abruptly cuts himself off.

Regret and shame and hesitation pulse across his entire face for a second. Then he awkwardly clears his throat and glances down at the floor.

"I'll, uhm . . ." He clears his throat again and starts drifting toward the door. "I'd better go and get ready too."

Draven opens his mouth to say something, but Galen has already slipped out. He heaves a deep sigh.

"Well," Isera drawls from where she's still leaning against the wall. "This is going to be an interesting dinner."

7

Warm evening winds sweep gently between the sandstone houses. I draw in a deep breath, relishing in the extraordinary pleasure of being able to breathe properly without coughing up blood, to walk on my own, to once more feel the warmth of my own body, and to not be slowly but surely dying in a haze of freezing, burning pain. What an absolute luxury.

"The fuck are you scowling about?" Draven demands.

Opening my eyes again, I find Alistair stalking out of the small house we've been staying in with a deep scowl on his face. Behind him, Lyra practically skips across the threshold and pulls the door shut behind her. A glittering smile shines on her lips.

"I wrote half a fucking essay before I realized she was just messing with me," Alistair huffs, and shoots an annoyed look at Lyra.

Lyra just grins wider.

"An essay?" I ask, confused.

"To introduce himself for the *official* meeting with the Unseelie King," Lyra replies, her eyes sparkling with mischief.

Draven snorts and gives Alistair a sideways glance. "You're so fucking gullible."

"Shut up," Alistair mutters, but he sounds more embarrassed than angry. "How was I supposed to know—"

"Can you stop your incessant bickering so that we can get this dinner over with?" Isera cuts in, leveling an exasperated stare at all of us.

Without waiting for us to reply, she simply turns on her heel and marches up the street. After a collective shrug, we follow her.

The house the Unseelie King allowed us to borrow is located just outside the castle area—as if he wants us close so that his guards can keep an eye on us but doesn't trust us to stay in the actual castle with him.

Our street is deserted, but from just a couple of roads over, I can hear the faint murmur of a bustling city. It's evening, but the Unseelie fae seem to have plenty to do out in the city regardless. Casting a glance over my shoulder, I gaze in their direction, even though I can't see anyone because the rows of buildings are blocking the view. I can't help but wonder what it would have been like to grow up in this city instead of the Seelie Court.

A few clanking sounds come from up ahead. I turn my gaze back to the view in front of me.

The castle guards, dressed in dark blue and silver, could see us the moment we stepped out the door since they are stationed at the other end of the road, but all they do when we reach them is open the small steel gate for us. I glance between them before casting a look in the direction of the main gates, which are halfway on the other side of the castle. Not exactly a grand welcome for us here by the side gate, but I suppose nothing about our visit here is normal.

A beautiful garden, complete with colorful flowers in full bloom and gently rippling fountains, meets us once we step inside the castle grounds. I stare at it, once again trying to readjust my perception of the Unseelie Court. Why have I always believed that this court is dark and ugly and full of decay? Is it something that the dragon shifters have taught us? Or does this prejudice come from our own people?

We only make it two steps into the garden before a servant dressed in black and blue livery appears before us.

"Please, follow me," he says without preamble.

Gravel crunches faintly under our shoes as we follow the servant along a pathway through the lush bushes and swirling flower beds. Tilting my head back, I look up at the grand castle before us. In the bright moonlight, the pale stone facade shimmers like silver. It truly is beautiful.

The servant guides us in through a side door and then through a series of corridors before finally stopping in front of a surprisingly unremarkable door. When they said that we were invited to a dinner with the Unseelie King, this was not exactly what I had imagined.

Once we are all gathered outside the door, the servant lifts his hand and knocks twice. "Your Majesty. Your guests have arrived."

"Send them in," his voice comes from inside.

With a nod to us, the servant opens the door and motions for us to enter.

Worry flutters through my stomach, and I have a sudden feeling that we're about to walk into a trap. I glance at the rest of my companions. Based on the expressions on their faces, they are thinking the same thing.

In the end, Draven just shrugs and strides through the door. Pushing my gloomy premonition to the back of my mind, I quickly follow him. And so do the others.

To my surprise, there is no trap waiting for us inside. At least not one that I can see. It really is just a small private dining room.

A rich dark blue carpet covers the pale stone floor, and paintings of breathtaking night skies and scenery decorate the walls. In the middle of the room is a dark wooden table with nine chairs around it. Four plain chairs line each long side, and then a grand high-backed chair made of carved wood has been positioned at the head of the table. Faelight gems gleam from a chandelier above the table as well as from several swirling steel light holders along the tabletop.

The soft white light glints against the sparkling plates already piled with food, but my gaze snaps straight to the lone person waiting inside the room.

Orion Nightbane is standing with his hands clasped behind his back. His elegant garments are impeccable, the blue and black fabrics entirely spotless, and the silver details on them glint in the light. Even his long dark blue hair is done to perfection. Underneath his spiky black crown, his hair falls down over his back with not a strand out of place.

And when he slides his black-and-silver eyes over the six of us, I suddenly feel like a piece of mud he has just scraped off his shoe.

Before we left the borrowed house, I took a bath to get the worst of the dust and blood and sweat off my body. But my boots are still scuffed, my pants frayed, and my shirt stained and ripped. Even though it's warm in here, a shiver rolls down my spine when a draft slides over the naked skin of my back, clearly visible through the large hole in my shirt.

Never before have I felt my station in life more than I do at this very moment. A destitute, low-class fish cutter standing before a king.

I half expect him to throw us out. To tell us that our appearances are unacceptable. That it is a grave insult to look like this when dining with the Unseelie King.

But to my surprise, he doesn't comment on our ragged appearances at all. Instead, all he says is, "Welcome."

Unsure of what to do, I nod in acknowledgment. As do my friends.

A slight smile ghosts across Orion's lips, but he simply motions toward the table and then saunters over to that grand chair at the head of it.

Draven and I claim the seats closest to the king while Galen and Lyra take the empty ones on Draven's side. Isera sits down as far away from Orion as she can get, leaving Alistair standing in awkward hesitation for a moment. Since there are four chairs on either long side, and Isera and I occupy the ones on the ends, there will be an empty chair next to either me or Isera depending on where Alistair sits.

After a frown in Isera's direction, Alistair sits down in the chair next to me. Isera doesn't even seem to notice. Her hard eyes are locked firmly on the Unseelie King.

He holds her gaze, a knowing smile that is as sharp as a knife on his lips, for a few seconds. Then he breaks eye contact and sweeps his gaze over all of us instead.

"I will get right to it," he says. "The man I want you to kill is called Danzo Wolfstalker and—"

"You've been here," Isera cuts off, her voice cracking through the air like a whip. Her eyes burn with cold fury as she stares Orion down from across the table full of plates and food and glittering faelights. "This whole time, you've been living your best lives here in the Unseelie Court while we have suffered under the dragon shifters' rule for millennia."

Lyra winces at the venom in Isera's voice at the mention of the dragon shifters' role in our suffering. Next to her, Galen casts a worried glance between Isera and the Unseelie King.

For a few seconds, ringing silence descends on the dining room. Orion is watching Isera in a highly assessing way, as if he is trying to decide whether to play with her for his own amusement or to simply slit her throat.

I stifle a grimace at Isera's blunt accusation. It might not have been delivered in a very diplomatic manner, but I don't blame her for reacting like this. I said much the same to Nysara, the Unseelie spy back in Frostfell, when I learned that the Unseelie Court had been free all this time.

The entire room is holding its breath.

A slow and deadly sharp smile spreads across Orion's lips as he finally replies. And it's only one simple word.

"Yes."

Isera's fingers close around the dinner knife on the table before her.

Anticipation sparkles in Orion's eyes, as if he is excited to see what she does next. But before things can get too far out of hand, Draven cuts in.

"Keep the stabbing to a minimum," he growls, and levels a commanding stare on Isera. "We have a job to do."

Orion slides his tongue along his teeth, his eyes still on Isera. "Indeed."

"Why was your court never conquered?" Alistair blurts out before Isera can retort. Or stab someone. His pale brows are furrowed in genuine confusion as he looks at the Unseelie King. "Why did the Icehearts never try to conquer you the way they did us?"

For a few moments, Orion only keeps watching Isera. Then he at last tears his gaze from her and turns to the rest of us.

With a mocking glance in Draven's direction, he replies, "Oh, they tried. They just never succeeded."

"Because you've been hiding behind your wards," Draven counters.

"Precisely." He doesn't sound offended. He sounds proud. After a cold smile in Draven's direction, he slides his gaze back to Alistair. "You want to know why your court was conquered all those millennia ago while ours has remained free all this time? Because we had wards. You didn't. You just let anyone in." His tone turns cruel and mocking. "Because you're *nice* like that."

Isera slams her fist into the tabletop. I jump at the loud bang and the rattle of silverware, and an apology is halfway to my tongue before I catch myself. I'm so used to always apologizing and doing everything I can to make sure no one is upset that it takes me a second to remember that I don't have to do that anymore. I don't have to make myself less and try to please everyone else just so that they will like me. But the instincts are still there, even though I'm working on ignoring them.

Wood scrapes against stone as Isera pushes her chair back and gets to her feet. That terrible bottomless rage burns in her eyes, making her look like a vengeful goddess risen from the pits of hell as she stares Orion down.

"You son of a bitch," Isera growls, her voice low and vicious as she presses her palms against the table and leans forward to glare at Orion. "You could have done something. You could have helped us. If both of our courts had fought together, the Icehearts would never have won."

"Firstly, I was not king back then. I wasn't even alive back then. My great-grandparents weren't even alive back then." He smiles, his eyes gleaming with cruel anticipation as he holds her gaze. "But if I had been the king back then, do you know what I would have done?"

He pauses for a few seconds, but Isera doesn't humor him with a reply. Once the crackling silence has started to stretch, he finally continues.

"I would have conquered your court while you were busy fighting the dragon shifters." His smile turns ruthless. "Then I would have warded it, just like our court was warded, and then I would have made you all kneel at my feet while I ruled it all."

Next to me, Alistair grinds his teeth while anger pulses across his face. But it's nothing compared to the cold fury in Isera's eyes. Very slowly, she pushes her chair all the way back and takes a step away from the table. Her shoes produce slow, ominous thuds as she starts toward the Unseelie King.

Orion's smile widens. It's a cold thing. Full of challenge and wicked taunting. "I suggest you sit back down." His eyes glint as he drags his gaze up and down her body. "Before I put you on your knees instead."

Ice explodes through the room.

I gasp, leaping to my feet in panic as Isera shoots a shard of ice straight at Orion.

But it doesn't even make it halfway to him before the room around me disappears.

Panic crackles through me like a lightning bolt as I suddenly find myself standing in the kitchen of my parents' house back in the Seelie Court. There is a pile of broken glass on the floor right next to me. My chest tightens at just the sight of it. Broken drinking glasses. Those are irreplaceable. We weren't allowed to have money, so we couldn't just buy new ones. And getting replacements for things that broke sometimes took years. Which means we would be forced to drink from our hands for years to come after I broke these.

"I'm sorry," I hear myself saying.

The sound of my own voice sends a bolt of shock through me. I sound so young.

"I'm so, so sorry," my younger self keeps saying in a choked voice.

I can feel tears rushing down my cheeks.

At last, my younger self looks up from the pile of broken glass, which lets me see the rest of the room. My heart jerks as I find both of my parents standing there, staring down at the destroyed glasses in shock, as if they'd broken just seconds before this.

Then they look up at me.

For a moment, only that surprise remains on their features. Then it starts.

I can see their expressions start to shift. Can see every excruciating change as their faces transform into mirrored masks of pure resentment.

Pain spears through me, so intense that it feels as if someone just punched straight through my chest and ripped my heart out. The force of the heartbreak makes me stagger away. But the scene before me doesn't change. The younger me remains standing in the exact same place. I try to look away from my parents' expressions, but I can't. No matter how much I move my head, the younger version of me keeps looking in the same direction. Which means that I am forced to watch it too.

"No, no, no, please," my younger self pleads in a voice full of panic and desperation. "Please, don't hate me. I didn't mean to . . . Please, I didn't mean to—"

"You always ruin everything!" my mother snaps from where she is standing on the other side of our kitchen table. That awful, soul-shattering resentment burns in her eyes like flames as she stares at me. "Why can't you—"

The scene around me disappears in a flash. It's so jarring that I jerk back. My foot gets caught on the edge of a carpet, and I just tumble down on the floor in a heap of limbs.

My head spins and my heart aches with pain. Blinking, I try to clear my vision and get my wits back, but the room around me is blurry. I wipe a hand over my eyes and it comes back wet. Stunned, I slide my hand down my cheek and find that it is wet too. I must have started crying at some point.

"You bastard!" Isera screams, her voice hoarse and sounding like it's going to break any second. "I will fucking kill you for—"

Her words are cut off abruptly.

I snap my gaze in the direction her voice came from.

For a few seconds, I can't make sense of anything that has just happened this past minute. Then, at last, realization comes crashing into me.

Orion has nightmare powers. He can pull bad memories from our heads and make us relive them. I can't remember the exact day that I just saw in my vision, but there have been plenty of days like that in my life, so I know that it is a real memory that Orion has dug out.

He must have done the same to everyone else, because they are all scattered across the room, looking dazed and disoriented.

My gaze darts to Isera, who must have figured out what Orion did to us faster than we did. But she is no longer threatening him. Instead, she is cowering on the floor, gasping and whimpering in fear. Orion towers over her, his black-and-silver eyes glowing with magic.

Then he cuts off the flow of his magic again, and Isera collapses to her hands and knees.

I drag in an unsteady breath, still trying to clear my own head.

Orion leans down and wraps his hand around Isera's throat. With commanding moves, he pulls her up by the throat so that she is on her knees looking up at him instead.

"Watch your mouth," he warns. Threats drip from his voice like dark poison, and his expression is one of merciless power. "With my magic, I could break you within a matter of hours. I could make you so desperate that you would kneel and suck my cock just for a chance at a moment's reprieve from my power. You live and breathe only because of my mercy, so I would be very careful if I were you."

Isera drags in ragged breaths, her chest heaving. But there is no fear on her face as she holds Orion's stare. Quite the opposite. She is glaring up at him with a promise of pain and death in her eyes.

A vicious smile slides across her lips. "If you ever stick your cock in my mouth, I will bite it off."

I tense up, half expecting him to kill her right then and there. But to my surprise, he just slides a slow and deliberate look up and down her body.

"Yes, you really would, wouldn't you?" he muses.

But he doesn't look angry.

He looks *intrigued.*

I stare at him. At Isera. At the beautiful but now messy dining room with knocked over chairs and dazed fae and dragon shifters scattered across the floor.

What kind of madhouse have we ended up in?

8

"Well, that was . . . interesting," Lyra comments once we're finally back in the small house we're staying in.

Isera, who is leaning against the pale living room wall with her arms crossed over her chest, gives the rest of us a flat look. "We survived, didn't we?"

"No thanks to you, ice lady," Alistair mutters from where he is sitting on the brown couch by the other wall.

She shoots him a pointed look. "As if you didn't want to confront him about that as well."

For a moment, it looks like he's going to argue. But then he just tips his head to the side and lifts his toned shoulders in a shrug, conceding the point.

"If you're done bickering, we have an assassination to plan," Draven says.

He is seated in the armchair next to the couch. Lyra and Galen have squeezed themselves down on the couch beside Alistair, but I still feel too on edge to sit, so I pace across the wooden floorboards on the other side of the low table instead.

The rest of the dinner with the Unseelie King was a short and tense affair. We ate, he explained who we needed to kill and reminded us that we needed to make sure we were seen doing it, and then we left. And all the while, Isera and Orion were watching one another as if they were imagining carving each other's hearts out with a dull knife.

"What's there to plan?" Isera counters with a scowl. "It's an assassination. We go in, we slit his throat, and then we get out."

Alistair shrugs and hikes a thumb in her direction. "I'm with the ice lady on this one. I can just torch his entire house. Boom. Job done."

"That's arson," I point out. "Not assassination."

"Does it matter? Dead is dead."

"How are you even going to set his house on fire?" Galen asks. "In case you hadn't noticed, all buildings in this city are made of stone."

"So? Everything melts if the temperature is high enough."

Galen casts him a dubious look, which is mirrored by most of the rest of us. But before anyone can say anything, Draven tries to push the conversation back on track.

"Orion said to assassinate the guy, so that's what we're going to do," he declares.

"Since when do you take orders from anyone?" Galen teases, a grin on his mouth.

Draven blinks in surprise.

Then Galen seems to realize what he just said, because panic and regret crash over his features like a bucket of cold water. Quickly averting his gaze, he clears his throat awkwardly and suddenly begins studying the pattern in the yellow and brown carpet with single-minded determination.

It looks like Draven is going to say something, but before he can, Isera speaks up again.

"Who cares about the stupid assassination," she snaps. "What we need is to figure out a way to force Nightbane and his entire court to help us take down the Icehearts."

Heaving a deep sigh, I finally stop pacing and instead plop down on the carpet in front of the low table. "I don't think that's going to be possible."

They all turn to me. Draven raises his eyebrows in silent question.

I adjust my position so that I'm sitting cross-legged and then drag a hand through my hair to push a few strands out of my face. "Okay, so a few weeks ago, while you were otherwise occupied, I kind of snuck out into the city and talked to Orion's spy in Frostfell."

A sly smile tugs at Draven's lips as he narrows his eyes at me. "Did you now?"

"Yes." I give him a knowing look. "And while I was doing that, you were also sneaking out so that you could be a secret legendary rebel leader, so don't even start with me."

He lets out a silent huff of amusement.

"Anyway, the point is," I continue, "when I talked to Orion's spy, Nysara, the first time, she told me that the Unseelie Court was free." I flick a glance at Isera. "I reacted in much the same way you did. But a little less . . . murderous."

She only continues watching me with those sharp eyes of hers.

I clear my throat and slide my gaze back to the others. "When I asked why they never helped us, she said that the Unseelie Court doesn't get involved in things outside their own realm. And also that relations between our courts were strained even before all this." Glancing at Isera again, I lift my shoulders in an apologetic shrug. "So I doubt that they would ever help us. But maybe the dryads can."

"Dryads?" Alistair says, stunned, at the same time as Lyra asks, "You've met a dryad?"

Draven and I exchange a glance.

"Yes, we have," I reply. "Several of them, in fact."

Even Isera stares at me in surprise as I summarize our meeting with the dryads in the underground forest during the Atonement Trials. When I'm finished, I can feel them all wanting to ask questions, but I realize that *I* have one too. A question that somehow got lost in all the craziness of the past few months.

Frowning, I turn to meet Draven's eyes. "They caught me and then let me go because of what I told them. But how did *you* escape the dryads without getting caught?"

His eyes gleam in the glowing faelights around the room. "I didn't."

"What?"

"They caught me too. But they let me go as well."

I stare at him, my eyes wide. "Why? They hate dragon shifters."

"They mainly hate the Icehearts. They just hate the rest of us by association. Once they realized who I was, that I am the Red Hand who has been working against the Icehearts for decades, they let me go."

My mind spins. Shaking my head, I try to clear it. It doesn't really work. "Wait. Stop. How in Mabona's name did the dryads know that you're the Red Hand? Your own people didn't even know!"

Galen and Lyra wince, and I immediately regret bringing that up.

"The dryads are . . . ancient," Lyra begins carefully, and casts an uncertain glance at Draven. When he gives her a nod, she sits up a little straighter and continues. "They're connected to this world in a way that the rest of us aren't. From what I've heard, they can . . . communicate, or something, through a network across the continent. Like a hive mind, almost."

Next to her on the couch, Alistair frowns so deeply that a long crease appears between his brows. "Yeah, no, I can hear that words are coming out of your mouth, but I have no fucking clue what you're actually saying."

"The trees in Frostfell told the trees in the Seelie Court that Draven was on their side," Isera snaps impatiently from the wall.

"A bit simplified, but yeah," Lyra says. Then she glances uncertainly toward Draven again. "Right?"

"Yes," he confirms. "I'm assuming so, at least."

"Huh," Alistair comments.

My mind churns. Shifting my weight on the soft carpet, I lean forward and rest my arms on the low table before me. Outside the window, soft night winds whirl between the stone buildings, creating a faint whistling sound.

"If the dryads are that ancient," I begin, thinking out loud, "then they might have a lot of answers that no one else does. Well, no one except the Icehearts, anyway. Like why the partnership between the dragon shifters and the fae ended." I abruptly look up from the table and glance between the three dragon shifters. "Unless you already know?"

"Know what?" Galen asks.

Draven blinks at me in surprise. "What partnership?"

I frown at them all. "The one between the dragon shifters and the Seelie fae, of course. Look, Nysara has already told me the truth. That only a small minority of entitled assholes used dragon steel to control the dragon shifters and that the vast majority of Seelie fae were dragon riders because we had a mutually beneficial partnership with you guys."

Shocked silence descends on the room.

The sight of everyone's stunned expressions makes my stomach drop and my mouth dry out. Because it can only mean one thing. They didn't know either.

"What are you saying?" Lyra blurts out.

Alistair and Isera look stricken.

Then rage starts building in Isera's eyes again. "We were punished for something our ancestors didn't even do?"

"Yes." I quickly explain what Nysara told me about our past. When I'm done, Draven, Galen, and Lyra are all staring at me with wide eyes.

"You didn't know," I say. It's more of a statement than a question.

They all answer anyway. "No."

"We were taught that you forced us all with dragon steel," Galen says. "Well, not our clan specifically since we weren't a part of your politics on the mainland. But all the other clans on the continent."

Alistair lets out a low whistle under his breath. "Shit. They lied to you too."

"How?" I demand. "How is that even possible?"

Draven flexes his hand, his features darkening. "You'd be surprised how easy it is to rewrite history. If enough people repeat the same thing, spreading it far and wide and for long enough, it eventually becomes fact. Regardless of how blatant the lie was when it began."

Tense silence settles over the cozy living room. The couch creaks slightly as Alistair shifts his weight.

Lyra heaves a sigh and rubs her forehead. "Well, this is depressing."

"Why don't we just leave?" Alistair suddenly says.

Sitting up straight again, I turn to look at him in surprise. To my utter shock, he blushes a little when everyone stares at him, but he forges on anyway. Sweeping out a hand, he gestures to our three dragon shifters.

"You said it yourself," he begins. "You don't want to get involved with the mess on the mainland. And we've all escaped the Ice Palace now." He motions at me. "Selena is fine. We're all safe. Why don't we all just disappear and leave the world to its fate?"

His words stun me so much that I can't even form a reply. I could never just . . . leave. I would spend the rest of my life looking over my shoulder, fearful that the Icehearts might have at last caught up to me. And more importantly, I can't just leave the rest of our people trapped in the Seelie Court.

I know that it's stupid and ridiculous and selfish, but I want to prove them all wrong. After how they have treated me all my life, I want to see the look in their eyes when they realize that *I* am the one who saved them. When they realize that they were wrong about me. That they should have trusted me. Should have let me in. Should have let me be a part of their community instead of shunning me for something that I had no control over.

Deep down, I know that a real hero would want to free their people solely for unselfish reasons. So the fact that I want to do it partly because I want the recognition I deserve but never received from my own people and partly because I simply want revenge on the Icehearts, rather than for any heroic reasons of the greater good, makes me sick to my stomach. I'm supposed to be a good person, aren't I? So why, when I open the lid and peek down into the dark pits of my soul, do I only find burning rage and festering hatred in there?

Draven clears his throat, shattering the tense silence that has fallen. "Let's just get through this assassination first."

Paper rustles as Draven pulls out the map the Unseelie King gave us and spreads it out across the low table before us. Schemes glint in his eyes as he smooths down the map and then looks from face to face.

"Here's how we're going to do it."

9

The night lies dark and still around the imposing manor before us. Hidden in the shadows outside the garden wall, the six of us move until we are positioned at the back of the property. Draven rises up on his toes and casts a quick glance over the top of the tall stone fence before yanking his head back down.

"Two more here," he whispers as he meets our gazes. "That makes six total in the gardens. Just like Orion said." His eyes lock on mine. "Selena, how many inside?"

Calling up my magic, I throw it across the house. First, I aim it at the gray sparks of boredom. Then tiredness. Then impatience and suspicion and several other emotions that the guards inside might be feeling. Each time my magic connects with a different person, I add it to my mental count.

"Eight, most likely," I reply as I let my magic fade out again.

Draven nods.

"That also matches what Orion said," Galen comments. A pensive expression blows across his features. "Maybe he's not trying to screw us over after all."

"Who even needs *fourteen* guards?" Alistair huffs and casts a scowl in the direction of the house. "Who does this guy think he is?"

"Someone who knows that he has pissed off the Unseelie King," Lyra replies with a shrug.

Next to her, Isera scoffs and rolls her eyes. I raise my eyebrows in silent question, but she doesn't elaborate. However, I think I can guess. Her animosity toward the Unseelie King was plain for everyone to see during that disastrous dinner yesterday evening.

"Just stick to the plan," Draven says, his voice pulsing with authority. "The faster we get this done, the faster we can get the hell out of this court."

Alistair narrows his eyes at him. "Anyone ever tell you that you give a lot of orders? Who even made you team leader anyway?"

Draven slides his gaze to Alistair, and a sharp smile plays over his lips as he flicks a deliberate look up and down Alistair's body. "Remind me again how many assassinations you have carried out?"

"I . . . That's not—"

"Enough with the dick-measuring contests," Isera snaps. She shoots the two of them a pointed look. "Let's just get this over with."

Alistair crosses his arms and scowls but doesn't argue. Draven gives him one last smirk before turning back to the rest of us.

"All right," Draven begins. "Everyone understands their part in the plan?" When we all nod, he adds, "We need to time this perfectly. The Unseelie fae are very particular about their bargains, and Orion requested an assassination where we get seen. Which means that it needs to look like an assassination gone slightly wrong and not like we were trying to get caught from the beginning. And that means stealth. Especially for this first part." He locks eyes with Alistair again. "So keep the fire small."

"Look, bossy pants, I've already told you." Alistair gives him an exasperated look. "I don't do stealthy. My magic is loud and messy."

"Adapt," Draven simply orders before turning back to the rest of us. "Let's go."

Alistair mutters under his breath and shakes his head but sneaks along the stone fence toward the front of the mansion. Isera simply spins on her heel and starts in the other direction in silence.

Still lingering by the wall, Galen and Lyra cast hesitant glances at

Draven, as if they want to say something, but Draven doesn't appear to notice because he, in turn, is looking at me. When they notice that, Lyra swallows while Galen clears his throat before both of them slip away after Isera without another word.

"Ready?" Draven asks.

I nod. Calling up my magic, I once more throw it across Danzo Wolfstalker's mansion. But this time, I only aim it at the six guards who are positioned across the grounds outside. All of them feel a flicker of suspicion as they keep watch. I latch on to it and start to steadily decrease it. We don't want them to spot Alistair before he can start the fire.

While we wait for the others to get into position, I tilt my head back and glance up at the tall stone wall that separates us from the gardens inside.

"You know," I begin, shifting my gaze back to Draven, "getting over this wall would be a lot easier if you could fly."

Draven's eyes glint, and a knowing smirk ghosts across his lips. "You mean like this?"

A small cloud of black smoke erupts before me. My jaw drops as Draven's wings suddenly appear from his back. He spreads them out slightly, looking very pleased with himself. For a moment, I just stare at those imposing black wings before I lock eyes with him again.

"But . . . ," I begin, completely bewildered. "I thought Orion said that you couldn't shift in here."

"We can't. While you were still unconscious, all three of us tried to shift into our dragon forms. It doesn't work. The magic from the wards makes it impossible." That smug smile on his lips widens. "But this form is half human, so the wards apparently can't suppress it."

"That's—"

My sentence is cut off as suspicion tries to spike through one of the guards at the front of the mansion. I flick a glance in that direction, even though I can't see anything from behind the stone wall. While still lowering the guard's suspicion, I turn back to Draven.

"Alistair is in position," I explain.

He nods and shifts his stance so that he's ready to fly us over the wall at a moment's notice.

A warm night wind caresses my cheeks as I wait another ten seconds for Alistair to start his fire. Suspicion tries to flare up from the second guard at the front of the mansion. A smile blows across my lips. *Showtime.*

With a rapid push of my magic, I make the flame of suspicion that all six guards are feeling erupt into a massive fire. Raised voices come from the front of the grounds, though we're too far away to hear what they're saying.

Then the screaming starts.

"FIRE!" a voice bellows from where Alistair snuck off to.

Clanking noises echo from the other side of the stone wall as the two guards who were stationed there leap into motion and rush toward the screaming voice. I cut off the flow of my magic and turn to grin at Draven.

"Well then," I say. "Shall we?"

He lets out a breath of amusement before wrapping his arms around me. My stomach lurches as he quickly flies us over the wall.

The moment our feet touch the grass, he shifts back into his fully human form and summons his magic. Storm clouds gather around us. In the dark of night, they add further shadows to the already darkened garden and hide us almost entirely from view.

After exchanging a nod, we dart across the grass and toward the back door. Alistair should be making his way here right now as well, while Isera, Lyra, and Galen are securing our escape route.

I cast a quick look toward the front of the gardens while Draven and I cut across a patch of neatly trimmed grass. Yellow and orange flames flicker faintly from one of the outbuildings at the front. All six guards who were stationed in the gardens are converging on the small fire.

My heart patters in my chest. *So far so good.*

Gravel crunches and clatters slightly as Draven and I skid to a halt outside the back door. His storm clouds are still rippling around us, keeping us hidden from view. I shove down the handle and yank the door open. Except it doesn't move.

"It's locked," I state, rather superfluously.

"Of course it is," Draven replies, looking entirely unworried about that fact.

While keeping his magic swirling around us, he reaches into one of his belt pouches and pulls out a pair of lockpicks. I draw back slightly and stare at him in surprise as he gets down on one knee in front of the door and begins picking the lock.

"You know how to pick locks," I blurt out. Again rather superfluously. If there was a queen of obvious statements, I would surely steal the crown from her tonight.

Draven casts a quick glance up at me before continuing his work. "That surprises you?"

"Uh, yes. I've always taken you for more of a kick-the-door-down kind of guy."

A surprised laugh escapes his throat, making him almost drop one of the lockpicks. With a smile on his lips, he shakes his head and shoots me a look before concentrating on his task again. "Kind of hard to pull off a stealth assassination if you simply kick the door down."

"True." I slide a considering look over his body. "Got any other secret talents I don't know about?"

The lock clicks open.

Draven gets to his feet and slips the lockpicks back into the belt pouch. Mischief sparkles in his eyes as he replies, "Oh, lots."

Warmth fills my soul. It's followed by a sudden burning hunger. A desperate craving that sears through my entire being. Because I want to learn everything there is to know about Draven Ryat. I want to spend *centuries* getting to know every single part of him. Unraveling all aspects of him. Every secret talent and every odd quirk and every wonderfully complex emotion. Everything that makes him who he is. I want to know it all.

"You—" I begin, but the sudden sound of crunching gravel interrupts me.

Draven and I whirl toward it.

Outside the dark clouds that Draven is keeping around us, a figure rapidly moves toward us. I let out a relieved sigh when I realize it's Alistair. He squints and turns his head from side to side. It takes me another moment to realize he can't see us in the darkness of the clouds.

Draven moves the clouds aside a little so that we become visible from his direction. It makes Alistair jump since he was much closer to us than he apparently thought. Then he quickly closes the final distance to us.

"It's done," he says.

"Good," Draven replies. "Then we—"

An explosion booms across the grounds.

I duck and throw an arm up to protect my head, and it takes me another second to realize that it wasn't an attack on us. Straightening, I dart to the corner of the building and peek around it in the direction the explosion came from. Draven and Alistair appear next to me a moment later.

My mouth drops open as the three of us stare at the scene at the front of the gardens.

The outbuilding where the small fire was located is now . . . gone. And the three buildings next to it are all engulfed in flames. Dancing firelight illuminates the entire estate, and red and orange flames lick their way up the walls of the outbuildings and toward the dark night sky.

For a moment, no one says anything.

Across the grass, the guards are running around and screaming in panic.

Then both Draven and I slowly turn to stare incredulously at Alistair.

He scowls back at us and lets out a huff. "What part of loud and messy did you clearly not understand?"

Draven flexes his hand and then rubs his face in exasperation. "Azaroth's fucking flame."

"Call for reinforcements!" the guards bellow. "The liquor storage just exploded! The fire is spreading! Water magic! Get people with water magic! Call for reinforcements!"

The three of us exchange a glance.

Reinforcements.

This was so not part of the plan.

10

"A small fire," Draven growls. "I said a *small* fire."

With that half-offended scowl still on his face, Alistair throws his arms out in exasperation. "How was I supposed to know that that exact building was full of highly flammable alcohol?"

"You could've looked through the window!"

"Guys," I interrupt before Alistair can retort. I give them both a pointed look. "Maybe we should save this argument for another time?"

All around us, the night is filled with chaos. Half the guards have sprinted out through the gate to no doubt bring those reinforcements they talked about, and servants in nightwear pour out of the mansion's front door with buckets and pitchers of water from the kitchen. Low hissing noises sound when they toss the small loads of water onto the raging fire, but it has practically no effect. Orange and red flames stretch toward the starlit heavens above as the fire keeps climbing.

A moment later, the guards return with a host of people dressed in uniforms. They spread out across the grass while several of them shoot water from thin air and straight toward the fire.

"Spread out!" one of the original guards snaps. "And find the one who did this!"

Alistair heaves a deep sigh and rolls his eyes. Then he turns back to us. "I'll keep them busy. So go and kill that guy." He slides his gaze to Draven, and a note of amused challenge laces his voice as he adds, "I'm sure you can manage to kill one man without me, Mr. Remind-Me-How-Many-Assassinations-You've-Pulled-Off."

Draven snorts. Then he shoots Alistair a pointed look back. "Don't burn the whole city down."

"You know I can't promise that." He's trying very hard to scowl, but there is a distinctly amused glint in his eyes. "All right, get going. I'll meet up with the others at the extraction point."

Before we can reply, he darts back out of Draven's protective dark clouds and disappears around the other corner of the building. We exchange a glance and then hurry back to the now unlocked back door. It opens without a sound. Slipping inside, we find ourselves in a short corridor lit by a few faelights that have been turned so low they barely illuminate the space.

The moment we close the door behind us, the chaos from outside is cut off. It's so abrupt that the sudden silence makes my ears ring. Shaking my head, I try to clear it and instead concentrate on my task.

According to the maps and the information we got from the Unseelie King, our target's bedroom is on the top floor. There is supposed to be a hidden stairwell that was built as an emergency escape route and therefore runs straight from the bedroom to this back door. The only problem, of course, is that it's supposed to be quite well guarded.

Draven keeps a small dark cloud around us, hiding us in the already gloomy corridor, while I summon my magic.

We had planned to do this differently, but because of Alistair's unnecessarily conspicuous pyromancy, the circumstances have now changed. In our original plan, the guards inside the house shouldn't be aware of the fire outside. But it would've been impossible for them to miss the huge explosion that just happened, which means that they are now alert in a way they weren't before. And all their emotions are now different.

I throw my magic across the mansion.

Just as I suspected, none of the guards are feeling bored or sleepy anymore. Instead, all of them are slightly worried.

I bite my bottom lip and drum my fingers against my thigh while trying to figure out how to solve this. Our plan was for me to make them feel so bored and sleepy that they didn't notice us when we snuck past. But that won't work now.

Next to me, Draven is silently watching the hallway while still keeping his magic up. It's not lost on me that he isn't questioning me. He hasn't asked what I'm doing or how I plan to solve this new problem. He is simply trusting that I will figure it out.

That realization distracts me for a moment. Because no one has ever trusted me like this before. No one has ever considered me dependable. No one has ever had this kind of faith in me and my skills.

Blinking, I give my head a quick shake to pull myself back to the present as an idea finally hits me like a lightning bolt.

Distracted. That's it. That's the solution to our problem.

The guards in the house are no doubt worried that the fire is going to spread to this building as well. And if they're too worried about something else, it will distract them from what they're supposed to be doing.

Pushing with my magic, I increase all those sparks of worry until they're burning brightly. For a few seconds, nothing happens. Then they start to move.

I have to suppress a satisfied whoop.

Faint footsteps and the soft sounds of creaking leather armor drift through the otherwise silent house as all eight guards move from their positions and toward the windows at the front of the mansion so that they can no doubt cast a glance at the fire outside to reassure themselves that it won't spread to this building.

"Now," I whisper to Draven. "The stairwell is clear."

He nods. While he keeps a small cloud around us, and I keep my magic pouring into the guards, we sprint down the hall and then skid around the corner. Just as I said, the door to the secret stairwell is now unguarded.

Yanking the door open, we dart into the stairwell and run up the steps two at a time.

A few of the guards start moving back to their positions.

Alarm crackles through me.

I pour more magic into their worry.

It makes two of them drift back to the windows, but the third one, the one who is supposed to be guarding the middle section of this stairwell, continues back toward his post.

"Hurry," I hiss at Draven.

He picks up the pace, taking the steps three at a time. And that's when I realize that he was slowing his pace earlier so that I could keep up, because now I'm the one falling behind. Pushing myself, I run with everything I have up the steps.

My breath saws through my throat and my heart pounds.

The guard is almost back at his post now.

We just need to make it past his floor.

Just a little more.

Draven darts past the second-floor landing.

To his right, the door the guard left through begins to open.

Panic pulses through me.

I leap the final three steps up to the landing and then throw myself up the next couple of steps. Right below me, the door opens fully. A strong hand wraps around my wrist and hauls me up the next five steps. I suppress a gasp.

My heart slams against my ribs as my feet connect with the steps again and I find Draven right there in front of me. He slowly releases my wrist. Standing still as statues, we listen to the guard close the door and then shift his weight on the landing inside the stairwell right below us.

I let out a silent sigh of relief.

After exchanging a nod, Draven and I quietly sneak up the final set of steps.

Another plain door meets us when we reach the final landing. The guard who was supposed to be standing on the other side of this door is still anxiously watching the fire from a window two rooms away. I keep pouring my magic into that flame of worry in his chest to make sure that he remains there, and then I give Draven a nod.

He gently pushes down the handle.

Opening the door, he slips into the room in a silent and fluid motion. I follow quickly behind.

Then I draw up short.

Blinking, I stare at the luxurious bedroom around us.

It's empty.

I frown. How can it be empty? This is supposed to be Danzo Wolfstalker's bedroom. And it's the middle of the night. There is no reason for him to be anywhere else.

Then it hits me.

Of course. The explosion woke *him* up too. That spark of worry I felt from this room wasn't a guard. It was him. In hindsight, it makes sense. I wouldn't want a person standing *inside* my bedroom watching me sleep every night either.

Draven, who once again doesn't look the least bit worried, simply turns to me in a silent request for directions. The sight of it makes my heart squeeze tightly. His faith in me and my abilities is unlike anything I have ever experienced, and it makes my soul thrum with something so steady and warm that I almost forget how to breathe.

Pulling myself together, I quickly point toward a location two rooms away, where I can feel a person standing and staring anxiously out the window.

Draven nods. Sliding out a knife from his belt, he starts in that direction. I follow him. Once we reach the right room, I motion toward the door. With very slow and careful movements, Draven pushes down the handle while I flood Danzo's chest with so much worry that he shouldn't be able to concentrate on anything else.

The door opens to reveal a neat study. And there, standing with his back to us and staring out a window, is a fae man matching the exact description we got from the Unseelie King. Danzo's red hair is illuminated by the fire that still rages outside the window, and his tall and slim body is tense as he grips the windowsill before him.

"Hey," Draven says.

Danzo whips around.

I only have time to see that his face matches the drawing we received.

Then a white bolt of lightning hits him straight in the heart.

His eyes widen for a second, and his body begins spasming violently. Then his knees buckle and he crashes down on the ground. I quickly cut off my magic so that the guards will no longer be distracted by their worry, but they apparently didn't hear the thuds from Danzo's body, because none of them start moving in our direction.

"Well, he's dead," Draven announces while watching the guy lie there and stare unseeing up at the pale stone ceiling. Then he turns to me. "Are they coming?"

I throw my magic across the house again, but those smalls sparks of worry are only moving back to their previous positions.

"No," I reply. Then I glance down at the blade in Draven's hand, which he unsheathed but never actually used. "What's with the knife?"

"It's for dramatic effect when we get caught."

A laugh escapes my chest. Raising my eyebrows, I give him a dubious look. "Seriously?"

"Yes. When people hear the word *assassination,* they most often think about someone getting their throat slit." He shrugs. "So I'm just making sure these people understand that this was in fact an assassination."

I let out another soft chuckle and shake my head. "Go signal to the others where we are. I'll make sure the guards are coming."

While Draven walks over to the window and shoves it open, I hurry to the pale wooden bookshelf by the door. Grabbing the ceramic pot on the middle shelf, I unceremoniously throw it down on the ground while reaching out with my magic toward the yellow-green sparks of suspicion.

The pot crashes down on the stone floor at the same time as Draven shoots a small bolt of lightning out the window.

I push with my magic at the guards' suspicion. It flares up in their chests, but to my surprise, they don't start moving in our direction. I scowl. They're probably just suspicious about who started the fire. Not the crash from the pot. Did they seriously not hear it?

With a sigh of annoyance, I grab the bookcase by the side.

And then I yank the whole thing forward.

It topples like a felled tree.

A loud bang echoes through the entire house as it hits the stone floor.

Draven turns to me and arches an eyebrow. "Subtle."

"Shut up," I huff.

He chuckles.

Those sparks of suspicion that I'm increasing finally start running in our direction.

I grin. "They're coming."

"All right, get to the window and get ready."

While I dart across the room and position myself right in front of the now open window, Draven drags our already dead target over to the toppled bookshelf so that it will look like it happened during the struggle. Then he positions himself behind the dead guy and lifts Danzo's chest up from the floor a little so that he can place the knife against his throat from behind.

Footsteps thud against the floor outside the door.

Draven flexes his hand on the hilt of the knife.

Then the door is yanked open.

And I have to give it to him, it is indeed very dramatic when he slits Danzo's throat right as the guards charge into the room.

"Assassins!" the first guard screams, his eyes wide with shock and panic.

The two guards behind him begin drawing their swords while he starts channeling some kind of magic. But I never get to find out what kind, because all three of them are hit in the chest with a blast of wind from Draven. It sends them tumbling back out the door.

"Go," Draven says as he whirls around and sprints toward me.

I scramble up onto the windowsill and then leap out the third-story window.

Winds rush in my ears for a second.

Then my feet hit a bridge of solid ice with a thud. I crouch down to regain my balance while Draven jumps out the window and lands behind me. Shouts rise from the guards outside in the gardens as the two of us take off across Isera's ice bridge.

Magic is summoned from below, but before they can shoot it at us, Alistair throws a torrent of fire at them from a roof to our right. Flames roar through the air, and the guards dive for cover.

My boots are slipping on the slick ice bridge as I hurtle down it. As if Isera could see that all the way from where she is waiting on the other side of the stone wall, she changes the texture of the ice so that it becomes rough and pebbled.

Alistair shoots another blast of flames at the guards below.

And then jumps from the roof and toward the bridge.

I gasp, because there is no way he will make it all the way there.

But before he can plummet down to the ground below, Isera stretches the ice bridge in his direction. He hits the pale ice with a thud and rolls with the motion. Then he's up and running. Draven and I reach him a second later.

An absolutely ridiculous laugh rips from my throat as we leap off the ice bridge on the other side of the stone wall and disappear back into the darkened city.

II

The armchair lets out a huff as I drop down on the soft brown cushions and lean back while raking my fingers through my hair. On the other side of the low table, Draven claims the remaining armchair while our four other companions are still making their way into the living room.

"I can't believe that actually worked," Alistair says as he throws himself down on the couch and swings his legs up across the cushions.

Galen unceremoniously pushes Alistair's legs back down on the floor and sits down next to him.

From the other armchair, Draven turns to Alistair while a smug smile plays over his lips. "Like I said, not my first assassination."

Alistair rolls his eyes, but instead of taking the bait, he shifts his gaze to Isera. "Would you sit down for once? You're always lurking by the door like a little . . . lurker."

Isera, who is leaning against the wall with her arms crossed, gives him a flat look. "Your extensive vocabulary dazzles me."

He huffs. "It's not . . ." Trailing off, he instead turns to frown at Lyra, who is strolling away from the living room. "And where are *you* going?"

She spins around gracefully to face us while continuing to walk backward toward the kitchen. "To get some glasses, of course."

On the couch, Galen sits up straighter and frowns at her. "Glasses? For what?"

A mischievous grin spreads across her mouth as she holds up a bottle. Both Alistair and I raise our eyebrows in surprise. Draven doesn't look particularly surprised, and Galen just groans.

"Seriously?" Galen questions and flaps a hand in her direction. "Where did you even get that?"

Her orange eyes gleam. "I stole it from the mansion, of course."

Galen sighs and rubs a hand across his face.

"What?" Lyra shrugs, a grin still on her mouth. "The guy's dead. It's not like he's going to miss it."

While Galen groans again and lets out a breath of amusement, Lyra winks and then disappears into the kitchen. The sound of clinking glasses drifts through the open doorway a few seconds later.

I turn to Alistair and arch an eyebrow. "I thought you blew up all the alcohol."

"I didn't blow it up," Alistair says with a huff. Though there is slight embarrassment hiding underneath his scowl as he crosses his arms. "I just . . . accidentally set it on fire."

"It was a pretty loud bang." I raise my hands. "Just saying."

He draws his eyebrows down farther. "Yeah, well, you try setting the fire next time, Soulstealer."

"All right," Lyra announces before I can reply. "Victory drinks!"

She saunters back into the living room with two tall stacks of drinking glasses gripped in the palm of one hand and the bottle in her other. Galen sucks in a sharp breath between his teeth and lurches up from the couch. Darting forward, he grabs the two stacks that were tilting precariously and rescues them before they can topple to the floor and fill the room with broken glass.

"Azaroth's flame, Lyra," Galen begins, sounding exasperated, as he sets the glasses down on the low table. "You do know that you don't have to make every activity into an extreme sport, right?"

"*Tsk.*" She flashes him another grin. "My grandma always says that living on the edge is much more fun that living responsibly."

"Yeah, well, your grandma is crazy."

"How do you know? You haven't even met her."

"She's related to you. That's all the proof I need."

I smile as they continue bickering while Lyra pours dark red wine into the water glasses that Galen has now positioned in front of everyone. Then my eyes slide to Draven, and a pang hits me right in the heart.

There is an awful mix of both hurt and desperate longing on his face as he watches the two of them. The sight of it makes my chest tighten. This kind of friendship and familial love is what he could've had. What he *should've* had. But because the Icehearts trapped him with dragon steel and forced him to do their bidding, he lost two centuries of friendship. He spent two hundred years being treated as a traitor by the people he was trying to protect. And now none of them seem to know how to act around each other.

Draven starts slightly, and his gaze darts to me, as if he can feel me watching him. In a heartbeat, he wipes the forlorn expression off his features and instead gives me a smile. I force myself to smile back as if nothing is wrong, because I know he didn't want anyone to see what he was really feeling. But inside, my heart aches for him.

"Now then," Lyra says, setting the now empty wine bottle down on the table with a thud and raising her full glass. "To victory."

Couches creak and clothes rustle as the rest of us quickly reach for the glasses on the table. Only Isera remains standing immobile by the wall. Her blue-and-silver eyes are as cool and sharp as always as she watches us lift the glasses.

"To victory!" Lyra repeats, even more forcefully.

"To victory," we all echo with a smile while holding our glasses in the air. There is something infectious about Lyra's joy.

I take a sip of wine. And almost cough it back up. Slapping a hand in front of my mouth, I forcibly swallow the mouthful of alcohol. A shudder rolls down my spine. The wine is incredibly dry and almost . . . bitter.

While checking to make sure that Lyra hasn't noticed, I carefully set the glass back down on the table.

"Does anyone else feel like this was way too easy?" Galen suddenly asks while everyone else sets down their glasses too.

Lyra shoots him an incredulous look. "Dude, I literally just said *to victory*. You couldn't wait two more minutes or something before you start with the grumpy gloom-and-doom comments?"

He shoots her a half-offended look back. "What? Someone had to say it."

"I agree with Galen," Draven says before Lyra can reply. "It was a lot easier than I expected it to be."

Both of them turn to him in surprise. I slide my gaze to him as well, but there is nothing left of the painful emotions on his face. Now there is only an expression of calm authority on his features. Just like always. And now that I know about the dragon steel, I suddenly understand why he has trained himself to expertly block out emotions.

"But you know as well as I do," he continues, "that Unseelie fae always honor the bargains they make. They saved Selena, and now we have killed this Wolfstalker guy. Orion is expecting us to deliver this news at dawn. Once we have, our deal is done. We have what we came for, and Orion got what he wanted."

Alistair sits up straighter. "And then we can leave."

Draven slides his gaze to him. "Yes."

"We shouldn't leave," Isera growls from the wall.

The sharpness in her tone makes me jump. Blinking, I turn to face her. And so does everyone else.

That terrible fury burns in her eyes like blue flames as she stares us all down. "We're inside the wards. This is our chance to force Nightbane and the entire Unseelie Court to help us take down the Icehearts."

"Force him?" Alistair counters. "How the hell are *we* supposed to force the Unseelie King to do anything? We have no power here. No leverage." He flings out an arm and stabs a hand in Draven's direction.

"Mabona's tits, the fucking Shadow of Death had to grovel on his knees for us to even be allowed in through the wards."

Draven winces ever so slightly, but everyone else is looking at Alistair, so they don't notice that. I do, though. And I once again swear to any goddess or god who will listen that I will make sure that Draven never has to do anything like that ever again.

"We have to do *something*," Isera snarls back. "We can't take down the entire Iceheart Dynasty on our own. You know it. I know it. We need allies. Powerful allies. Dangerous allies." Uncrossing her arms, she stabs a hand toward the window and the castle sleeping in the darkened night outside. "He's an arrogant, ruthless bully, but he has nightmare powers. And most importantly, he has a healer *and* a guy with portal magic. We need them."

"No, what we need is to get the hell out of here." Alistair throws his arms out and looks between the rest of us. "Right?"

I hesitate. The problem is that both of them are right. Isera is right that we need powerful and dangerous allies before we can even hope to go up against the Icehearts. But Alistair is also right. We have no way of forcing the Unseelie King to help us.

Isera clenches her jaw in anger. Pushing off from the wall, she stalks across the room without another word and disappears into the corridor that houses the bedrooms. Galen lets out a long sigh and rakes a hand through his blond hair while Alistair once more crosses his arms and scowls.

Sitting on the floor on the other side of the low table, Lyra stares after Isera for another few seconds before she turns her head back. She looks incredibly disappointed as she glances from face to face and then down to the still full wine glasses on the table.

"Well, there goes that celebration."

12

Brisk morning winds wash over us as we sneak in through the side gate and into the Unseelie King's castle without any civilians noticing. I stifle a shudder as the winds caress my naked back through the hole in my shirt. I still need to figure out how to get new clothes. Maybe before we leave, I can somehow manage to convince someone here in the city to trade me another shirt.

The servant who met us at the gate guides us through several corridors. I glance at him in surprise when I realize he isn't taking us to the same dining room we met Orion in last time. Instead, we seem to be moving in the direction of the main entrance.

When we reach a set of open double doors that lead into a massive throne room, I can't help but tense up. The last time I was escorted into a throne room in this way, I ended up with an iron collar around my neck.

Draven brushes a hand down my arm, seemingly without even thinking about it, because his eyes are locked on the throne room ahead. And it's such a comforting and natural gesture that I almost lose track of where we are.

My heart squeezes and warmth washes through my body.

This has to be real. These emotions . . . they have to be genuine. They have to.

But before I can fall deeper into that pit of uncertainty because of the mate bond, the servant comes to an abrupt halt by the doors and raises an arm to tell us to go inside.

The six of us exchange a glance. Then we walk through.

Once again, the Unseelie Court manages to surprise me. Those images in my head of a harsh and ugly court are thoroughly squashed underneath the sheer beauty that is the Unseelie King's throne room.

Just like the rest of the castle, the walls and floor of the high-ceilinged throne room are made of beautiful white stone. Tall windows along the room's long sides fill the space with golden morning light that makes the faelight gems sparkle. The entire ceiling has been painted to depict a breathtaking night sky with glittering stars and northern lights in green and purple.

Vibrant vines with flowers in shades of violet, dark blue, and silver climb up the stone pillars that line the dark blue carpet that runs from the door and all the way to the throne on the other side of the large room. The throne itself is a masterpiece carved from some kind of shining black stone. Intricate swirls and curving shapes make it look like night shadows that have been frozen in time.

I can't help but gape at the entire room.

Then my gaze slides to the fae man seated on the throne, and I promptly snap my mouth shut and wipe the amazed expression off my features.

Orion Nightbane isn't sitting on his throne. He is *lounging* on it. His legs are spread and he is leaning a little to the side to rest his chin against his fist while his elbow is propped up on the armrest. His other arm is draped nonchalantly along the other armrest. That, along with the half smirk on his face, makes him look like the very definition of lazy arrogance.

I grind my teeth in annoyance but keep my mouth shut as the six of us come to a halt a short distance in front of him.

"Well?" he drawls.

Next to me, Draven flexes his hand but keeps his tone neutral as he replies, "Danzo Wolfstalker is dead. And they saw me slit his throat."

"Excellent."

"As if you didn't already know that."

A slow and incredibly sharp smile spreads across Orion's mouth, but he doesn't confirm or deny it.

"We've upheld our end of the bargain," Draven declares.

The Unseelie King slides his gaze over all of us for a moment before finally replying, "Yes, you have." His eyes find mine. "Selena's life in exchange for Danzo's."

"Then that concludes our business." Draven narrows his eyes. "I suggest you—"

"Are you truly content just hiding in here behind your wards?" Isera cuts him off, her blazing eyes locked on the Unseelie King.

His black-and-silver eyes slide to her. I hold my breath. The silence thrums against the white stone walls as Orion slowly drags his gaze up and down Isera's body before locking eyes full of challenge on her.

"Who's hiding?" he counters.

"You know damn well that you're hiding in here." Her eyes are as hard and merciless as the ice she wields as she glares back at him. "So why not take this chance to do something about it? The Icehearts have lost the Commander of the Dread Legion. The Shadow of Death and the entire Black Dragon Clan are on our side." She flicks her hand toward me and Alistair. "We are the three strongest magic users in the entire Seelie Court. And we're all ready to fight."

On her other side, Alistair whips his head around and stares at her. But her eyes are still only locked on Orion as she continues speaking.

"You will never have a better opportunity than this. Join us. Together, we can take down the Iceheart Dynasty once and for all."

The silence that descends over the beautiful throne room is so thick that I can almost feel it pressing against my skin. My heart beats so loudly in my chest that I'm certain everyone must hear it in this dead-quiet room. If Orion actually agrees, it's going to change everything. With the Unseelie Court on our side, we might actually stand a chance.

I try to remember to breathe as Orion Nightbane studies us all in silence for another few seconds.

Then he laughs.

It's a vicious and mocking sound.

Lightning flashes in Isera's eyes, and she takes a step forward. But Alistair grabs her by the arm, stopping her from launching across the floor and strangling the life out of the snickering king. A snarl rips from her throat, and she yanks her arm out of his grip, but she doesn't have time to move again because Orion finally replies.

"Why should I?" he demands. Flicking his wrist, he indicates all of us. "You are the most miserable group I have ever seen." His eyes lock on Draven. "A former commander who trusts no one." His gaze slides to Galen and Lyra. "Two magicless soldiers who are drowning in guilt."

Both of them flinch.

But Orion's eyes just shift to me. "One emotion wielder who is terrified of her own power." His gaze moves to Alistair. "One fire wielder who doesn't even want to be here." At last, he locks eyes with Isera again. And his gaze seems to spear through her like a blade. "And one ice lady who is so consumed by vengeance that she has shut off all her emotions."

My heart pounds in my chest. How does he know so much about us? About *me?*

Then realization slides down my spine like ice. He can rifle through all our bad memories. He knows more about us than we do.

The Unseelie King flicks his wrist in a dismissive gesture. "You are weak and broken, and I will not risk my court by backing the losing team."

"Then our business here is done," Draven declares. Without so much as a nod to Orion, he turns and jerks his chin at the rest of us. "Let's go."

"I will not—" Isera begins, and starts taking another step toward the throne.

But before she can even lift her foot, Draven grabs her by the front of her silver tunic and yanks her face closer to his as he growls, "I said, *out*. Now."

The sheer power and command in his voice pulse through the room like a physical blow. That was not a request from an ordinary dragon shifter. That was an order from the Commander of the Dread Legion. A command issued. A command obeyed.

The utter authority in his voice stuns even Isera so much that she hesitates. Draven uses his grip on her shirt to shove her in the direction of the doors. She stumbles several steps before managing to find her balance again. Fury flares up in her eyes, but when Draven stalks toward her, she just grinds her teeth and then storms toward the doors as well.

For a moment, I just remain rooted there on the white stone floor. Then I hurry to catch up with them. The others do the same.

While walking briskly toward the door, I cast a quick look over my shoulder.

Orion Nightbane is still lounging on his throne. But instead of that cruel and dismissive look in his eyes, his beautiful face is now full of amusement and wicked anticipation. It makes a bolt of alarm shoot up my spine, and I quickly snap my gaze back to the doors ahead.

But as we make our way out through the castle's main entrance, I can't get his words out of my head.

A former commander who trusts no one.

That's what he said about Draven.

But he's wrong.

The more I think about it, the more I realize something that should have been glaringly obvious but that I haven't even noticed until now.

Draven trusts *me*.

During the assassination last night, he trusted me with his life. Trusted me to get us through the house without anyone spotting us.

But it's more than that.

He has been trusting me for months now. Trusting me with important things. Even when I hated him.

Even though he has had his wings savagely whipped for years, decades, he still trusts me to touch them. I didn't even realize it until now. After all the brutality and pain he has suffered, he must be incredibly wary of letting people touch his wings. But he lets me touch them. Even as far back as that time in the underground forest during the Atonement Trials when I still considered him an enemy. Even then, he still trusted me not to hurt him.

And he trusted me with his freedom. While we were in the Ice Palace, he gave me clues, trusting me to figure out the answer. That comment about why the furniture in his room was gray and not black. Telling me to question things that don't make sense.

Something else he said slams back into me and clangs through my mind like a giant bell. *I knew that I had found someone who understood what it's like to be hated for something that you haven't chosen.* He couldn't tell me what was really going on, so he left me little clues like that in our conversations, trusting me to figure out that the Icehearts were controlling him with dragon steel.

And most of all, he trusted me with his heart.

And I stomped all over it.

Pain slices through my chest at the memory of that night.

He told me that I was his mate, and I just screamed back at him that I didn't want to be his mate. I can still remember the hurt that pulsed across his face when I said that.

I swallow against a sudden thickness in my throat as I watch Draven where he walks down the white stone steps that lead from the castle's main entrance.

The Unseelie King said that Draven trusts no one.

But he has trusted me with everything.

His life.

His body.

His freedom.

His heart.

All my life, no one has ever trusted me with anything. But he does.

I grip the fabric of my shirt right over my heart to try to stifle the ache that suddenly pulses through my entire chest. It's followed by a flash of burning rage. I have never been this angry with the universe in my entire life.

All the suffering I have endured in the Seelie Court is nothing compared to the sheer injustice of knowing that some mystical force in the universe chose who I should love. There is not enough fire in hell to describe the utter rage I feel when I think about how I wasn't allowed to choose Draven on my own. Because now every time something like this happens, there is always a seed of doubt buried deep in my chest.

A seed of doubt that is always asking things like, *Does he trust you because he loves you or because the mate bond has conditioned him to trust you?* And, *Do you actually love him back or is everything you feel just the result of the mate bond tampering with your emotions?*

A snarl threatens to escape my throat, so I snap my mouth shut. Dropping my hand from my shirt, I shake it out in frustration and then stalk down the steps after Draven and the others.

If I ever meet the being who invented the concept of fated mates, I'm going to rip their fucking heart out and make them eat it.

13

A red sun rises over the tall rock formations that wrap around the back of the sprawling city as we leave the castle grounds. The red light reflects against the canal to our left, making the rippling water look like blood. I suppress a shudder.

Trying to shake off the sudden ominous feeling that crawled up my spine, I turn to my companions, who have all stopped on the street a short distance from the wrought steel gates of the castle. For a few moments, the rushing water from the waterfalls behind us is the only sound that fills the brisk morning.

Then Isera snaps, "Why did you interfere?"

Both Lyra and Galen start slightly at her sharp tone and glance uncertainly between her and Draven, but Draven doesn't seem particularly offended by her harsh demand. He just shifts his gaze to her furious face and locks serious eyes on her.

"Because Orion likes to play games," he replies. "Since he's always hiding behind his wards, I've only had limited interactions with him, but even then it's impossible to miss. He fucking loves to play games with people. Talking circles around them, making them admit things they never wanted to admit, pulling them into dangerous bargains, getting them to do things for his own amusement. He lives for it."

Isera clenches her jaw, but she sounds more annoyed with Orion than angry with Draven as she presses out, "I can handle that arrogant little pretty boy king just fine."

"No, you can't," Draven says, though not unkindly. There is no cruelty in his voice as he holds her gaze. Only simple facts. "We all saw how badly his nightmare powers affected you."

She flinches, and for a moment I swear I can see embarrassment flash across her face. Then the rage returns. "As if you didn't—"

"I'm not saying that we weren't affected too. I'm saying that whatever memory he was using against you is worse than what he was using against us. It affects you more than our memories affect us. And part of being a good soldier is knowing your own limits."

"I'm not a soldier. And I don't give a shit about limits."

"Then you will die before this war even starts."

"If you think—"

"Is it true?" Galen suddenly interrupts.

The question jolts everyone out of Draven and Isera's argument. Blinking, I turn to face him, but he is looking at Alistair. The sudden change seems to confuse Isera as well, because the burning fury in her eyes banks a little as she also turns to frown at Galen.

Another brisk morning wind whirls between the pale stone houses, and somewhere on the street next to ours, several doors are opened and closed. The faint thuds are almost drowned out by the rushing waterfalls.

I flick a quick glance at Draven, who, just like everyone else, is looking at Galen. But as opposed to the rest of us, he doesn't look confused. Instead, he is studying his friend with an expression I can't read. Shifting my gaze back to Alistair, I find him looking strangely guilty.

"Is what true?" he asks, glancing uncertainly between Galen and the rest of us.

"What he said in there," Galen says. "Was he right when he said that you don't even want to be here?"

Alistair starts, looking caught for a moment. Then he draws his pale brows down in a scowl and crosses his arms over his chest. There is a note of challenge in his voice as he replies with a single word. "Yes."

That moment right before we crossed the border into the Unseelie Court drifts through my mind. That moment when we were all moving toward the wards while Alistair glanced around the open grasslands instead.

So he *had* been about to leave.

Cocking my head, I study him as he glares back at the rest of us. I wonder why he stayed.

"You don't care about freeing the Seelie Court?" I ask, making sure to keep my tone neutral and free from judgment.

"Or getting revenge?" Isera demands.

She, on the other hand, isn't checking her tone. Her question comes out like an accusation. It immediately sets Alistair's anger aflame too.

"No." He practically spits the word back at her. "I don't."

"But you said that we would kill them all," she growls back at him. "You said that you hated them."

"I do hate them."

"Then why—"

"Because I hate everyone!" His chest heaves, and he uncrosses his arms and instead throws them out wide in a show of frustration. "I hate everyone! I hate people." Dragging in a deep breath, he rakes both hands through his hair. And suddenly, he just looks . . . exhausted. A hint of desperation creeps into his green-and-orange eyes as he says, "I just want to be left alone."

The pain and desperation and tiredness in his voice as he says it throw me off so much that I don't know what to say. Apparently, everyone else is struggling with the same thing, because we all just stand there staring at him for a moment.

When the awkward silence begins to stretch, Alistair clears his throat and drops his arms. That desperation disappears from his eyes in a heartbeat as he instead draws his eyebrows down in a scowl once more.

"Remember when you asked me what I would do if I won the Atonement Trials?" he demands, looking at me and Isera.

"You never answered," I reply.

"My plan was to buy a huge fucking mansion in some remote place far away, and then I was going to live there alone for the rest of my life. Away from everything and everyone. Forever."

The silence that descends over our group pulses with tension. Isera looks like she's about to punch him in the face, and Alistair is glaring back at her as if he is daring her to try. It makes my chest tighten and my stomach roll with nausea. I hate it when people who are supposed to be friends fight like this. It reminds me too much of how my parents always fought. And just like those times, I get ready to mediate in order to de-escalate the conflict.

But before I can so much as open my mouth, someone else breaks the tense silence.

"So you're a little grumpy," Lyra says in a light voice. "That's all right." Her black dragon scale armor shifts slightly as she reaches into one of her belt pouches and pulls out a small pastry, of all things. Holding it out, she offers it to Alistair. "Here, have a snack."

Alistair stares at her as if she has grown a second head.

To be fair, so do I.

If it had been anyone else, I'm pretty sure that Alistair would have turned them into a pile of ash at this point. But Lyra didn't say it mockingly. It wasn't a taunt or an insult. Instead, as I watch her hold out that absolutely ridiculous little pastry with a smile on her face, it becomes crystal clear that Lyra is being completely genuine.

Alistair seems to realize that too, because he hesitantly reaches out and takes the offered pastry. Lyra's grin widens, and she brushes a few crumbs off her hands while Alistair just stands there, holding the pastry and looking even more bewildered than before.

"Well, are you going to eat it?" Lyra asks, and nods toward the pastry.

Blinking, Alistair starts in surprise. When she just raises her eyebrows, he slowly lifts the pastry and takes a bite.

"There you go." Her eyes glitter in the morning sun as she nods. "My grandma always says that the way to a man's heart is through his stomach."

Alistair chokes on the pastry. Coughing violently, his entire chest shakes as he tries to breathe and dislodge the bite of food at the same time. His face is bright red.

"And besides," Lyra continues, and gives Alistair's back a brisk thump, "my oldest brother always gets *hangry* too, so I know how to recognize the signs."

The firm thump on his back makes him at last cough out the bite of pastry that had gotten stuck in his throat. He gulps in a breath and then straightens before turning to stare at Lyra once more. His cheeks are so red that I swear he's about to catch fire any second now.

For a few moments, no one seems to know how to react.

Then Draven bursts out laughing.

It's such a wonderful sound of genuine mirth that it fills my entire soul. Goddess above, I could live off that sound for weeks. Warmth floods my chest, and I once more find myself swearing to any deity that will listen that I am going to carve out a future where Draven laughs like that often.

"God, I've missed this," he says while dragging in a deep breath and composing himself again.

For one glorious second, both Lyra and Galen grin brightly. Then in a heartbeat, their smiles dim, and shame and regret slam across their features instead. Draven immediately notices, of course, and in the span of a few seconds, that wonderful atmosphere is gone again.

"You—" Draven begins, but he never has a chance to finish.

Alarm crackles through my veins as an arrow suddenly speeds through the air straight toward the side of Draven's head.

"Watch out!" I scream, shoving him straight in the chest.

I normally wouldn't be able to push him back like this, but he must trust my warning, because he doesn't try to keep his balance. Instead, he stumbles backward from the shove.

A moment later, the arrow speeds past in the space where his head used to be.

My heart jerks in my chest as I whirl around toward the attacker.

Panic lurches through me as I find a horde of fae soldiers pouring out onto the street. They swarm around us like a flood. Half of them are carrying bows, and the other half are—

Before I can even finish the thought, a blast of water hits me in the chest. It slams into me with such force that I fly backward, crashing into Draven, who was trying to straighten from my earlier shove. Air explodes from my lungs as my unprotected back hits his firm chest and the hard dragon scale armor that covers it. Since Draven was already off-balance, the hit makes both of us crash down on the ground in a heap of limbs.

Shaking my head to clear it, I try to blink my surroundings back into focus and scramble off Draven at the same time.

My stomach lurches as someone grabs me by the arm and hauls me off Draven's chest. I just barely have time to see Alistair being hauled off Isera in a similar manner, both of them on the ground, before I'm shoved down on my knees so hard, my teeth rattle.

A moment later, cold steel is pressed against my throat. I still.

"Don't," someone warns from a few steps behind me to the right.

Since there is a sword across my throat, I can't turn my head fully, but from the corner of my eye, I can see Draven on one knee, as if he had been about to get to his feet. Two Unseelie fae soldiers are standing behind him, and one of them is pressing a sword to his throat as well.

When I shift my gaze back, I find that the rest of our companions are in similar positions.

And suddenly, the street is dead silent.

People who look like normal civilians have cracked open windows all along the street, and they are watching us with a mixture of curiosity, confusion, and anticipation on their faces.

Footsteps echo between the pale stone buildings, coming from the direction of the palace. And even though I've barely spent any time with the guy, I already know who it is before he reaches us. The simultaneously lazy and commanding footsteps give him away.

"This is how you would repay me?" Orion Nightbane demands, his voice echoing across the whole street as he strides around our captured group so that he is standing in front of us.

He is wearing the same dark blue and black garments that he wore when we left him in the throne room a few minutes ago, and his dark blue hair lies neatly down his back, as if the wind itself wouldn't dare to rustle a single strand of hair on his royal head.

"What the hell do you think you're doing, Orion?" Draven growls back at him. "We had a—"

Before he can finish the sentence, the second soldier behind him shoves a gag into his mouth. I barely have time to even open my mouth before they do the same to me. Isera almost bites the finger off one of her captors, but with a sword to her throat, she can't do much else as she and the rest of our friends are gagged tightly as well.

The Unseelie King watches us all with a wicked glint in his eyes. I snarl a curse at him through the fabric of the gag, but it only comes out as garbled mumbling. And it makes the soldier behind me press his sword harder against my throat. I glare at Orion but make no other attempt to speak.

Once all of us have been firmly gagged, Orion continues speaking. And just like before, he talks loudly enough for the entire street to overhear.

"We had a deal," the Unseelie King declares. "I allowed my healer to save Selena's life in exchange for information about the Icehearts. I helped you, and you repay me by trying to weaken my court."

I draw back, staring at him in confusion.

"Don't look so shocked," he continues, and spreads his arms wide to indicate the city around us. "This is *my* court. I have eyes everywhere. And I know that you murdered one of my people last night. Several guards even saw you do it."

My mind spins as I try to figure out what in Mabona's name is going on.

"Danzo Wolfstalker was a high-ranking member of my court and an asset to this city," Orion says, stabbing an accusatory hand in our direction. "And you sought to undermine me, undermine us all, by killing him."

The expression that descends on his dangerously beautiful face is so cold and cruel that I would have shivered if I weren't so angry. Instead,

I glare back at him, my eyes blazing with rage. He is the one who told us to assassinate that guy. We upheld our end of the bargain, and Draven said that Unseelie fae always honor the deals they make. So why the hell is this backstabber arresting us for it now?

That ruthless expression remains on Orion's face as he stares us all down. "You betrayed my hospitality."

A few of the soldiers start putting on thick gloves before pulling out something that clanks metallically.

My stomach drops as I watch them approach us with iron manacles.

The Unseelie King flashes us a cruel smile.

"Let me show you what we do to traitors in the Unseelie Court."

14

Strength drains from my body like water through a sieve. I want to pace across the dark stone floor or slam my fists against the iron bars of our cell or murder the guards who have now fled up the steps to escape Draven's wrath. But with a massive iron manacle around my ankle and a thick iron chain locked to that manacle and then secured to yet another iron ring in the floor, all I can do is sit there on the ground and lean my back against the cold stone wall behind me.

Next to me, Isera and Alistair are doing the same. With the iron suppressing our magic and draining our strength, just standing up would be a challenge.

On my other side, Draven has been shackled with manacles and chains around both his wrists and ankles, as well as around his waist and neck. But the iron does nothing to suppress his magic, so a furious lightning storm is raging outside the wall of iron bars that separates our cell from the rest of the underground prison. The two guards who were stationed there fled up the steps a few minutes ago, but it unfortunately still doesn't help us escape.

Lyra and Galen, who are similarly shackled, yank uselessly against their restraints.

I draw in a long breath, trying to muster enough strength to lift my arms. The iron burns cold against my skin where it is clamped around my ankle. If they had shackled us fae the way they did Draven, we would all probably be unconscious by now.

A sudden urge to laugh pulses through me. It's so intense that I have to press my lips together to stop myself. But the absurdity of it all is staggering. Am I actually feeling grateful to those damn soldiers for only shackling me with a little iron instead of rendering me unconscious? Mabona's tits, if the bar falls any lower, it will be beneath the floor.

The door at the top of the stairs opens.

Draven immediately lets his storm magic fade. Better to draw the person down the steps and then knock him out with a lightning strike. That way, we might somehow be able to reach a pair of keys.

Footsteps echo between the dark stone walls.

Tilting my head back, I find a pair of spotless black shoes descending the steps. Once again, I try to muster enough strength to stand, but all I can do is raise my chin as the Unseelie King saunters down the stairs and comes to a halt outside the bars to our cell.

"Well, well, well," he drawls.

A bolt of white lightning zaps through the air.

It passes through the space where Orion was standing a fraction of a second too late and slams into the wall on the other side of the room. Dark storm clouds immediately start gathering again as Draven summons his full power. But right before another lightning bolt can split the air, Orion raises his hand and holds up something that looks like a short metal rod. It starts glowing faintly at the same time as Orion's eyes begin glowing.

Draven jerks back and sucks in a sharp breath between his teeth. The churning storm clouds evaporate in a flash.

"Oh, you recognize this, I see," the Unseelie King says, waving the little metal rod in the air.

I gasp as I finally realize what it is.

Whipping my head down, I stare down at my own clothes. At my belt. Where that piece of dragon steel used to be tied before I fell off

Draven's back and almost died from the ice flames. In the chaos of it all, I forgot that I had tied it to my belt before we escaped from the barracks.

"Yes, Haldia took it from you while she healed you," Orion says as if he could read my thoughts. "Very careless of you to leave something so powerful unattended like that."

Dread and shame wash over me like cold waves. Because he's right. How could I have forgotten about something so important?

Orion's eyes continue glowing as he shifts his gaze back to Draven. Still holding the also glowing piece of dragon steel in his hand, he levels a stare full of threats and challenge on Draven.

"All I need to do is touch you with it," he declares. "And then you belong to me."

Draven clenches his hand into a fist but says nothing.

A vicious smile spreads across Orion's face. "So keep your lightning to yourself."

The silence thrums around us as the two of them stare each other down. Draven doesn't drop his gaze or lower his chin, but he also doesn't summon any more magic. Amusement sparkles in Orion's eyes, and he seems to consider Draven's behavior an admission of defeat, because he stops channeling magic through the dragon steel and instead spins it lazily in his hand before lowering it again.

"You treacherous fucking backstabber," Isera growls from the wall to my left. Chains rattle as she tries to stand up, but she just collapses back down on the floor. Fury crackles in her eyes as she locks them on Orion. "We had a deal, you piece of shit-stained vermin."

I gasp as the dungeon disappears from around me.

Instead, my parents' kitchen once again appears before my eyes.

Panic and dread flood my chest as I once more hear myself apologize for breaking the glasses. My chest tightens so hard that I can barely breathe as I am yet again forced to watch, second by second, how the look in my parents' eyes changes. How that deep resentment blooms until it fills their entire faces. I squeeze my eyes shut, but the vision doesn't change, because in the memory I'm forced to relive, my younger self is still watching it happen. A sob threatens to rip from my throat as I hear myself begging my parents not to hate me.

Halfway through a sentence, the memory is suddenly ripped away.

I gasp in a breath as the cell around me comes back into view. A tear slides down my cheek. Goddess above, why did he have to show me that day again? There have been many days like that one. So many that I didn't even remember this specific one. But now that I'm being forced to relive it, I know that this is by far the worst one. That look in their eyes, that pure resentment that starts growing there, makes me want to rip my heart out.

Once more, I try to lift my arm. I want to clutch at the fabric of my shirt to stop the pain in my chest, but I'm still too weak from the iron.

Next to me, Isera is curled up on the floor, her entire body shaking. She drags in a breath before raising her head. Her eyes are wild as she meets Orion's gaze. But before she can say anything, he does.

"Watch your mouth," he warns.

She curls her fingers into a fist on the floor.

"She's right, Orion," Draven says before Isera can respond. "We did have a deal."

The Unseelie King slides his gaze to him. "Yes, we did."

"You always honor them."

"Yes, we Unseelie fae always keep our end of the bargain." His smile sharpens. "Which is why you need to be very careful how you word them. The deal was for you to kill Danzo Wolfstalker and be seen doing it." His eyes glint. "I never promised that I was going to let you get away with it."

Chains rattle as Alistair kicks out his leg in anger. "You son of a—"

"Go ahead," Orion cuts off, his voice like sharpened steel, as he levels a stare full of challenge on Alistair. "Finish that sentence. See how that works out for you."

For a few seconds, it looks as if Alistair plans to do just that. But then he forces in a breath, swallows, and glances away. Orion snickers.

Draven locks eyes with him. "I will kill you for this."

A chill rolls down my spine at the way he says it. It's not a threat screamed in anger. It's a statement of fact. Cold and hard as a knife slipped between the ribs.

It only makes Orion's wicked smile widen. "Tread carefully, Shadow of Death." He holds up the dragon steel and spins it once in his hand. "Or I might make you kill your friends." His gaze slips to me. "Or your mate."

A low snarl rips from deep within Draven's chest.

Orion just lowers the dragon steel again and flicks a glance over all six of us. "But I am not without mercy. I could allow you to win your freedom back."

"How?" Galen demands. He has been silent up until now, and it almost feels as if he is trying to draw Orion's attention away from Draven before the Unseelie King can make good on his threat.

Orion's eyes gleam in the faint light of the few faelight gems that have been set into the stone ceiling, and the smile on his face is so sharp that it could draw blood. "Care to make another bargain?"

"What kind of bargain?"

"Every few months, we host the Great Games. People come to the capital from all across the Unseelie Court to watch six teams play against each other."

The image of that massive amphitheater in the middle of the city flashes before my eyes.

"Like the Atonement Trials?" I ask.

He slides his gaze to me. "No, not like the Atonement Trials. That is a punishment. This is a national sport. This is entertainment, betting, faction loyalty."

"It's a distraction," Isera cuts in, her voice smug and vicious as she levels a mocking stare on the Unseelie King. "An event created to distract your people from the fact that you are all *trapped* in here."

Lightning flashes in Orion's eyes as he snaps his gaze to her. She just stares him down from the other side of the iron bars. A muscle flickers in his jaw, but he doesn't deny her mocking accusation.

Instead, he simply turns back to the rest of us. "This is the deal. If you play the games and win, I will allow you to leave the Unseelie Court. No tricks this time."

Silence falls across the darkened underground prison. For a few seconds, only the muted sound of dripping water breaks the stillness.

"This was your plan all along," I say as understanding finally clicks into place.

Isera is right. The Great Games that Orion hosts are a desperate scheme to keep his people from rioting. They have been trapped inside these wards, completely cut off from the rest of the world and unable to leave, for *millennia* now. It would drive people mad. Unless they have something to distract them.

And what better way to distract the entire Unseelie Court from their stifling reality than to have dragon shifters and Seelie fae play these Great Games for probably the first time ever. It will be the talk of the century.

"The assassination was never the real price," I continue. "You just wanted an excuse to arrest us."

"I wanted both." He slides his tongue along his teeth. "So why not get two bargains for the price of one?"

"Asshole," Lyra mutters under her breath.

Orion, however, thankfully doesn't appear to have heard it. He just arches a dark eyebrow at us and demands, "Well? Do we have a deal?"

"If we win, you will let us leave the Unseelie Court and you will help us take down the Iceheart Dynasty," Isera says, her entire face blazing with challenge as she holds Orion's stare.

"Don't push it." He drags his gaze over her body. "Or I might rescind the entire offer and decide to put you in the arena and *break you* for entertainment instead."

She looks like she wants to rip his throat out. But before she can say anything else, Draven instead speaks up.

"If we win the Great Games, you will release us and let us leave the Unseelie Court straightaway and without issue," he declares.

Orion slides his gaze to him. "Yes. The team selection for the next

Great Games starts in three weeks. Until then, you remain here."

"Fine."

"So, do we have a deal?"

Draven glances at the rest of us. When we all nod, he turns back to the treacherous Unseelie King.

"Deal."

15

The three weeks we waited for the team selection to start felt like three months. After Orion left, we were split up and locked in separate cells instead. Probably to prevent us from being able to plot an early escape together. Fortunately, they also changed my restraints from the heavy manacle to a much smaller one that wasn't locked to the floor. It was enough iron to block my magic but not to leave me completely drained of energy. So with nothing better to do, I spent the past three weeks working out in my cell.

Now, as we are led into the grand arena in the middle of the city, I feel surprisingly strong and confident. Especially considering the fact that I was lying face down on a table with a broken spine and ice flames destroying my body three weeks ago.

"You're number nine," declares a male fae with several rings in both of his ears.

He shoves a piece of paper with the number nine written on it at Alistair's chest. Alistair barely has time to grab it before it can flutter to the sand below. With a scowl, he grips the paper in one hand and looks between it and the man who handed it to him.

The Unseelie fae gives us all a look full of suspicion but then just raises a hand and points toward the open space in the middle of the arena. "Stand over there. Between teams eight and ten."

Before any of us can so much as ask a single question, the guards who escorted us here from the dungeons begin herding us toward the spot the man indicated. I study the arena around us.

The massive structure has been built using the same pale beige stone as the rest of the city. But as opposed to the houses with their colorful red roofs, this building doesn't even have a roof. Craning my neck, I glance up at the blue sky above. A few wispy clouds drift lazily across the heavens, and the bright midday sun warms my cheeks. I shift my gaze back down to the tall walls that frame the flat sand ground.

Shaped like an oval, the arena has also been built in several tiers. The ones closest to the ground are located farther in, and then each tier of seats is placed a little farther back so that the arena slopes outward slightly. At the top, decorative arches have been set.

It's an incredibly impressive structure and much larger than the amphitheater in the Seelie Court. As I shift my gaze back down from the walls, I can't help but wonder if our court also hosted games like this before we were conquered. Why else would we have a similar arena?

My heart twists painfully. So much of our own history and culture has been lost. So much that we might never be able to relearn.

"Didn't he say that there are only six teams competing?" Galen suddenly asks, keeping his voice low.

Pulled out of my own distracting thoughts, I give my head a quick shake to clear it and then glance around the arena. Surprise flickers through me when I realize that it's full of people. Each group consists of six people, just like ours, but there are far more than six groups. I do a quick count as our guards position us in an empty spot between two teams. There must be something like twenty teams in here.

"Yes," Draven replies.

"He also said *team selection*," I add, still studying the groups around us while our guards withdraw. "So I'm guessing they will choose six teams out of the ones who are here."

Tense silence falls over our group for a few seconds. My stomach twists with worry as a sudden thought slithers through my mind.

"But we're guaranteed a spot, right?" Alistair says, voicing what we are all no doubt thinking. When no one is able to confirm it, he repeats a bit more forcefully, "Right?"

"If we don't get selected, we won't even have a chance to win," Galen says. "We'll be stuck here until the next team selection. And then the next. And the next."

Draven curses under his breath. "That fucking asshole."

"Welcome!" a female fae with long red hair suddenly calls from the platform by the wall. "Today, you will all be given a chance to be chosen for the incredible honor of competing for one of the six factions."

A rush of excitement sweeps through the gathered teams.

"There are a few new teams this time around," the woman continues. "You'll figure it out. The rest of you know the drill. Get ready for inspection." Sweeping out her arm, she motions toward six people who are standing on the platform beside her. "Faction owners, feel free to move around the arena and inspect the teams available for this round's Great Games."

My heart starts pattering in my chest. We need to get one of those faction owners to choose our team. If we can't even compete, we won't be able to win our freedom back.

Four of the six people who were standing on the platform descend the steps and start toward the closest groups. The other two, a man wearing a red tunic and a woman wearing a white dress, remain standing on the dais, just watching everyone else with smirks on their faces.

"Looks like the Red Faction and the White Faction don't even need to think about which teams to choose," the redheaded organizer says with a grin.

Two of the teams, one a little in front of us and to the right and the other on the far left, let out cheers and salute the two faction owners on the platform.

"Shit," Lyra breathes. "We need to make one of them choose us. I can't take one more day in isolation like that." For the first time since I met her, I can hear clear dread in her voice. "Let alone several months."

We all keep our eyes on the four faction owners who are moving across the sand, but a ripple of worry washes through our group. There are eighteen teams left and only four factions.

"Selena," Draven says without looking at me.

"On it," I reply.

Lowering my chin, I adjust my body language so that it looks like I'm just staring down at the sand beneath my feet because I'm nervous. But as soon as the people around us can no longer see my eyes, I summon my magic.

When the guards took us from our cells, they also removed all our restraints, which means I can finally access my magic again. Isera and Alistair would never be able to use theirs without attracting attention. But I most certainly can.

After a discreet glance to check where the faction owners are, I throw out my magic toward the beige sparks of uncertainty in the others' chests. As they study the other teams, I increase that flame to make them doubt those teams.

Three of them begin moving away from the teams they were inspecting and toward others next to them. But the fourth one, a female fae wearing black pants and a black tunic, raises her head and looks from side to side for a few seconds. Her long and straight hair is so pale blond in color that it's practically white.

My heart leaps as she starts in our direction.

"She's coming," Galen whispers softly.

I make sure to keep my eyes firmly on the ground as she walks straight toward us. Releasing my grip on the uncertainty in the others' chests, I instead focus solely on her.

Once she reaches our group, I latch on to the burgundy spark of courage in her chest and begin increasing it. Since we're outsiders, I need to make her feel bold and confident so that she will choose us anyway.

My heart slams against my ribs as she comes to a halt in front of Isera, who is standing on the far left of our little row. With slow steps, she begins walking the line. Alistair crosses his arms when she passes him but thankfully says nothing.

I barely dare to breathe as she reaches me. My eyes are locked on her black shoes as she stops right in front of me.

Her hand shoots out.

I gasp as she suddenly grips my jaw and wrenches my chin up.

The moment her hand connects with my chin, I release the grip on my magic, so once my eyes are visible again, they are no longer glowing. There is no way that she had time to see it.

Her eyes, a stunning mix of pink and gold, sear into mine. Then a knowing smile as sharp as a blade spreads across her mouth.

"It's about a hundred years too soon for you to try to manipulate *my* emotions, girl," she says.

My heart leaps into my throat. How in Mabona's name did she have time to see that my eyes were glowing?

I stare back at her, my pulse thrumming in my ears.

She tightens her grip on my jaw, digging her fingers in more firmly.

Draven's hand shoots up and wraps around her wrist in an iron grip. Threats drip from every word as he growls, "Take your hand off her or I'll snap your fucking wrist."

Keeping her grip on my jaw, she just slowly turns her head and locks eyes with Draven before giving him a cold smile brimming with challenge. "If I tell Rosea that this sneaky little girl used magic to influence the faction owners, your entire team will be disqualified."

From the other end of our row, Lyra whips her head toward us in panic.

With my chin still trapped in the faction owner's grip, I reach out blindly with my hand until I find Draven's other arm. Brushing my hand down his forearm, I give his wrist a squeeze as I whisper, "Draven."

He stares daggers at the faction owner for another second before reluctantly releasing her wrist.

She chuckles. "Good boy."

Draven clenches both hands into fists but thankfully doesn't rip her throat out.

After watching him with amused eyes for another moment, she uses her free hand to flip her long white hair back behind her shoulder before she returns her gaze to me.

"I can see why you would need to cheat in order to get someone to pick you, though," she says, mocking amusement lacing her voice. "You're the weakest team here."

Behind her shoulder, the other three faction owners glance in our direction before moving on to other teams.

The woman still gripping my jaw once more slides her gaze to Draven. "*You* are powerful, of course. The infamous Shadow of Death. But you can't shift in here." She flicks a glance over the rest of us and then clicks her tongue. "And the rest of you? Two with no magic at all and three *Seelie* fae."

She says *Seelie* as if the word itself tastes disgusting.

"Even before you were conquered, you were weaker than us," she continues. "You were never ruthless enough to actually develop your powers to their full extent. And now when you've been starved and oppressed for millennia? Your powers will be nothing compared to ours."

I grind my teeth as I glare back at her.

"Glare all you want," she says, holding my stare. "It still doesn't change the fact that it's true. And everyone here knows it. Which is why no one will ever pick you."

If I had my knife, I would shove it between her ribs. But unfortunately, I don't have a weapon. And there are eight guards looming a few steps behind our backs.

At last, she releases my jaw. Dusting off her hands, she takes a step back and then levels a look full of threats and challenge on me. "If you use your magic again, I will tell Rosea." She jerks her chin in the direction of the female fae with red hair who appears to be the organizer for these games. "And then you will be disqualified. Got it?"

I glare back at her in angry silence for a second before forcing myself to nod.

"Good." She chuckles and then starts toward another team.

Clenching and unclenching my hands, I stare at her retreating back and imagine the sound she would make if I rammed a blade into it.

"Mabona's fucking tits," I snarl softly under my breath. "How the hell did she know that I was using magic?"

None of the others know either, of course, so they don't reply. Instead, the six of us are forced to just stand there silently and watch as the other three faction owners inspect all the teams except for ours.

"They're not going to pick us," Galen says as the four faction owners at last start walking back to the platform.

"No," Draven confirms. Shifting his weight slightly, he casts a discreet glance over his shoulder at the guards lurking there behind us. "We need to make a move before we get back to the dungeon."

"We're not waiting for the next games?" Lyra asks, sounding incredibly relieved.

"No. There's no point. It will be like this every time. Better to try to fight our way out."

"Agreed," Alistair says from my other side. "And without—"

"All right, listen up!" Rosea, the games organizer, calls across the arena. "It's time to choose teams." She reaches into a small brass bowl and pulls out a folded-up piece of paper. Opening it, she reads, "Green Faction."

The male fae wearing a fancy green tunic steps forward. "Team twelve."

A cheer rises from the indicated team.

Rosea pulls out another small piece of paper. "White."

The woman with the white dress, who never even left the platform, immediately looks toward the team on the far left and declares, "Team two."

They salute her.

The same thing happens when Rosea calls the Red Faction. The owner of the Blue Faction picks team eighteen and the Yellow Faction chooses team six.

"Remember that fountain we passed?" Draven whispers while Rosea unfolds the final piece of paper. "That's where we make our move. We can disappear into the narrow alley on the left and block it before they can follow."

I hadn't even noticed that there was a narrow alley close to that fountain when we were escorted here, but Draven apparently never turns off his scheming brain.

"And last but not least," Rosea calls. "Jocasta, which team will you choose for your Black Faction?"

Jocasta, the white-haired fae who confronted me earlier, steps forward.

"If we can get out of the city, I can fly us one at a time to the border," Draven continues. "Then from there, we can—"

"Team nine," Jocasta declares.

Dead silence falls over the arena.

Next to me, Alistair glances down at the paper in his hand.

Then clothes rustle as every single team turns to stare at us.

My stomach lurches.

Up on the platform, Jocasta flashes us a sharp smile that looks slightly threatening.

"Uhm . . . ," Alistair says as he looks up from the paper in his hand, which has the number nine clearly written on it.

I stare at the strange white-haired woman in absolute bewilderment.

What the hell just happened?

16

Jocasta frowns at the eight guards around us as they form up again once the other teams start moving out. But then she just jerks her chin in the direction of the main entrance.

"Let's go," she says.

Without waiting for a reply, she turns around and strides toward the now open doors that will take us back out into the city.

"What do we do?" Galen whispers hurriedly.

"Follow her for now." Draven casts a discreet glance at the guards around us. "Until we know which route she takes."

Isera is the first one to stalk after Jocasta. The rest of us hurry to catch up as well.

Indecision swirls inside me. Should we try to escape while we are escorted through the city? Or is it better to take our chances with these games? But Jocasta said that we are the weakest team, so do we even stand a chance at all? But then why did she pick us?

I glance at my companions. All of them seem to be thinking the same, but no one offers any solutions.

Warm midday winds tug at my hair as we step through the final set of doors and walk out onto the street outside the arena. Jocasta has stopped a short distance ahead. She speaks briefly to another female fae who then takes off at a run.

After once more frowning at our guards, Jocasta jerks her chin at us again and starts down the street to our left. Draven and I exchange a glance. We came from the right, which means that we won't know the layout of the streets we're about to pass.

On Draven's other side, Galen and Lyra look to him in silent question as well. He considers for a moment and then shakes his head.

All right, follow the strange fae it is.

The owner of the White Faction and the team she chose walk along the street a little farther up ahead. When they pass, citizens cheer and some even lean out windows to wave at them. They raise their right arms in greeting, which makes one of the spectators blush and fan herself with her hand.

I study them curiously. People act as if they are celebrities. Orion was apparently telling the truth. These Great Games are something like a national sport for these people. And given that the owner of the White Faction didn't even look at the other teams, this one must be her usual team. Maybe even a crowd favorite.

Jocasta walks with her chin raised and her steps confident as we stride after them, but when we reach the same group of spectators, the change in behavior is palpable.

Instead of cheering and waving, they stare at us with a mix of suspicion and disgust on their faces.

My stomach twists, and I swallow down a familiar feeling of nausea. I try to block it out, but I still hate it when people dislike me. And now, I'm once again trapped in a city where people who don't even know me actively despise me for something I haven't even done.

A sudden overwhelming tiredness crashes over me like a tidal wave.

Does it ever change?

In the Seelie Court, people disliked me simply because I had emotion magic. They didn't even know me and I had never done anything to them, but they still disliked me for something I hadn't even chosen.

In Frostfell, everyone hated me simply because I was fae. I had never enslaved any dragon shifters, but still they hated me for it.

And now, here in the Unseelie Court, people yet again dislike me simply because I'm a Seelie fae.

I blow out a long sigh and rake a hand through my hair. Is this what the entire world is like?

After a few more streets, we reach a freestanding three-story building made of the same pale stone as the rest of the city. The red roof almost shimmers in the bright sunlight. Jocasta walks up to the carved wooden door and pulls out a key. It unlocks with a distinctive click. Then she turns back to us.

"All right, scram," she says, and makes a shooing motion with her hands at the guards.

They start slightly in surprise and blink at her.

"I'll take it from here," she says. Without waiting for them to reply, she simply flicks her wrist at us and then strides into the building. "Let's go."

The guards look just as shocked as we do. Exchanging an uncertain glance, they hesitate before they start to back away.

"First things first," Jocasta is saying from right inside the door. "Baths and new clothes."

Despite myself, I immediately perk up. The others seem excited about that prospect too, because we all follow Jocasta in through the door.

What meets us on the other side is a very large room that looks to be a combined living room and kitchen. Warm sunlight falls in through the windows and illuminates the pale wooden furniture, making the entire space feel bright and inviting.

"Kitchen and living room on this floor," Jocasta says. Then she points to a staircase by the back wall. "Bedrooms one to three on the next floor. Bedrooms four to six on the top floor. All of them have bathrooms attached. Choose whichever you like and start by taking a long bath." She flicks her gaze up and down our bodies and crinkles her nose. "You smell like you haven't bathed in weeks."

That's because we haven't, I mutter sourly in my head. We've been locked in a dungeon for the past three weeks. Not exactly a haven for personal hygiene.

I frown in confusion as a sudden thought drifts through my head. Does Jocasta even know who we are? Does she know that we are prisoners bargaining for our freedom and not volunteers? If she doesn't, we might have an edge.

"I've sent my assistant to acquire new clothes for you," she continues. "So leave the ones you have outside your doors while you bathe."

"No," Draven simply says.

Jocasta arches a pale brow. "Excuse me?"

"I will be keeping my armor."

She scoffs and shakes her head. "Oh will you now?"

Draven just holds her gaze with a commanding stare. "Try to take it. See what happens."

For a few seconds, they remain standing like that, staring each other down. Then Jocasta lets out something between a sigh and a huff, and drags a hand through her long white hair. "Oh this team selection really is going to bite me in the ass, isn't it?" Flicking her wrist, she clicks her tongue. "Fine. Keep your armor. At least it's the right color." She glances up and down Draven, Lyra, and Galen's bodies. "And rather badass, I suppose."

Galen almost blushes a little at her intimate scrutiny, while Draven just gives her a flat look. She turns to me, Isera, and Alistair.

"But you three are definitely changing your clothes," she declares. She scrunches up her nose in disgust again as she looks us over. "You two are dressed like pleasure slaves for some reason."

Both Isera and Alistair flinch.

But before they can say anything, she shifts her gaze to me. "And you look like a beggar." She heaves a sigh. "Malachi's balls, maybe I shouldn't have picked you after all. Oh well, too late now."

Before I can ask why she did pick us, she lifts both hands and makes a shooing motion toward the stairs.

"Get to it," she commands. "Take a bath. A long one. Clothes will be delivered in a couple of hours. Food is in the kitchen. Eat. Rest. I will be back again in the morning. Feel free to explore the city if you want, but we only have a week to train before the games start, and you will need all the rest you can get, so I recommend using the day to recover your strength and get ready." Raising her eyebrows, she looks from face to face. "Any questions?"

But I can barely concentrate on her words because that middle part of her instructions is still ringing inside my head like a bell. *Feel free to explore the city.* Staring at her, I try to make sense of the words. Are we actually allowed to leave?

My friends seem equally stunned, because they also just stare at her in silence.

When no one asks a question in the first five seconds, she claps her hands. "Excellent. See you in the morning, then."

And with that, she strolls back out the door and closes it behind her.

I wait for her to lock it.

She doesn't.

Her footsteps quickly fade as she walks away down the street.

My heart is beating so hard that I can hear it pounding in my ears.

She doesn't know. She doesn't know that we are supposed to be prisoners. Oh Goddess above, she *doesn't know*.

Hope and excitement surge inside me as I tear my gaze from the unlocked door and meet my friends' eyes. They look equally stunned and relieved and hopeful.

"Are you thinking what I'm thinking?" Lyra asks, a conspiratorial grin on her face.

"Yes," Alistair immediately replies.

I nod. "We escape."

17

My heart pounds against my ribs as I stand there hidden in the shadows of a tree. The woods lie dark and still around me. A few strides away, Lyra, Alistair, and Galen are waiting silently as well.

Since we didn't want to risk being spotted in the city, regardless of what Jocasta said about us being allowed to explore it, we had to wait for nightfall before we made our escape. Thankfully, that at least meant that we also had time to eat, take a bath, and change into the clothes that Jocasta's assistant brought us.

I glance down at the black fighting leathers I'm now wearing. They look similar to Draven's armor, except they're made of leather instead of dragon scales, obviously. But they're sturdy and flexible and fit me perfectly. And most surprisingly, I feel different wearing them.

It's strange how much your clothes affect how you feel about yourself. For decades, I've been wearing frayed and dirty worker's clothes, and I've felt that in every fiber of my being. I've felt poor and ragged and . . . *less* than others. As if I should hunch my shoulders and keep my head down so that people won't look too closely at me. But now, wearing these badass fighting leathers, I feel strong and powerful and confident. I feel like I could conquer the world. The unexpected change in how I feel about myself honestly stuns me.

Glancing over at Alistair, who is also wearing black fighting leathers, I find him standing a little taller too.

And I'm struck by the sudden realization that this is probably why they did it. This is why the Icehearts had such strict regulations on clothes. They wanted our clothes to be worn and dirty and full of holes so that we would feel even more beaten down. So that we wouldn't get too confident.

Shaking my head, I blow out a long breath. If I weren't so angry, I would be impressed. They truly have thought about every single detail. Planned their conquest and how to keep us in line meticulously. Nothing has been left to chance.

They are strategic masterminds. And I must never forget that. Otherwise, we will never win.

A flash of indecision pulses through me.

Shifting my position, I look through the trees in the direction Draven will be returning from. He flew back to the city to get Isera, and once they're here, we will leave. But now that we're here right by the borders of the Unseelie Court, I can't help but think about what Isera said earlier. About how we need to get Orion on our side now that we have the chance.

She's right. But I also have no idea how we would even accomplish something like that.

Footsteps echo between the silent trees.

I jerk my head up.

"They're back," Alistair whispers.

But alarm shoots up and down my spine, and my heart rate picks up. Because I recognize those footsteps. Those arrogantly lazy yet commanding footsteps.

"No," I breathe, my pulse thrumming in my ears. "It's the Unseelie King."

The others whip their heads toward me.

"Shit," Galen curses under his breath. His gaze darts from the direction of the footsteps to the wards, which rise only a short distance to our left. "Get to the wards. We need to get out. Now."

"I'm not leaving them," I hiss back.

"We're not leaving them." He grabs Lyra by the arm and pushes her in the direction of the wards while casting another alarmed glance in the direction of the footsteps. "Draven and Isera can fly through them. But we need to already be on the other side when he does. Otherwise, it'll be too late."

I stare at the dark sky above the trees, wishing I could at least see them approaching. But I know that Galen is right. Lingering here would just risk us all getting caught, so I reluctantly push myself away from the tree trunk and hurry after the others.

To my surprise, Alistair waits to make sure I follow before he starts moving as well. But once he has seen me start sneaking forward, he barely looks at me. I really can't figure him out. He says that he hates everyone, and he had been about to leave earlier, but then he does things like this.

Shaking my head, I push the thought out of my mind for now. Right now, we need to focus on getting out before Orion finds us.

The forest ends a few steps ahead. After that, there is only an open stretch of grass before the wards.

I cast a panicked look over my shoulder.

Crossing the grass will leave us entirely without cover. But there is no other way to reach the wards.

Orion's unhurried footsteps continue to echo between the trees.

Dread curls inside me. It's almost as if he wants us to hear him. Wants us to scurry away like rats while he toys with us like a cat. As if he is enjoying this game. It makes me want to punch him in the face.

"We need to make a run for it," Galen says as the four of us come to a halt by the tree line. He looks from face to face before giving us a nod. "Go."

We sprint out of the forest and dart across the grass.

My heart thumps hard in my chest. We need to make it through the wards and far enough out onto the grasslands before Orion reaches the edge of the forest. If we don't, he's going to spot us.

I try to run as quietly as possible, but I can barely hear if my feet are making noise or not because my heart is pounding so loudly. How did Orion even find us? How did he know that we snuck out of the city? How did he know which direction we went in? Which side of the wards we're using to get out? Goddess damn it, there is so much I don't know.

The wards appear before us. Like water moving slowly across glass. I resist the urge to glance over my shoulder. If Orion had seen us, we would know. Just a few more steps. Then we'll be—

Galen reaches the wards.

And slams right into them.

The crash is so violent that he actually flies backward several steps before slamming into the ground.

I gasp as we skid to a halt.

"Galen!" Lyra darts over to him and quickly pulls him back up. "What did you—"

"We can't get out," Alistair interrupts.

The sheer panic in his voice makes me whirl toward him. He is standing right in front of the wards, slamming his hands against them. And when he turns to meet my gaze, his eyes are filled with dread.

"We can't get out," he repeats, one hand still pressed against the wards.

Ice spreads through my chest. The wards are locked from the *inside*. Why the hell are they locked from the inside? It makes no sense. Aren't they there to make sure dragon shifters can't get in?

A mocking laugh ripples through the night.

Spinning around, we find Orion Nightbane sauntering toward us at an unhurried pace. There is a wicked smile on his beautiful face. He opens his mouth to say something, but right before he can, another sound cuts through the night. The sound of beating wings.

For the first time since I met this snake of a man, there is something other than lazy arrogance on his face. Utter shock pulses across his features for a second as he whips his head around to stare at Draven.

Draven, who is carrying Isera in his arms, flies through the darkened night like a wraith. His massive black wings pound the air as he closes the final distance in a matter of seconds and slams down on the grass in front of me.

While setting Isera down, he gives me a quick once-over to check me for injuries. The sight of it makes my heart squeeze.

"Well, this is a surprise," Orion drawls from where he is still standing across the grass.

He tries to make his voice as arrogant as before, but there is a hint of genuine surprise lacing his tone. Narrowing his eyes slightly, he studies Draven.

After making sure I'm unharmed, Draven turns around to face the Unseelie King and flares his massive wings wide.

"A half-shift," Orion continues, still studying Draven intently. "I didn't know that was possible. The wards should block all dragons from shifting."

"Tough luck. In this form, I'm half human," Draven replies. Dark clouds gather around him as he spreads his arms in a cocky challenge. "Still think fighting me is a good idea?"

Orion doesn't say anything, but the hint of a smirk lurks at the corner of his lips. The sight of it makes ice skitter down my spine.

"Just open the fucking wards, Orion," Draven orders. "You will never win a fight against us like this."

Orion's smirk widens. "Oh, won't I?"

The moment the words leave his mouth, an entire horde of soldiers steps out from the darkened tree line. Fire flares up in the hands of half of them, while the others summon water and stone.

Next to me, Alistair's jaw drops.

With his eyes wide, he gapes at the mass of fire wielders.

On Draven's other side, Isera immediately summons ice. It floats around her arms like shards of glass. The sight of that makes Alistair snap out of his shock, and fire rushes down along his arms as he too summons his magic. The dark storm clouds grow, and lightning crackles around Draven, while I call up my magic and get ready as well.

My pulse hammers in my ears. There are a lot of Unseelie fae here. We're outnumbered at least four to one. And all of them have magic. I draw in short breaths while worry flickers inside my chest. Can we actually win this?

"You cannot fight your way out of this, Shadow of Death," Orion says.

"Watch me," Draven growls back.

The Unseelie King lets out another one of those mocking laughs. "You can't get in, *or out*, through the wards without the correct passphrase."

"Aww." Isera flashes him a smile so sharp it could draw blood. "Afraid your own people are going to desert you if they had the choice?"

Orion's eyes glint like a blade as he locks them on her. "Careful with that tongue, little viper. Lest someone cut it out."

Holding his gaze, she slides her tongue along her teeth in a clear challenge.

Dangerous light glints in Orion's eyes, and his threatening smile widens.

However, before they can start trying to kill each other, Draven cuts in. "Then I suppose I'll just torture the passphrase out of you."

The gathered soldiers start in shock at the threat. But Orion just snorts, looking more amused than angry. And what worries me the most is that he hasn't even summoned his magic yet.

Glancing around, he appears to search for something on the ground. I frown in confusion as he bends down and pulls something out of the dirt a couple of steps away.

A shudder rolls down my spine when I see the large insect he has picked up. It looks like a cross between a centipede and a spider. I shiver again as he lifts it up closer to his face and whispers something to it. That creature has far too many legs to be normal.

We all tense up as Orion starts toward the wards. But neither he nor his soldiers attack. Instead, he just walks up to the wards a short distance from us and sets the centipede spider down in front of the rippling wall. Then he straightens and turns to face us.

"This is what happens if I give you the *wrong* passphrase," he says.

I glance down at the gross insect that has started scuttling toward the wards.

The moment it reaches the shimmering magical barrier, it bursts into flame.

Jerking back, I gasp as all those spindly legs shrivel up in a flash. Barely a second after it reached the wards, the insect is no more than a tiny pile of ash.

I swallow, meeting Draven's gaze for a second before dragging my eyes back to the smirking king.

Orion spreads his arms wide, mimicking Draven's cocky pose from earlier. "Still want to try to torture it out of me?"

Next to me, Draven flexes his hand and clenches his jaw in frustration. Alistair and I exchange a glance. And so do Lyra and Galen. Isera just continues watching Orion as if she can kill him with her glare alone. But none of us say anything. Because we all know the truth.

Even if we were to win a fight against all these soldiers and capture Orion and torture him, there is no way for us to know if he gave us the right passphrase or the one that will incinerate us. He holds all the cards right now. He knows it. And so do we.

"The only way you are leaving my court is if I allow it," he declares, rubbing that fact in our faces with his smug tone. Then he lifts one shoulder in a nonchalant shrug. "But I do keep my bargains."

Isera scoffs.

His eyes gleam again as he watches her, but he lets the insult slide and instead shifts his gaze back to all of us. "Play the games. And play them well. Entertain my court. Make this the most interesting Great Games in a century. Win. And then, I will allow you to leave." He meets Isera's furious eyes again and smirks. "As promised."

"Fine," Draven grinds out.

Orion arches an eyebrow and looks from face to face, waiting for us to acknowledge his power as well. The others reply. I manage a nod. Isera barely dips her chin in confirmation, but he seems satisfied anyway.

"Excellent," he says. Then that spark of vicious authority returns to his eyes, and his voice drops dark and low. "But you were about to break our deal by leaving. And actions have consequences. So now you have just earned two *hours* in your nightmares."

I don't even have time to gasp before the world around me disappears and I'm plunged into the cold, dark depths of my worst memories.

18

When we finally stagger back in through the door and into Jocasta's faction house, I feel like a used dishrag that someone has wrung out too forcefully. The Unseelie King certainly followed through on his threat. And this time, he didn't just show me that one horrible memory. He showed me everything.

For two hours, I was stumbling around blindly on the grass by the wards, trapped in my worst memories. Memories of my parents, of all the shitty things people did and said to me in the Seelie Court, of my time in the Ice Palace, of those soul-crushing hours when I was paralyzed and dying from ice flames.

And now I feel so tired and wrung out that I'm afraid a gentle breeze is going to knock me over.

A thud comes from the door.

Collapsing down on the white couch, I slowly turn my head toward the sound.

Isera, who was the last person through the door, only managed to close it behind her before her legs give out. She sits down hard on the pale wooden floorboards right inside. Dragging in an unsteady breath, she draws her knees up to her chest and leans her back against the carved wooden door.

"I'm going to fucking kill him," she whispers, her voice hoarse.

The couch creaks as Draven sits down next to me. I didn't even realize I was tilting to the side until his firm body is there next to mine, giving me support. He wraps his arm around my shoulders, holding me tightly. It makes warmth flood my body and gives me a burst of energy. Without thinking, I lean my head against his shoulder. He tightens his arm around me even more.

"He's using your claustrophobia against you, isn't he?" I ask, my gaze returning to Isera.

She meets my gaze in silence for a few seconds before finally replying, "Yes."

"What happened?" Alistair asks from where he is sitting by the wall across the room.

He looks as exhausted and raw as the rest of us. Galen and Lyra, who are sitting on the other couch, have been watching Draven with pained eyes, but now they also shift their attention to Isera.

Still seated by the door, she tips her head back to rest it against the slab of wood behind her. Her blue-and-silver eyes stare up into the ceiling. And she says nothing.

Just when I think she's not going to reply, she heaves a sigh.

"I was eleven," she says, still looking at the ceiling. "I was trying to figure out how to control my powers. One day, I accidentally created a small box of white ice around myself. But I didn't know how to make it disappear again."

My stomach drops.

Her bottom lip trembles for a moment before she forces out another breath. "The ice was so thick that I couldn't break through it with my hands. And since it was white instead of clear, I couldn't see out either."

"Couldn't anyone break it from the outside?" Galen asks, his violet eyes filled with sympathy.

"Who?" She curls her hands into fists and cuts him a look. "My father was killed by dragon shifters when I was two."

Galen winces.

"And my mother won the Atonement Trials when I was ten and never came back." She schools her features into a blank mask. "I was alone. I have always been alone." She cuts him another look. "So no, no one even knew that I was trapped in there for five days, licking water from the ice walls to survive and beating my fists bloody trying to break through it."

I stare at her, my heart aching. Goddess above, I had no idea.

She draws her eyebrows down and shoots us a hard look. "Any other questions?"

Galen shifts awkwardly on the white cushions and clears his throat, and Lyra glances away. But Alistair and I continue watching her intently. When she notices that, she scoffs and goes back to staring at the ceiling.

For almost an entire minute, no one says anything. We all just sit there, drained and exhausted, in tense silence. Moonlight that falls in through the window paints pale shapes on the wall opposite me. We haven't even bothered to turn on more than the lone faelight by the door.

"Were you purposely killing all the fire wielders?" Alistair suddenly asks, shattering the oppressive silence so abruptly that it startles me.

Blinking, I turn toward him and find him looking at Draven with eyebrows raised.

Draven scowls. "First of all, *I* wasn't purposely doing anything."

On the couch opposite us, both Galen and Lyra flinch at the venom in his voice and the reminder of what he has been through. They quickly begin studying the fluffy white carpet beneath us as if it's the most fascinating thing they have ever seen. I resist the urge to sigh. Mabona's tits, maybe Orion was right. Maybe we *are* broken.

"And secondly," Draven continues, his scowl morphing into more of a frown. "What are you asking?"

From where he is sitting on the floor by the wall, Alistair draws his knees up and rests his elbows on them before dragging a hand through his hair. He looks uncharacteristically uncertain.

"Well, it's just . . ." He waves his hand in the air. "Fire is supposed to be a really rare power. But here, *a lot* of people have fire magic. Are the Icehearts purposely killing them in our court or why is it so rare there?"

Draven's frown clears. Leaning back against the cushions, he adjusts his arm around me so that his hand is resting on my hip instead. Then he lets out a long sigh. "No, the answer is much simpler than that." He meets Alistair's gaze. "Since fire magic is so destructive, the fae who wield it often win the Atonement Trials. And since they die in the Ice Palace, their magical bloodline dies with them."

Alistair stares at him, his eyes wide. "Oh."

Uncomfortable silence once again falls across the room. It makes me feel nauseous, and my old instincts immediately start thinking of how I can make everyone feel at ease. But I'm so exhausted myself that I have no idea what to say.

"Well, sounds like you need to get laid, then," Lyra suddenly says in a cheerful voice. "A lot."

Alistair's jaw practically hits the floor as he whips around to stare at her. For a moment, it looks as if he's trying to figure out if she was serious. Based on the expression on her face, she was. And Alistair seems to realize that too, because his face flushes bright red.

I burst out laughing.

In a heartbeat, the tense atmosphere shatters and warmth seems to flood the light and airy living room. Draven chuckles, his firm chest shaking against mine as he still holds me tightly. On the couch next to Lyra, Galen shakes his head and slaps her arm with the back of his hand, but there is a smile on his face. And I swear that even Isera's lips shift ever so slightly upward for a second too.

On the floor, Alistair scowls at us all, his cheeks still red, but he doesn't appear particularly angry. Instead, he casts confused glances at Lyra when she isn't looking.

Galen heaves a deep sigh that seems pulled from all our chests. "So, what do we do now?"

"The only thing we can do," I reply, and look from face to face.

They all appear to know what I'm going to say before I even say it, because they nod as soon as I meet their eyes.

"We win the games."

19

Jocasta tosses her long white hair back behind her shoulder and claps her hands once. "Alrighty, I hope you're well rested."

The six of us exchange a glance. Because of our escape attempt and Orion's punishment last night, we didn't get more than a few hours of sleep. But it's probably best not to tell her about that.

"Like I said, we only have a week to train before the first game starts," she continues. "And since you're the weakest team here, we're going to need all the time we can get."

The massive arena is filled with the distant clang of swords and rush of magic. All six teams have been given separate rooms so that they can train in private without the other teams spying on them. Ours is a decent-sized rectangular room with arched windows along one wall and packed sand on the ground.

"So, first we'll—" Jocasta begins, but Alistair cuts her off.

"Why did you pick us, then?"

She blinks, her pink-and-gold eyes shifting to him.

"If we're the weakest team here, why did you pick us?" Alistair clarifies.

"Ah." A sly smile spreads across her lips. "Well, for one, I picked you because it will draw a huge crowd. It will also make for very interesting betting opportunities."

He frowns. "Are you saying that people are going to bet on us?"

"No. *I'm* going to bet on you. No one else will likely do so, since, as I said, you're the weakest team here."

"Again, then why the hell did you pick us?"

"Because of *you,* you sneaky little manipulator."

I start in surprise when I notice that she is looking at *me*. Suddenly feeling everyone's attention on me, I clear my throat a bit self-consciously. Holding Jocasta's shrewd stare with my own bewildered eyes, I ask, "Why?"

"Because you have emotion magic."

"I, uhm . . . Yes. But most people think that's a bad thing. You don't?"

"No." Her sly smile widens. "Because I have emotion magic too."

My jaw drops.

She chuckles at the utter shock on my face and then winks. "I told you, kid. It's about a hundred years too soon for you to try to manipulate *my* emotions."

Kid. I will turn 168 in three months. But sure. Kid.

Cocking my head, I study Jocasta intently. Both fae and dragon shifters generally live to be around a thousand years old. I wonder how old she is.

"So I know just how powerful and dangerous emotion magic can be," she finishes with a confident smirk.

My heart does a backflip in my chest, and a sudden overwhelming sense of hope surges through me. I have never met anyone else who has emotion magic, so everything I know about my own powers, I've had to figure out myself. But if Jocasta is both older and more skilled than me, she might be able to teach me things about my magic. She might be able to help me become even more powerful. Powerful enough to take on the Icehearts, even without the Unseelie Court's assistance.

My pulse thrums, and I suddenly feel a world of possibilities open up before me.

"And besides, the crowd wants entertainment," Jocasta continues while lifting her slim shoulders in a shrug. "And what better way to provide that for them than to give them a team consisting of three Seelie fae and three dragon shifters. That has never happened. Not once since our borders were closed. And *that* will make for some great betting." Her eyes glint. "Everyone will be betting against you. Everyone except me. And if I can somehow whip you into shape in time, this will be my ticket to fortune."

For a few seconds, we all just stare at her in silence while trying to figure out how to feel. In the end, I decide to be grateful for the opportunity. Another person with emotion magic. Someone who wants me to get as strong as possible and will help me train. It's far better than anything I had ever dared hope for.

Jocasta claps her hands again. "All right, then. Let's get to it. I need to see what each of you can do so that I can plan a strategy." She flicks her wrist at Galen, Lyra, Alistair, and Isera. "You four, go get the practice dummies from the storage room. It's the door just to the left of this one." Without waiting to see if they obey, she simply turns to me. "You, I want to see what you can do first."

Next to us, our four companions frown at her bossy command. But, just like me, they seem to realize that Jocasta wants us to win just as much as we do and that she will give us our best chance to do that. So in the end, they just shrug and walk toward the door to get the practice dummies.

Draven watches them for a few seconds before shifting his attention back to Jocasta. The white-haired fae, however, is solely focused on me.

"All right," she says, her eyes still on me as she motions for Draven to take a few steps back. "I want to see how you create emotions. So demonstrate on him and create whatever emotion you want."

After moving a little back as requested, Draven just turns to face me, looking completely relaxed. Yet again, I'm practically stabbed by the realization of just how much Draven actually trusts me. But I can barely concentrate on that right now, because I'm so confused by Jocasta's order.

"You mean *manipulate*, right?" I begin hesitantly. "Choose one of the emotions he's already feeling and manipulate it?"

"Well, I suppose we'll get to that too. But first I want to see you create emotions."

Frowning deeply, I shake my head in confusion. "What do you mean *create emotions?*"

She draws back, blinking at me in surprise. Then she rolls her eyes and blows out a frustrated sigh. "You haven't even learned how to do that yet? Malachi's balls, you're much weaker than I thought." She massages her brows. "This is going to be difficult."

"No, I . . ." I almost trip over the words trying to get them out of my mouth fast enough. "I've been practicing with my magic for over a hundred and fifty years. I'm good at what I do. But it's not *possible* to create emotions from nothing. There needs to be a spark there first. That's how it works."

Jocasta stares at me as if I've just told her that wearing pants outdoors is overrated. Then she lets out another long sigh. Breaking eye contact, she instead turns to Draven and flicks her wrist. "Come stand closer to her."

I turn to Draven as well when he starts toward me. And even before my gaze lands on him, I can feel the irresistible pull of his body. Can feel the way his entire presence just consumes me. And when my gaze finally finds him, it sets my blood aflame.

His muscular body moves with lethal grace as he advances on me. I rake my gaze over his powerful body, suddenly desperate to touch him. I want to run my hands all over him. Trace his sharp abs and rake my fingers down his back and lick that absolutely sinful V that I know hides underneath his armor until I reach his cock. Fuck, I want to wrap my hands around his cock. I don't want to wait anymore. I want him now.

Fire rushes through my body as I drag my gaze up to Draven's eyes and find them burning with lust as well. He comes to a halt right in front of me. His chest heaves, as if he is struggling to contain himself. But I don't want him to contain himself. I want him to rip my clothes off and fuck me hard against the wall. No, I want to rip *his* clothes off and fuck him hard. I want everything. Everything. And I want it now.

Lust burns through my entire soul like wildfire.

And my restraint snaps.

Grabbing the back of his neck, I yank his sinful mouth down to mine and kiss him desperately. He kisses me back as if he's starving. As if he has waited millennia for this. I press myself harder against his firm chest. Fuck, I want to feel everything.

There is a hunger inside me. A new hunger. A desperate hunger. Something that feels different from before. Stronger. More mindless. More irresistible.

Fuck, I want him. I'm going to die if I don't get him.

I rake my fingers down his chest, but all I can feel is the hard dragon scale of his armor. I want to feel *him*. I need to feel him. Right now.

My fingers fumble with the clasp of his belt, practically yanking it open while Draven continues to steal the breath from my lungs with furious kisses. I try to shove his pants down, but because it's his armor and not normal pants, I only manage to get them open enough to reach his cock. It hardens instantly in my hand as I wrap my fingers around it.

A delicious moan rips from Draven's chest as I slide my hand up and down his cock. That burning lust inside me flares up even brighter. Oh fuck, I need him. I need him more than I need air. I can't even wait another twenty seconds for him to take his clothes off. If I don't get him now, I'm going to die.

Breaking the desperate kiss, I drop to my knees in front of him. His golden eyes burn with uncontrollable lust as he watches me kneel before him and slide my hand down along his throbbing cock. With my hand still gripping the base, I lean forward and take his thick cock into my mouth.

Another desperate moan rips from deep within his chest. The sound makes my clit throb with need.

I slide my lips back up and then lick along the side of his cock before swirling my tongue around his tip. His hand shoots out and grips my hair. Lust burns through me as his fingers tighten, holding my hair in a firm grip. I draw my hand up and down the base of his cock while I work my lips and tongue on the other half.

That fire inside me is so intense that I can't concentrate on anything else. I could spend my entire life like this. On my knees sucking Draven's cock. I don't need anything else. I don't need—

In a flash, that all-consuming wildfire of lust inside me disappears.

It evaporates so abruptly that it feels as if someone forcibly ripped the emotion out of me.

The experience is so jarring that I just sit there, still on my knees with Draven's cock in my mouth, and stare up at him. He stares back down at me, his eyes wide, looking just as shocked as I feel.

A smug chuckle cuts through the strange ringing in my ears. "And that's how you create an emotion. Lust, in this case."

The sound of Jocasta's voice jolts me out of my stupor. I quickly release my grip on Draven's cock and slide it out of my mouth. That seems to snap him back to reality too, because he blinks several times and gives his head a hard shake.

"Girl, have you ever even sucked a cock before?" Jocasta says from where she is still standing a couple of steps away. Amusement laces her voice. "You're supposed to suck it. Not lick it like an icicle."

Embarrassment crashes over me like a tidal wave. My entire face flushes bright red. It's so intense that I feel like I'm going to catch fire any second. Whipping my head around, I stare at Jocasta with my cheeks burning with mortification. She just grins down at me, her eyes sparkling with satisfaction.

And that's when my stunned mind finally catches up with what happened these past couple of minutes. Jocasta created lust in my chest. In Draven's too. Since I can't manipulate my own emotions, I have never known what it feels like from the other side. And since I know that I'm changing someone's emotions, I've always thought that there was something about it that would feel artificial. I had no idea that it felt this . . . organic. When she created the lust inside me, I had no idea that it wasn't my own emotion. I truly believed that it was all me.

That thought sends another shockwave through me, because it leads me to the most mind-blowing realization of all.

Jocasta *created* lust inside me.

If it had happened when I turned and looked at Draven, I would have doubted her word. I would have thought she just manipulated the spark of lust that is always present when I look at Draven. But it began before that. That all-consuming sense of lust began before I even laid eyes on him. Which means that it was created out of nothing.

And that should not be possible.

"Uhm . . . What's going on here?" Galen's voice suddenly echoes through the room.

I whip my head toward the door to find Galen, Lyra, Isera, and Alistair standing there frozen on the sand, staring at the three of us in stunned silence. The practice dummies they have brought stand motionlessly beside them.

Draven quickly pulls his pants all the way back up and fastens his belt again while I scramble off my knees and take a few steps back. Heat once more sears my cheeks.

"No need to hide it," Jocasta says, her eyes sparkling with amusement as she nods toward Draven's crotch. "It's a very impressive cock."

In a heartbeat, Draven has closed the distance between them. Lightning crackles down his arms and storm clouds churn around him as he grips her by the collar and yanks her up on her toes.

"If you ever do something like that again, I will fucking kill you," Draven growls in her face.

"Oh, come now," Jocasta replies, smirking back at him. "It was very educational. Or at least, it will be. Because now you can start teaching her how to suck cock properly."

"Watch your mouth." His fist tightens in her black shirt. "And for your information, her technique is fucking excellent."

Heat once again flushes my entire face, turning it bright red, and I send a desperate prayer to Mabona that the ground will open up and swallow me.

Jocasta just gives Draven a knowing smirk. "Uh-huh."

He shoves her backward and releases her shirt.

Our four companions, who have now reached us, come to a halt on the sand two steps away while glancing between the three of us.

"Did we . . . miss something?" Lyra asks, looking genuinely bewildered.

"Yeah, what's going on?" Alistair adds as he meets my gaze.

I draw my eyebrows down into a scowl, desperately trying to force the searing heat out of my cheeks. "Don't ask."

A few steps away, Jocasta chuckles and brushes her hands down her shirt to smooth it after Draven's manhandling. Amusement glitters in her eyes, and she wiggles her eyebrows at us. I shoot her a glare.

"And what even is this court's obsession with sucking cock?" I huff, remembering how Orion threatened Isera earlier.

Alistair raises his eyebrows. "You sucked his cock?"

"I said don't ask," I mutter, embarrassment heating my cheeks once more.

"It's the ultimate power exchange," Jocasta replies with a hungry look in her eyes.

At first, I think that hunger in her eyes is directed at Draven, and the urge to ram a knife through her ribs hits me like a landslide. That violent urge to kill her just for thinking about Draven shocks me a little, which in turn dampens the murderous rage enough for me to see that her eyes aren't focused on Draven at all. Quite the opposite. She's staring out across the room, as if looking through the wall and toward whoever she's fantasizing about.

"One person is kneeling at the other's feet, sucking his cock," she says, her tone laced with deep craving. "An act of absolute submission." Her gaze remains on the pale stone wall across the room as she slides her tongue along her teeth. "While at the same time, she has the most vulnerable part of his body in her mouth. Right between her teeth." Her eyes gleam and a sigh escapes her chest as she repeats, "The ultimate power exchange."

The six of us just stare at her in silence, unsure of how to reply to that. My question had been more a comment of frustration. I hadn't expected her to actually answer it.

At last, she tears her gaze from the wall and shifts her attention back to us. "That's why it's so hot." She lets out a small chuckle and gives us all a knowing look. "Just imagine how hot it would be to do that with someone as powerful as the Unseelie King."

Isera's gaze sharpens. "He likes that?"

"Of course. Complete submission, especially from someone powerful, is what he craves most."

"I see."

I glance at her, trying to meet her gaze. But her calculating eyes are focused on Jocasta.

For a few seconds, the room is dead silent. Somewhere outside the door, the distant sounds of clashing swords and rushing magic fill the warm air inside the arena. Gray light from the overcast sky filters in through the windows, painting lighter patches on the pale stone wall on the other side.

"Uhm . . . ," Galen begins, looking distinctly uncomfortable.

Jocasta yet again claps her hands. "Anyway." She shifts her gaze to me. "You can't create emotions yet. That's fine. We have a week to work on that before the first game. For now, at least show me how you manipulate emotions."

Yet. Can't create emotions *yet*. I stifle a scoff. I don't know what kind of extra power the fae have here in the Unseelie Court, but it is not possible to create emotions. I know. I have been practicing with my magic for over 150 years. I know that it's not possible to create emotions. There needs to be a spark there first. That's just how it works. At least for us.

I glance at Jocasta. Maybe she was right. Maybe the Unseelie Court has always been stronger than us and that's why she can create emotions while I can't.

"Well, get to it," Jocasta says, and raises her eyebrows at me.

Since I don't want to manipulate my friends' emotions, I walk over to the window instead.

Below, people are strolling through a large market square. Colorful awnings flutter in the breeze, and bright flowers rustle in the wooden planters that have been placed in strategic places throughout the square. Carts and booths full of wares line it in neat rows. I crack the window open so that I can hear their chatter and laughter.

Jocasta comes to stand next to me. "The city instead of your friends, huh? Smart."

"Yeah." I keep my eyes on the people outside. "But I can't do the whole city. Well, technically I can. But only for about ten seconds."

She laughs. "The whole city. Right. Good one." A wistful smile blows across her lips. "Wouldn't that be something, though? An entire city."

Confusion pulses through me, and I turn to look at her properly. She just looks back at me, seeming equally confused.

"What?" she says at last.

"I wasn't kidding." I frown at her, now completely bewildered. "I can manipulate an entire city. But only for about ten seconds. I did it back in Frostfell right before we came here."

Dead silence falls over the training room. Standing there by the open window, she stares at me for several seconds, as if trying to figure out whether I'm messing with her or not. Color drains from her face when she realizes that I am indeed being serious.

"That's not possible," she says.

Turning back to the window, I push it open wider. Then I summon my magic. After a deep breath, I throw it across the entire city in search of the glittering silver sparks of excitement. Not everyone feels it, of course. But with the Great Games on the horizon, the majority of them seem to possess at least a tiny spark of that emotion. I blow it into a wildfire.

The people in the market square below, and on all the streets that we can see from here, suddenly seem to lighten up. Laughter becomes louder. Joy infectious. People get a spring in their steps. Anticipation seems to vibrate from the whole city. And not the tense kind that hung over the city before. Just simple, pure excitement this time.

I quickly cut off my magic after only three seconds so that I won't drain all my energy.

Then I turn back to Jocasta.

For a while, she just continues staring out the window, where everyone has now started to return to a more normal state. Then she turns to me. And when her wide eyes meet mine, I can't tell if she's shocked or terrified or impressed.

"It's not possible," she blurts out. But it sounds more like a desperate attempt to hold on to her worldview rather than a declaration of fact. Her pink-and-gold eyes are still wide as she shakes her head at me. "It shouldn't be possible."

"But it is," I reply gently. Then I nod in the direction of the city while I close the window again. "You saw."

She works her mouth a few times, but no sound makes it out. Then she suddenly whirls around to face the others. Her stunned eyes lock on Alistair. "You. Fire wielder, right?"

"Yeah," Alistair confirms.

"Show me."

He drags a hand through his hair and then jerks his chin toward the short wall where the door is located. "You're gonna wanna stand over there."

When only Jocasta starts toward the wall, he flicks a glance at the rest of us. "You too."

We all lurch into motion and hurry toward the indicated wall. Alistair follows at a more leisurely pace. Once we have reached it, we all stand so that we are looking at the short wall on the other side of the rectangular room.

Alistair draws in a breath, and his eyes begin to glow. Then he shoves outward with his hands.

Yellow and orange flames roar across the sand, reaching two-thirds of the room.

Jocasta's jaw drops.

Heat washes over us as Alistair keeps the fire going for another few seconds. Then he releases the grip on his magic, and his eyes stop glowing again.

"Malachi's balls," Jocasta blurts out as she turns to gape at him. "That's your full power?"

He blinks in surprise and then frowns at her. "Full? That wasn't even half."

She just stares at him, her mouth still open. Then she spins toward Isera, her eyes wild. "And you?"

Isera gives her a cool look for a moment. Then she calls up her magic and flicks her wrist.

A rushing, clinking, crackling sound echoes between the pale stone walls as she fills the entire room before us with ice. Then with another flick of her wrist, she makes it disappear. Crossing her arms, she leans back against the wall and just holds Jocasta's gaze with impassive eyes.

Jocasta drags in a shuddering breath. Raising her hands, she rakes them through her long white hair while she turns to stare at the now empty room before us. The rest of us exchange a glance.

Then a wide smile spreads across her face, and she lets out a laugh so genuine that I can feel it all the way in my soul. Turning to look at us, she grins.

"I'm going to be so fucking rich."

20

The heavenly scent of baking bread and grilled meat drifts through the air and fills my lungs as I draw in a deep breath. Above us, the fresh green leaves rustle in the lone tree as a gentle breeze sweeps across the market square. The other patrons at this outdoor tavern cast suspicious glances in our direction, but we are already sitting as far away from them as possible.

"Took three tries to get them to accept our order," Lyra says as she plops down on the wooden chair next to Alistair. "Even though we paid up front."

Galen, who claims the final remaining seat, rolls his eyes at her. "Can you blame them though? We were literally sent to kill them every time one of them set so much as one foot outside the wards."

"Still," she huffs as she tosses her wavy brown hair, pulled up in a ponytail, back behind her shoulder. "It's rude to let people starve."

"You're not starving."

"Well, if I don't . . ."

I tune out their good-natured squabbling as I instead study the market square before us. It's the same one that we saw from the windows of the training room earlier. We had planned to return to our house once training was done, but Jocasta gave us some money and told us to go out and eat dinner and enjoy the city tonight.

Since I have never been allowed to own, let alone handle, money before, I had no idea how to use it without looking like a fool. And neither did Alistair and Isera, of course. So we sent Lyra and Galen to order for our entire table. Though they apparently had trouble doing so for a different reason.

The massive walls of the grand arena loom above us, and I glance up at the windows of our training hall again, even though Jocasta is no longer there.

Once she learned of our powers, her entire demeanor changed. Gone was the amused and slightly mocking tone and the smug superiority. Instead, she began taking us seriously in a way that she never had before. And also rewarding us. Hence this dinner.

I still haven't been able to truly grasp that we are apparently much more powerful magic users than the average Unseelie fae. On the one hand, it makes sense because the Icehearts have been breeding us for millennia to create people with strong magic for them to drain. Of course that would make our magical bloodlines stronger than the Unseelie fae, who have just been living normally and having as many children as they like.

But at the same time, if I'm supposed to be stronger than Jocasta, then why can she create emotions from nothing while I cannot? Is there something wrong with me? Despite having more raw power, am I somehow defective?

"Are you okay?"

I'm jolted back to reality as Draven leans closer and brushes his hand gently down my thigh. His casual touch sends a flood of warmth through my body and makes the uncomfortable storm of emotions inside me calm again. I let out a long sigh.

Tearing my gaze from the market before us, I instead meet Draven's beautiful eyes. "Yes. I was just . . . lost in thought."

He brushes his hand over my thigh again, making my spine tingle. But before he can say anything else, Isera surprises us all by speaking without being forced to.

"They're restless," she says, her cold eyes on the people strolling through the large market square. "Can you feel it?"

"Yes," I reply immediately.

I don't even need to use my magic to feel the restless tension that seems to hover over this entire city like a cloud. I've spent my entire life reading the situation around me, always alert and on the lookout for that moment when the mood in the room shifts and someone is about to get angry, so that I can try to defuse the conflict before it happens.

"Isn't it just anticipation?" Galen asks, glancing between me and Isera. "Excitement before the games?"

"No," I reply. "This feels different. There is a tension in the air that isn't there if it's only positive emotions."

Isera nods. "They're bored. Restless. Crawling up the walls waiting for something to happen."

"It's why people are arguing so much about which faction will win," I finish.

Alistair gives both of us a look as he drawls, "And why is this relevant again?"

I watch Isera, waiting for her to reply. She doesn't. And that dangerous glint remains in her eyes as she just slides her gaze back to the restless market before us.

"Because *we* need to win these games," I reply, shifting my attention to the others instead. "This is entertainment for these people. Their favorite type of entertainment. The contestants on the regular teams, like the White Faction, are practically celebrities." Resting my elbows on the wooden table before me, I draw both hands through my hair before heaving a sigh. "You all heard what Jocasta said before we left. It's not just about winning. It's about making sure the crowd is entertained."

"And everyone hates us," Draven finishes with a shrug.

I shoot him a half-hearted glare at his awful pep talk. But he is in fact right, so I just sigh again and echo, "And everyone hates us."

"All right, how should we play this, then?" Galen asks, looking from face to face. "There are six teams with six people on each team. Our entire team needs to win these games." He focuses on me, Alistair, and Isera. "You three have done something like this before during the Atonement Trials. So, what's the best move?"

Alistair scowls at him and shakes his head. "How should I know?"

"You're one of the few people who actually had a group of allies during the trials."

"Allies. Right." He snorts as if the idea is laughable. Then a sharp glint appears in his eyes. "And where are those *allies* now?"

It takes me a second to realize.

"Dead," I blurt out, staring at Alistair. "Maximus, Jeb, Tommen, and that other guy too . . . They all died during the Atonement Trials."

Alistair meets our shocked stares with unapologetic eyes. "Yeah."

Across the table, Galen watches him, his expression now slightly guarded.

"What?" Alistair challenges. Crossing his arms, he leans back in his chair. "I'm not a team player."

Isera cuts Galen a flat look. "Neither am I."

I shrug. "Yeah, I have no idea how to win properly either. I practically cheated my way through the whole thing."

Draven lets out a huff of amusement. "Don't I know it."

Drawing my eyebrows down in a mock scowl, I elbow him in the ribs. But he's still wearing his dragon scale armor, so it does absolutely nothing to make him wince. He grins at me, clearly pleased with his win.

"True," Lyra muses, her gaze sliding to Alistair. "In terms of pure strength, I suppose Trevor should've been the third winner."

"Don't look at me," Alistair says, raising his hands. "That one wasn't actually *my* fault." Then he nods at Isera instead. "She's the one who almost cracked his head open with a block of ice so that he had to drop out."

A sharp smile spreads across Isera's lips.

Galen groans and throws his arms up in an exasperated gesture. "Great, so we have two people who are entirely incapable of teamwork and one who shouldn't even have won."

"You're looking at it wrong," Draven says. A sly smile plays over his lips as he looks from me to Isera to Alistair before meeting Galen's gaze again. "We have two people who were strong enough to win completely on their own and one person who was smart enough to win even though she shouldn't have."

"Ha!" Lyra exclaims, a wide grin on her face as she points at Draven. "I knew there was a little optimist hiding underneath all that brooding."

Draven begins turning toward her, but before he can even meet her gaze, panic and hesitation blow across her features. She swallows and clears her throat before awkwardly glancing away.

Tension starts settling over the table like a death shroud. Thankfully, the waitress chooses that exact moment to arrive with our dinner. I stifle a sigh of relief as the heavy atmosphere is forced out by the heavenly scents of food.

My stomach growls as the waitress sets down a plate full of grilled meat, fried potatoes with what smells like garlic and herbs, and a slice of fluffy white bread. I didn't realize how hungry I was until now. These past two days, with the team selection, the escape attempt, Orion's nightmare punishment, and this entire day of training, have felt like three weeks. Not to mention the actual three weeks we spent in Orion's dungeon.

Thuds drift through the air as the waitress sets down wooden tankards of ale in front of us. I glance down into mine while she sets the last one down in front of Draven.

"Thank you," I say.

She doesn't reply. Only shoots me a disapproving look and stalks away.

It makes my stomach twist uncomfortably, but I block out the emotion and instead dig into the food.

A moan escapes my lips as I put a bite of grilled meat and potatoes into my mouth. The meat is so perfectly cooked that it practically melts. Closing my eyes, I savor the taste of garlic and herbs.

My eyes snap back open again as I suddenly feel a warm breath caress my ear, and I find that Draven has leaned in close. His lips brush the shell of my ear, sending lightning skittering across my skin.

"I thought only I could draw those sounds from you," he whispers in my ear.

Warmth curls around my spine, and I give him a sly smile as he draws back and sits upright again. While holding his gaze with eyes full of teasing challenge, I spear another piece of meat and put it in my mouth. Then I close my eyes and moan softly again as if the food is the best thing I have ever tasted.

Draven's hand grips my thigh under the table. And I, in turn, have to grip the table as he slides his strong hand up toward my hip and then sideways until it's resting on my inner thigh. My clit practically tingles from the near touch. He leans in again.

"Careful now, little rebel," he whispers in my ear, so softly that only I can hear. "Unless you want me to bend you over this table right here and fuck you so thoroughly that everyone will know what you *really* sound like when you moan."

My heart flips, and heat licks through my veins.

He once more pulls back, but he doesn't remove his hand. I struggle to swallow the bite of food as his fingers skim along the inside of my thigh. Coughing, I force the food down with a gulp of ale. I cast a worried look around the table, but everyone else is either engaged in their own conversations or focused on the food.

Draven's hand remains possessively on my thigh, his fingers teasing me, as I cut another piece of meat and potatoes. This time when I eat, I make sure to do it without moaning. Draven gives my thigh an approving squeeze, and he briefly leans closer again.

Another shiver of pleasure ripples down my spine as he places his lips right next to my ear.

"Good girl."

I choke on the potato.

Coughing violently, I lurch forward to grab the tankard of ale to wash it down while shooting the bastard next to me a glare. My cheeks are blazing red. Draven gives my thigh a couple of satisfied pats and lets out a smug chuckle under his breath as he pulls back again so that he is sitting normally.

From my other side, Galen glances at both me and Draven in confusion. "You okay?"

After forcing down the potato with several gulps of ale, I cough again and croak, "Yes."

He frowns at both of us. But before he can ask any more questions, Lyra's voice rings out.

"Are you going to drink or what?" She raises her eyebrows at Alistair, managing to somehow look both cheerful and half offended at the same time. "I'll have you know that I spent a lot of time choosing the best type of ale to go with this spice blend for the meat and potatoes."

"Oh we know," Galen mutters from across the table.

"Shut up," she says, but she's still smiling. Then she shifts her gaze back to Alistair and nods toward his still full tankard. "So why aren't you drinking it?"

Crossing his arms, he gives her a dubious look, as if the reason should have been obvious. "They hate us."

"So?"

"So they probably spit in it."

Lyra pauses with her tankard halfway to her lips. And so do the rest of us. I quickly put mine back on the table while trying to remember if the ale tasted strange or not when I drank it earlier. It's hard to tell. But then again, spit is tasteless. Isn't it?

"Huh." Lyra glances down at the ale in her mug, already half empty, before cocking her head. "I didn't think about that." She meets Alistair's gaze again. "How'd you figure?"

He draws his eyebrows down, trying to scowl, but ends up almost looking a bit embarrassed. Then he shrugs. "It's what I would've done."

A laugh rips from her throat. It's so unexpected that the rest of us draw back and blink at her in surprise. But she just keeps laughing, almost making the ale slosh over the top of her tankard before she manages to set it down on the table. Her orange eyes glitter as she turns to meet Alistair's gaze fully.

"We should totally team up sometime," she says, a sparkling grin on her mouth. "Can you imagine the level of trouble we could make together?"

"Oh no," Galen interrupts, raising a finger at her in warning. "Don't rope him into that. You alone are enough of a menace."

"Menace?" She presses a hand to her chest in an exaggerated look of shock. "Me? I would never."

"Uh-huh. Remember that time when—"

"I don't get you," Alistair blurts out, interrupting their argument. His orange-and-green eyes are wide and filled with such genuine bafflement that it's almost comical. Shaking his head, he stares at Lyra with those wide eyes. "Like, at all."

Lyra turns back to him and blinks in confusion. "What?"

"Why are you being nice to me all the time?" There is an almost desperate note to his voice. Holding her gaze, he shakes his head in disbelief again. "I'm a rude, angry bully."

Surprise flits across Lyra's face, as if she's shocked that he would describe himself in such a way. Then that easy smile returns to her features, and she slaps Alistair's arm with the back of her hand. "Nah. You're just a little grumpy." She shrugs. "And I happen to like grumpy people." A conspiratorial grin spreads across her mouth, and she nods toward Galen. "Why do you think I'm friends with that one?"

"I'm not grumpy," Galen protests.

"Oh please. You've spent two hundred years sulking because Draven—" She cuts herself off, panic flashing across her face as her gaze darts to Draven.

I brace myself, waiting for that awkward tension to yet again settle over us and strangle the previously pleasant mood.

But instead, Draven slams both palms down on the table so hard the utensils rattle and two of the mugs jump in surprise.

"Enough!" he snaps. "Enough with the guilt!"

Both Galen and Lyra draw back, looking stunned.

Draven rakes both hands through his hair and forces out a long breath, composing himself again. Then he looks between his two friends and repeats in a softer voice, "Enough with the guilt. It's not your fault that I was ambushed and trapped and enslaved with dragon steel."

"But we—" Galen begins.

"Listen to me." He holds their gazes one at a time, his expression pulsing with calm authority. "It was not. Your. Fault."

Pain and heartbreak swirl like a storm in Galen's eyes. And Lyra bites her lip, her own eyes glistening, as if she has to physically hold back tears.

"We should have known," Galen says, his voice barely more than a broken whisper. "*I* should have known."

Draven shakes his head, his gaze softening. "How could you have known? No one knew that dragon steel was still in play. That they had kept some of it and used it in secret these past six thousand years. I didn't know either. And without that, there was no other explanation for my behavior."

"I should have figured it out."

"You tried. I know you." A small smile ghosts across Draven's lips for a moment. "I watched you. You spent the first forty-two years trying to figure out why I was acting the way I was before you gave up. Forty-two years, Galen."

Galen swallows hard, a tear escaping the corner of his eye and slipping down his cheek. His voice is thick as he glances away and repeats, "I should have figured it out."

"Look at me."

Wiping away the escaped tear, he turns back to meet Draven's gaze.

"What I said back in the barracks after Selena cut out the dragon steel," Draven begins, holding his best friend's gaze with serious eyes. "I didn't mean it. I was angry and frustrated and worried because everything had just gone to hell, and I took it out on you. But I didn't mean it. It wasn't your fault. And you couldn't have known about the dragon steel."

Galen draws in an unsteady breath. "I am so, so sorry."

"Me too. And I hate how much time we've lost because of this." He looks from Galen to Lyra and then back again. "So please, stop with the guilt and the hesitation and all the walking on eggshells around me.

We've already lost two hundred years of friendship. I don't want to lose a single day more."

Lyra swallows thickly and then nods, her eyes brightening again. Across the table, Galen draws in another shuddering breath as he holds Draven's gaze.

And then he smiles.

Warmth floods my soul. Draven deserves this. He deserves everything. Friends. Family. Love. Freedom. Good food and lazy days and happiness. Winds and open horizons. A future full of endless possibilities.

A sudden overwhelming urge fills me.

Draven deserves *everything*. And I'm going to make sure he gets it.

21

Ice and fire roar through the air. I wince as the two forces almost cancel each other out instead of working together against Draven, Lyra, and Galen, who are facing Alistair and Isera from across the room. Sand rises from the ground, whirling like a tornado, as Draven throws a blast of wind back at them.

Jocasta snaps her fingers in front of my face. "Pay attention."

Blinking, I give my head a quick shake to clear it and focus on my own training instead. "Sorry."

"I know you wanna fuck him, but keep it in your pants until you're back at the house at least."

A jolt shoots through me, and my cheeks practically catch fire as I snap my gaze away from Draven. Shaking my head, I blurt out, "What? No, that's not what I—"

"You didn't even ask *who*."

Heat sears my cheeks even deeper.

Jocasta chuckles and shakes her head at me, but there is a smile lurking on her lips. "Kid, even my blind and dead grandmother could see it from a mile away." Her gaze turns pensive. "So what's stopping you?"

My heart twists uncomfortably at the question.

What's stopping me? Before all this craziness started where I almost died and we got trapped in the Unseelie Court, Draven told me that he *loves* me. And I didn't reply.

I don't want him to feel as if I'm just playing with him. He has had enough people manipulate him already. So first, I need to figure out how much of my feelings are my own.

That is what's stopping me.

But I can't tell Jocasta that, of course, so I just clear my throat and reply, "Can we just focus on the lesson, please?"

"Oh, now you want to focus on the lesson?"

I give her a flat look.

She chuckles again but thankfully lets the issue drop. Drawing in a long breath, she motions at me. "All right, this frustration that you're feeling right now. Try to share it with me."

"Share it?" I frown at her. "What's there to share? I'm frustrated because I can't do the things you're telling me to do. But you already know that. So what else is there to share?"

She laughs. "No, I mean share the emotion. So that I feel your frustration too."

I stare at her, my eyes wide.

She stares back at me, looking confused. Then she heaves an endless sigh. "Malachi's balls, you don't know how to share emotions, do you?"

"No."

"All right, it works like this. You take an emotion that you're feeling, and then you reach out with it toward—"

"What do you mean *reach out*?"

She ponders for a second. "Visualize it like you're stretching the emotion."

"All right."

"And then you attach it to the other person. Once it's attached, that person will feel half of that emotion while you feel the other half of it. So it decreases the feeling for you but makes them feel it too."

I raise my eyebrows in surprise. "It decreases the feeling for me and they feel the other half?"

"Yes."

"That's cool," I begin hesitantly. "But also kind of . . . useless. What am I supposed to use it for?"

"I've mainly used it while being tortured."

I stare at her. The casual way she said it makes me wonder if I actually heard her correctly. "Tortured?"

"Yeah. If they inflict pain on me, they feel half of it too. Great way to make them reluctant to do it."

That had not been what I was asking at all, so this time, I spell it out. "You've been tortured a lot?"

"Well, yeah, of course." She looks at me as if that should've been obvious. "Everyone in the Unseelie Court has been trained in how to withstand torture."

And just when I thought our courts might not be so different after all, she hits me with something like this.

"Uhm . . . right. Of course." I clear my throat, trying to focus on the task at hand again. "All right, stretch the emotion and attach it."

She nods encouragingly.

I know that I am frustrated. We've been training every waking hour of the day for three days now, and I still haven't been able to create emotions from nothing like Jocasta does. Which is why we switched to other techniques today. But I am apparently bad at those too.

Frustration burns inside me, eating at my soul and making me feel like a failure. I know it. I can feel it. But how do I take that emotion and stretch it out to attach it to someone else?

When I reach out with my magic to manipulate someone else's emotions, I just cast it toward them. So I try doing the same to my own chest.

It doesn't work.

A snarl slips from my lips. Clenching my jaw, I flex my hand in annoyance and then try again. I have no idea how to even connect the magic to my own emotions.

"I can't even see them!" I snap.

Jocasta, entirely unfazed by my outburst, just raises her eyebrows in question. "See what?"

"My emotions."

"Hmm." She taps her chin, considering in silence for a few seconds.

Across the sand, Draven, Lyra, and Galen are working in perfect synchronization as they try to advance across the room and make it past Isera and Alistair. The two fae, however, look to still be having massive issues working together. They're stopping the dragon shifters' advance separately instead of trying to coordinate their attacks.

Embers flutter through the air as Draven forces Alistair's flames away with a blast of wind. Outside the windows, soft white clouds drift across the heavens and temporarily block the midday sun. It makes the light inside our training room dim and brighten at irregular intervals.

"What do they look like?" Jocasta finally asks. "When you see the emotions in other people's chests, what do they look like?"

"Like flames, of course," I reply, frowning at her in confusion.

"Really?" She raises her eyebrows. "Huh. That's interesting." She cocks her head, making her long white hair slide across her shoulder. "I see them kind of like balls of water."

Shock clangs inside my skull as I stare at her, mouth open. "What? You don't see fire?"

"No. Mine are elegant orbs of liquid that ripple and shift softly."

I gape at her. "Mine are raging fires."

She laughs and slaps my shoulder playfully with the back of her hand. "You must be one angry girl, then."

Her words strike something deep inside me. Not hurt or any sense of being offended. But instead . . . panic.

When I don't immediately reply, she gives me a look and smiles. "I was kidding."

"Yeah, I know," I press out, and then also force out a laugh for good measure.

But her words still rattle me to the core. Because I'm terrified that she might be right. I barely dare to acknowledge all the emotions I've suppressed throughout my life, but the few times that I have dared to peek down into those hidden depths of my soul, all I've found is burning rage and festering hatred.

Thankfully, Jocasta doesn't seem to notice my panic, because she just claps her hands and declares, "All right, let's get back to it. So visualize those fires in your own chest, and then—"

A chunk of ice shoots through the air. We throw ourselves backward, barely managing to get out of the way before the wayward shard can hit us. It flies through the air in the space we used to occupy and then slams into the pale stone wall to my right.

Jocasta whips around and stabs a hand at Isera and Alistair. "That's it! I've had it." Stalking forward, she advances on them. "You two, with me. Right now."

"We just—" Alistair begins, but she cuts him off.

"I don't want to hear it. We only have three and a half days left before the first game starts. And I am going to make you work together if it's the last thing I do. I've bet my entire fortune on you, and if you don't win, I will be forced to suck the Red Faction's cock for the rest of my life. And guess who will be right there on your knees sucking cock with me? That's right. *You*. So you *will* work together if I so have to tie you together for the next four days."

"I thought you said there were only three and a half days left," Alistair drawls.

A growl of frustration rips from her lips. While still stalking toward Alistair and Isera, she stabs a finger at the rest of us. "You four, practice sparring while I beat some sense into these two."

Galen quickly hurries out of her way so that he won't get mowed down by our furious faction owner while Lyra flashes Alistair a grin, which only makes him scowl deeper. To my surprise, Isera doesn't object. Rather the opposite. She walks up to meet Jocasta halfway, and there is an intense look in her eyes.

"Well then," Draven suddenly says from right next to me.

I jump and whip my head around to stare at him. How someone so big can move so quietly still baffles me. And when I meet his gaze, I find a slight smirk on his lips as if he's way too pleased with himself for sneaking up on me and startling me like that. I shoot him a glare.

"Two against two?" he asks, shifting his attention to Lyra and Galen, who are standing opposite us.

"Sure," they reply, unsheathing their swords.

Next to me, Draven does the same. I still don't know how to fight with a sword, so I take out my dagger instead.

Two days ago, Jocasta managed to persuade the Unseelie King to return our weapons to us so that we would be able to give the audience a more entertaining show during the games. Though I have a feeling that she might have had to bribe him a little too. Regardless, I'm glad to have my familiar dagger back.

"So, how should we—" I begin.

Draven spins around and lunges at *me* instead.

I yelp, leaping back and out of range. "What the hell?"

He grins at me while thrusting his sword at me again. "First rule of battle. Always be on your guard."

From a few strides away, Lyra chuckles. "I knew it!"

Galen nods. "Does the same thing to all the new recruits."

"I'm not a new recruit," I huff as I try to parry his thrust.

But because of how massive his sword is, I only manage to redirect it a little and then I'm forced to duck instead. Behind Draven's back, Lyra and Galen form up and begin sparring with each other instead.

"Aren't you?" Draven replies, his eyes gleaming with challenge and his lips curved in a sly smile. "I seem to remember you addressing me as *sir*."

My cheeks flush. "That was when I was handcuffed to your bed."

His smile turns positively villainous. "I'm sure I can locate another pair of handcuffs."

"I've been using a knife every day for the past one hundred and forty-nine years to gut fish." A grin full of challenge spreads across my mouth. "I could demonstrate on you, if you want?"

"Come try it, little rebel. I bet I can put you on your back and make you submit in the next two minutes."

"You want to have me on my back, huh?"

"I want to have you in all positions."

My heart flips, and heat rushes through my veins.

And of course the bastard chooses that exact moment to launch an attack at lightning speed. I throw myself sideways, barely managing to escape before he can trap me. While he was teasing me, he was slowly but surely backing me into the corner of the room. And I was so focused on him in front of me that I didn't even notice.

Rolling across the warm sand, I jump back up to my feet and raise my knife to defend myself again. But I don't find Draven swinging a sword at me. I blink in surprise as I watch him sheath his massive sword instead.

"You're forfeiting?" I ask, arching a smug eyebrow at him.

A dark chuckle rolls from his muscular chest. "You wish." His eyes glitter as he rakes his gaze up and down my body. "I don't even need the sword to win."

I let out a stunned laugh. "You are one cocky bastard, aren't you?"

"As if you didn't already know that."

"You—"

He lunges for me again.

I leap backward.

Shock pulses through me as my back hits a wall. I cast a panicked look over my shoulder. How the hell did he manage to steer me back here without me even noticing? I will die before I ever admit it to that smug bastard, but damn, he's insanely good at this.

The wall cuts my escape short, and I'm forced to try to dive sideways instead. I land on the soft sand and try to roll away. But I barely make it more than two strides away from the wall before it's too late.

Draven's knees hit the ground on either side of me, stopping my movements and trapping me underneath him. I yank my arms up and try to get my knife in a better position. But of course, Draven has already anticipated that.

His strong hands wrap around my wrists at the same time as he settles his weight on my hips. My muscles shake as I try to force my knife toward his throat. But no matter how badass I think I am with my knife and my fish-cutting skills, it unfortunately doesn't change the simple biological fact that Draven is much, much stronger than me.

He just sits there on my hips, smirking down at me, as he holds my wrists trapped in his hands. The bastard doesn't even look at all winded, as if he barely needs to exert any effort at all to hold me down, while I'm using every smidgen of my strength trying to break free.

"I think there's about thirty seconds left of those two minutes I gave you," he says, his tone light and his eyes sparkling.

"Oh you smug little—" I growl, but it's interrupted by a noise of frustration from my throat as Draven starts to effortlessly push my arms down.

I squirm desperately underneath him as he moves my hands up over my head and then shifts his grip so that he is holding both my wrists with one hand.

"Now you're just showing off," I huff, shooting a half-hearted glare at him.

He smirks and pins both my hands to the ground above my head. Leaning down over me, he wraps his free hand around my throat. He isn't cutting off my air in any way, but his hand is firm. A clear reminder of who holds the power here now.

Wiggling, I once more try to yank my hands free or get his weight off my hips or . . . something. Anything. But with his muscular body straddling my hips, his hand pinning both of mine to the ground above my head, and his other hand locked around my throat, I am so thoroughly trapped that all I can do is kick my heels uselessly at the ground.

"So, little rebel." Draven flexes his hand around my throat, that devilish smile still on his lips. "Now what?"

I moan. "Choke me again, sir."

He blinks in shock.

And in that second of absolute stunned bafflement, his grip on my wrists loosens just a fraction. But I was waiting for it.

Yanking my left hand free, I press the edge of my dagger against his throat.

He starts in surprise, staring down at me in utter shock.

I grin up at him, still holding my blade across his throat. "And now you're mine."

A dark laugh, full of approval and wicked promises, escapes his throat. Desire flares up like flames in his eyes as he holds my gaze. His right hand is still resting around my throat, and he brushes his thumb over the side of my neck. Pleasure skitters down my spine. His other hand still pins my right hand to the ground above my head. But with my dagger to his throat, I've won. And he knows it.

He leans forward, and I move my knife with him, allowing him to bring his face closer to mine.

"You really are a little menace, you know that?" he murmurs.

I stop moving my hand, forcing him to stop as well, when his lips are just a breath away from mine. My spine tingles as his warm breath caresses my lips with every breath. And his firm weight on my hips is making my clit throb with need. I purposely roll my hips, grinding my body against his. His eyes shutter, and a soft moan comes from deep within his chest.

Tilting my chin up slightly, I close a little more of the distance between us so that my mouth almost brushes his. "Now, about that submission."

Another one of those amazing laughs full of approval and wicked promises rolls from his muscular chest. And his breath is like a gentle caress as he whispers against my lips.

"I submit."

22

The entire arena practically vibrates with anticipation. Cheering and shouting and clapping echoes from the other side of the door. We can't see them from where we're waiting in this small room adjacent to the main section, but it sounds as if the whole place is filled to the brim with people.

"Remember," Jocasta says from where she is standing next to the door that leads out into the main section of the arena. "*Entertain* them. Shock them. Delight them. Make them crave you."

Draven narrows his eyes at her. "Why is this so important?"

"Because during this first game, members of the crowd can . . . *affect* the course of the game."

"In what way?"

"I'm not allowed to say." She casts a discreet glance at a man who strides in through the other door behind us. "But remember what I've said."

"All right," the guy who just walked in says. It's the same man who gave us our number at the team selection earlier. The rings in his pointed ears glint in the faelights as he comes to a halt in front of all six of us while Jocasta moves out of the way. "Welcome to the first game."

The week we had to train before this game passed faster than I feared. We got a little better at working together, but I didn't improve much in terms of magical ability. Yesterday, I finally managed to figure out how to stretch my own emotions toward someone else. But I still don't know how I'm supposed to attach them. Learning new skills takes time. And a week was not nearly enough.

Not to mention my continued utter failure to create emotions from nothing. It doesn't matter how many times Jocasta explains it and tries to guide me through it. It doesn't work. I can't even do the very first step. And I can't help but worry that it's because I'm somehow defective.

"The objective of the game today is to get both keys and make it through the door at the center of the arena," the administrator continues. "There are two types of keys. One black. One white. Half of the teams have the white key, and the other half have the black key." Reaching into his satchel, he pulls out a white key. Then he thrusts it into Alistair's hands. "This is your key. You need both keys to open the door, so you need to take a black key from one of the other teams."

"How do we know which team has which key?" Alistair asks.

"You don't."

Alistair rolls his eyes. "Great."

"Any questions?"

"Yes," Galen replies, frowning at the brusque man. "What are the rules?"

He scowls back at him. "I just explained them. Get both keys and make it through the door. Those are the rules."

We exchange a glance. So they don't exactly care about foul play, then.

When no one immediately asks another question, he spins on his heel and stalks back out the door without another word.

Jocasta approaches us again while Alistair hands the key to Draven. Draven arches an eyebrow in surprise and silent question.

Alistair draws his eyebrows down, looking slightly embarrassed. "I don't want to be responsible for it."

Thankfully, Draven simply takes the key without commenting on it. Our teamwork is hanging by a thread already, and we really don't need Alistair and Draven to get into another dick-measuring contest right now.

"You understood the rules, right?" Jocasta asks. "Half of the teams have the white key and the other half have the black key, which means that only half of the teams can move on to the final game."

"Or less than half," Alistair says. When we all turn to him, he explains, "If you take more than one key, there are fewer pairs left for the others."

Isera cuts him a knowing look. "Like you did during the coin trial."

"What?" He lifts his toned shoulders in an unapologetic shrug. "I was being strategic."

"He's right," Jocasta says before Isera can reply. "But don't focus on that. As soon as you have both keys, run like hell to the door."

"Why?" Draven asks, his eyes narrowing.

"All teams who make it through the door will progress to the final game. But the team who makes it through first will also be invited to the castle for a celebration hosted by the king, which will raise your standing with the crowd."

Several of us exchange sharp looks. If we're invited to the castle, we will finally have a chance to solve a problem that we have been discussing every night this past week. How to get the piece of dragon steel back from Orion so that he can't use it against Draven. Or any other dragon shifter.

"Plus," Jocasta continues, an innocent smile on her lips. "The bets I've placed will yield even more money."

"Oh, we'll make it through first," Isera promises. Schemes glint in her eyes as she turns to stare at the door that leads into the main arena. As if she can see Orion through it. "I'll make sure of it."

"Excellent," Jocasta says.

A loud horn blares three times from somewhere on the other side of the door. I jump in surprise and spin around to face it while a jolt of both anticipation and worry shoots through me.

"It's time," Jocasta says.

Leather creaks as the rest of my friends turn to face the door as well. I quickly check my knife at my belt and then make sure that my hair is tied back properly. My pulse thrums, and I suddenly feel like there is a flock of erratic birds fluttering around inside my rib cage.

The horn blares again. Only twice this time.

"Any final advice?" I ask, flexing my fingers nervously.

A few steps to the left, Jocasta casts a quick glance toward the other door, as if checking to make sure that no other administrator is about to walk through it and catch her saying something that she shouldn't. The room is empty except for us, but she still lowers her voice so much that I can barely hear her.

"Don't split up," she whispers.

I glance briefly at her from the corner of my eye. "Why?"

On the other side of the door, the horn blares once in one final call.

"Because the walls have a way of moving."

The door before us is thrown open.

Bright sunlight streams into the room as the main section of the arena becomes visible before us. I draw in a nervous breath.

And then we stride out into the arena.

23

A deafening cheer echoes through the massive arena as we step out onto the warm sand, though I already know it's not for us. The other five teams have no doubt walked into the arena at the same time as well, but in different locations around the oval structure. Looking from side to side, I stare at the space around us in confusion.

"Where the hell did all these walls come from?" Alistair asks, echoing my exact thoughts.

During the team selection, the entire floor of the arena was one massive open space. But now we find ourselves standing in a small room. There are two openings, one straight ahead and one to the left, that lead out of the room and into what look like short corridors. Tilting my head back, I stare up at the open sky above. It's an incredibly disorienting feeling.

The stone walls around us section off the floor of the arena, making it feel as if we are indoors. But there is no ceiling. And above the walls that box us in down here, there are of course the actual walls of the arena. Which also have no ceiling, so the bright blue sky is visible high above us.

The tiered walls of the massive arena, curving slightly in an oval shape, rise up high outside the walls we have down here on the floor. So everyone in the audience can see down into the labyrinth of rooms and corridors we are standing in, but we can only see inside the room we're currently located in. Which is empty, except for us.

"So, left or straight ahead?" Lyra asks, drawing my attention back to our present problem.

She looks to Draven. As does Galen. But I decide to answer anyway.

"Since all the teams start at the edges, the one on the left will likely lead us toward another team pretty quickly." I turn and motion at the opening straight ahead. "And that one will likely take us faster to the door at the center. Since everyone will be heading toward the center, we will run into a team sooner or later anyway if we choose that direction, while at the same time, it will also take us closer to the finish line."

Draven glances at me, a smile full of approval lurking on his lips. "Agreed."

"All right." Lyra shrugs. "Straight ahead it is, then."

Next to her, Alistair frowns and motions at Draven. "Can't you just fly up over these walls and check where the other teams are?"

Draven gives him a flat look. "What an excellent way to get us all killed."

His frown deepens. "What?"

"If I fly up there, then yes, I will see where all the other teams are. But do you know what else will happen? All the other teams will know exactly where *we* are. And then all five of them will be coming straight for us."

"Oh. I didn't think about that."

"Uh-huh."

"I can track them with my magic," I say before Alistair can retort. "Or most of them, at least."

"Good." Draven nods. "Do it."

"We should get a move on," Isera says, her eyes on something up in the audience. Then she tears her gaze from whatever it was and cuts us all a look. "Now."

We nod and hurry toward the corridor straight ahead. While we walk, I summon my magic and throw it across the arena floor. I aim for feelings of apprehension, since that should be something that most of the other players are experiencing right now. To my surprise, I only find one.

With a frown, I release that emotion and instead throw out my magic in search of glittering silver sparks of excitement. I blink in surprise when my magic connects with twenty-three sparks.

They're *excited* about this? Shouldn't they be worried?

Then I remember that most of these people are celebrities. They play variations of these games every few months. The crowd adores them, and they're probably eager to show off their skills and settle rivalries with other teams. We are the only ones whose lives actually depend on this.

"You have them?" Draven asks as we sneak down the corridor.

"Yes," I reply. "Enough of them, at least."

Aside from us, there are thirty other contestants, and I only have a connection to twenty-three of them. But the connections are coming from five separate locations, so I'm fairly certain that I have at least one person from all teams.

We reach the end of the corridor and arrive inside another room. This one is bigger and shaped like a rectangle, but it's still empty. Three openings stare back at us. The one we just walked in through, one to the left, and one to the right. Nothing that leads toward the center.

Everyone turns to me.

With my magic still connected, I decrease our opponents' excitement slightly while I estimate distances. The closest team on the right seems to be heading farther in while the closest team on the left is heading in our direction.

"Left," I say.

They nod, and we start through that opening.

High above, the crowd is yelling and cheering. I glance up at them. Half of them aren't even sitting in their seats. Instead, they're standing and waving flags and banners. I study them while we sneak through the corridor.

On the other side of the arena is a large section where everyone seems to be wearing white, or at least waving white banners. There is a slightly smaller group of people in red opposite them. The rest of it appears to be more neutral territory, because banners in yellow, green, and blue, along with some more white and red, are scattered across every tier all the way around the arena. It's with dismay, but not surprise, that I notice no one is waving black banners.

Some people in blue are yelling and pointing as if they're trying to tell the blue team where to go, but it's impossible to hear what they're actually saying through the noise from the rest of the crowd.

I shift my gaze back to my friends. "We should—"

My stomach lurches.

For a moment, I can't figure out what's happening.

Then I'm plummeting downward after the ground has suddenly disappeared underneath my feet, revealing a mass of sharp spikes below.

I cry out, trying to grab on to something. All around me, my friends are plummeting downward as well. Half the floor in the corridor that we were passing through is gone, and the walls are too smooth to offer any handholds. There is nothing I can do to stop my fall.

Fear crackles through me at the overwhelming sense of helplessness.

Then my feet slam into something solid.

It's so abrupt that the hard landing sends me crashing down on my knees. I gasp, bracing myself against the cold surface beneath me.

My head is still screaming with panic, so it takes me a few seconds to understand what it is that I'm looking at.

A thick sheet of ice has materialized halfway between where the floor used to be and where the sharp spikes are waiting to impale us.

"Azaroth's flame," Galen gasps out from my right.

Raising my head, I look up at Isera where she is crouched on one knee a little in front of me. She straightens and then uses the front part of her ice sheet to create a set of steps back up to the section of the floor that still remains.

"Nice catch," I say.

She gives me a nod but then just jerks her chin toward the steps she created. "Get going."

I begin to stand up but stumble back down. That's when I realize there is a hand gripping my wrist tightly. Blinking, I glance down at it and then up at the man attached to it.

Draven, seeming equally surprised to find himself still holding on to my wrist, quickly stands up and uses his grip to help me to my feet as well. As if that is the reason he has been holding on to me for so long.

Giving me a quick smile, he at last releases me and motions for me to start up Isera's ice steps. I nod in thanks and do as requested. But in my chest, my heart is beating erratically.

When we fell, his first instinct was to catch *me*. Not Galen, who has been his best friend for over 280 years. Me. He grabbed *me*.

My heart pounds.

It's real. It has to be.

Or it's just the mate bond driving him to protect you by instinct, that foul voice whispers in the back of my mind.

But this time, a third voice adds another small whisper. *Does it matter?*

"I thought she told us to watch the *walls*," Alistair grumbles as he climbs up onto the floor ahead of me.

I quickly make my way up as well, with Draven and Isera bringing up the rear.

"Looks like both the walls and the floor have a tendency to move," Lyra replies, glancing at the pale stone around us.

Once Isera has reached the real floor as well, she dismisses the thick sheet of ice she used to save us all.

From the stands above, the audience boos loudly, as if they're disappointed we didn't get impaled, while another smaller group laughs and points at us. Cold fury burns in Isera's eyes as she stares up at them.

Alistair clicks his tongue and nods to the group who were laughing. "How much you wanna bet that those assholes up in the audience are the ones who control the walls and the floor?"

Jocasta's words echo in my mind again. *During this first game, members of the crowd can . . . affect the course of the game.*

"Fuck," Draven growls, and rakes a hand through his hair.

I blow out a sigh. "They're going to do everything they can to screw us over."

"Yeah."

The sound of grinding stone fills the corridor as the floor slides back out from where it had disappeared into the wall earlier. It moves until only solid ground, topped with a layer of sand, is visible in the hallway once more.

Tearing my gaze from it, I turn to Isera but find her still staring daggers at the audience. Or, not the audience. A specific person. Following her gaze, I realize who she has been glaring at this whole time.

Orion Nightbane is sitting on a throne in a private section in the middle of the arena. The silver details on his black and blue clothes gleam in the bright sunlight, and his long midnight-blue hair falls perfectly down over his shoulders to rest on his toned chest. His head is turned in our direction, as if he was watching us struggle earlier. And even from this distance, I swear I can see a smirk on his lips.

"Selena," Galen begins. "Where's the team we were tracking?"

My heart leaps into my throat.

Shit. When the floor disappeared, I lost the grip on my magic and the connection to the other players.

Scrambling to get it back, I summon my magic and throw it out across the arena toward those glittering silver sparks of excitement.

Alarm crackles down my spine, and I whip my head toward the next opening up ahead.

"They're here," I blurt out. "They're right around the corner."

"Fuck," Draven curses. Lurching into motion, he grabs Galen and Lyra and practically throws them toward the opening up ahead. "We need to make it into the next room before they do. Otherwise, we'll be trapped between them and the floor that those assholes up there can remove at any time."

Alistair leaps into action as well, sprinting after the two dragon shifters. Isera, Draven, and I follow them.

Our boots pound against the sand as we hurtle through the corridor and toward the next opening. Draven is right. If they make it to the opening before we do, we will be trapped. We have to make it there first. We have to.

My pulse thrums in my ears as I sprint down the corridor.

The opening gets closer.

And so do the people whose emotions I can still feel.

Please, Mabona, I beg in my mind. *Come on. Please.*

Galen, Lyra, and Alistair reach the opening.

Yes!

Just a few more steps. A few more, and then we will also—

The wall next to us flips.

24

Stone slams out in front of us as the wall to our right spins as if it has been secured to a pole in the middle of it. It makes the section ahead of us rotate into our corridor while the section behind moves in through the space on the other side. And it happens so fast that it crashes into us, shoving us with it as it whirls half a turn before slamming back to a halt.

The maneuver pushes us out of the corridor we were in and deposits us in the room that was on the other side of the wall.

We stumble into each other from the force of the shove, and Isera and I go sprawling on the ground as I crash into her from behind. Draven lands on his hands and knees above us, barely managing not to crush us with his body.

For a second, the three of us just stare at each other, trying to process what just happened. Then Draven quickly climbs off us. I toss my hair out of my face as Isera and I disentangle our limbs.

"Assholes," I growl while shooting a glare up at the audience.

The entire section around us is now laughing and pointing in our direction.

"We need to get back through the wall," I say as I struggle to my feet. "The others made it into the room, and the other team is—"

"Here," Draven interrupts, sounding exasperated. "The other team is . . . here."

Straightening, I whirl around to stare in the direction he is looking.

My stomach drops.

Just like he said, the team we were tracking is standing there on the sand right in front of us. All six of them are scrambling to their feet as well, casting confused glances at the wall. They must have been shoved into this room from the other room that Galen, Lyra, and Alistair are now waiting in alone.

I whip my head from side to side.

There are no openings inside this room. Only tall walls on all four sides. No way out. And a full team of six Unseelie fae facing us while our team is split in half.

Narrowing my eyes, I stifle another snarl as I shoot a glare at the laughing and whooping audience. *Fucking assholes.*

The team before us, all dressed in yellow fighting leathers, at last notices us as well and quickly forms up into an attack formation.

"You're outnumbered," the leader, a man with dark brown hair, calls in a shockingly loud voice. "How about you crawl up to us and surrender your key, and we'll consider not maiming you too badly."

The people waving yellow banners in the audience above us whoop and cheer. And even some people wearing green and red scarves yell and clap as well.

That's when I realize why the team leader of the Yellow Faction is screaming so loudly even though the room we're in is not that big. He's putting on a show. Not for us. For *them.*

Of course. Jocasta's words yet again echo through my brain. It's not just about winning. It's about entertaining the crowd.

Next to me, Draven gives the six Unseelie fae before us an unimpressed look while saying to me and Isera, "Well then, shall we?"

Isera throws a block of ice at them.

Half of them start in surprise at the sudden attack, and I don't waste a single second. Shoving my magic out, I lock on to those sparks of surprise and fan it into full-blown shock. They gasp, and the unnatural shock that I just forced them to feel makes them just stand there and stare.

The other three throw themselves out of the way and summon their own magic. Fire roars through the air toward Isera's block of ice, but it only manages to melt part of it. The rest slams into their three stunned companions.

A flash of smug victory pulses through me as they cry out when the ice crashes right into them.

But the other three are already moving.

Water blasts through the air straight toward us.

I dive sideways, cutting off my magic as I roll across the sand to escape the torrent. Draven does the same, but dives in the other direction, while Isera just raises an ice wall in front of her. The water smacks into it with enough force to send chips of ice flying.

Rolling to my feet, I yank out my dagger. The three people I stunned in the beginning have recovered from both my magic and Isera's ice, and they are charging toward us.

Draven summons his storm magic, shoving a blast of wind at them long enough for us to get to our feet. I leap back, barely managing to get out of the way before a stream of fire crackles through the air where I used to be. My heart slams against my ribs, and blood rushes in my ears.

Dread suddenly curls around my spine.

Yes, our raw magic might be stronger than the average Unseelie fae, but it makes no difference in here. In an open space, where magic needs to reach far and wide, the power difference would be vital. But here, in a small cramped room where it doesn't need to reach too far, their magic is just as deadly as ours.

And we are outnumbered two to one.

Fuck.

I duck and summon my magic again as another blast of water hurtles toward me. A few steps away, Draven is shooting lightning at three of the players while Isera is throwing spears of ice at the other two.

My mind churns as I scramble upright again while trying to figure out how to help them and also take down the sixth member of the enemy team. The guy, his black-and-purple eyes locked on me, shoots another blast of water at me from across the room, forcing me yet again to leap to the side to evade it.

Panic and dread twist inside my stomach like cold snakes.

Because it's with horrifying clarity that I'm coming to realize that I am practically useless in one-on-one fights like this.

I'm not a warrior. I'm a spy.

I have no magic that can kill or block attacks. The best I can do is distract an opponent with my magic. Or make them flee. But even that is difficult. Because first, they need to actually feel fear for me to be able to increase it so much that they flee or surrender.

Throwing myself to the side, I evade another water blast. A dull ache pulses through my body as my shoulder hits the ground yet again before I roll to my feet.

It would be different if I could create emotions from nothing. But this . . . The way my powers are now, it's not enough.

Anger flares up inside me, shocking in its intensity. The rage that consumes me is so furious that my vision blacks out for a second. Fucking hell, I *need* to figure out how to create emotions the way Jocasta does. I need to get stronger. More powerful. I will not—

Water slams into my chest.

The blinding rage distracted me so much that I wasn't keeping track of my surroundings.

Pain pulses through my back as I crash into the stone wall behind me. My ears are ringing, with both anger and pain, but I still hear the crowd cheer above me. Rage sears through me, setting everything on fire. Fuck, I want to kill them all.

I jerk back, stunned by my own thoughts.

It distracts me enough that I manage to shove the rage back and focus properly on my surroundings again.

Draven has managed to knock out two of his opponents and is now fighting hand to hand with the final one. A few steps away, Isera is still battling the other two. Both of them are fire wielders, which is of course the worst kind of opponent for her. They smirk as they shoot torrents of fire at her one after the other.

A sudden idea strikes me.

I summon my magic, but then have to yet again dive sideways as my own opponent tries to drown me with a wave of water. It slams into the wall behind me, creating a sloshing sound as it washes over the stone.

Rolling across the now wet sand, I leap to my feet and throw my magic across the room.

Just as I thought, my magic connects with the sky-blue flames of confidence in the chests of both my opponent and Isera's two. With a shove, I turn them into raging wildfires.

Their grins widen as the two fire wielders start attacking Isera with more fervor. But their attacks are sloppy now. Isera flicks a glance in my direction. I keep increasing their confidence until they start blocking Isera's attacks far later than normal.

Across the sand, the water wielder who has been facing me abandons his ranged attacks and instead sprints toward me, a confident grin on his face.

I flex my fingers on the knife in my hand while still continuing to manipulate their emotions.

To my right, Isera shoots two sheets of ice consecutively, followed quickly by two smaller chunks. Her opponents, overconfident in their own abilities, block the sheets with lazy waves of fire right before they can hit. But when they lower their flames again, the two chunks of ice are far too close. They crash into their faces with sickening cracks. Blood gushes out of their noses as they collapse to the ground.

The water wielder before me draws a sword as he charges across the sand. I force out a calming breath, getting ready to fight him in close quarters, since that will significantly increase my odds.

He closes the final distance.

I grip my knife hard.

His head snaps to the side as a block of ice slams into it.

I jump out of the way as his feet continue taking him a few steps forward before his brain realizes that he is unconscious. He hits the sand next to me in a heap of limbs.

For a few seconds, I just stare down at him. Then I glance up at Isera. She gives me a nod, a knowing glint in her eyes. I flash her a smile back.

It worked.

Overconfidence will kill you faster than any blade.

Not that these people are dead. Just unconscious. But still. The insane levels of confidence I forced them to feel made them sloppy and arrogant, which ultimately led to their downfall.

A scream shatters through the air.

I turn to find Draven pinning the team leader, the one who told us to crawl earlier, to the stone wall across the room. Isera and I exchange a glance before starting in that direction.

"Last time I'm asking nicely," Draven says. "Give me the key."

"Fuck you," the team leader snarls back. "You filthy dragon shifter whore of a—"

Draven snaps the guy's wrist.

Another scream rips from his chest.

Stopping halfway across the room, I summon my magic and shove it at the guy. Latching on to that violet flame of pain, I blow it into a raging inferno.

His scream turns into a cry of pure agony. It's so loud that his voice breaks halfway through. And he shakes violently against the wall.

Draven turns his head and glances at me over his shoulder. I give him an unapologetic shrug. He tilts his head to the side in a half nod, approval lining his features. Then he turns back to the Unseelie fae.

"The key," he commands.

The guy sobs and gasps in breaths through the intense levels of pain I'm forcing him to feel. Draven digs his fingers into the guy's broken wrist, and another world-ending scream of pain tears from his throat.

"Okay, okay," he blurts out.

"No," I say before Draven can reply.

The Unseelie fae snaps his gaze to me, and a flash of fear pushes out the pain in his eyes for a second. I quickly release my grip on his pain and latch on to that fear instead. Something terrifyingly vicious awakens in my chest as I flash him a ruthless smile while I start to increase his fear.

Glancing at me over his shoulder again, Draven arches an eyebrow in silent question.

"Let him go," I say, still continuing to increase the guy's fear.

Draven doesn't even hesitate. He immediately releases his grip on his captive.

The Unseelie fae lets out a whine as his now broken wrist falls back down to his side, and his eyes are filled with fear as he just stands there, staring at me. I keep increasing his fear until he is shaking against the wall. Then I cast a discreet glance at the audience.

Everyone seated in this section is watching our confrontation with bated breath. The ones who were standing up appear almost frozen as they stare intently down at us, while the ones who were still sitting down have all leaned forward in their seats, as if they want to get as close as possible.

I let a smirk curl my lips.

They wanted a show.

I'll give them a show.

With my magic still turning the team leader into a trembling mess, I lock hard eyes on him.

"Crawl up to me and surrender your key, and I'll consider not maiming you too badly," I order, echoing his own words from earlier with a mocking smirk on my lips.

He immediately drops to his knees.

A gasp rips through the audience above us. Apparently, this isn't something the team leader for the Yellow Faction would normally do. But with me manipulating his emotions, he doesn't exactly have free will anymore.

Whines of pain escape his lips as he crawls across the sand on his broken wrist. Once he reaches me, he sits back on his knees and reaches into his yellow fighting leathers to get the key. His undamaged hand shakes so badly, he almost drops it.

I soak up the terror in his eyes like a fucking psycho as he drops the key into my waiting palm. But it just feels so good. This power. This absolute power I have over him right now. It's intoxicating.

White lightning crackles through the air.

The kneeling man jerks as it hits him in the back. His eyes go wide and his body spasms before he topples to the side. He hits the ground with a thud, sending a small cloud of sand swirling up.

Draven glances down at him as he steps over his unconscious body to reach me. His golden eyes burn like wildfire when he meets my gaze. My heart flips as he leans closer and places his lips right next to my ear.

"Fuck, you're hot when you threaten people," he murmurs.

Pleasure crackles down my spine, and heat floods my veins.

"If you're done eye-fucking each other, we still have a job to do," Isera's voice comes from somewhere to my left.

A different kind of heat sears my cheeks as I remember that we're not alone. In fact, we're in a packed arena full of people watching us.

Clearing my throat, I take a step back to put some distance between me and Draven. He gives me a sly smile but then turns so that we are all facing the same way. Or rather, the same section of the audience.

We won the battle, but there is still no way out of this room unless the audience turns one of the walls for us again.

Standing there side by side, we stare up expectantly at the crowd. The ones who were waving yellow banners are glaring down at us as if they want to murder us. But the rest look more uncertain. A few of them look like they're about to give us a round of applause, or at least cheer, but then they glance hesitantly at the others. We gave them a nice show. But we're still outsiders.

When no one opens any of the walls for us, Isera lets out an annoyed sigh under her breath. Her eyes begin to glow again as she summons her magic.

Ice crackles and glints in the bright sunlight as she creates steps along the stone wall that the Yellow Faction came from. Then she gives the crowd an elaborate bow, which seems to surprise them as much as us, before she jerks her chin at us to follow.

A few scattered cheers of approval come from the crowd as we jog up the ice steps and onto the top of the stone wall.

From up here, I can see the layout of the entire arena. Countless rooms and corridors fill the entire sand ground except the very middle, where a round space has been left empty. It's impossible to tell from this distance, but I assume there is a door somewhere in that space.

While Isera forms another staircase on the other side of the wall, I quickly sweep my gaze over all the rooms in search of the other teams. A jolt shoots through me when I realize how close both the red team and the blue team are to our location. The White Faction is on the other side of the arena, but the green one is about halfway between us and them.

And all of them jerk their heads up to stare at us where we're standing on top of the wall.

"Let's go," Isera says, and hurries down the ice steps as soon as they are finished.

We dart down after her.

"Azaroth's flame," Galen exclaims as we reach the room below, where he, Alistair, and Lyra were pacing like restless wolves. "What the hell happened?"

"We got the key," Draven replies, and nods to me.

A grin spreads across my mouth as I hold it up. They all stare at it.

"It's white," Alistair says.

"Uhm, yes," I reply, frowning at his strange tone. "It's . . ." I trail off as realization finally slams into me before I manage to end with a miserable, "white. The key is white."

A collective groan escapes us all. Because the key we started with is also white.

Shoving the useless key into one of my new belt pouches, I rake a frustrated hand through my hair. "After all that, the key is fucking white."

"So now we have two white keys," Alistair summarizes rather superfluously.

"Yeah."

"Guys," Isera interrupts. Her eyes are fixed on the openings on the other side of the room.

But she doesn't need to say anything else, because realization floods my chest like icy water.

All the other teams saw our location when we were forced to climb over the wall.

I curse under my breath, glancing between the two openings while my pulse thrums in my ears.

"We need to move. Now."

25

My heart slams against my ribs, drowning out the sound of my pounding feet, as we hurtle through the corridors and deserted rooms. We don't even know where we're going. We just need to put as much distance between us and our previous location as possible. Otherwise, we're going to have to fight three teams at once. And we won't survive that.

I keep my magic attached to the excitement in their chests as we run, but it doesn't matter that I decrease it. They're still coming. I can feel them. Three entire teams. All eighteen of them, converging on us.

Shit.

Picking up speed, I throw myself around the corner after my friends.

The farther into the arena we get, the more decorated the rooms and corridors become. Where we started, they were all empty. But now furniture has started to pop up. Tables and chairs and pedestals with ceramic pottery and even full-length statues of Unseelie fae warriors now line the walls at various locations. They haven't been arranged like someone would decorate a real room or hallway. Instead, the mismatched furniture just stands in random spots. As if they're meant to be used as tools to create a more interesting fight.

We sprint through the next opening and into a room full of chairs. They have been placed all across the room, and I slam right into one before I even realize it. Wooden clattering echoes between the walls as the chair crashes into another one, but it's barely audible over the cheers and mocking laughter from the crowd above.

Shoving the chairs out of the way, I ignore the jeering of the audience and instead whip my head from side to side. There are three openings inside this room. Those glittering silver sparks of excitement in our opponents' chests are still getting closer. My pulse pounds in my ears as I snap my gaze to the right. The group in that direction has picked up speed.

"Left," I yell to my own team.

They don't even hesitate a second. Isera leaps over a cluster of chairs while Galen tries to shove another one out of his way. A growl of frustration rips from Draven's throat, and a moment later, storm winds whirl through the room.

A deafening sound of snapping and clanking wood echoes around us as Draven blows the sea of chairs straight into the stone wall and the opening to the right. The chairs hit the stone with a crash, wooden legs and armrests snapping in half from the force until the cluster blocks the entrance from that side.

Above us, a few cheers of approval rise from the audience. But most of them call out curses and threats that we'll be wiped out by whatever other team they're rooting for.

With the mass of chairs finally out of the way, we dart toward the opening on the left unhindered. The yells from the crowd grow louder, as if they're furious that we got out before the team hunting us from the right could reach the room.

Skidding out through the opening, we find ourselves in a long and wide corridor that is completely empty.

Strangely, the crowd above us roars in excitement.

Damn. Was this a trap? Did they actually want us to go left?

We sprint down the corridor.

"I have a bad feeling about this," I yell to my friends. "We should—"

A slab of stone shoots out from the wall behind us. I yelp as it slams into the wall on the other side of the corridor, blocking off our way back into the room with the chairs. The crowd cheers again.

While still hurtling down the corridor toward the next opening, I cast a quick glance behind me. I have a really, *really* bad feeling about this.

"Isera," I call. "Create another staircase! We need to get out of this corridor. Right now!"

Stone grinds against stone.

I gasp as a flat slab of stone shoots out from the wall to our right again. But this time it's above us. Dread crackles through my every nerve as a thick ceiling made of stone shoots out and then slams in place against the other wall. It blocks out the previously open sky above us entirely.

It also blocks out the light.

Air escapes my lungs in a huff as I slam right into someone. The corridor is now pitch-black around us except for the faint light coming from the opening up ahead. I stumble, throwing out my hands to steady myself as I try to regain my balance. My hands meet a slim body wearing fighting leathers. Isera.

I frown at her in the darkness. Why did she stop like that? We need to make it to the opening.

Grabbing her by the arm, I start pulling her with me toward that faint light from the doorway up ahead. "Come on."

A low whimper comes from her throat.

The pitiful sound, coming from someone as strong as Isera, stuns me so much that I whip my head toward her. But I can barely see her face in this darkness. The others are still running up ahead, getting closer to the opening.

"Come on," I repeat. "We need to—"

Stone slams against stone.

And then all light disappears.

Isera lets out a strangled noise.

"Fuck!" Draven screams from up ahead.

I turn in his direction while still keeping my hand around Isera's wrist. Her hand, and her entire arm, has started shaking uncontrollably.

In the thick darkness, I can't see anything. But I can hear someone pound against a stone wall.

"The bastards blocked off our only way out!" Draven calls back to us.

Isera starts hyperventilating.

Then light returns as Alistair summons flames along his arms. Yellow and orange firelight illuminates the corridor, which has now become radically shorter. Stone walls box us in from every direction, and with the ceiling now in place, we're trapped in here.

"Can you break through it?" Galen asks, looking at Draven. "With your lightning or wind?"

"I can try," Draven replies, dark storm clouds gathering around him. "But if the lightning hits wrong, it could cause the whole stone ceiling to collapse right on top of us." He turns in our direction. "Isera, create another ceiling of ice above us to protect us in case that happens."

But Isera doesn't answer. She just stands there next to me, her eyes wide with terror as she stares at the stone enclosing us. Her breathing comes in short, shallow bursts.

Releasing her wrist, I gently stroke her arm instead. "Isera, can you—"

A low rumbling starts. The sound of rock scraping and gears grinding.

Then the walls on our left and right start to move.

Fear drops like a stone in my stomach as the corridor begins to *shrink*.

Isera's knees buckle.

"No, no, no, please," she gasps out, throwing her hands up over her head and rocking back and forth in panic. "Make it stop. Make it stop."

"Hold the walls!" Draven bellows.

Leaving Isera there on the ground, I rush over to the wall on my right and throw my weight against it. Alistair joins me while Galen and Lyra do the same on the other wall.

White lightning cracks through the air as Draven tries to break through the unmoving wall up ahead. The lightning bolt slams into the stone, leaving a charred mark on the wall, but doesn't break through. He shoots a blast of wind at it.

My heart pounds in my ears as I press my palms against the right wall, but it just keeps moving inward, making me slide across the sand. I try to dig my heels in, but the soft sand provides little support.

"Isera!" I call. "You need to create a block of ice between the walls to stop them!"

She just shakes uncontrollably while hyperventilating on the ground.

"Isera!" I scream. "Please! We need you!"

Lightning slams into the stone wall again, the sound ricocheting through the shrinking corridor. Draven shoots another bolt.

The stone cracks.

Ice spreads through my veins as that crack spreads across the wall and up through the ceiling. Stone groans above us.

"Mabona's fucking tits," Alistair growls.

And then he releases the wall.

I cry out as the wall starts moving faster without Alistair pushing against it too. Spinning around, I press my back against it and try to dig my heels in instead to get a better grip.

"Alistair," I call as he darts away. "What are you—"

"Stand aside," he snaps at Draven, ignoring my question.

Draven leaps aside as Alistair stalks up to the wall.

"Farther back," Alistair says as he comes to a halt. "And use your wind to direct the heat away from the five of you."

My boots slide across the ground, leaving deep ruts in the sand, as the wall pushes ever closer. There are only a few strides left now before it reaches the other wall. Panic pulses inside me like shock waves. We're going to be crushed between them.

"Fuck," Alistair growls as the fire along his arms shifts down to his palms instead. "This is going to take everything I have."

Draven runs back to me, throwing his weight against the wall next to me. It stops the rapid sliding and forces the wall to move slower. But it's still not enough.

"Wind!" Alistair snaps. "Now!"

While still bracing the wall, Draven summons his magic and sends gusts of wind rippling in the space between us and Alistair. Once

Alistair's curly blond hair is whipping with it, he positions both hands so that they're facing the unmoving wall in front of him.

I just stare at him in disbelief. This will never work. If it was wood, sure. But it's stone, for Mabona's sake! It's not even flammable.

Fire erupts through the corridor.

It bursts from his palms and streams through the air in one thick torrent before it hits the stone wall in front of him. Orange and yellow flames crash against the stone. Alistair clenches his jaw. Then the color of the fire starts changing. First toward white. Then the fire turns blue.

Even with Draven's winds keeping the worst of it away from us, the heat that radiates from the fire is still insane. It fills the cramped corridor like thick fog, so oppressive that it's almost difficult to breathe. Sweat slides down my temples and rolls down my spine as I continue to press myself against the wall, trying to keep it from crushing us.

Alistair, who is immune to his own fire magic and the effects of it, just stands there, his spine straight, and continues to pour violet-blue flames straight at the wall before him.

On the ground, Isera seems to be barely conscious. Her chest rises and falls with jagged breaths.

We slide closer toward the middle. Toward the other wall.

I stare desperately at Alistair. This will never work. It will never—

The stone before him begins to *melt*.

My jaw drops.

I stumble, almost losing my grip on the wall before I manage to steady myself again. While pushing harder against the wall behind me, I stare at Alistair in shock.

Stone starts dripping away from where his flames hit, creating a hole.

But our walls continue pushing closer.

A strained grunt rips from my chest as I throw my entire weight against the wall, trying to force it to stop. Sand shifts around my boots as I slide steadily inward.

Panic pulses in Lyra's and Galen's eyes as we are pressed so close to each other that it's barely more than a few strides. Draven lifts his legs and places his feet flat against the opposite wall. With his back bracing our wall, he groans in exertion as he pushes hard with his legs. Galen quickly does the same from the other side. And so do Lyra and I.

The walls grind to an almost halt.

On the floor between us, Isera is lying on the sand, barely breathing through waves of terror, as her worst nightmare and most terrible fear has become reality.

Then a pair of strong hands grips her shoulders.

I snap my head up.

Alistair drags Isera toward the other wall, where a hole roughly the size of a person is now visible. His face is pale and lined with exhaustion, and he stumbles slightly before he manages to pull Isera out through the hole.

"Go!" Draven snaps at the rest of us.

Lyra and Galen quickly obey, dropping their legs back down to the floor. Then they're sprinting toward the hole.

The moment they're gone, the walls start pushing harder against our feet and backs again.

"Now," Draven growls at me, command pulsing from his voice like thunder.

"You'd better be right behind me," I snarl back at him. "Or I will come back in here and kill you myself."

Then I drop from the wall and sprint toward the hole. Draven's boots hit the ground right after mine.

The walls start sliding faster.

Our feet pound against the sand.

Air saws through my throat as I gasp in desperate breaths.

The walls close in on us faster. Panic lurches inside me as the stone brushes against my shoulders on both sides.

I dive through the hole.

Sand puffs up in a cloud as I land hard on the ground outside.

A boom echoes through the air.

I whip around, fear turning my blood into ice. Draven. Where is—

A massive weight lands right on top of me.

I let out a huff as the air is knocked right out of my lungs. But in my chest, my entire soul is vibrating with relief. Because the big lump of muscle on top of me grunts and struggles to get to his hands and knees so that he isn't crushing me. And then a pair of glittering golden eyes meet mine.

Relief shatters through me, and a wide smile spreads across my lips as I hold Draven's gaze. "Graceful as a boulder."

He lets out a huff of what seems to be equal amounts amusement and relief, and a smile curves his lips as well. "Shut up."

After raking a hand through his messy black hair to get it out of his face, he climbs off me and rolls over so that he is sitting on the sand next to me instead. I sit up as well. Isera is seated by the wall a short distance away, dragging in deep breaths. But color is once again returning to her face.

Next to us, Galen and Lyra are staring at the hole in the wall with stunned expressions. I shift my gaze toward it too.

The walls are now fully closed, and we can see them pressing against each other through the hole that Alistair created. I stare at that hole, because from this side, I can see how bloody thick the stone wall was. Turning my head, I gape at him.

He's busy brushing sand off his legs where he's seated on the ground, so he doesn't notice our attention at first. Then he looks up as if to say something, but he stops when he finds us all gaping at him. Uncertainty floods his exhausted features.

"What?" he asks, glancing from face to face. When no one states the obvious, he lifts a hand and rubs the back of his neck in a surprisingly self-conscious move. "I've already told you. Everything burns if the fire is hot enough."

"Oh, we know," Lyra says, watching him appraisingly, as if she's seeing him in a different light this time.

"I'm sure you've melted stone thousands of times too."

"Well, yeah, but we're dragons. Like, actual dragons." She nods toward the hole in the wall. "You melting a wall this thick, this fast, is impressive as hell."

He blinks. Then a hint of red creeps into his cheeks.

"I'm sorry," Isera suddenly whispers from the wall. "I just . . ." She swallows, looking like she's still trying to claw her way out of her nightmares and back to reality. "I'm sorry."

"It's—" I begin, but then a startling sound cuts me off.

Loud cheering explodes through the air.

I whip my head around, remembering where we are. Large parts of the crowd are cheering and pointing at us, looking as shocked as we are. They apparently didn't think we would make it out of there.

Alarm shoots up my spine.

The other teams.

Quickly summoning my magic again, I throw it across the arena. It latches on to twenty-four sparks of excitement. And eighteen of those sparks are just one or two rooms away.

All color drains from my face.

I snap my gaze back to my companions.

"They're coming."

26

Sand whirls around us as we leap to our feet and sprint the final distance through the corridor toward the room up ahead. From all sides, three teams are converging on us. The crowd roars in excitement.

We skid into the room right as the Green Faction pours in through one of the other openings. They jerk back, seeming surprised to find us for a second. Then wicked grins spread across their lips.

I snap my gaze toward the other opening. "Shit. Another team is coming."

"Then cut them off before they can flank us." Isera shoots a block of ice at the Green Faction. "Alistair."

"Yeah, I know," he replies, but I can hear the exhaustion still lacing his voice.

He hasn't recovered fully after all the energy he had to expend to melt the wall, but he still summons his magic and shoots a torrent at the Green Faction in order to block their flames before they can melt Isera's ice attacks.

"Help them," Draven orders, jerking his chin from Galen and Lyra to Alistair and Isera. Then his gaze slides to me. "We'll intercept the other team."

Before we can even see them nod in confirmation, we take off toward the other opening. If we get trapped between two teams who block the only exits, this is going to go to hell very quickly. We need to make it out into the corridor and stop the other team from reaching the room. We'll have a better chance if we face them in a narrow corridor where they can't surround us.

The crowd cheers and screams above us, creating a deafening noise that drowns out the sounds of the fight we just left. With my magic still attached, I can feel our opponents' excitement spike as they reach the corridor from the other side.

"They're here," I press out as Draven and I skid into the corridor.

And just as my magic has already told me, we find another team jogging into the corridor from the opening on the other side. The Red Faction. They trail to a halt when they see us.

Light from the bright sun above gleams against the white stone of the statues that line this entire corridor. Fae warriors in imposing armor stand carved from stone, watching impassively as our two teams face each other.

"We should—" Draven begins.

The wall to our left flips.

Yelps and clanks from weapons fill the air as three people in blue fighting leathers are shoved into our corridor by the spinning wall. They stumble, crashing into each other from the force of the shove, before hitting the wall inside our corridor and steadying themselves.

To our left, the wall continues spinning back and forth. And through those gaps when it moves, I can see the final three members of the Blue Faction, who are still standing in the corridor running parallel to ours. They stare at the rapidly spinning wall, looking stunned.

For a moment, nothing happens.

All of us just stare at each other.

Then Draven throws a blast of wind at the three people from the Blue Faction.

It slams into them, catching them unawares, and throws them backward toward where the Red Faction is standing. They crash into them, knocking over several of the people from the red team.

Draven gives me a nod. Then we're running toward them.

We can't let them trap us this far back in the corridor; we need to make both their teams share the same tight space so that it will be harder for them to fight properly.

Screams of excitement echo from the crowd above, almost drowning out the dull *whump whump* sounds from the still violently spinning wall. The three remaining players from the Blue Faction are still trapped on the other side, trying to time a jump in through the gap before it closes again.

The Red Faction shoves away the members of the other team who crashed into them. I quickly reach out with my magic, latching on to their anger and increasing it in order to make them fight each other instead.

Rage flares up in their eyes.

Draven and I skid to a halt on the sand right next to the flipping wall. We can't move any farther down in case the three remaining people on the other side make it through. If they do, we can't risk them getting behind us.

Steel sings in the air as a few members of the blue team draw swords while others call up magic. They glance from side to side, now caught between us and the Red Faction, as if they're not sure who to fight first. I keep increasing the anger in the Red Faction members' chests while Draven at last shifts into a half-shift.

Jocasta told us to keep it a secret for as long as possible that Draven can perform a half-shift. But if we're going to hold off nine people on our own, we need every advantage we can get.

A gasp rips from the crowd above. And the shock is mirrored on the faces of our opponents.

Unfortunately, it also draws their attention away from each other.

Both teams stare at Draven with stunned expressions. Then malice seeps into their eyes.

The Red Faction flashes Draven a cruel smile and yanks something off their belts before flicking their wrists.

Whips crack through the air.

And Draven *flinches*.

My heart stops.

Our enemies couldn't see it because they're standing too far away. And they don't know Draven like I do. They don't know about the torture the Icehearts put him through for years. But I do. And I saw it. I saw the Shadow of Death fucking *flinch*.

And I decide then and there that I won't let this happen. He has been through enough. He has sacrificed enough. Done enough. It's time someone protected *him* for a change.

My gaze darts around the corridor while plans spin through my head like a raging storm.

The Red Faction draws their whips back again and summons magic while the three members of the Blue Faction do the same but with swords instead. Draven starts taking a step forward.

I make a decision.

The moment he is off-balance from lifting his foot to take that step, I slam my entire body weight into his side. It catches him completely off guard, and he stumbles sideways. And right into the still spinning wall.

He cries out—in surprise or anger, I can't tell—as the wall shoves him into the other corridor next to ours. The players on our side hesitate, staring at me in utter shock. But I'm already moving. Sprinting over to the statue closest to the spinning wall, I place my palms against it and shove.

Through the brief gaps in the spinning wall, I can see Draven straightening on the sand. His golden eyes are wide with disbelief as he stares at me.

I topple the heavy statue.

It hits the sand with a thud, sending a cloud swirling up into the air. And the last thing I see before the wall is forced to slam closed against the statue now blocking its way is Draven whirling around to block attacks from the three members of the blue team who remained in that corridor.

The crowd in the stands above us scream and clap, thoroughly entertained by this unexpected turn of events.

I turn toward the players blocking the corridor before me. Nine of them. Six members of the Red Faction and three from the Blue Faction. There is no chance in hell that I will ever win against all nine of them if they attack me at the same time.

But I don't even care anymore.

No one will come near Draven with a whip ever again. I will burn down hell itself before I ever let that happen. He is *mine*.

The Blue Faction lets out a battle cry and launches themselves toward me.

The Red Faction cracks their whips.

Diving sideways, I shove a blast of magic into the anger in everyone's chests.

A few of the whips graze the members of the blue team instead, and rage lights up inside them, fueled by my magic.

Snarling, all three of them whirl around and attack the people on the red team instead. I pour my magic into them, turning them crazy with fury. Swords clash and whips crack and magic roars through the air as the battle frenzy turns into full madness.

But through it all, one man in red fighting leathers locks eyes with me instead. I quickly cut off my connection to him, but the damage is already done. Elbowing his way through the throng, he charges toward me.

"Shit," I curse.

He flicks his wrist, and the whip cracks through the air.

Leaping backward, I barely manage to evade it. It snaps through the air right in front of my face. I flinch, almost losing my grip on my magic. Gritting my teeth, I yank out my dagger and pour even more magic into the others. I need to keep them focused on each other, at least.

My opponent flashes me a vicious smile and raises his free hand.

Lightning shoots toward me.

I gasp, throwing myself down on the ground as the bolt of lightning streaks past over me.

Mabona's fucking tits! He has a whip *and* lightning magic?

Rolling across the sand, I leap to my feet right before another lightning bolt hits the ground where I used to be. Panic clangs inside my skull. I need to keep my magic connected to the eight other people and keep them distracted and focused on each other. Otherwise, they will remember that it's me they're supposed to be fighting. But that means I can't use my magic on my own opponent. Other than to make him angry. Which won't exactly work in my favor right now.

I duck, throwing myself in behind one of the statues as another bolt of lightning splits the air. White stone shatters, exploding before me, as the lightning hits the statue. I dive sideways to escape it. My opponent keeps his distance, remaining far out of my reach as he attacks with his whip and his magic.

Leaping to my feet, I snap my gaze around the corridor, trying to figure out a plan.

Goddess damn it. Think! How can I make him—

Pain shoots up my forearm.

I yelp as I'm suddenly yanked forward.

Snapping my gaze down, I find the end of his whip wrapped around my forearm, trapping me after it struck. I'm pulled off-balance and stagger forward as my opponent yanks hard on the rope. Blood rushes in my ears. I yank up my dagger and slice through the whip right before he can pull me all the way to him.

But lightning splits the air again, forcing me to dive blindly to the side. The dagger flies from my grip as my elbow hits the sand on impact. I roll over, pushing up to my knees while desperately searching for my knife.

A thin rope wraps around my throat from behind.

I choke on my breath as it's pulled tight.

Still on my knees, I claw at the whip that now encircles my throat. But my opponent, who is now standing right behind me, just pulls it harder. A strained gurgle comes from my throat.

The crowd roars.

Or it might be my own pulse pounding in my ears.

It's hard to tell.

"You'd better pray to your little goddess Mabona that you are the one carrying the key," the man snarls in my ear.

I claw desperately at the thin rope. Draven has the key. How can I—

The spare.

Oh Goddess above, I have the spare key. The second white key that we took from the Yellow Faction.

My head pounds as I stop trying to get the whip away from my neck and instead reach into my belt pouch. I can barely concentrate enough to get it out, and my fingers fumble so much that I nearly drop it, but I at last manage to pull out the white key.

"Well, look at that," the man behind me says in a smug voice. "Just what we need."

I choke, still trying to get air into my lungs. He doesn't let up for so much as one moment.

"Hand it over," he orders.

And through the ringing panic in my skull, a sudden breath of clarity hits me like a blow to the gut. He is going to kill me. Even if I give him the key, he's going to kill me.

Choking and gasping weakly, I try to think through the pain and terror. My vision is starting to turn black at the edges.

Before me, the other eight players have stopped fighting each other and are instead now watching me. When he started choking me, I lost the grip on my magic, which means that they are no longer distracted. Fuck, I need to—

An idea smacks into me.

Raising my hand, I hold up the key.

The guy behind me reaches for it.

I throw it across the corridor.

It lands there on the sand, halfway between us and the three members of the blue team. Their eyes light up.

"Shit," the guy behind me snaps.

Releasing me in a flash, he sprints forward and dives toward the key while the three players from the Blue Faction lurch toward it as well.

I gasp in air, ripping the whip away from my neck. Pain pulses around my entire throat, and I can barely swallow, but I continue forcing air in and out of my lungs. The flickering blackness at the edges of my vision begins retreating.

Up ahead, my attacker snatches up the key right before the Blue Faction can reach it. His team members immediately start shooting magic at the three Blue Faction players, forcing them back while their companion darts back toward them. Once he reaches them, they sprint back out through the opening that leads deeper into the arena.

For a moment, it looks like the Blue Faction is going to pursue them. But then they cast uncertain glances toward the corridor on the other side of the wall where Draven is fighting their three other companions.

Still on my hands and knees, I drag in strained breaths.

The three members of the Blue Faction turn toward me.

Murder shines in their eyes.

And now, there are no members of the Red Faction left to distract them. And no more keys to trade.

Sunlight glints against their swords and magic crackles in the air as they take a step toward me.

Oh, shit.

27

Still trying to gasp air back into my aching throat, I snatch up the dagger I dropped on the sand earlier and scramble to my feet. Panic pulses inside me as I try to come up with some kind of plan for how to survive this. I'm outnumbered three to one, and there is nothing in this corridor except for stone statues.

The crowd yells from the stands. It's a deafening, rumbling sound that rolls over me like thunder. Bright sunlight streams down from the open ceiling high above, heating my black fighting leathers. A bead of sweat rolls down my spine.

Water magic swirls in the air as two of my opponents make their magic dance. It seems to be the most common type of magic in the Unseelie Court. Or at least in this city. Though given that the city is surrounded by waterfalls and full of rivers, I suppose that shouldn't be too much of a surprise.

My mind churns as I try to think of a plan. Can I somehow use—

Torrents of water shoot toward me.

I jerk back, trying to get away, but the streams of water are so massive that they almost cover the entire corridor.

A shadow of death and fury slams down on the sand in front of me.

I suck in a sharp breath as Draven lands hard on the ground in front of me, his massive wings still flared wide from when he flew over the wall from the other corridor. He shoves a blast of storm winds right into the water.

The two forces collide with a wet slapping sound that cracks across the arena. Water crashes right back into all three members of the Blue Faction, sending them flying through the air and slamming into the stone wall behind. Two of them gasp and struggle to their feet. One of them doesn't.

Draven uses the element of surprise to the fullest and doesn't waste a second as he shoots a bolt of lightning at one of the two remaining players. The one on the left, a female fae with short red hair, is struck before she has even managed to raise her head. Her body shakes uncontrollably as she collapses back down on the sand, her chest rising and falling in jagged breaths while her limbs continue twitching from the lightning.

Our final remaining opponent snaps his head up, and his eyes widen in shock as he stares at us. Raising a hand, he gets ready to shoot magic back at us.

Ice explodes into the air before him.

It shoots up from the ground, crawling up his legs and encasing his entire body all the way up to his neck.

I spin around, staring at the corridor behind me.

Isera is stalking down the corridor toward us, her face a mask of cold power, while Galen strides along next to her with a sword in his hand and an assessing look in his violet eyes as he scans the scene before him.

Behind them, Lyra is bracing Alistair, her arm around his waist and his over her shoulders, as they make their way toward us. Lyra looks energetic as always with a grin on her mouth, but Alistair looks like he's going to collapse any second. Exhaustion clings to every line of his face, and he is leaning heavily on Lyra in order to stay upright. After the energy he was forced to expend in order to melt the wall, and then a battle with the Green Faction right afterward, he must have used up basically all his magical energy.

"The key," Isera demands, her eyes locked on the now trapped member of the Blue Faction.

"Fuck you, you worthless Seelie cunt," the guy snaps from the wall.

Isera doesn't even blink at the insult. Her features remain as ruthlessly cold as ever as she simply flicks her wrist. The ice crawls up over the guy's throat and jaw until it covers his mouth and nose.

Panic crackles in his eyes like lightning.

Sand swirls around Isera's boots as she strides up to him, stopping two steps away. Then she just stands there, watching him with impassive eyes. He begins jerking. Or trying to, at least. Only the top of his head moves as he tries to break free from the ice. It doesn't work.

A ball of water starts forming in the air, but it wavers and then disappears as the guy can't concentrate enough to keep his magic up while he's choking to death at the same time.

Terror shines in his eyes, and his head jerks more violently.

Isera still doesn't allow him to breathe.

Above us, the crowd is cheering in excitement. Apparently, this kind of violent and cruel power demonstration is exactly what they wanted to see.

"The key," Isera demands again, her voice splitting the air like a blade.

The trapped man quickly shifts his gaze and starts desperately pointing with his eyes toward the woman with short red hair who is still lying on the ground, twitching from Draven's lightning strike.

Taking her time, Isera bends down and starts searching through the woman's blue fighting leathers. The guy by the wall struggles hard against the ice, desperation pulsing in his eyes.

Above, the calls from the crowd turn even more frantic. Only the people who are wearing blue scarves or holding blue banners are yelling in anger. Everyone else is leaning forward in their seats, clapping and pointing and cheering in approval.

At last, Isera pulls out a black key from the woman's belt pouch.

Relief washes through me. A black key. Exactly what we needed.

Isera straightens and then flicks her wrist. The ice shrinks back down to the guy's throat. He gasps in deep breaths. Above, the audience laughs mockingly.

"You fucking—" the guy presses out, still trying to breathe at the same time.

But it's cut off by a yelp as Isera suddenly makes the ice encasing his body evaporate. The sudden loss of support makes his knees buckle, and he crashes down on the ground. Before he can so much as catch himself, Galen rams the butt of his sword into the guy's stomach. He gasps again, his body convulsing, as he crumbles the final distance down on the sand.

Draven whirls toward me.

Hellfire burns in his eyes as he locks them on me. "You and I are going to have words later."

About the fact that I shoved him through the spinning wall and then locked it behind him, no doubt. But we have more pressing problems.

Breaking his murderous stare, I sweep my gaze over all my companions. "I was forced to hand over our spare key to the Red Faction, so they now have both keys."

"And the Green Faction didn't have any key at all," Galen says. "Which means that the White Faction probably has both keys too."

"Shit." I ram my dagger back in its sheath and rake both hands through my hair in frustration. "We need to be the first to reach the door." My gaze flits to Draven for a second. "Otherwise, we'll lose the opportunity to steal back the dragon steel."

"Then stop yapping and let's go," Isera interrupts. "I'll scout the way from atop the wall. That way we'll know exactly which corridors lead straight to the door."

"That way everyone will also see you and attack you," I challenge, staring at her in bewilderment. "You'll be completely open for attacks in every direction."

"I have ice magic." She forms a staircase made of ice leading up to the wall. "It's the best defensive magic out of all of us."

Before we can get another word out, she darts up the ice steps and straightens atop the stone wall. Turning, she scans the arena before her. The crowd lets out a whoop.

"Straight ahead," she calls down at us. "Let's go."

She doesn't wait for us to reply. Instead, she simply starts jogging forward on top of the wall. We exchange a quick glance and then scramble to follow her.

My heart pounds as we run through the corridors and rooms, sprinting as fast as we can toward the center of the arena.

Fire roars through the air.

Instinctively I duck. But the flames just stream past above me. I suck in a sharp breath as they shoot straight for Isera. Still running atop the wall on our left, she yanks up a thick sheet of ice.

The fire slams into it, creating a hissing sound as the flames hit the cold ice, and washes out into the air around Isera instead of hitting her. With a flourish, she shifts the sheet of ice, sending the remaining fire shooting up into the sky instead. The crowd cheers in excitement.

"Take the right," she calls down at us as we reach another room.

All across the floor of the room is a sea of tables and paintings in thick wooden frames, and a piano, of all things. We leap and weave through the mess, hurrying toward the opening on the right.

Lightning crackles through the air above.

Isera dives forward, rolling across the top of the wall, to evade it. Leaping to her feet, she twists and leans to avoid another bolt of lightning. A stream of ice shoots through the air as she fires back at the person who shot the lightning. The crowd screams in anticipation.

I shove a cluster of paintings aside and then dart through the opening on the right.

Atop the wall, Isera is pelted by attacks from two different directions, evidence that both the Red and the White Factions are now within range.

My heart slams against my ribs as we sprint down the next corridor. I cast panicked glances up at Isera, worry crackling through my veins like lightning. But she just dances out of the way of the attacks, leaping and twirling and raising spiked shields of ice. It's effortless, graceful, and so fucking incredible to watch that I almost stumble when I realize what she's actually doing.

She's entertaining the crowd.

Roars and cheers thrum inside the massive arena as the audience hangs on Isera's every move, watching her incredible display of both magical and physical abilities.

I gape up at her as we dart down the next corridor.

Out of all the people who I thought would take Jocasta's words to heart and focus on entertaining the crowd, *Isera* most certainly wasn't one of them. She never lets anyone bully her into doing something she doesn't want to. And performing before a crowd is definitely not something that she would ever agree to do willingly. So it stuns me to see her sacrifice her pride in order to help us win like this.

"Hurry!" she suddenly yells down at us. "The White Faction is almost at the door!"

Alarm shoots up my spine.

"Fuck," she snaps. "The Red Faction is coming too!"

We pick up speed, running with everything we have toward the next opening ahead. My breath rasps through my throat, and Alistair looks like he's about to pass out after the long run. His eyes glide in and out of focus as we draw closer to the opening.

"The door is right here!" Isera calls. "Go, go, go!"

She reaches the edge of the wall up ahead and then spins to the left.

We sprint through the opening and into a large circular room right as figures become visible in two of the other corridors leading into it.

"Ryat," Isera snaps, and tosses the black key at Draven.

He spins around, skidding to a halt, and manages to catch it in one hand before it can hit the sand.

Isera yanks both arms upward.

Ice shoots up from the ground and blocks both of the other openings.

"Get the door open," she calls right before blasts of fire slam into her ice walls.

I gasp in desperate breaths as we dash the final distance to the middle of the room. A wide trapdoor, painted white with a large black X in the middle of it, has been set into the ground. There are two keyholes on it. One white and one black.

The ice walls blocking the openings begin to melt at an alarming rate as fire crashes into them from the other side.

Draven yanks out the white key we began with while shoving the black one into Galen's waiting hands. After a quick nod, they ram the keys into both locks at the same time.

The ice walls shatter.

Shards of ice explode into the room, clattering against the stone walls inside while melted ice sloshes down on the ground in puddles.

Unseelie fae in white and red fighting leathers pour into the room.

"Turn!" Draven snaps.

Isera jumps from the wall.

The crowd gasps as she plummets toward the ground.

Draven and Galen turn the keys at the same time.

Two loud clicks ring out.

"Lift!" Draven calls.

Ice appears underneath Isera's boots, stopping her fall. She spins around, shooting blocks of ice at the two teams rushing across the sand toward us.

The crowd screams.

We dig our fingers into the gaps along the front of the trapdoor.

And then we heave.

Wood groans as the trapdoor begins rising from the ground.

Fire roars through the air, slamming into Isera's ice. Boots pound against the sand. My muscles strain as we shove the massive trapdoor upward. With a push, we throw it back.

"Get in," Draven orders.

Alistair lets out a yelp as Lyra practically shoves him through it before leaping after him herself. While Galen jumps down as well, Draven turns and shoves a blast of wind at the White Faction. They have almost reached Isera, who is jumping through the air across the room from one block of ice to the next. The wind slams into them, sending them crashing back right before one of them can grab Isera's ankle as she leaps past them.

She lands on the sand instead, tucking and rolling before leaping to her feet. Draven sends another blast of wind at the two teams, slamming them back against the ground.

Twisting around, Isera raises her chin and looks up at something in the crowd above instead.

My heart leaps when I realize what it is.

Orion Nightbane.

He is still sitting on his grand throne in the otherwise empty section reserved only for him. Even from this distance, I can almost feel him stewing in silent annoyance as he watches us.

Isera summons an ice spear.

And throws it straight at him.

I gasp as the ice spear shoots through the air and slams into the wood of the Unseelie King's throne. Right next to his head. To his credit, he doesn't so much as flinch. But I swear I can still see the shock in his eyes, even from this impossible distance.

Down on the sand, Isera spreads her arms wide with dramatic flair and gives the audience a theatrical bow. Then she flashes Orion a wicked grin and blows him a kiss.

The crowd completely *erupts*.

Whoops and cheers and screams of approval explode across the whole arena. They're so loud that the very air practically vibrates.

My stomach lurches as a strong hand suddenly grabs my forearm and yanks me down. I half jump, half fall down through the trapdoor with Draven next to me. Two seconds later, Isera leaps through as well.

A jolt shoots up my legs as we hit the soft sand below, but Draven quickly wraps his arm around me, keeping me steady. Tilting my head, I glance back up through the trapdoor.

From down here, we can see the space where Draven, Isera, and I used to stand. I stare up at it for a few seconds before the trapdoor slams shut again.

Two distinctive clicks echo as the locks reset, waiting for the next team to unlock it. Given that both the Red Faction and the White

Faction are up there, they will likely be forced to battle each other for the privilege of being the second team through the door.

Behind me, Alistair lets out a low whistle. "Throwing a spear at the Unseelie King and then blowing him a kiss?"

We all turn to face him, even though his gaze and his question are clearly directed at Isera. She just looks back at him, her expression unreadable.

He chuckles and shakes his head at her. "And here I was, thinking *I* was the drama queen in our group."

A laugh rips from my lungs. A laugh full of mirth and exhaustion and utter relief. We did it. We made it through the door first. And now we will be the team that is invited to the Unseelie King's celebration, giving us a chance both to woo the crowd so that we will have a better chance to win the final game and also to steal the dragon steel back from Orion.

The others laugh as well, sounding as exhausted and relieved as I am. And even Isera almost smiles before she manages to hide it behind an impassive expression again.

She lifts her slim shoulders in a nonchalant shrug. "We were told to entertain them. So I did."

Oh, she sure did.

I let out a long sigh.

Now we just need to figure out how to actually steal the dragon steel back from a no doubt furious Unseelie King.

28

I don't make it more than three steps into my room back at Jocasta's faction house before the door is slammed shut and I feel a thunderstorm looming behind me.

"What the hell were you thinking?" Draven snaps, stalking up behind me.

We were allowed to eat and bathe in the private rooms underneath the arena while we waited for the other teams to finish the game, which took longer than I expected. So I'm fed and clean and the ache from when the Red Faction tried to strangle me with a whip has already healed, but I'm still exhausted and not in the mood for this argument. So I drag in a long breath before turning to face the furious dragon shifter behind me.

He's standing there, tall and powerful like the ruthless commander he is, still in his black dragon scale armor and with his wings spread wide, looking incredibly out of place in this elegant room. Sheer white drapes flutter gently in the warm breeze that blows in through the open windows, and bright sunlight glints in the unlit faelight gems that have been placed into swirling holders made of gold. The bed, covered in sheets in cream and gold, has been made perfectly by the people who came in to clean while we were at the game. And in the middle of all that serenity stands a furious Shadow of Death.

"You're gonna have to narrow that down," I reply, meeting Draven's gaze.

His golden eyes flash with lightning. "You know exactly what I'm talking about!"

"We won, didn't we?" I retort, feeling the anger rise in my own chest.

"You could've been killed!"

"So could you!"

"Don't fucking start with me. You and I both know that *I* would've had better odds against nine people than you did."

Frustration rips at my chest. Mostly because he's right. Grinding my teeth, I cross my arms to protect myself against the storm of emotions that has been raging inside me for months now and that is threatening to break free.

"Instead of getting angry, you could've just said thank you," I snipe back at him.

Disbelief pulses across his face. "For what? You almost getting yourself killed?"

"I was *protecting* you!"

He blinks, looking stunned.

Forcing out a harsh breath, I uncross my arms and instead rake my fingers through my hair in frustration. That knot of pent-up emotions twists like snakes in my chest. Behind me, the gauzy curtains ripple again, and a warm wind smelling of blooming flowers and warm stone ripples through the room, making my hair flutter. I let my arms drop again.

"I was protecting you," I repeat, glaring up at Draven. "You once confronted me about how I always take care of everyone else while no one takes care of me. Well, you're the same, you stubborn idiot. You're so used to doing everything on your own. But you don't have to do everything on your own anymore!"

Draven just stares at me for a moment, looking uncertain. But then that frustrated anger returns, and he blows out a forceful breath. "But that's the problem. You didn't try to *help* me. You shoved me through a fucking wall and then locked it behind me so that you could do it on your own. Our best chance of beating them was *together*!"

Logically, I know that he is right. But I wasn't thinking logically when I made that decision. Those furious emotions thrum inside me, threatening to break through my rib cage. I drag in a deep breath, trying to calm the storm.

"So why the hell did you lock me out to face them on your own?" Draven snaps, throwing his arms out in frustration.

Anger crackles through me. "Because they had *whips*!"

"I can handle—"

"I don't care! I'm not letting anyone near you with a fucking whip ever again!"

"That's why you did it?"

"Of course it is!"

"That's insane! The whips weren't going to kill me. But *you*, you could have died! Why would you risk your life like that?"

"Because I love you!"

He jerks back, staring at me with wide eyes. His mouth is still open, stuck on his next argument, but no words make it out.

My chest heaves, and everything inside my soul is thrumming with desperate tension, but I can't stop now. The words keep pouring out of my mouth like an unstoppable flood.

"I love you," I repeat, my heart beating out of control. "And I have loved you ever since we fell through the ceiling of that underground forest and you flipped us over to protect me from the hits and then handcuffed me and pulled me close and held me as I slept and then challenged me about why I treat my own dreams as less important than everyone else's and then when the dryads attacked, I couldn't bear the thought of something happening to you." My chest heaves, and I drag in another breath, still holding Draven's stunned gaze. "I have loved you for *months* now, but I've been too much of a stubborn coward to admit it."

He draws in an unsteady breath, staring at me as if he's afraid that if he takes his eyes off me for one second, I will disappear and none of this will have happened. "What about the mate bond?"

"Fuck the mate bond! I don't care that some mystical force has decided that we're supposed to be together." Fire burns inside me as I hold his gaze, letting him see that I mean every word of this. "Do you know why?"

"Why?" he breathes, the word barely more than a whisper.

"Because I would have chosen you anyway. There is no world, no universe, no version of reality where I wouldn't have chosen you. I would always. Choose. You."

He draws in a shuddering breath, emotions pulsing in his glittering golden eyes.

"I have—" I begin.

But then something breaks free in my chest. Like an explosion of color and light, it shatters the thick stone walls that I have kept around my heart these past few months.

The experience is so intense that I gasp and stagger a step back.

Emotions flood my chest.

And not all of them are mine.

Pressing a hand against my chest, I stare down at it as if I can see all the emotions swirling in there. My heart pounds underneath my palm. I can feel my own emotions. The thrill, the vulnerability, and the utter relief of finally having admitted, both to Draven and to myself, how I really feel. The searing love for him that threatens to consume me. The excitement and nervousness about the future.

But I can also feel . . . *him*.

There, deep inside, I can faintly feel the echo of another set of emotions. Shock. Disbelief. Hope. And love so deep it could burn the world down. And from it all is an invisible thread. A physical tug more than something visual. Raising my head, I look up toward where it leads.

Straight to Draven.

"This . . . ," I begin, trying to think through the shock of this realization. "*This* is the mate bond, isn't it?"

He smiles then. And the smile is so bright and so full of devastating hope that my heart squeezes tight.

"The mate bond finally snapped into place for you too," he says.

My head is spinning. I realize that I'm still pressing a hand to my chest, so I force myself to remove it and instead rake my fingers through my hair. My heart beats hard against my ribs. Blowing out a long breath to steady myself, I let my hand drop back down before I meet Draven's gaze again.

"But if this is the mate bond," I begin, staring at him with wide eyes. "Then everything I felt before . . ."

"Was all you." His gaze is serious as he looks back at me. "The mate bond only snaps into place *after* you have already fallen in love with the person."

"After," I echo, feeling shell-shocked.

Amusement tugs at his lips, and his eyes glitter as he adds, "Though you have apparently been fighting against it for months now."

Shock still clangs inside my skull like a bell. After. The mate bond only snaps into place *after* you have already fallen in love with the person. It doesn't draw you to them. It doesn't force any feelings onto you. It happens afterward.

My heart beats so hard against my ribs that I fear it might bruise them.

But nothing can stop the sense of relief that washes over me like a warm ocean wave.

My emotions are my own. His emotions are his own. We have, and we always have had, free will to choose on our own. It's real. Everything he's said and everything he's done for me. It's all real.

Looking up, I stare at Draven again, my soul feeling both full and cavernous at the same time. "Why didn't you tell me? You knew that I hated the thought of not choosing on my own. Why didn't you tell me that it only happens after you've already fallen in love?"

"Because I wanted you to choose me too." He glances away for a moment, looking uncharacteristically uncertain, before he meets my gaze again. "I didn't want you to settle for me. I wanted you to choose me. Despite it all."

"Settle?" A stunned laugh escapes my chest. Staring up at him, I shake my head in disbelief. "Do you seriously think it would be even remotely possible for anyone to *settle* for you?"

"Anyone? No. You? Yes." He steps closer, his eyes searing into mine as he slides a hand along my jaw. "How could I possibly be enough to deserve you when the gods themselves would go to war to have you?"

My heart stutters.

Yanking my hand up, I slide it behind his neck and pull his perfect mouth to mine.

A moan rips from deep within his chest as his lips crash against mine. His hand slides down from my jaw to instead rest against the side of my neck, his thumb underneath my chin to keep my head tilted back as he claims my lips. I tighten the grip on the back of his neck and draw my other hand up his chest, wishing that I could feel his warm body against my palm.

The mate bond thrums inside me, and that tug I feel toward him intensifies. I moan into his mouth as he slides his other arm around my waist, pulling me tight against his muscular body.

Desire burns through me like wildfire.

I want him. I want all of him. All the time. Forever.

That storm of emotions, finally free of its shackles, rages inside my body and consumes everything in its path. Rages like wildfire until the only thing that remains, the only thing that will ever matter in this whole universe, is me and him.

The pull toward Draven is so intense that I can barely breathe.

Gasping, I break the kiss to drag in a few desperate breaths. My chest is heaving.

"Is it always this . . . intense?" I gasp out, gazing up at him.

He smiles, his arm still around me and his eyes burning with just as much fire as mine. "Yes. Like I said, once the mate bond snapped into place for me during the Atonement Trials, keeping my hands off you has been the hardest fucking thing I have ever had to do in my entire life."

I grin back up at him. "Well, luckily, you no longer have to."

Reaching down, I start undoing the fastenings on my fighting leathers. Lust flares up in Draven's eyes, burning even brighter, and he immediately starts stripping off his own armor.

Our final garments have barely hit the ground before I flash Draven a smirk full of challenge.

"Now, how about you make good on that promise you made?" I say.

He advances on me while he rakes his gaze over my naked body. "And what promise would that be, little rebel?"

Grinning, I jerk my chin toward the desk by the wall. "I see a perfectly good table right there."

His eyes glint.

Anticipation ripples down my spine as he backs me toward it. He slides his tongue along his bottom lip, his eyes drinking me in. The sight of it makes my clit throb.

Holding his gaze, I purposely slide my hand up my thigh. "You'd better hurry up and bend me over that table before I take matters into my own hands."

A sly smile curls his lips, and dark storm clouds ripple around his powerful body. "Was that a threat?"

I grin back. "Did it sound like a suggestion?"

My stomach lurches as a storm wind suddenly whirls into me from the side, making me spin around so that my back is to Draven and I'm facing the table instead. Before I can even get my bearings again, Draven wraps a hand around my throat from behind. With a firm grip, he moves me until my back is pressed against his muscular chest. His naked skin is warm against mine.

"So bossy," he murmurs in my ear.

Pleasure curls around my spine as his breath caresses the shell of my ear with every word, and his commanding hand around my throat makes my clit ache with need.

He slides his other hand over my hip. "But you know that I like hearing you beg first."

A shudder of pleasure rolls down my spine at his possessive touch. His hand slips lower, dipping down between my thighs.

"Widen your stance," he commands, his voice low and dark.

I bite my lip, suppressing a moan, and then carefully spread my legs wider. He lets out a hum of approval. It vibrates against my ear, making my spine tingle.

A jolt shoots through me as he brushes his fingers over my already throbbing clit. He lets out a low chuckle and then kisses that sensitive spot behind my ear while he rubs his thumb over my clit. I drag in a shuddering breath. Pleasure pulses through me as Draven starts teasing my clit with expert precision, and a moan escapes my lips.

Throwing my head back, I rest it against his firm shoulder while tension starts building inside me. Draven keeps his hand around my throat, holding me firmly in place as he continues drawing moans from my mouth. A whimper spills from my lips as the tension inside me reaches unbearable levels.

But Draven only continues stroking my clit with those excruciating moves that are fast enough to push me toward the edge but slow enough to not let me fall over it.

Raising my head again, I reach down and grab his wrist, trying to force his fingers to move just a little faster.

Draven tuts. "So greedy."

Since I can't make his fingers do what I want, I adjust my stance and try to rub my thighs together instead.

"Oh, I don't think so," Draven murmurs, a smirk in his voice.

With his hand still firmly around my throat, he moves it upward, forcing me up on my toes. My free hand shoots up and wraps around his wrist. But he just keeps his commanding hand where it is while his other one continues to tease my clit. And now, balancing on my toes, I can't do anything other than stand there and take whatever sweet torture he gives me.

"You ruthless villain," I press out. It comes out like something halfway between a curse and a moan.

He lets out another dark chuckle that dances over my skin. "Ready to beg for mercy yet?"

"You—"

A gasp interrupts my curse as he traces his index finger around my entrance. Pleasure crackles through me, and the storm of tension inside me thrums harder. Every nerve in my body is wound so tightly that I can barely concentrate. Draven toys with my clit while teasing his finger over my entrance again. A desperate moan rips from deep within my chest.

"I'll settle for a *please* this time," Draven whispers in my ear.

I try to shift my position, but his firm hand around my throat is still keeping me trapped and balancing on my toes. Squirming against his firm chest, I drag air into my lungs while the tension inside me thrashes like a lightning storm.

"Please," I gasp out.

He smiles against my skin. Moving his hand, he lowers me down gently until I'm standing firmly on my feet again. Then he releases my throat and slides his hand away from my clit. The loss of his hands against my skin is so jarring that I just stand there, dragging in desperate breaths while pent-up tension still crackles inside me.

Draven draws a finger down my spine. "Now, are you going to bend over that table or should I do it for you?"

His voice snaps me out of my stupor, and I blink repeatedly until I can once again see the desk before me. It's a sleek thing, made of pale wood, and positioned so that one of the short sides sticks out from the wall, providing whoever wants to sit in the chair a view out the windows across the room instead of making them stare into the pale stone wall.

Taking a half step forward, I bend over the table's short side and brace my forearms on the smooth wood before widening my stance.

"Good girl."

A desperate noise rips from my throat.

Draven slides his hands up my thighs and then takes my hips in a firm grip. My clit throbs as he adjusts my position. Then another desperate gasp escapes my lips as I feel the crown of his cock press against my pussy.

"So wet," Draven murmurs.

Frustration and pent-up need crackles through me. "If you don't—"

He gives my ass a firm slap.

I gasp, forbidden pleasure shooting straight through my spine and making my clit throb with desperate need.

Then he thrusts inside me.

A moan spills from my lips as Draven's thick cock slides into me in one firm stroke, filling me completely. Pleasure curls around my spine, and I squeeze my hands into fists. Draven tightens his grip on my hips but keeps his cock in place for another few seconds, letting me adjust to his size.

Then he draws out and slams back in again.

Another moan tears from my chest as his cock hits a spot deep inside me.

That mind-bending pleasure starts building inside me again as he starts up a commanding pace. My thighs push against the edge of the desk with every thrust, and the desk slams against the wall, making the painting above it rattle.

I drag in shuddering breaths at the incredible friction his cock creates. The pent-up tension inside me soars, sending me tumbling toward an orgasm. I tilt my head down, pressing my forehead against the cool surface beneath me.

"No," Draven says.

A strong hand slides into my hair.

Another burst of forbidden pleasure crackles through my veins as Draven takes a firm grip on my hair and then winds it around his fist, forcing me to raise my head again. He keeps twisting my hair around his hand until I have to crane my neck back.

"I want to see every flicker of pleasure on your gorgeous face when you come," he declares.

My heart skips a beat. And then beats twice as hard to make up for it.

With his hand still firmly gripping my hair, he pounds into me. I suck air into my lungs as the pleasure inside me intensifies until I can barely see straight. All I can feel is his commanding grip on my hair and my hip, and his thick cock inside me.

There is something primal about the way he is claiming me. And I fucking love it.

I gasp as his cock hits the perfect spot inside me.

He thrusts hard, hitting it again. And again.

Pleasure explodes inside me.

Stars flicker before my eyes and my legs tremble as the orgasm sweeps through my body with enough force to leave me breathless. Desperate moans and whimpers drip from my lips as Draven continues fucking me through the orgasm, intensifying it so much that I can barely see straight.

When the final waves of pleasure at last begin to fade, my chest is heaving and my mind is so scattered that it takes me a moment to remember where I am. I press my palms against the smooth tabletop beneath me as I drag air back into my lungs.

Draven has stopped thrusting, leaving his thick cock still inside me. Releasing his grip on my hair, he leans down and kisses my spine. "You're so fucking perfect."

A sudden realization pushes its way to the front of my mind. Blinking, I try to focus my eyes as I turn my head to gaze up at Draven over my shoulder.

"You didn't come," I press out, still breathless.

His eyes gleam in the warm sunlight as a truly villainous smile spreads across his lips. "No. Because I'm not done with you yet."

Before I can reply, he pulls out in one smooth motion. The sudden loss of him inside me leaves me feeling shockingly empty. I try to straighten from the desk, but my knees are still weak, so I wobble slightly. Draven immediately slides his arms behind my knees and back and lifts me into his arms.

My heated skin is flush against his as he carries me toward the bed. He places me gently on the smooth sheets before climbing onto the mattress so that he is kneeling between my legs. I gaze up into those beautiful golden eyes of his as he reaches down and brushes a lock of hair out of my face. His eyes burn with emotion as he watches me.

Reaching up, I slide a hand over his muscular chest. He wraps his fingers around my wrist and lifts my hand up so that he can kiss my fingers.

"Can't get enough of me, huh?" I tease.

"Never."

And the thick emotions in his voice make my whole soul thrum. I draw in an unsteady breath. He moves my hand back down and presses it against his chest so that it's right over his heart. It beats hard underneath my palm.

"I meant what I said," Draven begins, his eyes serious as they lock on mine. "If something ever happened to you, I would rip out my own heart and follow you into the afterlife. I would kill both of our gods to take you back if I had to." His grip tightens around my wrist. "So don't ever do something like that again."

I swallow, suddenly feeling guilty about pushing him through that wall and locking it behind him. It wasn't because I didn't trust that he could handle the whips. I just didn't want to see him hurt like that again. But in hindsight, I know that it was reckless and stupid.

So I nod.

"Good." He releases my wrist and instead leans down, slanting his lips over mine. "When there is danger, we face it *together*. Understood?"

"Together," I whisper against his lips.

"Always."

He kisses me. Slow and luxurious at first. Then faster and desperately, as if he can't breathe without me.

Fire lights inside my blood. I spread my legs wider, rolling my hips against his.

A deep moan rips from his chest, and his wings flare out wider. They block out the bright sunlight that streams in through the open windows, casting shadows over the pale sheets. He adjusts his hips, making his cock press against my entrance. While still kissing him senseless, I lift my hips slightly in response.

He thrusts inside me. I moan into his mouth as his thick cock fills me yet again. Goddess above, he's so fucking perfect.

Reaching up, I draw my hand over the soft membrane of his wings.

A shudder rolls through his body, and another desperate moan escapes his sinful mouth. I steal that glorious sound from his lips as I kiss him furiously.

He slides his cock halfway out and then thrusts in again. Lifting my hips, I meet him thrust for thrust as he starts up a commanding pace. My fingers trail down over his wing, drawing the most incredible sounds from his mouth. His revenge is swift as he pinches my nipple before rolling it between his fingers. I bite his bottom lip in return. He smirks against my mouth.

Pleasure builds inside me again as he teases my nipple while fucking me just the way I want him to. Hard and dominantly and completely without mercy. I gasp against his mouth as I careen toward another orgasm.

My spine tingles as he kisses his way across my jaw and then down my throat. I arch into him, moaning and gasping with every thrust of his hips and every brush of his lips.

His cock hits that perfect spot inside me right at the same time as he pinches my nipple.

Release crashes over me.

I squirm against the sheets, throwing my head from side to side, as pleasure crackles through my every nerve. Draven releases my nipple and instead wraps his hand around my throat, forcing me to keep my head still. Leaning down, he claims my mouth with a savage kiss while he continues fucking me through the orgasm.

Incoherent moans drip from my lips.

My fingers brush along the inside of his left wing.

He comes. Hard.

Pleasure flickers in his beautiful eyes as he breaks the furious kiss and gasps while his cock pulses inside me. I show him no mercy. Sliding my fingers along the soft membrane, I draw a shuddering moan from his lips. He flexes his hand around my throat, his cock still pulsing with release inside me.

And I can *feel* it. Through the mate bond, I can feel his emotions faintly. Like an echo of a memory. But the pleasure and love that flows through him as he gazes back at me still leaves me breathless.

I memorize it all. Every expression and every sound and every tiny movement of his powerful body against mine. The sight of it makes my heart swell. Even now, it still astonishes me every time. I did that. I can make the great Shadow of Death come completely undone like this.

When the release has faded for both of us, Draven drags in a deep breath. With his cock still inside me and his hand still around my throat, he remains where he is above me as he locks searing eyes on me.

My heart jerks at the desperate yearning in his eyes.

A knowing smile curves his lips as he slowly shakes his head at me. "Azaroth help you, little rebel."

I raise my eyebrows in question, fighting a smile as well. "And why is that?"

"Because you're mine now. Body, mind, heart, and soul. And I will never get enough of you."

Shifting my hand from his wing to the back of his neck, I yank his mouth down to mine in a possessive kiss. "Likewise, Shadow of Death."

He kisses me back furiously. Claiming me. Dominating my mouth. And in that moment, I know that he means it. He will never get enough of me. Just like I will never be able to get enough of him.

But there, together in that soft bed with a warm breeze drifting in through the open windows and the bright sunlight warming our skin, I can't stop a flicker of fear from entering my mind.

I want eternity with him. Just like this. But how are we supposed to get that eternity when the Icehearts will be hunting us for the rest of our lives?

29

The previous disgust and hostility have morphed into something like curiosity. And hunger. It makes me feel like a prized horse being assessed at an auction. But it's better than hatred at least, I suppose.

Light from the faelight gems casts glittering sparkles over the large room and makes the attendees' jewelry gleam like stars. With grand stone pillars and a high ceiling, this room should feel like a ballroom. But the plush couches and booths and cushions and other seating arrangements throughout the room instead create the impression that we've stumbled into an orgy. Not to mention the guests. The way they're looking at each other, and at us, makes it feel as if they're going to start indulging in their desires right here. Maybe they will. Who knows with these Unseelie fae?

I suppress the urge to cross my arms over my chest as a group of partygoers ogles us from a short distance away. The attire Jocasta forced us to wear isn't exactly helping either.

All six of us are dressed in black and gold. Black to signal Jocasta's faction and gold to rub it in her rivals' faces that we won the first game. And that's fine. But it's the style of dress that makes me feel incredibly exposed.

Isera, Lyra, and I are wearing short skirts made of gold-trimmed strips of black leather that overlap, forming a full skirt together rather than being one solid piece of fabric. The top, also made of black leather, only has two thin straps over our shoulders, and it ends a little below our breasts, leaving our stomachs bare. Bands of gold twist around our bare arms like snakes, and we're wearing these absolutely ridiculous sandals made only of straps that reach almost all the way up to our knees.

Draven, Alistair, and Galen wear even less. They're only wearing that skirtlike garment, though theirs is a little longer than ours and reaches almost to their knees, and those sandals made of straps. Bands of gold circle their upper arms as well, but as opposed to us, their chests are completely bare.

On Jocasta's suggestion, Draven has his wings out as well, and they loom menacingly over his shoulders.

I have to admit, he is insanely hot in this outfit.

But the fact that other people are staring at his half-naked body as well is making me want to stab something.

"How much longer?" I mutter under my breath.

Jocasta, who is standing in the middle of our row, casts me a glance from the corner of her eye. "He should be arriving any minute now."

We're standing side by side in the middle of the large room, arranged in a straight line and facing the grand stairs that the Unseelie King will saunter down soon. Apparently, he needs to congratulate us on the win before the actual party can begin. But the infuriating monarch is fifteen minutes late, which has forced us to just remain standing here while the rest of the guests appraise us like livestock.

"You said that ten minutes ago," I huff.

Jocasta doesn't reply.

A low murmur fills the room as the crowd, dressed as scantily as we are, continues studying us. I can almost feel them reassessing their previous opinions of us. The fact that we won the first game proved that we are strong. And these outfits we're wearing now make them see us as desirable. Though I will never admit it to Jocasta, she did know what she was doing when she picked these outfits for us.

The quiet murmurs disappear in a flash as a figure appears at the top of the stairs.

Clothes rustle and jewelry clinks as everyone bows to the Unseelie King. Well, everyone except the six of us. With a growl of frustration, Jocasta grabs my arm with one hand and Draven's with the other and yanks. We exchange a glance before bowing slightly. The others do the same. Though Isera's so-called bow is barely a dip of the chin.

Orion Nightbane saunters down the white stone steps and toward the packed room below. There is a satisfied smirk lurking on his lips as he watches his people bow to him. Then his eyes find Isera, and his gaze sharpens. But he thankfully doesn't press the issue.

The crowd straightens again as he reaches the final step. He remains there, watching us with a haughty expression on his face for a while. Once the silence has started to get uncomfortable, he finally speaks.

"Congratulations, Jocasta," he says, his voice echoing across the whole room, "on the Black Faction's surprising win. We were all wondering what you were thinking when you picked these outsiders as your team, but you have trained them well and given us a most entertaining first game." A knowing glint flickers in his eyes as he briefly sweeps his gaze over the six of us. "I look forward to seeing how they will perform in the final game." That wicked gleam disappears as he shifts his attention back to Jocasta. "But for now, enjoy all this night has to offer."

Jocasta bows deeply. "Thank you, Your Majesty."

He waves his hand, giving her permission to withdraw, before strolling toward the luxurious dark blue sofas that have been set aside behind a golden rope. Thick curtains of the same royal blue color frame the private area, sectioning it off from the rest of the massive room and providing privacy. The crowd waits until Orion has taken a seat in the middle of the comfortable seating arrangement before they start moving and talking again.

As soon as everyone's attention is at last elsewhere, Jocasta turns to us. "All right, we need to start making the rounds so that people can meet you. The more you—"

"Jocasta," Orion calls from where he lounges on the dark blue cushions. Raising a hand, he twitches two fingers in arrogant command. "Send over the Shadow of Death and his mate."

She immediately snaps her gaze to us. "You heard him. Get over there." Steel creeps into her tone as she gives us a pointed look and adds, "And behave."

I suppress the urge to roll my eyes and instead simply turn around and start toward Orion with Draven next to me. Clenching my jaw, I try to force down a burst of anger. *The Shadow of Death and his mate.* I hate the fact that he defined me only by who I am to Draven, but I know that he did it for exactly that reason. Draven has already explained that Orion loves to play mind games and get inside people's heads, so I try to block out the anger. He wants to get a rise out of me, and I refuse to let him. We have a mission to accomplish, and it starts right now.

Several groups of people watch us with excitement in their eyes as we approach the Unseelie King's private section. He just watches us with a smirk from where he's lounging on the dark blue couch, his legs spread and both arms draped nonchalantly along the backrest. When we reach the gold rope, we simply walk around it and then come to a halt right in front of the sofa. It makes us tower over him.

Annoyance flits across his face and a muscle flickers in his jaw for a moment before he manages to hide it.

"Sit down," he orders.

"No, thanks," Draven drawls, spreading his wings a little wider.

It blocks Orion's view of the rest of the party, and everyone else's view of him too. Lightning flashes in his eyes as he tries to stare us down even though he has to tilt his head back to even meet our gazes. We just look back at him, smirks full of challenge on our faces.

Come on, I urge silently in my mind. *Come on, do it. You have to have brought it with you. Come on. Do it.*

Fury burns in his eyes.

Then he lets out a scoff before reaching into a pocket in his fancy shirt.

Victory pulses inside me as he pulls out a short piece of metal. *Yes!* He did bring the dragon steel. Now we just need to steal it from him.

"Sit down," Orion orders, a vicious smile on his face as he spins the dragon steel nonchalantly in his palm. "Before I make you."

Draven, who I now know is an incredible actor, glares very convincingly at Orion before tucking his wings in tighter and dropping down on the sofa to the king's right. I shoot Orion a, in my opinion, very convincing scowl before I sit down on the sofa to his left.

"So cocky when you're waving that little stick around," Draven challenges, his eyes locked on Orion. "Because without it, you know I'd mop the fucking floor with you, you preening little princeling."

Orion lets out a cold laugh, his eyes still pulsing with smugness. "Is that what you think?"

"You wouldn't even last two minutes in a one-on-one against me."

He laughs again. It's an arrogant sound, full of challenge. "In a one-on-one, you would be weeping for mercy at my feet within the first minute, you brooding beast."

"Put that little stick down, then, and let's see who's right."

For a moment, it looks like Orion is actually considering it. Which shocks me. It's Draven fucking Ryat. Only the most suicidal of people would agree to fight him one-on-one.

But then Orion clicks his tongue and flicks a dismissive hand. "Maybe later." But he does slip the dragon steel back into a pocket inside his shirt. Then he locks commanding eyes on us. "For now, I have a simple order for you."

"And what's that?"

"Keep your little ice lady in check." His intense gaze locks on Isera where she is standing next to Jocasta across the room, being introduced to a group of people who all look very pleased to see her. Orion shifts his attention back to us, his tone sharpening. "I can't have her challenge me like that in public."

I use that as an excuse to make eye contact with Isera as well and give her an almost imperceptible nod. She doesn't nod back, but she holds my gaze for another few seconds to signal that she saw it. Now, we just need to keep Orion distracted until she gets here.

On the couch opposite me, Draven smirks at Orion. "You mean throw a spear of ice at you and then blow you a kiss in front of an entire arena packed with people."

Narrowing his eyes, he gives Draven a vicious look, not even bothering to reply.

"Then why not just tell *her* that, then?" I ask, interrupting their staring contest.

Orion slides his gaze to me but doesn't reply to that, either. Instead, he looks to Draven again. "Keep her in check, or I will vent my displeasure on your mate instead."

Draven goes preternaturally still. Like the calm before a violent storm. Then he sits forward, closing some of the distance to Orion, and spreads his wings slightly.

"Threaten her one more time," he growls, his voice low and vicious. "I fucking dare you."

Orion's eyes glint in challenge. "You—"

"Enough." I cast an exasperated glance between the two of them. "It's fine. We'll make sure she doesn't humiliate you in public again."

Red flushes Orion's cheeks, and he snaps his gaze to me, looking stunned. "She didn't *humiliate* me." He practically spits out the words.

"Sorry, I meant *challenge* you."

He grinds his teeth but doesn't call me on the lie. I flick a quick glance toward Isera. She is trying to leave Jocasta and the group currently fawning over her, but they keep blocking her escape route while asking more questions. Her eyes find mine. I stifle a groan. *Shit*. I need to stall for time.

"Good," Orion says with finality. He flicks his wrist. "Then you can leave—"

"What was the partnership between fae and dragon shifters?" I blurt out, just to keep him talking. And if I'm being honest, because I really want an answer too.

He frows, looking confused for a second.

So I press on before he can dismiss us again. "Before the war, the fae and the dragon shifters apparently had some kind of mutually beneficial partnership. What was it?"

His frown deepens, and annoyance laces his tone as he replies, "How should I know?"

"You're fae, aren't you?" I retort, now equally confused.

"*Unseelie* fae."

"So?"

"The dragon shifters only entered into partnerships with the Seelie fae."

I blink. "Really?"

"Yes." He looks between the two of us as if he can't figure out if we're taunting him or if we truly didn't know. He appears to see the genuine surprise on our faces, because he lets out a forceful sigh and adds, "It's the main issue that drove a rift between our courts."

Raising my eyebrows, I stare back at him. "You wanted to be dragon riders too?"

"Of course we did." Deep resentment laces his tone. "Both the Seelie fae and the dragon shifters became incredibly powerful when they formed those partnerships, so we naturally wanted it too." He shoots me a sharp glare. "But you refused to tell us and guarded that secret fiercely." His gaze slides to Draven. "And the dragon shifters didn't want to bond with us on their own because they didn't trust us."

Draven scoffs. "I wonder why."

A considering look blows across Orion's face. "Don't you know how it's done? You're a dragon shifter."

"No," Draven admits, somewhat reluctantly. "We were also only taught that the fae forced us and enslaved us."

Orion lets out a short chuckle and then clicks his tongue again. "Ah, changing history. Smart."

Frustration washes over me. The Unseelie Court doesn't know either. It's looking more and more like the only ones who are old enough to still know the truth are the dryads. But how in Mabona's name are we going to persuade them to help us?

Orion suddenly sits up straight and snaps his gaze to something directly ahead. It yanks me back to the present. Turning my head, I find a stunning Seelie fae woman with long black hair and sharp blue-and-silver eyes striding toward us. Isera.

A small smile steals across my lips as I glance between her and Orion.

This is going to be fun.

30

The air practically crackles with tension as Isera saunters over to the royal blue sofas we're occupying. Her hips are swaying more than I have ever seen since the day I met her, and there is a knowing smirk on her lips as she locks eyes with the Unseelie King. Orion narrows his eyes at her.

"You have not been summoned, little viper," he says, his voice laced with both authority and threats.

Isera arches an eyebrow while the smirk on her lips widens. "Do I look like someone who is summoned?"

"No." He rakes his gaze up and down her body, and his eyes glint. "Which is why it will be so much more satisfying when I finally make you submit to me."

"You couldn't make me submit to you even if you spent the rest of eternity trying."

"Is that a challenge?"

"No. That was a fact. The ice spear was a challenge."

A dangerous expression flickers across his handsome features for a second as he no doubt relives the memory of the ice spear Isera threw at him in front of the entire arena. But to my surprise, he doesn't look angry. He looks more . . . intrigued. As if he enjoys playing these dangerous games.

"And the kiss you blew me?" he asks, his intense eyes locked on Isera as she closes the final distance to him.

"Oh, that?" She stops right in front of him, standing between his spread legs. That sharp smirk remains on her lips as she casts a pointed glance down at his crotch before meeting his eyes again. "That was a threat."

His eyes glint, and he shoves to his feet. Isera just places a hand on his chest, pushing him back down. And because she is already standing in the exact same spot that Orion would need in order to get to his feet, he's off-balance when he tries to stand, and the shove makes him sit back down hard on the cushions again.

A sharp intake of breath comes from my left. I snap my gaze toward the sound, finding a group of Unseelie fae watching the unfolding events with rapt interest. The thick blue drapes that frame the sides and back of this private seating area are still open at the front, leaving us all visible to the rest of the room.

My gaze flits to the Unseelie King, who seems to realize the same thing. Reaching behind him, he pulls on a golden rope. The dark blue drapes at the front flutter closed, leaving only the glittering faelight gems mounted on gold candle holders next to the sofas to light the space.

In the dim light, Draven and I exchange a glance. He gives me a nod before casting a distinctively impressed look in Isera's direction. We discussed this plan before we left the house, but neither of us was certain if Isera would actually be able to do what she said. Looks like we were wrong to doubt her.

During those few seconds when Orion is distracted with pulling the curtains shut, Isera presses her advantage. In one fluid motion, she climbs up so that she is straddling Orion's lap. He whips his head back to stare at her, the rope still dangling behind him, as she slides her hands over his shoulders and interlinks them behind his neck.

For a moment, it's as if Orion can't process what is happening. He just sits there, staring at her with stunned eyes. Isera uses that moment well.

Leaning forward, she brings her lips almost all the way to his, stopping only a breath away. "This is what you want, isn't it?"

He sucks in a sharp breath.

Isera smirks against his mouth and then abruptly pulls back again. "Too bad you can't have me."

Emotions flash in his eyes, and I can't tell if he's angry or embarrassed or turned on. Lifting his arms, he grips her bare waist with both hands as he grinds out, "I am the king. I can have whatever I want. I can do whatever I want. Especially with my prisoners."

"I didn't take you for someone who had to force a woman."

His grip tightens on her waist, and frustration pulses across his features. "I'm not. I have never forced anyone into my bed. Ever."

"Thought so. Because with this pretty face of yours, you have never been rejected by anyone before, have you?" She gives him a knowing smile. "People have thrown themselves at your feet, begging for just one single night with you. Haven't they?"

"That's right."

"Hmm." Her smile turns mocking as she unlinks her hands from behind his neck and instead slides them down his toned chest. "Then my rejection must really sting." She tuts. "Such a fragile ego you have, pretty boy."

His hand shoots up, wrapping around her throat. "Careful, little viper."

"Or what?" She rakes her hands down his chest before slipping them underneath the dark fabric. "You'll come in your pants from my mere touch?"

Fire flares in his eyes, and he shifts his grip on her throat so that his thumb is pressing underneath her chin, forcing her to tilt her head back. "Oh, the things I would do to you."

"You couldn't handle me even if you tried."

She rolls her hips, grinding herself against him, right at the same time as she slides her hands back out of his clothes.

My heart jerks as something metallic catches the light. *She did it!*

Leaping to my feet, I grab at Isera's wrists as if to pull her off Orion's lap in a panic. Just as we agreed earlier, she shoves me off while discreetly slipping the piece of dragon steel into my hand. I pretend to stumble back and bend over to catch my balance on the sofa while I ram the thin piece of dragon steel down between my breasts, hiding it beneath the thick leather of my top.

Draven, who has also jumped to his feet, blocks Orion's view of me while I perform the maneuver as he launches himself at Isera as well. Grabbing her by the shoulders, he wrenches her up and yanks her off Orion's lap.

"I'm so sorry," I blurt out, making my voice sound frantic and worried.

"Get off me," Isera snarls, very convincingly, as Draven throws her to her feet behind him.

On the sofa, Orion blinks, looking disoriented.

"We'll keep her in line," I continue in that deliberately panicked voice, trying to keep him from realizing that we just stole the dragon steel from him. Pressing my palms together, I hold them pleadingly in front of my chest. It's both to sell the worried act and as an extra safety precaution so that he won't see any outlines of the dragon steel underneath my clothes. "Please. I promise. Just don't . . . Don't use your powers on us again. Please. I can't handle another night like the last one."

Orion at last seems to recover. Shifting his weight, he sits forward to hide the very distinctive bulge that is now pressing against the front of his pants. We all pretend not to see it.

"I *should* punish you all for this insolence," he threatens, his voice hard. But he looks . . . flustered. Clenching his jaw, he drags in a controlled breath before locking commanding eyes on Draven. "Keep her in line." His gaze darts to me. "Or my previous threat stands."

Draven flares his wings wider, a snarl on his face at the threat to me.

But we have what we came for, and now we just need to leave before Orion realizes it, so I hurriedly reply, "Understood."

Before anyone can say anything else that might screw this all up, I whirl around and start pushing Draven and Isera toward the front curtains. They thankfully follow along, and we beat a hasty retreat out of the Unseelie King's private section.

Light and music and laughter meet us as we step back out into the massive room. Some people have started dancing closer to where the musicians are playing. Though it's not the orderly ballroom dancing that I experienced in the Ice Palace. This is wilder. More uncoordinated. And more intimate. I raise my eyebrows as I notice a surprising number of people raking their hands over each other and making out in the other seating arrangements across the room. Maybe my first impression of this feeling like an orgy wasn't all that wrong after all.

Halfway across the room, I spot Jocasta and the rest of our team. She is explaining something to a group of male fae while motioning expressively at Alistair. They appraise him, looking impressed as they nod. Alistair, in turn, looks like he can't decide whether to puff his chest up with pride or run away and hide from the intense scrutiny.

We set course for them.

"That was . . . ," Draven begins, glancing down at Isera.

She walks between us, her spine straight and her chin up, looking entirely unaffected by what she just did. At Draven's words, she flicks a sideways glance at him.

"Surprising," Draven finishes at the same time as I say, "Impressive."

Isera casts a glance over her shoulder, back toward the Unseelie King's still closed-off section. Then she lifts her slim shoulders in a shrug. There is an entirely unreadable expression on her face as she turns her head back and simply replies, "Whatever it takes to win."

Apprehension flutters through my stomach as I'm reminded that we still have an entire game left to get through. A game that we still don't know what it will entail. And if we fail, it won't matter that we managed to steal back the dragon steel from Orion. We will still be trapped in here behind the wards.

I blow out a long, steadying breath.

Whatever it takes to win, indeed.

31

"Concentrate!" Jocasta snaps.

"I *am* concentrating," I growl back.

Across the sand, the others are sparring. Isera and Alistair against Draven, Galen, and Lyra. The three dragon shifters are a sight to behold. They fight together so effortlessly that it almost looks as if it was scripted beforehand. Light from the tall windows glints against their swords as they move in perfect synchronization, always anticipating each other's moves and backing each other up without the need to speak. Draven's storm magic crackles around him, the lightning illuminating the already bright stone room as it cleaves the air.

On the other side of the rectangular room, Isera and Alistair are trying to push them back. While not nearly as synchronized as their opponents, they have figured out how to work together enough to not hinder each other at least.

It would be an incredibly interesting battle to watch if I weren't already busy failing my own training quite spectacularly.

"If you were concentrating, you would be creating emotions right now," Jocasta snipes back at me.

Letting my magic fade out again, I shoot her a frustrated look. "It has nothing to do with concentration. I just can't do it!"

She forces out a breath and rakes her fingers through her long white hair in exasperation. Letting her arms drop back down again, she straightens her spine and pins me with a hard stare. "Yes, you can. We have the same magic, and I can do it."

"Well, apparently I'm different."

"That's just an excuse."

"It's not an excuse!"

"You're just not trying hard enough!"

"I *am* trying!"

"Listen to me," she snaps, her own frustration boiling over. Throwing out her arm, she stabs a hand toward where our three dragon shifters are fighting. "Apart from Galen and Lyra, who have no magic at all, *you* are the weak link in this team."

Her words hit something deep inside me. So deep that I stagger a step back. My anger and frustration evaporate as a rolling nausea takes their place. I hate failing. All my life, just the thought of not being able to live up to people's expectations of me has made me almost physically ill. And I can barely breathe through the disappointment that I can feel radiating from Jocasta.

But it's more than that.

That twisting pit in my stomach isn't just because of my constant need to be liked and accepted. It's also because I know that she's right.

"Draven has storm magic *and* wings," Jocasta continues, her voice still hard. "Even without his full dragon form, he is still the literal embodiment of his nickname. The Shadow of Death." She flicks her wrist in Alistair and Isera's direction. "Alistair has fire magic. Incredibly powerful fire magic at that. He has the most destructive power out of all of you. And Isera has ice magic. Perfect for both attacking and defending. The ultimate battle magic." She blows out a harsh breath as she turns back to me. "And then there is *you*."

My chest tightens uncomfortably, and I try to swallow down that sickening feeling in my stomach.

"If I had your raw power, I would be one of the most dangerous people in this city." She shakes her head at me, but the hard edge to her voice is gone. Replaced instead by bewildered frustration. "But despite all the power you possess, you are severely limited by the fact that you can't create emotions from nothing." A hint of desperation bleeds into her voice. "So you need to figure this out. You need to try harder."

I am trying, I want to snap at her again. But I swallow down the petulant outburst. We've been at this for four days now. After the first game, she sat us all down at the kitchen table in her faction house and went through our performance. Overall, she was satisfied. Especially with Isera and the show she put on. She even commended the show I put on when I made the Yellow Faction's team leader crawl to me and hand over the key. But she also identified our weaknesses, which were Lyra and Galen's lack of magic. And me.

I already knew that, of course, since I was thinking the same thing during my battles with the other factions. So I threw myself into the training. Jocasta has been working one-on-one with me every day this week, and while I've made progress with my ability to share emotions, I still haven't figured out how to create them.

Swallowing down the hurt inside me, I give Jocasta a nod in acknowledgment of her statement.

She blows out a short sigh and nods back. "All right, then let's try again."

Straightening my spine, I draw in a steadying breath and then summon my magic once more. For these training sessions, I usually use joy as the emotion I'm trying to create, since I know that Jocasta doesn't already feel it due to all the frustration she harbors instead.

"Now, visualize the emotion like we talked about," she says. "Then just move it toward me and put the emotion in my chest." Lifting a hand, she taps it against her chest. "Right here."

In my mind, I can see that warm yellow spark of joy right in front of me. It's a different shade than the yellow spark of panic. That one is cold and bright in a harsh way, while the flame of joy is a warm yellow tone, like summer flowers, with a slight sparkle to it. It's one of the more beautiful emotions to visualize.

I keep it there in my mind's eye, the small flame burning steadily, while I brace myself. Then I start moving it toward Jocasta's chest.

My magic immediately balks.

That warm and sparkly yellow flame is snuffed out in a flash, as if someone slapped a gigantic hand down over it.

A snarl of frustration comes from deep within my throat.

Forcing out a calming breath, I try again.

I visualize a burning flame of warm yellow joy. Every muscle in my body tenses as I start moving it toward Jocasta again. It recoils violently, as if hitting an invisible wall, and then disappears in a flash again.

"It doesn't work!" I snap, frustration crackling through me like lightning. "As soon as I try to move it, it disappears. Every. Fucking. Time."

Jocasta opens her mouth to no doubt scold me again but then stops. A considering look blows across her face.

Outside the windows, the golden afternoon sunlight hits the rooftops. It makes the red tiles look like they have been dipped in gold. People stroll up and down the rows of stalls down there in the market square, their voices a soft murmur that drifts in through the open window. A warm breeze slips in, washing over my heated cheeks. I wipe a bead of sweat from my neck.

"Maybe we're going about this wrong," Jocasta finally says. Her pink-and-gold eyes have turned pensive as she studies me. "I see my magic as a shifting ball of water, so I just *place it* in people's chests. But you see it as a flame." She taps her chin in consideration for a few seconds and then cocks her head. "What if, instead of moving the flame to my chest, you tried to simply light that flame in my chest straightaway. So you don't have to move it."

I raise my eyebrows in surprise, and a burst of hope flickers in my soul. Maybe I'm not a useless failure after all. Maybe we have just been using the wrong method.

Blowing out a breath, I straighten my spine and call up my magic again. Then I try to make a flame of joy spark to life straight in Jocasta's chest.

It doesn't work.

I grind my teeth.

Concentrating hard, I try to force that warm yellow flame into existence. My magic doesn't stir. Doesn't move at all. It just sits there inside me, waiting for me to do something with it. I flex my hand and try to light a flame in Jocasta's chest again, but I can't even see it in my mind's eye when I try that. And my magic just keeps flowing inside me, waiting for me to use it.

"Mabona's fucking tits," I growl under my breath, and release the grip on my magic.

Jocasta sighs and arches an eyebrow. "Doesn't work?"

"No. It's even worse than when I try to move it. Nothing happens at all when I try it this way."

She nods, looking more resigned than angry at the news. "Then I was right from the beginning. You need to do it the proper way and move it from the magic inside you to someone else. I'm not surprised. It's how our magic always works. It always starts inside ourselves."

"Then I really am a useless failure after all."

The words are out of my mouth before I can stop them. Embarrassed, I run a hand over my face and turn away. Walking over to the windowsill, I sit down and try to get my head back on straight.

Across the room, my friends are still sparring. Fire and ice rush through the air, met by storm winds and lightning across the sand. Weapons wielded with perfect precision gleam in the golden afternoon light. Perfect magic. Perfect sword skills. And then there is me.

Raking both hands through my hair, I tilt my head back and stare up at the pale stone ceiling above to hide the tears that suddenly press against my eyes.

I hate feeling like this. I hate failing. I don't want to be the weak link. I don't want to be a burden. I want to show the whole world that they were wrong about me. That they should have trusted me. That I can be an asset.

"Look, kid," Jocasta says, her voice now much softer than before. A thin trail of stone dust trickles down from the windowsill as she sits down next to me. "In all honesty, you're actually pretty good."

I scoff in disbelief.

She gives me a mock glare. "Hey, don't scoff at your elders."

"Elders," I echo with a chuckle while shaking my head. Turning my head slightly, I peer at her. "How old are you even?"

"Six hundred and forty-three."

My eyes widen. "Seriously?"

She dramatically sweeps her perfect hair off her shoulder in a theatrical move. "I know."

A surprised laugh escapes my chest.

She smiles as well. Then her eyes turn serious once more. "What I'm trying to say is, I not only have centuries more practice than you, I also had something even more important."

"Natural skill?" I quip, only half joking.

Rolling her eyes, she gives me a flat look. "A *teacher*."

"Oh."

"When I first manifested my magic, my parents sent me straight to a guy who also had emotion magic and who could teach me how to use it."

"When I first manifested my magic, my parents started resenting me and then kicked me out of the house the moment they could."

She turns fully to look at me, probably searching for signs that it was a joke. When she finds none, she lets out a low whistle under her breath. "Damn. Shitty parents."

"Yeah."

"My point is, I had someone to teach me how to use this magic properly and to its full extent from the very beginning. You have just been figuring it out on your own through trial and error." She holds my gaze, as if she truly wants me to understand what she's saying. "You're incredibly skilled at the things you *can* do. It's not your fault that you didn't know about all the other things we're able to do with this magic. Like create emotions from nothing."

I swallow through the sudden thickness in my throat. Breaking eye contact, I stare down at the sand beneath my boots while I once again fight against the tears pressing against my eyes. But for a completely different reason this time.

"Thank you," I whisper.

"You're welcome, kid."

We sit there in comfortable silence for another minute while I get my emotions back under control. She's right. There is so much I don't know about my magic, because I have been forced to figure it out on my own all this time. And learning new skills takes time. Just like training with a sword for three weeks wouldn't make me an expert warrior, I can't expect to perfect new skills with my magic in just a few weeks either.

The only problem is that I have hit a wall with this particular skill. With all the other techniques that Jocasta has been teaching me, like how to share emotions, I keep improving all the time. But with this, creating emotions from nothing, I can never get past the stage where I'm supposed to move it from me to her. It's as if some invisible force is blocking it. And I don't know what to do about it.

Jocasta draws in a breath and slaps her thighs. "But I did also bet my entire fortune on this team winning the final game, so let's get back to it."

A small laugh escapes me, easing some of the tension that had started to build again. Pushing off from the windowsill, I stand up as well. "Yes, let's get back to it."

But as I once more start trying to move that warm yellow flame of joy from my chest to Jocasta's, only for my magic to balk and be snuffed out every time, I can't help but feel that this is never going to work.

32

The door is thrown open and then slammed shut so hard that I nearly leap out of my skin. Whirling around, I face the intruder while dropping into a fight stance. My five companions do the same.

Surprise flickers through me when I realize that it's Jocasta. I start to relax my stance but then hesitate when I take in her face. Rage crackles across her beautiful features like lightning. It's so intense that the air around her practically vibrates with it.

"What the fuck did you do?" she screams at us as she stalks forward.

The small stone room is empty except for the seven of us. No other people. And no furniture either. Just a door with a long rectangular slot running horizontally across it at face height. Beyond it, the vast arena floor awaits. The crowd is already there. Thousands of people packed into the stands that slope down toward the flat sand ground in the middle, eagerly awaiting the start of the final game. Their excitement is a steady rumble that echoes through the entire stone structure.

"What in Malachi's fucking name did you do?" Jocasta repeats, her voice cracking through the room like a lightning strike.

We exchange a confused glance. We haven't done anything this entire week except train with Jocasta almost all hours of the day. And those few hours when we weren't training, we've only had time to inhale some food and then crash into bed for an exhausted and dreamless sleep.

"What do you mean?" Galen asks, frowning at her.

"This final game was supposed to be a team game," she snarls at us, fury still pulsing across her face as she comes to a halt in front of us. "Some kind of scavenger hunt. But by royal decree, it was changed last minute to a fucking one-on-one battle tournament! We had one of those during the last set of games, so it shouldn't have been used again for months. But His Majesty the King has now decided that it will be the final game this time as well to supposedly *give the people what they want*." She says the words mockingly, as if she doesn't believe it for a second. "But the king never does anything without a reason." Her eyes flash as she stabs an accusing hand at us. "So what the fuck did you do to piss him off?"

Confused, I just frown at her for a few seconds. We haven't done anything to him. What could he possibly—

Then it hits me.

I snap my gaze to Isera, who is just looking back at Jocasta with that usual chilly expression on her beautiful features, before I shift it to Draven. He meets my gaze, and I can tell that he is thinking the same thing.

The dragon steel. Orion has at last realized that we've stolen back the dragon steel.

But we can't exactly tell Jocasta that, so after exchanging an unfortunately very conspicuous glance, the six of us just shift our attention back to Jocasta in silence.

When no one responds, she growls, "Malachi's fucking balls!"

Draven crosses his arms and pins her with a stare. "Why is the one-on-one game a problem?"

"Because you're going to *lose*!" The words rip out of her chest in a scream. Dragging in a breath, she rakes both hands through her hair while she starts pacing back and forth in front of us. Her chest heaves, and panic bleeds into her voice as she snaps, "Fuck! I bet everything on you after I saw your raw power because I knew that there would only be team games this time around. And in team games, the strongest of you would be able to make up for the weakest of you." Her gaze flits to Galen and Lyra as she says that.

"Don't you dare call them weak," Draven growls at her, his voice dropping low and vicious.

"It's not an insult," she snaps back, frustrated. Looking to Lyra and Galen again, she adds, "You're excellent sword wielders. There's no question about that. And in your dragon forms, I'm sure you're fucking lethal. But in here, you can't shift into dragons." That panic seeps into her voice again, almost cracking it, as she all but screams, "And you can't win a magic battle with a sword!"

Her chest heaves as she rakes her hands through her hair once more. We say nothing, because we all know that she's right. Lyra and Galen are skilled, but in a one-on-one against a magic user, they're going to be at a severe disadvantage.

"And then there is *you*." Jocasta's pink-and-gold eyes are desperate as they lock on me. "Who still hasn't figured out how to create emotions."

My stomach twists. Next to me, Draven opens his mouth to no doubt defend me as well, but I grab his wrist and give it a quick squeeze. Because once again, Jocasta is right.

"The White Faction has never lost a one-on-one battle game," she says, stopping her pacing to instead stare at each of us in turn. "And only three of you have actual battle magic."

"How does it work, then?" I ask. "We fight one-on-one, but how is the winner decided?"

"The faction with the most match wins combined will win the game. If each of you were to win your individual matches, the Black Faction would have six wins, which would be a guaranteed game win."

Above us, the crowd continues cheering and yelling in excitement.

Jocasta heaves an endless sigh. "But that's never going to happen." She looks to Draven. "You have been matched against a member of the Red Faction. And they are notorious for using whips, so it's probably to stop you from using your wings." She slides her gaze to Lyra and Galen.

"You have been matched against the other two members of the Red Faction." Her eyes shift to me, Alistair, and Isera. "And you three have been matched against the three members of the White Faction."

And the White Faction has never lost a game like this.

Great.

Jocasta's rage seems to have bled away into hopeless desperation as she shakes her head at us. "It's the worst possible match selection for you, which means that you have been deliberately set up to lose." Panic and fear pulse in her eyes as she looks at us. "But you have to win anyway. Please. *Please*, you have to win."

Her begging stuns me so much that all I can do is stare at her. She has always seemed so strong and confident. But now . . .

"I've bet everything on this. On you." She draws in an unsteady breath. "Not just my entire fortune and my houses. I've bet my life on this." She stabs a hand in the direction of the remaining waiting rooms, where the other teams are located. "Kossian, the owner of the Red Faction, was so smug and insufferable about how his team was going to beat mine, so when I found out about your raw power, I made a personal bet with him. The one who loses has to *serve* the other. And I can't . . ." She shakes her head desperately. "So please, please, you have to win."

My heart aches for her. For the pain and fear I can see in her eyes. But I can't for the life of me figure out what to say, because I have no idea if we will actually be able to win.

"Yeah, well, you're not the only one whose life depends on this," Alistair says, though not unkindly. "If we don't win, we will be stuck here as prisoners too. So we'll win." His tone is confident, and his gaze is steady as he sweeps it over the rest of us. "Right?"

"Of course we will," Isera replies, her voice as smooth and cool as ever.

I want to reply too, but the words get stuck in my throat. My pulse thrums in my ears, and my chest is starting to constrict.

"Good," Jocasta says while nodding. It sounds as if she's trying to convince herself more than us. "Good. I'll see you on the other side, then."

Then she turns and walks back out the door. She shuts it much more gently than when she stormed inside. Once she's gone, we turn to face each other.

"We need to—" Draven begins.

"Ladies and gentlemen!" a voice booms from outside in the arena. It's Rosea, the organizer who oversaw the team selection. "Welcome to this round's final game. Since you loved the one-on-one battle game we played during the last Great Games, our magnificent king has decided to give you a mighty gift. We will be playing that game again today!"

The crowd roars in excitement and approval.

"Fucking Orion," Draven growls under his breath.

"In our first match, Draven Ryat from the Black Faction will be facing the unstoppable beast himself," Rosea calls across the sand. "The Red Faction's Fergai Bloodworth!"

Ecstatic screams erupt through the arena.

The door that leads out onto the sand swings open. Bright sunlight pours in through the opening, illuminating the floor of our room. Draven blows out an annoyed sigh and shakes his head. Then he shifts his gaze to us.

"You can do this," is all he says. Confident. Certain. As if there is no doubt in his mind that we will all win our matches.

Then he strides out the door. It swings shut behind him with a thud that is almost entirely drowned out by the excited roar of the crowd.

I hurry over to the now closed door, positioning myself so that I can see out through the horizontal slot. The others do the same.

Draven is striding toward the center of the arena with confident steps. Sunlight glints against parts of his black dragon scale armor and the scabbard strapped to his spine. But he doesn't shift into his half-shift form. Lingering fury ripples through me as I slide my gaze to the male fae in red fighting leathers who is stalking toward the middle of the arena as well. Because just as I remember from the last game, he carries a whip on his belt.

My heart beats hard against my ribs as I watch them come to a halt on the sand and face each other. I sweep my gaze over the rest of the arena.

White banners and scarves and clothes can be seen throughout most sections, while the Red Faction supporters seem to be more clustered together in groups this time. And to my surprise, there are quite a lot of black banners now being flown throughout the whole audience. Apparently, we made quite the impression during the last game. Or at least Isera did.

"You all know how it works," Rosea calls, her voice booming across the arena and silencing the crowd. "The match is over when one of them is unconscious, dead, or surrenders. Other than that, there are no rules."

My heart jerks. Goddess above, how the hell are we going to win this?

The crowd goes silent.

Anticipation crackles in the air.

I barely dare to breathe.

"Begin!" Rosea calls.

Draven shoots a bolt of lightning at Fergai. He dives sideways to escape it. With a snarl on his lips, he rolls to his feet and yanks the whip from his belt. But he barely even has time to stand up straight before a blast of wind slams into his chest. The force of it is so strong that he flies backward before crashing down hard on the ground. Clouds of sand whirl up from the impact before being blown away by Draven's winds.

I gape at the scene. Draven hasn't even drawn his sword yet. He's just standing there in the same spot, his arms crossed over his chest while his storm magic crashes over Fergai.

And the crowd is eating it up.

Screams of excitement pulse through the arena, and the very walls around us tremble as the crowd above stomp their feet and clap their hands.

Fergai struggles to his feet but then has to leap away again when Draven shoots another lightning bolt at him. The Unseelie fae bellows in frustration and then sends a torrent of fire toward Draven.

Still standing with his arms crossed over his chest, Draven simply shoves the flames aside with another blast of wind. Fergai flicks his wrist, trying to hit Draven from afar with his whip. But the lash is shoved off course just like the flames when Draven counters it with wind.

My heart swells with possessive pride as I watch him.

Mine. That lethal man is all mine.

The mate bond remains inside me, as it has every day since it snapped into place, feeling like a faint pull toward Draven. It took me some getting used to, but now it's not distracting anymore. Instead, it feels comforting. As if he is always with me.

Usually, I can also feel a faint trace of his emotions through it. But right now, I can't feel anything. It doesn't surprise me though. After the centuries he has spent deceiving everyone around him, he is an expert at blocking out all his emotions, which is no doubt very useful in a fight as well.

The man from the Red Faction is fighting desperately to get one single strike through, but against Draven's expert battle skills and overwhelming raw magic power, it's impossible. The crowd is cheering so loudly at the incredible display that I have to suppress the urge to shield my ears from the deafening roars.

Once Draven has thoroughly humiliated his opponent, he ends the match by hitting Fergai with two lightning strikes that leave him unconscious with his limbs shaking uncontrollably.

"Wow, what a show!" Rosea calls in the aftermath. "That has got to be the most one-sided match we have ever witnessed in the history of these games."

A wicked grin steals across my mouth, and that possessive pride returns. *Mine*.

Draven is escorted in through a door on the other side of the arena while two attendants have to carry Fergai in after him.

"But the day isn't over yet!" Rosea calls. "So hang on to your betting slips, ladies and gentlemen. Because now it's time for the Black Faction to face the White Faction."

Cheers erupt once more.

Alistair starts in surprise when his name is called but then straightens his spine and strides out into the arena as soon as the door swings open.

His match is not nearly as showy as Draven's was. Instead, Alistair practically mows his opponent down with sheer brute force within the first minute. It's brutal, efficient, and shockingly fast.

His opponent from the White Faction has water magic, which should have given Alistair trouble. But because of the difference in raw power that the Icehearts' selective breeding has created, it doesn't even matter.

The audience in white, who were so sure of their faction's win, gape in stunned silence as Alistair leaves their prized fighter gasping on the sand with severe burns.

Hope flickers in my chest. Maybe we do stand a chance after all.

After that, the White Faction fights the Red Faction. The spectators who are carrying white banners regain some of their enthusiasm as the female fae from the White Faction beats her opponent in a surprisingly close match. But a win is a win, and the crowd is once more cheering. Though not the Red Faction supporters. Several of them even drop their red banners and instead borrow black ones from their neighbors. Apparently, the rivalry between the White and Red Factions is strong, so cheering for our team instead appears to be the only suitable compromise.

Then Lyra's name is called.

She tenses. Her normally so cheerful face is filled with worry as she stares out at the sand. Then she quickly wipes the expression off her features and turns to give us all a beaming smile. It fools none of us, but I force a smile anyway. Isera gives her a nod, while Galen squeezes her arm. Then she's striding away toward the middle of the arena.

Hushed anticipation washes through the arena as Lyra faces the woman from the Red Faction.

"Begin!"

I gasp as stones shoot through the air toward her.

Next to me, Galen grips the edge of the door slot hard.

Lyra throws herself sideways, rolling across the sand with her sword already in hand. But her opponent shoots another hail of stones at her. She twists, and they slam into the side of her dragon scale armor.

Worry courses through me as the Unseelie fae woman rushes her. It turns into sickening dread as the match progresses. Lyra is skilled with the sword, but she barely manages to get any strikes through, since her opponent is hammering her with blocks of stone.

Galen tightens his grip on the door slot before us as Lyra cries out in pain when she's hit hard in the side. More stones are shot at her.

But Lyra doesn't surrender.

Pain pulses through my heart as I watch Lyra fight hard until a stone slams into the side of her head with a dreadful crack. She collapses onto the sand, her chest still moving but her eyes closed.

Galen lets out something between a growl of rage and a whimper of dread. Rosea calls the win in favor of the Red Faction, and then Lyra is carried away across the sand and in through the same doorway that Draven and Alistair left through.

"They'll take care of her," I find myself saying. "She'll be all right."

Neither Galen nor Isera answers.

Once the arena floor has been cleared yet again, Rosea announces the next match. Isera doesn't so much as blink when her name is called. Without a second look back, she simply strides out the door.

The crowd yells in anticipation when they see her.

And by Mabona, does she deliver.

Her entire match is pure entertainment. She toys with her opponent from the White Faction, making the Unseelie man look like a fool who challenged a goddess to a fight. Attacking and defending expertly with her ice magic, she makes the fight into such a spectacle that it's impossible to look away.

The crowd goes wild.

This time, I do have to press my hands to my ears to block out the deafening screams and cheers that fill the entire arena. It looks like Isera is about to become their new favorite celebrity.

Once Isera has finished entertaining the audience to the fullest possible extent, she knocks out her opponent with a block of ice and then bows theatrically to the crowd before blowing another kiss in what I assume is the Unseelie King's direction. Since it's located somewhere right above us, I can't tell for sure. But he was sitting in that section last time, so it must be aimed at him.

Another wild roar sweeps through the crowd.

Isera saunters away and disappears through the door while her opponent is carried in after her.

After that, the White and Red Faction fight another battle, which once again ends with the White Faction as the winner.

Then it's Galen's turn.

My heart sinks as I watch him fight a fire wielder from the Red Faction. It ends with Galen on his back, his leg broken and his hands burned. The crowd dressed in red cheers as Galen is forced to surrender with a sword to his throat.

I can barely breathe as the second-to-last match is called. The White Faction against the Red.

That dread in my chest turns into a furious storm of panic as I watch the guy from the White Faction beat the girl from the Red Faction.

There is only one match left now.

The Red Faction has two wins.

The White Faction has three wins.

We also have three wins.

And the match that remains is between me and a member of the White Faction. Which means that whoever wins this match wins the entire game.

My mouth is so dry that it feels like it's full of sand. I try to swallow, but I can barely get anything through the tightness in my throat.

It all comes down to me.

If I lose this match, we will be trapped here as the Unseelie King's prisoners forever.

Panic and dread crackle through my veins like bolts of lightning as I stare out at the bloodstained sand outside the door. I am not a warrior. My magic is meant for stealth. For sneak attacks. For spying. For intimidating. For distracting an opponent while an ally strikes them down.

So how the hell am I supposed to win in a one-on-one fight against someone with actual battle magic?

"And now," Rosea calls, "in the closest one-on-one battle game we've had in years, we will get to witness a thrilling finale that will determine who wins this round's Great Games. Will it be the White Faction?"

The crowd dressed in white screams in affirmation and waves their banners high.

"Or will it be the Black Faction?" she finishes.

The rest of the audience, both the ones wearing black and the ones who previously flew red banners, cheer in encouragement. It's so loud that it vibrates in my rib cage. But it does nothing to reassure me.

My hands shake, and I have to wipe my sweaty palms on my thighs as I drag in a shuddering breath.

"Let's bring in the fighters!" Rosea bellows. "Oleander Darkmane from the White Faction. And Selena Hale from the Black Faction."

The crowd screams.

And the door swings open.

33

I can't even hear the roars of the crowd anymore because of how loudly my own heart is beating in my chest. Standing there in the middle of the packed arena, I stare at the male Unseelie fae who stands before me.

Oleander Darkmane is massive. Almost as tall as Draven. The muscles in his arms and chest strain against the white fighting leathers he's wearing, the pale color somehow making him look even bigger. His long brown hair has been tied back in a bun, and his red-and-blue eyes are practically glittering with wicked anticipation as he studies me.

Two long daggers hang from his belt. But other than that, I have no idea what kind of attacks to expect. There is no way to know what his magic type is before the match begins.

My pulse thrums furiously in my ears as I stare at my imposing opponent. There is no way in hell that I will be able to knock him out. If I were to slam my fist against his skull, I would probably hurt my hand more than him. That leaves killing him, which seems highly unlikely to work for the same reason, and forcing him to surrender somehow.

Mabona's fucking tits. This is never going to work.

Dread rips at my chest.

Maybe we can somehow trick the Unseelie King into another bargain after this. Another way for us to regain our freedom after we lose. Maybe we can—

"Begin!"

I suck in a sharp breath between my teeth, yanked back to the present by Rosea's loud voice. Pulling out my dagger, I drop into a fight stance while I summon my magic.

My opponent, however, doesn't seem to be in a hurry to attack. He slowly unsheathes his long knives while a vicious smile spreads across his face. My stomach twists.

Gripping my dagger hard, I shove my magic toward him in rapid bursts, testing several emotions to see what I can use.

Ice spreads through my veins as I find . . . nothing.

Just like when I tried to manipulate Draven's emotions during that very first test for the Atonement Trials, my magic is met with a blank wall. I suck in a shuddering breath, unconsciously staggering a step back. This is a man who has trained himself to block out all emotions in order to better focus on the fight. Or maybe to protect himself from Jocasta or some other fae with emotion magic who he has fought earlier.

My gaze darts toward Orion.

The Unseelie King smirks down at me from where he is lounging on his throne.

He *knows*. That fucking asshole knows. It's no coincidence that I have been matched against this specific opponent. Goddess fucking damn it. He set us up to lose on purpose. Every single pairing in this game has been carefully chosen. The entire deck was stacked against us from the very beginning.

Something thin and black shoots toward me.

On instinct, I leap back and to the side.

My heart jerks as a sleek shadow snakes across the ground where I was only seconds before. Landing lightly, I'm already moving before the next attack happens. Shadows shoot toward me, aiming for my ankles, but they streak past through empty air since I dodged before the attack happened.

Across the sand, Oleander narrows his eyes at me.

I grind my teeth, wishing that I had some kind of ranged weapon.

A bow or some throwing knives or something that I could aim at his face, which is the only exposed part of his muscular body. But I don't dare to throw the dagger I have. Both because it's not suited for throwing and also because if I miss, I will have lost my only weapon.

Oleander lunges at me.

I yank my dagger up, barely managing to redirect his knife before it can spear through my chest. Metal grinds against metal as his long knife slides along the edge of my dagger. I flick my wrist, forcing it off. He twists and swings his other blade while shadows shoot for my wrist. Panic spikes up my spine as they brush against my skin before I manage to yank my arm away.

But the move makes me lose focus on his blades.

A hiss rips from my throat as his knife slides along the side of my ribs. Thankfully, the thick leather prevents it from drawing blood.

I throw myself backward before he can bring his other arm around and try again. Shadows flash after me across the sand. I jump, looking like a startled rabbit as I hop from foot to foot to escape the snaking tendrils.

The crowd whoops and laughs from the stands.

Clenching my jaw, I whip my gaze from the ground beneath me to where Oleander is standing.

He has two long knives, superior strength, better reach, and shadow magic. And I have one dagger and magic that doesn't work against him.

Goddess damn it, I need to think.

The shadows shoot up toward my wrists at the same time as Oleander lurches across the sand. I gasp. Yanking my arms down, I barely make it before the shadows can trap my wrists. But that leaves me unable to block the strike that Oleander swipes at my neck.

I duck, twisting sideways.

A knife whooshes through the air right above my head.

Throwing my arms out, I try to regain my balance again.

Think! Goddess damn it, think!

He recovers from the missed strike and swings his fist, still gripping the blade, toward my cheek in a backhanded strike.

How did I beat Draven when he was blocking out his emotions?

Shadows streak through the air toward my waist.

Diving to the side, I roll across the sand to escape both the fist and the shadows.

An idea strikes me. I shocked Draven into feeling something. I need to do the same now.

Sand flutters up around me like a cloud as I grind to a halt and spin up onto my knees. Oleander is already on me. He lunges, his blades aimed at my throat.

Snatching up a fistful of sand, I throw it right in his face.

He gasps as the sand hits his eyes and mouth, which then causes him to choke. Shooting to my feet, I call up my magic and shove it straight at his chest. I aim for panic. Then fear. Then shock.

Nothing.

A snarl of frustration rips from my throat as I can't connect with any of the emotions. I need to do something else. Something—

My stomach lurches as a shadow wraps around my ankle, yanking hard. I throw my arms out, spinning wildly as I try to regain my balance. Oleander is coughing and spitting sand from his mouth while wiping the back of his hand over his eyes. I swing my dagger at his face in a desperate attempt to make him lose focus.

Still blinking against the sand, he barely sees my blade in time to dodge. His focus wavers as he is forced to yank up his arm and block my strike with his forearm. It causes his magic to flicker, and I rip my ankle out of the constricting shadow. My blade barely scratches the leather on his forearm, but I wasn't trying to kill him with the blow anyway.

Now free from the shadow again, I leap out of reach while my mind churns.

I need to do something else to force an emotion into his chest.

He blinks the last of the sand from his eyes and then advances on me again, fury now crackling across his face.

My heart slams against my ribs.

I gasp.

Then whip my head back to stare up at the sky. "*Dragon!*"

A collective gasp rips through the whole arena as everyone snaps their gazes toward the sky. I shove with my magic.

This technique worked perfectly against Tommen during the battle royale trial, and I do the same now, aiming for the bone-white spark of fear in Oleander's chest.

I almost scream when I find nothing.

Quickly dropping the magic, I throw it out toward another emotion. Shock.

My heart jerks as I at last find a brass flame of shock in his chest. Latching on to it, I pour everything I have into it.

Oleander gasps, dropping his blades and throwing his arms over his head as his shock flares into wildfire.

I dart forward. If I can just get my knife against his throat, I can force him to surrender.

My boots pound against the sand as I practically throw myself the final distance between us. The shock is still wreaking havoc inside Oleander when he sees me coming and snaps his gaze to me. Just another step. Another step and then—

A fist slams into the side of my face.

The hit is so unexpected, and so powerful, that I'm thrown sideways across the sand like a doll. I hit the ground hard, my dagger flying out of my hand when my elbow smacks into the sand, and I roll several times before coming to a halt.

My ears ring, and I swear I can hear the sound echoing around in my empty skull. Blinking, I try to gather my wits. The stands above shift back and forth, as if duplicating and then becoming one again.

A figure in white fighting leathers becomes visible above me.

I'm so dazed that it takes me another few seconds to remember who he is and where we are. And Oleander uses those seconds well.

Puffs of sand rise up around my body as he drops to his knees over me, straddling my chest. I gasp in a breath, finally realizing that I've lost the connection to my magic, and scramble to summon it again.

Two strong hands close around my throat.

Panic rips through my chest.

Yanking my arms up, I try to ram my elbows into the crook of his to break his grip. He snarls. Then black shadows shoot out. I try to gasp as they wrap around my wrists, but only strangled gurgling noises make it out of my throat as he continues squeezing while his shadows force my arms away.

I yank furiously and kick my legs with everything I have as the shadows pin my hands to the ground on either side of my head. But it's futile. My arms are now trapped, and my legs can't reach him.

Oleander continues squeezing.

The panic inside me clangs like giant bells.

I'm going to die. Oh Goddess, I'm going to die.

Fear washes through me like cold water.

Then it's broken up by a sudden roaring feeling of fury.

My mind is spinning so much that it takes me a moment to realize that it isn't mine. The fury is Draven's. I can feel it through the mate bond. It's faint, like all emotions that trickle through the bond, but it still helps. That burst of sudden fury cuts through the panic for a second.

I need to do something. Something. Now. Right now!

Calling up a bone-white flame of fear, I let it burn before me.

Oleander tightens his grip on my throat.

A whimper escapes my lips.

Black spots start flickering across my vision.

I try to move the flame of fear to his chest.

It balks.

Panic streaks through my entire body like bolts of lightning. I kick my legs, slamming my heels into the sand, and yank at the shadows around my wrists. My lungs scream with the need for oxygen.

The fear and panic and frustration and the utter certainty that I am going to die explode like a storm inside me.

I scream in my mind.

I scream so loudly with my entire soul that I taste blood and iron.

And then I *shove*.

That bone-white spark of fear slams into Oleander's chest with enough force to send a shock wave through me.

He gasps, jerking back and losing his grip on my throat.

Air floods my lungs as I drag in a deep breath.

Pleasure floods my entire soul. It's unlike anything I have ever experienced before. It's like a warm hug. Like floating in a sparkling ocean. Like resting on a fluffy white cloud. It fills my entire soul.

Stunned, I pour an unstoppable flood of magic into that bone-white flame of fear in my opponent's chest.

He screams.

And this scream is audible.

It splits the air and echoes through the entire arena as he staggers backward. His shadows evaporate, and his body disappears from mine. I cough and gasp air into my lungs while that intense pleasure courses through me again.

It's addictive.

My entire soul is just chanting, *more, more, more*.

I increase that flame of fear that I forced into Oleander's chest until it practically consumes his entire body.

Urine trickles down his leg, wetting the sand underneath his boot. His eyes are wide with undiluted terror, and his entire body shakes as he screams.

Then he cuts and runs.

The entire arena stares in shock as Oleander runs like a bat out of hell toward the door where the rest of our teams are waiting. I stare after him, pleasure still coursing through me while my mind tries to process.

Then something inside me snaps free.

It's a violent shattering.

Like slamming a boulder through a building.

Walls that I didn't even know I had inside me shatter like an explosion.

Gasping, I stagger backward and lose the grip on my magic as memories flood my mind.

My parents. In our kitchen. The broken drinking glasses on the floor before me. Their faces as I look up. My pleading voice as I beg them not to hate me. Their eyes . . . Oh Goddess, their eyes as that slow but steady change starts. That moment when I can see their expressions change second by second until only deep resentment remains.

The memory that the Unseelie King has been using on me. The memory that I can't remember having before he forcefully showed it to me.

My legs give out and I crash down on the ground.

Somewhere above me, Rosea's strong voice booms across the arena. "What a shocking finale! Oleander Darkmane runs screaming off the arena, forfeiting the match. Ladies and gentlemen, with his shocking surrender, we have our winner. Selena Hale and the Black Faction!"

Screams and cheers and whoops sweep across the arena. But I can barely hear them.

Because now, a terrifying question has crept into my mind.

I *can* create emotions out of nothing. There is nothing stopping me from it. Nothing limiting my powers in any way. I am entirely capable of doing it.

Those crystal-clear seconds when my parents' eyes go from looking at me with surprise to glaring at me with sudden resentment flash through my mind over and over again. That memory that I had repressed until now.

And all I can think about is that one terrifying question.

What the hell did I do to my parents?

34

Chaos fills the waiting room on the other side. The entire Red Faction, and half of the White Faction, are arguing with their respective faction owners, trying to persuade them to in turn argue with the guards that we should be disqualified because we're technically not citizens of the Unseelie Court.

The guards themselves are busy glaring at Draven, who apparently almost shattered the door to get to me when he realized that I was truly in danger of dying. There are black scorch marks on the pale stone door where his lightning hit, and half the tables and chairs closest to the door look to have been smashed against the stone by a blast of wind. Isera is standing by that charred door, gazing out through the slot toward the Unseelie King's section with a slight smirk on her lips.

Draven, however, isn't acknowledging the guards' glares. Instead, he is seated on the ground next to where Galen and Lyra are lying on a pair of blankets. Galen's hands are badly burned, and his leg is sticking out at an odd angle. Next to him, Lyra is breathing, but her eyes slide in and out of focus. Alistair is kneeling next to her, his hand hovering over her arm but not quite touching it.

Jocasta, who was celebrating our miraculous win earlier, has promised to take both Galen and Lyra straight to Haldia and pay for their healing as soon as the guards give us all permission to leave.

The moment I stepped through the door, Draven was there, checking my injuries and demanding to know if I was okay. I assured him that I was, that he should focus on Galen and Lyra, and that I needed a moment to myself.

In truth, I need more than a moment.

Shock still clangs inside my skull like giant bells, and memories long buried are now rattling around in there. I feel off-kilter. As if something fundamental has snapped free inside me, and now I'm just flailing as I tumble through an open sky with nothing to grab on to.

Seated on a bench at the back of the room, I stare at Oleander Darkmane. He is hiding underneath a pale wooden table as far away from me as he can possibly get. His blue-and-red eyes are wide with terror as he stares at me from underneath that table, and his face is ghostly pale. The remaining two members of the White Faction who aren't currently arguing with their faction owner are looking between me and Oleander's shaking body. Confusion and fury mix in their eyes.

"Malachi's balls," Jocasta says as she plops down on the bench next to me. Leaning back, she stretches out her legs and rests her back against the stone wall behind us. "That was some finale, kid." There is deep approval in her eyes as she glances over at me and smiles. "I knew you could do it."

"Thank you," I reply, as sincerely as I can.

I want to mean it. I *do* mean it. But I'm just so shell-shocked right now that I'm having trouble functioning. That memory of my parents is still swirling around inside my mind. And I also can't stop thinking about that incredible feeling of pleasure that I got when I created the fear in Oleander's chest. And I can't stop staring at Oleander, huddled underneath that table and still terrified of me.

Jocasta follows my gaze and then nods discreetly toward the terrified man. "You must've used a lot of power if he's still this scared of you even after you've released the magic."

Jolted out of my stupor, I blink repeatedly as a sudden idea hits me. I can decrease his fear so that he won't have to hide under the table now that the match is over. Calling up my magic, I throw it out in search of that bone-white spark of fear.

Shock crackles up my spine when I find *two*.

There is a small spark of fear and a big one. The small spark feels the way it usually does when I connect to someone's emotions. But that big flame next to it, it's distinctly mine. I can both see and feel my own influence and magic in it. It's incredibly obvious that it's not his own fear. Leaving the small spark alone, since it probably has nothing to do with me, I instead latch on to the bigger spark and start lowering his fear at a rapid pace.

That massive bone-white flame decreases steadily.

Then it stops.

I scowl, trying again to decrease it. It's smaller than before, but it's still there, burning steadily. And no matter how much I try to decrease it, it doesn't get any smaller than that. I try instead to simply slam it down. Like a lid slammed onto a burning pot. That doesn't work either.

With that frown of confusion on my face, I turn to Jocasta. "How do I release it?"

She blinks, looking genuinely stunned by the question. "What do you mean?"

"I haven't removed the fear that I put in his chest. It's still there. I can feel my own magic in it. I managed to decrease it a little. But how do I turn it off completely?"

Silence falls over us for a few seconds as she just stares at me, her mouth slightly open. As if she's trying to figure out if I'm messing with her or not. When she sees the seriousness on my face, she blinks again and gives her head a quick shake.

"Like normal," she says, sounding hesitant. "When you disengage your magic, it disappears."

"No." My frown deepens. "It's still there."

"Just try it again. You looked a little dazed after the match, so maybe you just forgot."

I cut off the flow of my magic. Once Jocasta has seen that my eyes have stopped glowing, she nods. Turning toward Oleander, I throw my magic toward that bone-white spark of fear. Just like last time, there are two. One small spark and one steadily burning flame. The flame has my distinctive feel to it.

"It's still there," I say, cutting off the flow of my magic again and turning back to Jocasta. "And I can't decrease it beyond a certain point either."

Once again, silence descends over us. But this time, it's filled with tension. Jocasta turns to look at Oleander. After I decreased his fear slightly, he has at least stopped shaking and hiding underneath the table. But he's still staring at me with terrified eyes.

Through the open slot in the door, the murmur of the crowd drifts in like the rumble of the sea as they discuss the matches and wait for the victory presentation.

Next to me, Jocasta licks her lips. But all she says is, "Oh."

My heart jerks. I don't like the sound of that. "What do you mean, *oh*?"

"It's supposed to disappear when you withdraw your magic."

"But it doesn't."

"Probably because your magic is so much stronger than mine. With that much raw power, I guess there are . . . side effects."

Ice washes through my veins and my stomach drops. "It's permanent?"

"It would appear so."

"Can't *you* remove it from his chest? With your magic?"

"No. It's impossible to even manipulate, let alone remove, an emotion that another emotion wielder has created."

Dragging in an unsteady breath, I turn to stare at Oleander. I can create emotions, but once created, I can't remove them? Goddess above, what a terrifying thought.

That memory slams into me again like a punch to the gut.

And suddenly, I can't breathe.

My parents, standing there looking surprised. And then from one second to the next, resentment flashes to life in their eyes.

I run my tongue around my suddenly parched mouth. My heart is beating so hard against my ribs that I can hear the loud pounding in my ears.

What if I *made* my parents hate me?

Back when I was young, when I couldn't control my magic, it activated randomly. What if, back then, I accidentally made them resent me? And then I couldn't remove it?

My heart is beating so fast that I feel lightheaded.

What if my parents don't actually hate me? What if, all this time, they were just acting that cruel to me because I unwittingly created feelings of resentment in their chests?

The thought makes my head spin, and I have to grip the edge of the bench hard with my fingers to stop myself from just toppling sideways.

If I created the hatred in their chests, there will be no way to undo it, so it won't change anything. But at the same time, it will change *everything*. Because I will know that it's not actually real.

A small sob escapes my lips.

As soon as this is all over, I'm going to return to the Seelie Court and seek out my parents. Then I'm going to reach out with my magic and see if the flames of resentment in their chests are actually theirs, or if they have my dangerous magic all over them.

"They'll be okay," Jocasta says, misinterpreting my small sob as she glances between me and where Lyra and Galen are lying on the ground. "I promise, as soon as we get permission, I will take them straight to Haldia. I'll even skip the victory presentation with the king." Her eyes are full of gratitude as she glances at me while placing a light hand on my thigh. "You've made me more money today than I have ever made in my entire life. You've bought me life-changing freedom in this court in a way that I can't even properly explain to an outsider. If you ever need anything, all you have to do is ask."

Drawing in a calming breath, I push the world-altering memories and realizations and questions about my parents out of my mind. There will be time for that later. For now, there is something else I need to know.

"I have a question," I begin hesitantly, trying to figure out how to word this without sounding like a psychopath.

She nods. "Shoot."

"I, uhm . . ." I clear my throat. "When I created that flame of fear and shoved it into Oleander's chest, I got this intense rush of . . . pleasure. It was so addictive that I just wanted more and more."

Mabona's tits, that was the best explanation I could come up with? If that doesn't make me sound like a psycho villain, I don't know what does.

But to my surprise, Jocasta doesn't look at me as if I'm the King of Hell incarnate. Instead, she lets out a small breath of amusement and leans back against the wall again.

"Oh, that." She sucks her teeth and then shrugs. "Yeah, I get that too. We all do."

"When creating fear?"

"When creating all emotions."

I blink at her in surprise and confusion. "Why?"

"It's nature's way of creating balance. Our magic is much stronger than elemental magic." She chuckles. "Fire wielders especially will argue with you about that until the day they die if you ever mention it to them, but it's true. They can create elements. But we can *change* a person. It's one of the most dangerous types of magic there is."

Alistair's nickname for me suddenly flits through my mind. Selena Soulstealer. Maybe he wasn't all that wrong after all.

"That . . . makes sense," I reply, but my brows are still furrowed as I look back at her. "But why this addictive feeling of pleasure?"

"Because that's how emotions work." She lifts her shoulders in a casual shrug. "Everyone is addicted to something. It could be the comforting feeling they get when they eat, or the pleasure they feel when they have sex. Some people are addicted to anger. They actively seek out things to be angry about because it gives them a sense of purpose. Some are addicted to the feeling that people have wronged them, because it makes them feel righteous. And some people are addicted to that warm feeling when someone praises them for being good because it validates their existence."

Ouch. That one might have hit a little too close to home.

She shrugs again. "I could go on, but I think you get the point."

"Yeah." I rub my thigh, suddenly feeling anxious. Then I glance back up at her. "Does that . . . craving ever go away? Because I kind of already want to feel it again. It was like a warm sparkling hug, and I just . . . I can't stop thinking about how good it felt."

"Unfortunately not. You will have to manage that craving now. But don't worry too much about it. I've been successfully handling it for over six hundred years now. It's not too bad."

"Oh. Good."

She sits up straighter, blinking as if a sudden thought just struck her. Swallowing, she meets my gaze with eyes that have suddenly filled with a terrifying amount of sympathy.

"But," she begins, sounding hesitant for the first time in this conversation. "I suppose the craving will be even stronger for you than it is for me. Maybe significantly stronger, given the strength of your magic overall."

I stare back at her in silence, my mind spinning.

This just adds more weight to my suspicion that I accidentally made my parents hate me. My mind probably blocked out the whole thing and buried it deep inside where I couldn't reach it, both because of the sheer trauma of what I had done and also to cut off the memory of the pleasure I felt, so that I wouldn't continue doing it to my parents just to feel that rush of pleasure again.

A choked noise escapes my mouth.

I'm suddenly not sure whether to bawl my eyes out or burst out laughing like a crazy person.

Not only did I probably make my own parents hate me, I will now be fighting against an overwhelming urge to do it to everyone else around me too.

Splendid.

Just . . . splendid.

35

The sly smile on Isera's lips is making me increasingly nervous. We're standing outside the door to the Unseelie King's private section on the middle tier of the arena. The carved wooden door is still closed, and two guards are standing on either side of it, waiting for Orion's orders to send us in.

True to her word, Jocasta turned down this audience to instead get Lyra and Galen healed straightaway. Since neither of them could walk on their own, Draven is carrying Galen to Haldia's house while Alistair is doing the same for Lyra. That left me and Isera to face the Unseelie King and secure confirmation of our hard-won freedom.

And Isera has been smirking the entire way here.

Which is making me jittery.

We need to make Orion keep his end of the bargain and give us permission to leave. Not insult him or bait him into going back on his word.

"Send them in," Orion Nightbane calls from the other side of the door.

A jolt shoots through me, and I flick another worried glance at Isera. But that sly smile is now thankfully gone from her features, replaced instead by that usual mask of cold confidence.

The guards open the door and motion for us to step through.

Drawing in a bracing breath, I straighten my spine and then follow Isera in through the door.

The Unseelie King is standing in the middle of an elegantly furnished lounge. A cluster of sofas and divans in royal blue have been positioned by the wall to my left. There are several small wooden side tables scattered between them, and bowls of fresh fruit and platters filled with everything from bread and cheese to delicate pastries are waiting there. Several silver decanters of wine have been placed among them as well.

Behind Orion, two thick drapes in his signature royal blue separate this lounge room from the platform outside where he can sit on his throne and watch the games down in the arena. The drapes have been left slightly open, letting us see the throne and the arena beyond but still providing privacy for the three of us in here.

The door shuts behind me and Isera with a faint click.

Orion cocks his head, his black-and-silver eyes studying us intently. "You are the smallest party of seven I have ever seen."

"As you no doubt saw," I begin, careful to keep my tone neutral. "Two of our team members were badly injured in their matches, so our faction owner had to take them to Haldia straightaway."

"I see," he replies. And I can't tell if he's disappointed or amused or simply indifferent. His gaze shifts between me and Isera. "I suppose you speak for your entire team, then."

"We do," Isera says, her eyes locked on the Unseelie King.

Another flash of worry pulses through me, and I have to suppress the urge to glance at her. But she thankfully doesn't say anything else. Nothing to antagonize him. I let out a small sigh.

"Excellent." His eyes glint as he holds Isera's gaze. "Then you can start by giving back the dragon steel and begging my forgiveness for stealing it."

A sharp smile spreads across her lips. "Can't steal something that already belongs to you."

"Ah, but it didn't belong to you. The moment you committed a crime, all your possessions became property of the Crown."

"Can't commit a crime when the mission was sanctioned by the king."

"You have a lot of cocky retorts already waiting on that wicked tongue of yours, don't you?"

Her sly smile widens, and she runs her tongue along her teeth. "You should see what else I can do with it."

His eyes flash. But not with anger.

"We made a deal, Your Majesty," I interrupt with as much politeness as I can muster before this strange confrontation between them gets out of hand. "If we won these games, we would be allowed to leave the Unseelie Court promptly and without issue. You've already gone back on your word once. Do you intend to do it again?"

This time, it's most definitely anger that flashes in his eyes as he snaps his gaze to me and growls, "I did *not* go back on my word. You just didn't word the bargain carefully enough."

Irritation crackles through me at his damn word games, but this is obviously an important distinction to him, so I incline my head and diplomatically reply, "Of course. I apologize. However, this time, the bargain was clear. So, do you intend to honor it?"

Drawing in a long breath, he just watches the two of us in silence for a while. Then he finally lets out that breath again, sounding both annoyed and resigned. "Yes." His eyes slide to me. "While I am somewhat irked by your miraculous win . . ."

Since you deliberately stacked the deck against us and set us up to lose, I finish for him silently in my mind.

"I do always honor the bargains I make," he finishes, giving me a pointed stare. "So yes, you have my permission to leave the Unseelie Court. As soon as you're ready, I will personally escort you to the wards and let you through."

"Unless you want to strike another bargain," Isera cuts in.

I whip my head toward her. "What?"

Interest sparks in Orion's eyes as he locks them on Isera instead. "I'm listening."

"You like games and gambles, so here is one for you," Isera says. "We trade our freedom for another bargain. And if we win, you and your court will help us take down the Iceheart Dynasty."

"What?" I snap again, aghast.

We've just barely managed to win this one and get our freedom back. There's no way in hell we'll be able to win another one.

"Isera, what the hell?" I demand. "We haven't—"

She flicks her wrist.

And *ice* fills my mouth.

I jerk back in shock, trying to gasp, but the ice spreads out so that it prevents me from moving my tongue. Gagging, I try to spit it out. And then I try to pull it out with my fingers. It doesn't work. I can still breathe through my nose, but the chunk of ice inside my mouth is so wide and so tall now that I can't get it past my teeth and back out of my mouth.

Whirling toward her, I stare at her in shock and disbelief. But she isn't even looking at me. Her gaze is firmly fixed on the Unseelie King, who is watching her just as intently.

His eyes gleam like daggers as he flashes her a sharp smile. "My, my. Gagging your own friend so that you can bargain away her freedom? How very ruthless of you."

"So you accept the bargain?" Isera pushes.

Still fighting against the ice in my mouth, I grab Isera by the arm and pull hard, trying to force her to look at me. She just yanks her arm out of my grip and flicks her wrist again.

Ice shoots up from the ground, wrapping around my ankles and wrists. I try to gasp again, but only a gurgling sound makes it past the ice in my mouth. Now completely immobilized, all I can do is stand there and watch while shock at her betrayal clangs through my skull.

Orion slides his gaze to me for a second before locking eyes with Isera again. A sharp smile, full of approval, lurks on his lips. "Oh, you really are an interesting one, aren't you, little viper?"

"The bargain," Isera repeats. "Do you accept it?"

My heart pounds against my ribs as silence falls for an uncomfortably long time.

Then Orion chuckles. "No."

Relief crashes over me.

Lightning flashes in Isera's eyes.

"Why would I agree to something as dangerous and futile as trying to take down the Iceheart Dynasty just for a little bit of extra entertainment from you?" the Unseelie King asks, arching a haughty brow.

"Because it's not just entertainment," Isera retorts. "You can see it yourself. Everyone in here is crawling up the walls with restlessness. You and your entire court are bored in here behind your wards. If we take down the Icehearts, you could open your borders again and play with humans and dragon shifters and whoever you want to your heart's content."

"If that was something I wanted badly enough to risk my court, I would have taken action against the Icehearts long ago."

"You're not fooling anyone." She stabs a hand toward where the crowd is still waiting in the stands on the other side of the thick blue drapes. "Your city is on the brink of rebellion. One more push, and all their restless energy will explode into civil war."

Something incredibly dangerous flickers in Orion's eyes. "Careful with that tongue, little viper."

"The only thing distracting them right now is these games. You know it as well as I do. But one wrong word from the wrong person to the wrong crowd, and this whole city will erupt. It's why you were so desperate for us to take out that Wolfstalker guy."

"Watch your—"

"Admit it. You need these borders open just as badly as we do." She spreads her arms wide in challenge. "So take this bargain. And in exchange, we will give you the distraction of a century."

"I will not risk my court for a little entertainment."

"I wasn't finished." Her expression is dead serious as she holds his gaze. "The extra game we play for your people is just the staging ground for the bargain. I've told you what we get if we win, but I haven't said what you will get if we lose."

He opens his mouth as if to refuse yet again, but there is a hint of interest in his eyes now. It sends a bolt of panic through my spine.

Yanking against the ice trapping me, I try desperately to get free. But it doesn't let up for even one second. I push my tongue up at the ice in my mouth, trying to force it to move. But that doesn't work either.

Frustrated, I consider using my new power of creating emotions on Isera. But the terrifying knowledge that I won't be able to remove it afterward stops me. I'll just have to hope that the Unseelie King keeps refusing her.

"If we lose, you won't just get to keep us from leaving the Unseelie Court," Isera says, her intense eyes burning holes through Orion as she holds his gaze. "If we lose, you can have *me*. And the Seelie Court."

His eyes widen in surprise for a fraction of a second before he composes himself again. Then he flicks a dismissive hand. "The Seelie Court isn't yours to give."

"Ah." She lets out a mocking chuckle and shakes her head at him. "You truly haven't figured it out yet, have you?"

"Figured what out?"

"Who I really am."

Confusion pulses inside me as I stare at her. Orion watches her in silence as well, his eyes slightly narrowed. Then sudden realization seems to flicker in his eyes for a moment before he manages to hide it.

"The Seelie Queen was publicly executed by the Icehearts at the end of the war," Orion says. "And both of her daughters had died fighting in the battles before that."

"But . . . ?" Isera prompts.

My heart starts pounding in my chest. She can't possibly mean . . . ?

"But," Orion begins slowly, "there were always rumors that the Seelie Queen's second daughter survived, because her body was never recovered."

"The rumors were true."

Shock and disbelief thrum inside my chest like a violent storm. It's not possible. It can't be. Is she actually—

"I am a descendant of the Seelie Queen's second daughter." A knowing smile curls Isera's lips. "And because of the selective breeding system of only one child that was imposed on our court, I am the *only* currently living descendant." She lets out another slightly mocking chuckle and raises her eyebrows at Orion. "Which means that the Seelie Court is in fact mine to give."

I gape at her. Or I would, if my mouth weren't full of ice. My mind spins and my heart slams against my ribs as I stare at Isera.

But it makes sense.

The names of the Seelie Queen and her family have been erased from our history books by the Icehearts, so it's impossible to tell by her last name. And even if the names hadn't been erased, the daughter who survived would no doubt have changed her name to escape notice. But it's more than that.

The Seelie Queen's second daughter was said to have an incredibly rare type of magic that made the Icehearts hunt her relentlessly.

Isera has ice magic, for Mabona's sake! It's one of the rarest types of magic there is. And it's also *their* element. Bane and Jessina's clan magic. I still remember the fury on their faces when Isera shot that block of ice that slid onto their platform during that very first power demonstration during the Atonement Trials. If there was ever any kind of magic that would make them hunt the fae wielding it to the ends of the world, it's ice magic.

My head rings as I stare at Isera with wide eyes.

She is a descendant of the Seelie Queen. All this time, the bloodline has remained intact. Our royal family lives.

"It might be yours by blood," Orion says, now watching Isera with new eyes. "But you do not rule it. Your promise of surrendering the Seelie Court to me will only be possible if you actually manage to take down the Iceheart Dynasty. And that promise only comes into effect if you lose the bargain, which means that you won't have my help to do it. I might not even allow you to leave if you lose."

"And if that happens, you will have lost nothing," Isera presses. "If we can't take down the Icehearts on our own, you lose nothing. But if we can . . ."

She starts toward him. He watches her intently but remains standing there with his chin tilted in a slightly cocky manner. I yank against the ice again, but it keeps me mercilessly trapped. Outside the thick drapes, the murmur of the crowd has started to become restless as they wait for the victory presentation that still hasn't begun.

Surprise pulses across Orion's features as Isera drops to her knees right in front of him. Her face is only inches away from his crotch as she tilts her head back and looks up at him. A jolt shoots through him as she slides her hands up his thighs before gripping his hips.

Her eyes sear into his as she at last finishes with, "Then you get to have me on my knees, sucking your cock, while you rule my court for all eternity."

Desire flares up in his eyes like flames. It's a deep, insatiable hunger that threatens to set the whole room aflame. He wants this. He wants *her*. And the Seelie Court. Badly.

I try to scream, but only a garbled mumbling makes it through the ice. This is insane. He can't be considering this. Please, Mabona, he can't agree to this. We need to leave. We need to get the hell out of this court while we have the chance and try to find the dryads instead. Because based on how Orion manipulated this last game, there is no way in hell we're going to be able to win another one.

That terrible craving burns in Orion's eyes as he slides his hand over Isera's neck, wrapping it around her throat. "Oh, there is almost nothing I wouldn't do in order to have you submit to me utterly and completely, little viper."

My heart pounds against my ribs and I struggle hard against the ice.

Tension crackles between the pale stone walls as the two of them hold each other's gaze.

Then Orion lets his hand drop from her throat. "But unfortunately, risking my court is one of them." He straightens and takes a step back. "The answer is no."

Isera, still on her knees, clenches her jaw and flexes her hand in frustration. But she says nothing as she gets to her feet.

"Let's get this victory presentation over with," Orion declares. With a glance at Isera, he nods in my direction. "You might want to ungag your friend for this part."

Without even looking at me, she flicks her wrist again.

The ice evaporates.

I suck in a deep breath as the thick ice finally disappears from my mouth. Running my tongue along my teeth, I work my jaw to ease the strain in the muscles. Then I shift my gaze to Isera, glaring daggers at her. In fact, I have to suppress a sudden urge to stab her. When we get back to the faction house, she and I are going to have words about this.

Warm sunlight hits my face as Isera and I follow Orion out onto the platform. The crowd cheers when we become visible, but it turns into a slightly confused murmur when they notice that the rest of our team is missing. The heat inside the arena, with the bright blue sky and high sun above and the thousands of people packed into the stands around us, is so intense after the long minutes in the shade inside that I have to take a moment to steady myself again.

Isera, however, doesn't appear to need it. Instead, she strides right up to the edge of the platform where the Unseelie King is about to start speaking. I hurry after her.

"Good news, ladies and gentlemen!" Isera calls across the sea of waiting spectators before Orion can get so much as a word out. "Instead of a boring victory presentation, your generous king has decided to give you what you truly want. Another game with us against your two favorite factions!"

Orion and I whip around to stare at her.

The crowd goes wild.

Because they fucking love Isera. After the insane displays of power and skill and utter ruthlessness she has given them during these last two games, she has shot to the top of their favorite players.

Deafening screams of excitement explode across the whole arena as the audience surges up from their seats to leap up and down and pump their fists in the air at this unexpected news.

I just stare at them in stunned surprise, feeling my heart sink in my chest.

Next to me, Isera smirks and gives Orion a smug sideways glance. "Good luck trying to take that back without starting a civil war."

Fury flashes like lightning strikes in Orion's eyes. Gritting his teeth, he clenches his jaw and forces out a breath through his nose. Then he flicks a glance out at the crowd.

Black, white, and red banners are waving in the air, filling the arena with snapping fabric. People are cheering and jumping and screaming in excitement.

It seems to dawn on Orion at the same time it dawns on me.

Isera has fully and completely outmaneuvered him.

His entire court is so restless that they're crawling up the walls, and the only thing stopping them from turning on Orion in sheer frustration is the distraction that these games give them. The crowd loves Isera. They crave watching her fight again. So now, if Orion tries to refute what Isera just said and deny his people another game, it will surely spark violent riots.

Turning his head slowly, Orion locks eyes with Isera. He is furious. But also *impressed*. It's etched into every line of his face as he stares at her.

To be honest, if I weren't so angry, I would be too.

Because I realize that this has been Isera's plan all along. *This* is why she entertained the crowd so much during the games. Why she threw the ice spear at Orion. Why she blew him a kiss. Why she gave the crowd exactly what they wanted. She has been planning this move from the very beginning. Backup plans behind backup plans to make sure she got what she wanted.

Isera has managed to beat the Unseelie King at his own game.

And he knows it.

Dragging in a long breath between his teeth, he holds her smug stare in silence.

"So, about that bargain, then," Isera prompts, a wicked smirk sliding home on her lips. "Do we have a deal?"

And it seems to be dragged kicking and screaming from the very depths of the Unseelie King's dark soul as he grinds out one single word.

"Yes."

36

Draven leaps to his feet, instantly alert when I storm through the front door and into the combined kitchen and living room back at the faction house. Galen is lying on the couch beside him, his hands and leg now looking completely healed. Lyra is on the other couch, also lying down but looking much more alert than before. Exhaustion clings to their bodies though.

But they both sit bolt upright when Draven shoots to his feet. Alistair, who was about to hand Lyra a cup of tea, has to yank his hand back to stop Lyra from knocking it over in her haste. Tea sloshes over the rim of the cup to pool in the delicate saucer beneath. With his eyebrows drawn down in a scowl, Alistair looks up from the teacup to meet my gaze. Jocasta is nowhere to be seen.

"What's wrong?" Draven demands as I stalk into the living room.

Isera strolls in behind me, completely unfazed by my anger.

"What's wrong?" I echo. It comes out like a growl. Slamming to a halt on the floor, I spin around and stab a hand at Isera. "She just bargained away our freedom!"

"What?" Alistair snaps.

Panic and rage crackle through the light and airy room as he whips his gaze to Isera while both Galen and Lyra scramble to their feet. The teacup leaps and then rattles in fear as Alistair slams it down on the low table by the couch so hard that it almost shatters.

"You did *what?*" he demands.

Coming to a halt as well, Isera simply crosses her arms and meets everyone's shocked and angry stares with a cool expression on her features. "I did what needed to be done."

"And what is that exactly?" Draven asks. His voice is dark, an undercurrent of threats in his tone.

They all stare between me and Isera in shock and disbelief and anger as I explain the bargain she made with the Unseelie King.

"I'm going to fucking kill you!" Alistair yells. But he sounds more desperate and panicked rather than angry. His chest heaves as he swings his arm around and stabs it in the general direction of the wards. "We were out! We could finally leave. And you . . . you—"

"We were never going to win," Isera snaps back, her calm facade at last shattering. "We need the Unseelie Court if we're going to even stand a chance against the entire fucking Iceheart Dynasty."

"We agreed to—" I begin, but she cuts me off.

"I don't care. This was my decision, and I made it."

"But it was not your decision to make!" The words tear from my chest so violently that I have to suck in a deep breath to refill my lungs. Anger and frustration course through me as I stare at her while raking both hands through my hair. "Fuck. After Lavendera, I thought I was done getting double-crossed by people I thought were my friends."

"I am not your friend," she growls back at me. "I don't have any friends. I don't have anyone. No parents. No partner. No friends. No one I love and no one who loves me." She stabs her hand at us all. "And that is why I am the only person in this whole dysfunctional fucking group who can make the tactical decisions we need without letting emotions get in the way."

"It has nothing to do with emotions! It has to do with trust. And common fucking sense! There is no way in hell we'll be able to win whatever twisted game Orion comes up with for us."

"That's just a risk we're going to have to take. We *need* the Unseelie Court."

"We also *need* our freedom."

"Freedom is worthless without revenge. Or have you forgotten what they did to us in there?"

"Of course I haven't. But you didn't even give us a choice this time. You chose for us!"

"Because it's the right choice!"

"For *you*! What about—"

"You don't understand!" she screams the words at me. At us all. So shockingly loud that the windows rattle.

Her chest heaves, and her eyes are wild and desperate and so out of control that I actually stagger a step back. I have never seen her this unhinged before.

And then something inside her seems to just *crack*.

Pain floods her face. Pain and heartbreak and guilt so deep it could drown the world.

"You don't understand," she repeats, her voice breaking on that last word. "I hated her." She draws in a shuddering breath, her eyes desolate as she looks back at us. "I spent a hundred and fifty years hating her."

It takes a moment for my brain to catch up with this change in topic. Her? Who?

Then it clicks.

Oh. Elena Shaw. Her mother. She won the last Atonement Trials a hundred and fifty years ago, and before she left, she told a ten-year-old Isera that she was coming back for her. But, of course, she never did.

"And while I was hating her, she was *there*!" Isera stabs her hand toward the wall where somewhere far beyond, the Ice Palace sits on the roots of the mountain above the city of Frostfell. "Suffering. Being drained of magic and tortured and humiliated. And she was thinking about me!"

Her voice breaks again, and she sucks in another unsteady breath. Her blue-and-silver eyes are storms of emotion as she stares desperately at us all.

"And what did I do?" Pain pulses in her eyes. "While she was being tortured and humiliated and while she was thinking about me, what did I do? I was wishing her misfortune! Once I realized that she wasn't coming back, I spent a hundred and forty-three years praying every day that her life was fucking awful."

A sob rips from her chest. Then her knees buckle, and she crashes down on the ground. Bracing one hand on the smooth wooden floor for support, she presses the other over her mouth as more sobs tear from her throat.

"All this time, I hated her for abandoning me." Tears stream down her face. "But she didn't. She was trapped there, being tortured and humiliated, and suffering. And I hated her." She chokes out the words. "She died with me hating her."

For a few seconds, we all just stand there as if frozen in time, staring at her in shock.

My heart beats hard against my ribs. This is why she was catatonic those first few weeks in the Ice Palace. Not because we were prisoners or because of what the Icehearts were doing to her. But because she realized what had really happened to her mother.

Pain tightens around my chest, and I take a hesitant step toward her. "Isera—"

"No," she snaps, cutting me off.

Her eyes flash with fury again as she forcefully wipes the tears off her cheeks and struggles to her feet. That fury crackles across her whole face like ice until she once more looks like a goddess of death who has clawed her way out of hell to rain death and destruction down on whoever is unfortunate enough to cross her path.

"I don't want your sympathy," she says, her voice a soft snarl. "I don't care if you understand. All I want is to paint the fucking walls with Bane's and Jessina's blood. I am going to shatter that whole fucking ice castle if it's the last thing I do. And for that, I need Nightbane and his Unseelie Court."

We all just stare at her in silence, unsure of what to say.

"So I don't care if you hate me." Her eyes are cold and hard as she looks from face to face. "Because all I have left is hatred anyway. I hate the Icehearts more than I care about you. I hate them more than I care about my own life. So I will cling to that hatred. Because without the hate, I will drown in an ocean of guilt that is so deep that I will never be able to claw my way back out again." She forces out a long breath, her spine straight and her chin held high. "So I did what needed to be done."

The silence that falls over the beautiful living room is so loud that it's practically vibrating between the pale stone walls. Somewhere outside the windows, life goes on in the Unseelie Court. People are chatting, laughing, and strolling along the glittering canals. As if none of this is happening.

I swallow, trying to think of something to say. It appears as though everyone else is doing the same.

To my surprise, the one who at last replies is Draven.

"She's right."

Blinking, we all spin around to face him. Even Isera looks shocked for a second.

He heaves a long breath and drags a hand through his messy black hair. "Hate trumps everything. Pain, despair, heartbreak—it consumes it all. Gives you a purpose. Something to focus on." His eyes slide to me. "It's what I did to you when you first woke up in the Ice Palace with the collar. I tried to make you hate me so that you would focus on that instead of drowning in despair."

My mouth drops open a little, but no sound makes it out. Because I suddenly see the truth in it. Focusing on how angry I was with him helped keep the hopelessness at bay.

A few steps away, Isera is staring at Draven, looking taken aback by the fact that he understands her feelings so well. Or that he is backing her up. Or both.

"She's also right about the other thing," Draven continues. "We will need the Unseelie Court if we're going to have a chance to beat Bane and Jessina. I don't approve of the fact that she went behind our backs to make the deal." He cuts Isera a hard look. "But the deal is done. Now, we just need to make sure we win."

His words send a ripple through the room, and within a matter of seconds, the vibrating tension starts dissipating again. Everyone draws in a deep breath. Both Galen and Lyra nod. Alistair scowls but bends down to pick up the teacup for Lyra again.

I watch it all, completely fascinated. With a few words and a confident tone, Draven can make people accept their new reality and start thinking about how to solve the problems instead of arguing. No wonder he did well as the Commander of the Dread Legion.

Letting out a long sigh, I try to let go of my anger and do the same. To focus on the problem at hand. Because Draven is right. The deal is done. Now we just need to focus on figuring out how the hell we're going to win this.

37

Stars glitter in the dark blue heavens above me. Dangling my legs over the edge of the roof, I lean back on my palms and gaze up at the beautiful night sky. Warm winds ripple over the flat rooftop, making my long silver hair flutter. Even though I'm only wearing a short black nightgown and a thin silk robe, I'm not cold. We're starting to get close to the end of spring now, and within the Unseelie Court's wards, the temperature is even warmer.

I let out a sigh. Tilting my head back down, I stare out across the red tiled rooftops of the vast city around me. A strange sense of guilt twists in my stomach.

Draven and all my friends are trapped in this court because they had to come here in order to save my life. That is the sole reason we went to the Unseelie Court. To save me. And since then, we have been thrown into one dangerous situation after another. Been betrayed and tricked and deceived. Gotten tortured and suffered injuries in battle.

And despite all of that, I am actually *glad* that we came here.

Because of it, I managed to find an experienced emotion magic user who could actually teach me about my powers. With Jocasta's training, I'm stronger and more powerful than ever. I have also learned that my relationship with my parents might not be what I thought it was.

If we had never come here, I would have gone the rest of my life thinking that my parents genuinely hated me simply because of who I am. But now, there is hope.

And even though I'm still pissed at Isera for gagging me and trapping me in ice, we now also have a real chance at forcing the Unseelie Court to help us take down the Iceheart Dynasty.

Coming here, to this beautiful and dangerous court, has been more important than I could ever have imagined.

Guilt twists inside me again, and I tug self-consciously at the hem of my silk robe. Everyone I care about is in danger, and we might never even make it out of this court at all, but I'm still glad we came? The memory of that burning pit of rage and hatred deep inside me, the one that I barely dare look inside, flits through my mind again. And a sudden chill rolls down my spine. Goddess above, maybe, deep down, I really am a horrible person after all.

A dark shadow shoots up through the air right in front of me.

I yelp, almost toppling backward before I manage to brace myself on the flat roof behind me. Sitting up properly again, I shoot the shadow a mock glare and huff, "Show-off."

Draven smirks at me. His massive black wings beat the air with a rhythmic thumping as he hovers there in front of me for another few seconds before he flies over to the edge and sits down next to me.

I scoot over, making room for his muscular body so that he doesn't have to sit halfway over the edge. His wings rustle as he folds them in a little more and then shifts his weight until he's sitting comfortably. I keep my gaze on the starlit night before us while trying to push all those uncomfortable feelings from before back behind the mental walls where they belong.

Draven gives me a sidelong glance. "I thought I had exclusive rights to staring broodingly at the horizon."

A surprised laugh erupts from my chest. The last of those uncomfortable emotions evaporate from my mind like mist before a strong morning sun as a smile instead spreads across my mouth. Turning my head, I give Draven a knowing look.

"Well, you do excel at it," I admit.

"I know. I've spent a lot of time practicing."

I chuckle again and shake my head while jabbing an elbow at his ribs. Even though he's only wearing a black dress shirt and a pair of black pants rather than his dragon scale armor, my little jab doesn't even make him wince. I bet I even felt it more in my elbow than he did. The man is a marvel of rock-solid muscle.

"Are you thinking about your parents?" Draven asks, his voice now serious and his eyes softer.

Clearing my throat, I slide my gaze back to the rooftops before us. "Yes."

It's mostly true, anyway. I *was* thinking about them. Just not only about them. That rage and hatred inside me worries me. All my life, I have suppressed all my fury at how people have been treating me. I've only ever shown them positive emotions so that they will accept me and like me. But ever since I met Draven, I've started to actually express my real emotions instead of just stuffing them all into that pit inside me and slamming the lid closed on top of it. And that has started to make things . . . leak out.

But I don't want to tell Draven that. *Hey, ever since I met you, an overwhelming pit of rage and hatred has started to bubble up inside me* isn't exactly a compliment. And I don't want him to misunderstand. So for now, I just give Draven a small smile and let him think that this is only about my parents.

Once all the craziness of the past few days had settled, I told him about how I can now create emotions and how they're permanent and my suspicions about my parents. I left out the part about how using that power makes me crave it again like an addict, though. It's another thing that I don't know how to explain without sounding like a psycho. And I also don't want him to worry.

"Want to talk about it?" he asks, still studying me.

I shake my head. "No. It's only speculation, anyway. I will never know for certain until I go back there and check with my magic. And right now we're kind of busy with other things."

"Like trying to outmaneuver the slippery little snake called Orion Nightbane before he can deceive us again, and then win a war against the entire Iceheart Dynasty and all seven other dragon clans and all the human towns that they have conquered as well."

"Like that."

"Piece of cake."

"Right?"

We both chuckle.

Comfortable silence falls over us as we just gaze up at the glittering stars for a while. Draven drapes his arm around my shoulders, holding me close to him. His solid body against mine helps ground me in the present again and forget all the worries we still have to face.

"You couldn't sleep either?" I ask after a while.

A sad smile blows across his lips for a moment. "No."

I say nothing. If he wants to tell me, he will. But I know that he's not used to sharing things with others, especially after two hundred years of not being physically able to do just that, so I don't want to push him.

Stars glitter like silver dust in the canals that run through the city below us, and the soft rumble of the waterfalls in the distance fills the warm night air as Draven and I sit there in silence for another couple of minutes.

Then he at last heaves a long sigh and rakes a hand through his hair. "I don't know who I am." He hesitates for another few seconds before adding, "Now."

I turn to look at him but still say nothing.

He normally always looks calm and in control. The perfect image of command and utter authority. But now there is an uncharacteristically uncertain expression on his features as he stares out at the vast night sky.

"I just . . ." He lets out a small frustrated breath, as if it's hard to find the right words to explain. "I was someone. Back then. Before Bane and Jessina put the dragon steel inside me. But then I spent two hundred years without free will." Slipping his arm off my shoulder, he rakes both hands through his hair before turning to meet my gaze head-on. "I've spent two centuries either obeying commands that I physically couldn't refuse, or pretending to be a human rebel in Frostfell, or pretending to be a fae rebel in the Seelie Court. I haven't been *me*, just me without limitations, for two hundred years." His eyes are desperate as he holds my gaze. "And now, I don't know who that is anymore. I don't know who I am anymore."

My heart aches for him. Holding his gaze, I take his hand in mine. "I'm so sorry for everything you've had to endure. And that you've had to endure it alone."

He draws in a shuddering breath, and I swear I can almost feel a flicker of relief through the mate bond. As if he was worried that . . . that what? That I would think less of him because he's struggling? That I would say he was being ridiculous for feeling like this? Nothing could be further from the truth.

"Thank you," he says softly, and squeezes my hand.

I smile. "I look forward to getting to know you."

A surprised laugh escapes him. It's a wonderful sound of genuine mirth, and it breaks through the desolation in his eyes and chases away that haunted look on his face.

With light now twinkling in his eyes, he leans closer and slides his hand over my jaw. "Do you now? What if you get to know the real me and realize that I'm a domineering, territorial bastard who will kill anyone for even looking at you?"

"As opposed to the meek and mellow fop you've been up until this point, you mean?"

A dark chuckle rolls from his chest, making his warm breath caress my lips. "Oh, you haven't seen anything yet. Are you sure you can handle the real me, little rebel?"

"Oh, I think I can handle you just fine, Shadow of Death."

With his hand still gripping my jaw, he leans in and steals a possessive kiss from my lips. I moan into his mouth. The sound makes him draw in a shuddering breath. He breaks the kiss but doesn't pull back. Keeping his eyes closed, he leans his forehead against mine while drawing in another deep breath, as if breathing me in.

"You don't have to figure out everything straightaway about who you are now," I whisper against his lips, my tone serious again. "We have the rest of our lives to get to know every part, every quirk, and every corner of each other's souls."

He swallows. "What if you don't like what you find?"

A jolt shoots through me, and it takes all my willpower to keep it from showing. Because deep down, I'm terrified that *he* might not like *me* when he finds out about the hidden rage and the hatred that festers inside my soul. He has nothing to worry about. But I do.

"That's not possible," I reply, making sure that he truly hears the certainty and seriousness in my voice. "I love all parts of you." Before he can say anything, I pull back and lock eyes with him instead. "Can I show you something?"

He blinks, looking a little disoriented by the sudden change for a moment, but then nods. "Of course."

I summon my magic. Draven doesn't flinch, doesn't show so much as a hint of trepidation, when my eyes begin to glow. And that fact sends a pang right through my heart. Goddess above, what did I ever do to deserve this man?

Reaching inside me, I pull at the massive flame of love in my chest. I can't create or even manipulate feelings of love in other people, because it's too complicated an emotion. But I can use my own.

While holding Draven's gaze, mostly to see if he wants me to stop, I do as Jocasta taught me and reach that emotion toward Draven. Two days ago, a little after my breakthrough with creating emotions, I finally figured out how to share emotions too. I haven't tried anything like this before, though.

My heart patters nervously as I attach that feeling of love to Draven's chest.

He gasps.

Eyes wide, he snaps his gaze down to his chest and presses his hand over his heart. Then his gaze darts back up to mine, his expression completely stunned. "This . . . I can . . . I can feel . . ."

"My love for you," I finish for him with a smile.

He draws in an unsteady breath, his hand still pressed against his chest. Joy and disbelief and the most heartbreaking glimmer of relief shine in his eyes. "*This* is what you feel for me?"

"That's half of it. When I share an emotion, it cuts the intensity in half so that I feel half of it and you feel the other half."

But he doesn't appear to even hear the scientific explanation of it, because his mouth drops open slightly as he just stares at me for a few seconds. Then he presses out, "Half. This is just *half* of it?"

"Yes."

He draws in one of those unsteady breaths again, almost looking like he's about to fall off the roof. Raw emotions fill his eyes as he stares at me.

Smiling, I reach up and cup his cheek. "So remember this feeling, if you ever start to doubt again."

He closes his eyes. I leave the connection between us so that he can burn the memory into his very soul and never have to doubt just how much I love him. Then once he opens his eyes again, I let the connection fade and my magic disappear back inside me again. That burning flame of love inside me once more doubles in strength as all the feelings return to me.

His wings flutter as he suddenly moves so that he's straddling my thighs, his knees on the roof on either side of me. My heart flips as his powerful body, his handsome face, his imposing wings, his entire essence, blocks out the rest of the world until all I see is him. He slides his hands along my cheeks and into my hair, tilting my head back so that I meet his searing gaze.

"Azaroth's flame, Selena," he says, sounding breathless. "That was . . ."

"Very impressive, if I do say so myself," I joke, a grin on my mouth. "It's a very complex technique with an even more complex emotion, but I am quite brilliant after all, so."

He claims my lips, cutting off my teasing words with a possessive kiss. "You're a fucking goddess," he breathes against my mouth between furious kisses.

Lightning skitters across my skin, and my heart skips a beat. He drops one hand from my hair and instead braces it on the roof behind me. Leaning forward, he moves us down until my back is pressed against the warm stone. My short silk nightgown slides up almost to my hips as I lift my legs up from over the edge and instead brace my feet on the roof.

Still kissing me breathless, Draven slips one hand underneath my neck and the other underneath my back. Then he beats his wings. I gasp against his mouth as he flies us away from the edge and toward the middle of the flat roof instead.

My back hits the warm stone again as Draven lays me down gently before removing his hands. Still straddling me, he sits up straighter and locks eyes with me instead. Mischief glitters in his golden eyes.

"I've also been working on a new technique," he says. "Want me to show you?"

Anticipation ripples through my body, and a throbbing starts between my legs at the dark promises in his voice. "Yes." I rake my gaze over his powerful body. "But first, take off your shirt."

He wraps a hand underneath my jaw, holding me firmly, and leans down to steal another savage kiss. "So bossy," he murmurs against my lips.

But then he pulls back and starts unbuttoning his shirt. Pushing myself up on my elbows, I quickly slide the silk robe from my shoulders and toss it onto the roof. Then I just watch as Draven undoes the final buttons. The black shirt falls open, revealing his firm chest and sharp abs.

Fire sears through my veins, and I lick my lips.

"Fuck," Draven growls. "Do you have any idea how fucking difficult it is to keep a single thought in my head when you're looking at me like that?"

My heart flips, and I flash him a satisfied smirk. "The shirt."

His eyes burn with desire and approval as he shakes his head at me and then shifts into his fully human form. A small cloud drifts off into the night while Draven shrugs the shirt off his broad shoulders. He tosses it to the roof beside my robe.

"Your wings," I complain.

He gives me a long look, and then shifts back into a half-shift. His imposing black wings now spread out behind his half-naked body. They rustle slightly as he moves them into a better position.

Still leaning back on my elbows, I gaze up at his muscular body, drinking in the sight of the absolute perfection that is Draven Ryat.

"Azaroth's fucking flame," he groans, his voice hoarse. "What the fuck did I just tell you?"

Just to mess with him even more, I slide my tongue along my teeth as I deliberately rake my gaze down his body. A yelp slips from my lips, followed by a moan, as Draven grips my thighs firmly. Heat pulses through me as he draws his commanding hands up my thighs, pushing the short nightgown all the way up to my hips, and then curls his fingers over the top of my panties.

My skin prickles and my clit throbs as he slides my panties down my legs. Adjusting his position, he maneuvers the delicate fabric over my feet and then tosses my panties down on the roof next to my robe.

"Spread your legs for me," he orders.

The command vibrates through my bones, making my clit throb harder. I give him a sly look. "Yes, sir."

Lust flares up in his eyes like dark flames, and he flexes his hand while forcing out a long breath. "Fucking hell, little rebel."

With a satisfied chuckle, I lie down fully on my back and spread my legs as commanded. A nervous thrill courses through my body at being so exposed. But up here on the roof in the middle of the night, only the stars bear witness to our depraved cravings.

A jolt shoots through my body as Draven takes a firm grip on my hips and lifts my ass off the roof. I squirm, trying to get my balance back. Draven just drapes my legs over his shoulders. It leaves me lying on my shoulder blades with my ass in the air and my pussy right in front of his face. My nightgown slides down toward my tits, leaving me almost entirely naked.

"That's more like it," Draven muses, his voice dark and teasing.

This position leaves me entirely at his mercy. And the smug bastard knows it.

My heart pounds at the thrill of it, and my clit throbs with need.

"This is the new technique you were bragging about, huh?" I bait.

"Oh, no, we haven't gotten to that part yet." His mouth is so close to my pussy that every word sends puffs of air over my sensitive skin.

I squirm, trying to relieve the aching need that is pulsing inside me. "Then you—"

He licks my pussy.

I gasp, pleasure shooting up my spine. He lets out a smug chuckle, the sound vibrating against my clit as he takes it into his mouth. I moan and squirm desperately again. But in this position, he is in complete control of my body.

Pleasure streaks through me as Draven teases my clit with his lips and tongue before scraping his teeth lightly over the sensitive skin. Another desperate moan rips from my lungs. My hand shoots out, but I can't even reach him in this position.

Letting my arms slump back on the roof, I suck in shuddering breaths as Draven toys with my clit until I can barely see straight. Tension thrums inside me, begging to be let out. Draven slides his tongue along my pussy in a slow, luxurious stroke and then pulls back. My chest heaves, and it takes me a moment to realize that his lips are gone.

Then something *zaps* my clit.

I gasp, my eyes snapping open.

Pleasure crackles through me as my entire clit tingles with the after-effects of that zap. Lifting my head as much as I can, I stare up at Draven with wide eyes. My legs are still draped over his shoulders, but he looks up to meet my gaze. There is a wicked smirk on his lips as he holds up his right hand for me to see.

Tiny lightning bolts flicker over his fingers.

My jaw drops.

His smirk widens. "How's that for new technique?"

Only a gasp and a deep moan answers him as he zaps my clit with his lightning again. I throw my head back, rolling my hips as pleasure pulses through me. He slides his tongue along my pussy and then swirls it around my clit. A whimper drips from my lips.

He licks and sucks and works his mouth and then zaps my clit with lightning again and again until I'm writhing and panting and moaning his name. Pent-up tension crackles inside me like a storm. I gasp air into my lungs. It feels as if my mind is going to shatter.

Draven flicks my throbbing clit with his tongue before taking it into his mouth again. I can barely breathe through the pleasure as I tumble headfirst toward an orgasm. He slides his tongue around my entrance.

"Oh, God—" My words are cut off by a gasp and a pleading whimper as Draven zaps my clit with his lightning again.

"I prefer *sir*. Or *master*. But I suppose God will do."

My growled response is drowned out by another moan as he swirls his tongue around my clit with expert precision. I whimper, squirming desperately in the air. Draven tightens his grip on me as he continues his sweet torture. My entire body is trembling with pent-up release.

"Please," I beg, the word breaking on another breathy moan. "Oh, fuck, please."

He chuckles against my clit. Pulling back, he gently slides my legs off his shoulders and places them back on the ground. My chest heaves, and I just lie there on the warm rooftop, delirious with pent-up need.

On his knees between my legs, Draven smirks down at me. "You're so fucking pretty when you beg."

A desperate growl rips from my throat, and my hand shoots out to grab his belt. "If you don't start fucking me right now, I'm going to stab you."

Fire sparks in his eyes. Wrapping a firm hand around my throat, he leans down over me and claims my lips in a savage kiss before murmuring, "And even hotter when you threaten me."

While kissing him back furiously, I start blindly unbuckling his belt. My fingers fumble, but I finally manage to get it open and unbutton his pants. Shoving the fabric aside, I wrap my hand around his thick cock and then jerk up and down.

A moan rips from Draven's chest. He sucks in a sharp breath, his body trembling as I do it again.

"Fuck me," I order, smirking against his lips. "Right now."

He bites my bottom lip and slides his hand higher up my throat, locking it right underneath my jaw. I draw my hand up and down his hard cock again. Something between a moan and a growl escapes his lips.

"Next time, I'm bringing the fucking handcuffs," he threatens against my mouth.

But then he pulls back and starts quickly stripping out of his remaining clothes. I hurriedly yank the nightgown over my head and toss it aside as well. His eyes burn with desire as he gazes down at my naked body, and that look in his eyes takes my breath away.

"You're so fucking perfect," he presses out, staring at me as if the sight of my naked body still leaves him breathless every time.

Heat flushes my cheeks.

He bends down over me, and I spread my legs again as he braces his arms on the roof on either side of me while he positions his hips right over mine. His cock brushes against my entrance. I wrap my hand around the back of his neck and yank his mouth down to mine.

A moan tears from his chest. Then he thrusts into me.

I gasp against his lips as his hard cock slides into my soaking wet pussy. As always, he gives me a moment to adjust to his size before he slides out and then slams back in again. Pleasure shoots up my spine.

While still stealing the breath from my lungs and thrusting his hips hard, Draven takes one hand off the roof and slides it up the side of my ribs. My skin tingles as his fingers brush over my ribs and up toward my tits. I moan into his mouth as he rolls my nipple between his fingers.

He starts up a firm pace, thrusting into me with commanding strokes. That incredible tension starts building inside me again. I slide my fingers from his neck and up into his hair, gripping it hard. Lifting my other hand, I draw it over his wings.

His body trembles.

I smirk against his mouth and do it again.

He zaps my nipple with lightning.

Gasping, I arch up from the ground as my nipple tingles with pleasure. Draven lets out a smug chuckle that vibrates against my lips. I slam my hips up against his and bite his bottom lip. He just picks up his pace, fucking me harder.

Pleasure pulses through my body with every commanding thrust. I suck in desperate breaths as that pent-up storm of release thrums inside me. And the domineering bastard shows me no mercy. While continuing to fuck me hard, he alternates between toying with my nipple and zapping it with lightning while also kissing me completely senseless.

My body trembles with the onslaught of stimulation until my entire world narrows down to just him. His lips against mine, tasting like rain and wind and lightning. His intoxicating scent, like night mist and embers, filling my lungs. His muscular body against mine. His thick cock inside me. His commanding hands on my heated skin. I could drown in it, in him, forever. Never needing anything else.

He thrusts hard, hitting deep inside me.

Pleasure crackles through my body as release crashes through me. I gasp, my legs shaking around his hips as the intense waves of pleasure sweep through my every limb. Draven steals that gasp from my lips with a furious kiss while he continues fucking me through the orgasm, intensifying it.

My pussy tightens around his cock, my inner walls fluttering, as he pounds into me.

I draw my fingers along those extra sensitive lines on his wings where the soft membrane meets bone.

Pleasure explodes in his eyes.

A deep groan rips from his chest as release slams into him as well. As always, I memorize every sound, every expression on his perfect face, as it fills with pleasure when he comes hard as well. Because I will never get enough of that.

When the waves of pleasure have faded, he just stares down at me in amazement. As if I'm the most astonishing thing he has ever seen. The fact that he still looks at me like this, even after all these months and everything we've been through, makes my heart flip and my chest fill with sparkling warmth.

Pulling out gently, he maneuvers his powerful body to the side and then lies down on the warm rooftop next to me. I draw in a shuddering breath, lingering pleasure still skittering across my skin like tiny lightning bolts. Draven slides his arm underneath me and pulls me close.

Our chests heave, and for a while, our breathing and the low rushing from the waterfalls are the only sounds that fill the starlit night.

Draven pulls me even closer, his lethal body melding with mine. My heart flutters as he brushes a soft kiss against my temple.

"When all this is over, I swear that I'm going to give you the life you deserve," he promises, his voice solemn. "The life that you have always deserved."

My chest tightens.

"You deserve it all," he whispers against my skin.

I swallow against the sudden thickness in my throat. "So do you, Draven."

He hums and then kisses my temple again. "A promise, then. Let's get everything we've ever wanted."

A villainous smile spreads across my mouth as I lie there in Draven's arms and gaze up at the glittering heavens above. I nod, feeling his words settle deep inside me. A promise. A vow. A fucking defiant scream to this unfair world.

"Yes. Let's get fucking everything."

38

Once again, the excited roar of the crowd vibrates through the walls of the arena above us. We're standing in the same waiting room as last time, and just like during that game, the sands of the arena outside the door are completely empty. There are no structures. No weapons. No obstacles. Nothing to allude to what kind of game we will be playing for the crowd's pleasure this time.

The door opens behind us, and three people walk in from the corridor that leads deeper into the back rooms rather than the one that leads out onto the sand. We all turn toward it.

In the week since Isera pulled her stunt, we have all come to terms with it in our own way. Draven wasn't particularly angry from the beginning, so he just continued as usual. And once he had accepted it, Galen and Lyra did too. Alistair was scowling at Isera all the way up until last night, when he let out a dramatic sigh and grumbled something about how she could have at least let us know what she was going to do so that we could've helped.

To my surprise, Isera did actually apologize a few days ago. But only to me. And not for making the actual deal but rather for gagging and shackling me in ice while she did it. It was more than I was expecting to get, so I accepted it. To be honest, my irritation had already faded by then anyway. Because I know she is right.

We need the Unseelie Court in order to win this war. And we need to win this war so that Draven and I can have that future we promised each other. As long as Bane and Jessina live, they will hunt us to the ends of the world to get revenge for Draven's betrayal and the humiliation they suffered when we started a rebellion in their own city and then escaped. So we need to take them and their entire dynasty down. Which we won't be able to do without powerful allies like the Unseelie Court.

So, Isera was right, and I can't really be angry with her for it.

Deep down, there is also another reason. One that I barely dare to admit to myself. I can't be angry with how she accomplished her goal, because there is a secret part of me that wishes that *I* could be that ruthless too.

"Welcome to the special extra game," a male Unseelie fae with short silver hair says. "I'm Yster. And I believe you have already met Grey." He motions at the male fae next to him, who I recognize from somewhere.

He has shoulder-length brown hair pulled back in a ponytail, and eyes that are turquoise and yellow. It takes me a moment to realize that it's the guy who brought us into the city from the forest out by the wards. I blink, stunned. He has portal magic. So what in Mabona's name is he doing here?

"And this is Hana," Yster continues, and points toward a female fae with shoulder-length black hair.

The woman's eyes, which are vibrant shades of blue and green, study the room around her before she notices that everyone is staring at her. Then she snaps her gaze back and flashes us all an awkward but genuine smile.

"Hi," she says.

Alistair frowns at her, but I manage a small smile.

"For this extra special game, His Majesty has commissioned an extra special set," Yster says, beaming as if he is very proud on the king's behalf. "Grey here will open a portal into a pocket reality that Hana has created."

Stunned silence falls down over our group like a violent slap.

"They'll be doing what now?" Alistair at last blurts out.

"Well, we can't get you into the pocket reality without a portal. So that's why—"

"Yeah, not at all what I was asking about." There is a scowl full of suspicion on Alistair's face. "What the hell is a pocket reality?"

"It's, uhm . . ." Yster trails off, uncertain, and looks to Hana.

She is once again staring at the room around us, and she jumps a little when she notices Yster's glance. Giving her head a quick shake, she turns back to us.

"A pocket reality," she begins, her voice surprisingly gentle. "It's a temporary intrusion into a place that is separate from our reality but then pulled into our reality for a brief, or longer, moment in time, depending on the strength, while using certain measures to bend the edges around it and also—"

"No," Alistair interrupts, giving her a look that is somewhere between exasperation and disbelief. "Spell it out like I'm five."

She hesitates, her lips slightly parted as she just blinks at him for a few seconds. Then she hums hesitantly and begins glancing around. We all stare at her as she suddenly drops down to her knees and draws two circles in the sand. She points to the first one.

"Think of this as the Unseelie Court," she begins. Then she points to the other circle. "And this is some other place far away from here."

We nod. Once she has seen that we are following her explanation so far, she reaches down with both hands into the circle that represents the other place and scoops sand into her hands.

"When I create a pocket reality, I take a little bit of the place, like this." She nods toward the sand she holds in her hands. "That place still remains in the circle. Physically, at least. But I can move that reality into our reality over here." She nods to the circle representing the Unseelie Court. "So you see, the sand is physically still here. But now everything that is inside the walls of my pocket reality, which is the sand in my hands, now belongs to our reality. So no one can enter or leave this pile of sand in my hands until I release it." She lets the sand drop back down into the circle. "Then it goes back to belonging to the original realm again."

"That . . . actually makes sense," I say, somewhat surprised by that fact.

The others nod as well.

"Good," Hana says, flashing us all a bright smile.

Brushing sand off her hands, she stands up again.

"No, not good," Galen interjects before anyone else can say anything. "What does that mean? This game takes place in another reality?"

"No," she says, her tone pensive. "More like another world. Or perhaps another continent. I'm not entirely sure."

Alistair stares at her. "Is that supposed to make us feel better?"

She blinks, looking startled. Because apparently, it was.

Next to me, Draven crosses his arms and fixes Yster with a commanding stare. "We're being sent into another world for this game?"

"Yes," Yster replies with a nod. "As I said, Hana has created a pocket reality, and Grey will create a portal to take you there. I am a farseer, so I will be looking into that pocket reality and projecting it for everyone out there in the arena to see. We won't be able to hear you, unfortunately. But the crowd should probably be satisfied anyway."

My mouth drops open. A farseer can project what he sees for other people? The farseer we have in the Seelie Court, who watches for dragons atop the tower, can only, well . . . see far.

I let out an impressed breath. It's incredible what a difference it makes to have a teacher who can help you understand everything that your powers can do—something that most people have been sorely missing in the Seelie Court, since there are fewer people with magic in our city.

Yster apparently misinterprets my impressed noise, thinking it was for the no doubt brilliant combination of their three powers, and stands up a little straighter while another beaming smile spreads across his lips.

"So what's the objective?" Draven asks, his commanding stare still locked on the proud farseer.

"Oh, uhm, it's to find the portal that leads out," he replies.

"That's it?"

"Well, you need to find it before the Red Faction or the White Faction can find it. You see, as soon as one person steps through the portal that leads out, all members of that team will be instantly transported back here to the center of the arena. And the pocket reality will collapse."

Shock pulses through me, and my jaw drops. "Say that again?"

"Only one team will make it back. The other two will be left behind in the land that the pocket reality originally belongs to." Yster shrugs. "Or at least until His Majesty gives us orders to open it again and retrieve someone."

Which he will never do for us if we are one of the losing teams. Well, maybe he will open it to get Isera. But the rest of us? He will definitely leave us in there.

"Wow," Lyra says, and lets out a low whistle. "That's . . . intense."

Yster flashes us another beaming smile. "A very exciting game, don't you think?"

"Uhm," Galen says, giving him a sideways glance. "Sure."

"Well, get ready," Yster says, and claps his hands once. "All teams are starting from different locations that are roughly the same distance from the portal that leads out. And the other two teams have already gone through."

A jolt shoots through me, and I snap my gaze back to him. "What?"

"Yes, well, Grey can't open more than one portal at a time, so we had to send each team through one at a time. And since you are the crowd favorite, His Majesty suggested that it would make it even more exciting if you were the last ones in."

Of course he did. Fucking Orion.

We all exchange a glance, wondering how much of a head start the other teams have on us.

A shimmering blue rectangle begins to rise from the sand as Grey summons the portal into the pocket reality that Hana has created. I swallow down a sudden overwhelming flash of nervousness. This game has a lot higher stakes than I expected.

Above us, the excitement of the crowd rumbles like thunder. Much more understandable now that we know that the Red Faction and the White Faction have already started playing.

The rectangle at last stops moving, forming a doorway. Through it, a forest is visible.

"What world does the pocket reality belong to?" I ask, licking my lips nervously.

Hana starts in surprise, once again pulling her attention away from the room and back to us. "Oh, uhm, I'm not sure. I opened it by accident just last week."

I give her an incredulous stare.

Fantastic.

We step through the portal.

39

What meets us on the other side is like nothing I have ever seen. In terms of sheer strangeness, the forest before us is on par with that magical underground forest where the dryads live. I blink, turning my head from side to side.

There is not a single straight tree trunk as far as the eye can see. It looks as if someone has taken every branch and every tree trunk and then twisted them around, making them look like spirals that stick out in all different directions. Green leaves rustle in the canopy above, but most of the twisting branches are also covered in dark purple moss that hangs down like curtains that ripple in the gentle wind. The hanging moss paints the woods with splashes of color. In fact, everywhere I look, bright colors light up the forest.

Pink flowers dot the fresh green grass that covers the forest floor, and bright yellow lichen covers every stone and boulder. There are even a few pale blue mushrooms growing on the gnarled tree trunks.

I stare at the colorful vista.

It's like standing in the middle of a rainbow.

"Wow," Lyra says. "This is pretty cool."

I nod. "It's stunning."

Alistair draws his eyebrows down. "I hate forests."

The portal behind us drops back into the ground, sealing us in. I glance down at the grass where it used to be while a sudden sense of dread slithers through my stomach. I have a bad feeling about this.

"Ah, cheer up." Lyra jabs her elbow into Alistair's ribs. "We just need to find the other portal, and then we'll be back on that dry and barren sand you prefer."

He levels a flat look at her, but it's incredibly obvious that he's fighting a smile too.

"And we need to find it fast," Draven picks up. "Especially since the other teams have a head start. So listen up."

"And there you go, giving orders again, bossy pants," Alistair notes.

Draven fixes Alistair with a commanding stare until the snarky fire wielder raises his hands in mock surrender. With an exasperated sigh, Draven turns back to us.

"You heard Yster," he begins. "As soon as one person steps through the portal, the entire team is immediately transported back."

"Which means that we should split up to cover more ground," I finish for him.

He nods. "Exactly."

"Unless we're attacked by the other teams," Galen adds. "Then we'll be picked off easily if we're alone."

Leaves rustle above us as a warm wind sweeps through the strange forest while we consider his words in silence. He has a point. After the last game, both the Red Faction and the White Faction seem to have developed a grudge against us. I'm pretty sure that's a big part of why they agreed to play this high-stakes extra game. Not just to win back the crowd's favor but also to get revenge against us.

"Good point," Draven agrees. Crossing his arms, he considers in silence for another few seconds. Then he turns to Galen. "In pairs, then. You go with Isera. Lyra, you're with Alistair." He turns to me. "And Selena, you're with me."

We all nod in confirmation.

"Don't waste any time or effort doing things to entertain the crowd," Draven continues. "We just need to finish as fast as possible, and we're already behind." A sly smile tugs on his lips. "But fortunately, we have an advantage against the other teams this time."

A small cloud of smoke explodes in the air and then drifts away on the breeze as Draven performs a half-shift. His massive black wings rustle as he spreads them wide.

Lyra chuckles and rubs her hands excitedly while Galen smirks knowingly.

Draven jerks his chin at me. "All right, let's get going."

Lurching into motion, I run my hands down my black fighting leathers and check that my dagger is secure in my thigh holster. Then I quickly step over to Draven. He bends down and slides one arm behind my back and the other behind my knees. My pulse flutters as he lifts me into his arms.

His eyes are serious as he looks between Galen and Lyra. "Be careful."

Then he shoots into the sky.

My stomach lurches, and I wrap my arms tightly around his neck while squeezing my eyes shut. Winds rush in my ears, and my hair flutters behind me. Then the rapid ascent stops and Draven comes to a halt, hovering in the air. His massive wings create thumping sounds as they beat steadily.

Drawing in a deep breath, I pry my eyes open again and level a stern look at him.

"Bastard," I huff. "You really are doing that on purpose, aren't you?"

He just smirks at me, the wicked glint in his eyes answer enough.

With another half-amused, half-exasperated sigh, I shake my head at him and then turn to look at our surroundings.

The forest we've been dropped in is vast, but not all of it is accessible to us. Our playing field is limited to Hana's pocket reality, which takes the shape of a dome. Walls rise up from the ground and slope inward to meet in the center up in the sky. The walls look like some kind of thick liquid moving against glass. It's similar to the wards around the Unseelie Court, but these are less transparent. They distort the landscape outside the walls, letting us see only the general shape of what's out there. But what I see still takes my breath away.

Beyond the forest is a large city and a magnificent castle. Arches and twisting spires reach for the heavens, and the entire palace appears to be made of some kind of pale reflective stone. Even through the thick walls of Hana's pocket reality, the massive castle shines when the sun hits it, as if the building itself is radiating sunlight.

The sight of it shocks me. Because the effect is eerily similar to both our Golden Palace in the Seelie Court, which glows golden in the sun, and Orion's castle in the Unseelie Court, which glows silver in the light. This palace shines more like a never-setting sun rather than a precious metal like gold or silver, but still, the similarities are unnerving.

I stare from the castle to the city that spreads out before it while my heart pounds in my chest. Are there fae living here? Are there more of our people living here on this other world or other continent or wherever the hell we are?

"We're at the edge of the pocket reality," Draven says.

His voice snaps me out of my stunned thoughts, and I give my head a quick shake to clear it and to refocus on the problem at hand: finding the only portal out before the Unseelie King traps us in here.

"And Yster said that all teams were dropped at a similar distance from the portal," he continues. "Which means that the portal should be located somewhere in the middle of the pocket reality."

Glancing behind us, I find that there is indeed a thick half-translucent wall rising up from the forest a short distance behind us. I shift my gaze back to Draven's face. "Yes. It's probably hidden underneath a thick canopy, though. Since Orion knows that you can fly."

"True." He clenches his jaw in annoyance. "Well, let's see what we can find when—"

Magic shoots toward us.

And arrows.

Draven drops down through the air right before a lightning bolt and a hail of arrows speed past right in the space we used to occupy. I gasp, tightening my arms around his neck at the sudden drop.

A blast of water slams toward us. Draven jerks us sideways, but right as we move, another storm of arrows shoots through the air. He snaps his wings in to protect them.

My stomach lurches as we plummet downward at an incredible speed.

Fire crackles through the air as a torrent of flames streams toward us. It's followed almost immediately by another massive bolt of lightning. And then another swarm of arrows.

Draven summons his storm magic and narrowly manages to push the torrent of fire aside with a blast of wind while he flares his wings again. Our rapid descent comes to a halt as he steadies us in the air for a second. But more magic and more arrows are already speeding toward us, so he tucks his wings in again and drops us down through the canopy.

We land hard on the grass, the jolt pulsing through his whole body. But his eyes are locked on me, scanning my body for injuries.

"I'm fine," I assure him.

Footsteps thud against the ground behind us. Draven quickly sets me down on the grass, and we whirl to face our attackers.

Relief crashes into me when we instead find Isera, Galen, Alistair, and Lyra sprinting through the trees toward us.

"What happened?" Galen demands, his eyes wide as he flicks worried glances between us and the sky above.

"We were attacked," Draven replies.

"Yeah, we could obviously see that too," Alistair points out as the four of them come to a halt before us. "But by who? The other teams shouldn't be this close."

"Or have magic that strong," Isera adds, her cool eyes sharp as she scans the forest.

"Or have bows and arrows," Lyra finishes.

Galen shifts his gaze back to Draven. "Did Orion set us up?"

Draven considers the question in silence for a few seconds, storms brewing in his eyes. But all he says is, "Not sure."

My heart is still pounding fast after the sudden attack, so I draw in a deep breath to compose myself and then summon my magic. If Orion dropped the other teams close to us from the very start, and also gave them bows and arrows to use against us, I should be able to feel their excitement.

I throw my magic across the forest around us, looking for those glittering silver sparks of excitement.

It connects with eleven people. Six of them are moving in a cluster somewhere far across the forest straight ahead, and the other five, also moving together in a group, are somewhere to our left. Neither direction matches where the attacks came from.

Frowning, I keep my magic searching for another few seconds before I let it fade out again. If neither team is in a position to attack us, then who in Mabona's name just shot at us?

"The other teams are not close by," I say, silencing the confused discussion around me.

My friends all turn to me.

"Then who the hell was shooting at you?" Alistair asks, echoing my own thoughts.

Calling up my magic again, I once more throw it across the forest. But this time, I'm searching for yellow-green sparks of suspicion.

A jolt shoots through me, and I swallow as I look from face to face.

"Not sure. But they're heading straight toward us."

40

"Shit," Galen curses. But his violet eyes are steady as he turns to Draven. "Fight or run?"

"We're already behind," Draven replies, clenching his jaw in frustration. "We can't afford to get bogged down by a fight."

"So we run, then?"

"They're coming from that direction," I interject, and nod at the path toward the center of the dome. My heart slams against my ribs as I add, "Fast."

The others snap their gazes between the direction I nodded and the area behind us, where the curving walls of the dome rise up from the ground and block any escape on all three other sides.

Draven lets out a low growl of annoyance and then jerks his chin. "Then run. Fast."

We sprint forward.

Panic pulses inside me as we dart between the gnarled tree trunks, heading right toward our mysterious attackers. We need to make it past the cutoff point so that we can turn left before they reach us. But they're moving fast. Incredibly fast.

"They're coming," I press out as we hurtle between the trees.

Dark purple moss sways around us as we shove the rippling curtains aside in our mad dash. I leap over a stone covered in yellow lichen and then duck under another tree. The group of attackers closes in rapidly.

"Hurry," I plead.

Our boots thud against the grass, flattening delicate pink flowers and leaving a trail behind. Alarm shoots through me when I realize that. But we need to make it past the bend in the walls. Otherwise we'll be trapped between them and our attackers. But if they can see our footprints in the grass, they'll be able to keep hunting us.

"Isera," I gasp out between rapid breaths as we sprint through the trees. "Our footprints."

She snaps her gaze between me and the ground, realization sparking in her eyes. I catch her eyes beginning to glow for a second before she turns her head back toward the woods ahead. Then ice springs to life before her feet.

Lyra yelps, stumbling slightly, as she almost trips over the circular patch of ice that now hovers right above the grass. But she recovers quickly and jumps up onto it after Isera. Another patch forms ahead. And then another. And another. We all leap onto them, running in a line along the patches of ice. Isera creates new ones in front of her while letting the last ones disappear as soon as the final person has left them.

I keep my magic connected to the group of people up ahead. They're closing the distance faster than I thought possible.

"They're coming," I hiss again.

We pick up speed, sprinting so fast that the woods blur around us. My pulse thrums in my ears.

The group draws closer.

I suck air into my lungs.

We just need to make it past this point up ahead. Then the wall evens out, curving away wider in both directions.

Just a little more.

Alarm shoots up my spine.

"They're here!" I gasp.

The group is crashing through the trees straight to our right.

"In here," Draven snaps.

I don't even have time to turn my head before a storm wind slams into me from the side. My breath is knocked right out of my lungs as I fly through the air and slam into a tree trunk. Gasping, I try to get my breath back. But any air is knocked right back out again when Alistair crashes into me. Followed by Galen.

Blinking, I try to clear the ringing from my skull and figure out what the hell just happened.

"Stay down," Draven orders, his voice low but pulsing with command.

I stop moving.

Five of us are lying in a pile, our limbs all tangled up, blinking and looking dazed. Everyone except Draven, who orchestrated this move. He's on his feet, yanking a long curtain of that dark purple moss closed in front of us. The patches of ice are gone as well.

Gloomy darkness falls over our group.

Drawing in a soft breath, I glance around me. A twisted and gnarly tree envelops our messy pile. Branches stick out on both sides, and the thick curtains of moss hide us almost entirely from view in here.

Still on his feet, Draven summons his magic and fills the cramped space with dark clouds as well.

A moment later, a group bursts through the trees outside.

My heart leaps into my throat.

Lying there on the ground with Alistair half on top of me, I stare out between the small gaps in the hanging moss as nine people run out of the woods.

And my mind can barely comprehend what I'm seeing.

They look like us. Like fae. But at the same time . . . *more*.

Just like us, they have an ethereal beauty to their features. But these people look as if they have been sculpted by the goddess Mabona herself. Tall and muscular, they somehow manage to look both powerful and graceful at the same time. And based on their height compared to the trees around them, they look to be at least half a head taller than even Draven. And not just one or two of them. *All* of them.

Light glints against their polished bronze breastplates, and long pointed ears stick up from their shining hair that flutters behind them when they run. Arrows rattle in the quivers they carry, and eight of them are holding powerful bows. The ninth person, a severe-looking male who is running at the head of the squad, carries no bow. But lightning crackles along one of his arms, and fire burns along the other.

I gape at them.

What kind of beings are these people?

They thunder past, their boots thudding against the ground as they rush through the trees and toward the location where we landed earlier.

For a few seconds, all six of us just stare after them in shocked silence.

"Fuck," Alistair says at last.

A rather apt summary indeed, so I nod. "Yeah."

That seems to snap us all out of our stupor. Sucking in a breath, we start to detangle our limbs and push up from the ground.

Isera cuts Draven a look as she straightens and brushes blades of grass from her fighting leathers. "A little heads-up next time, Ryat."

He arches an eyebrow back at her. "Like you gave us with the ice path?"

For a moment, she just looks back at him with those cool eyes of hers. Then she lets out a huff, and I swear she almost smiles.

He smirks, looking satisfied with his win, before shoving the hanging moss aside and jerking his chin. "Come on. We need to put as much distance between them and us as possible before they figure out that we're not there."

"I'm creating some patches of ice now," Isera says in an overly explanatory tone while giving Draven a pointed look.

I chuckle, shaking my head at them, while Draven just rolls his eyes.

Circular ice patches appear outside the sheets of hanging moss, forming a pathway out. Isera jumps up on the first one, and the rest of us scramble to follow her.

We run across the ice until we've cleared the immediate area and disappeared farther into the woods. Then Isera lets her magic fade out, and we continue jogging across the soft grass.

My heart still pounds and my head spins with questions about those beings we just saw. They must be the native population of these lands, and they were probably caught inside the barrier when Hana created the pocket reality. No wonder they're so aggressive. They probably think *we* did it.

To calm the worried storm inside me, I throw my magic out again in search of those sparks of suspicion. They're still heading in the other direction. I breathe a small sigh of relief. Then I disconnect my magic and throw it out in search of sparks of excitement, just in case.

I suck in a sharp breath as my magic connects with five people heading toward us from the left.

"Another team is coming," I snap.

Galen curses under his breath and casts a sharp look over his shoulder. "We can't fight them here without those strange fae in bronze armor noticing it."

"Agreed," Draven grinds out. He shifts his gaze to me. "Selena, which direction and how far?"

"They're coming from the left. Based on the speed they're moving, they'll be here in less than two minutes."

"Fuck." But his breathing is even as he continues running while casting a glance at the rest of us. "We need to push ahead. Fast. Better to have them behind us than next to us, because that will at least put them between us and that group of natives."

We nod, still zigzagging through the mass of twisted trees.

"Aye, aye, captain," Alistair says.

Draven cuts him a look, but then just returns his gaze to the forest ahead and says, "Run."

My heart leaps, and I pick up speed. Pushing ourselves hard, we sprint through the woods so fast that I barely have time to check where I place my feet. I leap over a twisted root, almost slamming into a tree at the hard landing. The dark purple moss sways as I stagger into it. Shoving it aside, I keep running.

Our pounding feet and rapid breaths echo around me as we hurtle through the forest.

The other faction is getting closer, picking up speed as well.

Goddess damn it, we need to lose them. Or shove them into the path of the natives. Or somehow—

Air explodes from my lungs as I slam into Draven's muscular body.

The force of the hit sends me stumbling backward. I flail my arms, trying to regain my balance. Next to me, everyone has screeched to a halt.

"What are you doing?" I snap, staggering upright again. "The other faction is almost . . ."

Trailing off, I stare at what made them all stop.

A massive yellow cloud spreads out before us, swallowing the forest ahead.

41

We stare at that yellow mass that floats in between the tree trunks almost like fine sand. It obscures the view of the forest ahead, turning everything into a murky yellow haze, and it spreads out on both our left and right.

Alistair raises his hand. "I vote for *not* walking into the suspicious yellow cloud."

"Excellent idea," we all agree.

Cocking my head, I glance between the cloud and the trees to our left, where another faction is still drawing closer. "Speaking of ideas, I might have one."

Half a minute later, I'm standing alone in front of that swirling yellow cloud while footsteps echo between the trees on my left. Sunlight, though slightly distorted through the half-transparent ceiling of the pocket reality, filters down through the gaps in the thick green canopy above. It catches in that yellow dust, making the small specks appear brighter. I wonder what it is.

"You!" a furious voice snaps.

I gasp and whip around toward the source of the voice.

The entire White Faction stalks out of the woods. Anger now mixes with the excitement on their faces as they advance on me. Or at least on five of their faces. The sixth person only looks frightened.

"You *broke* Oleander," the leader growls.

The words catch me off guard, and I flinch at how unexpectedly hard they hit. My gaze darts to the tall and muscular man on the right. Oleander Darkmane moves with his teammates when they approach, but he keeps another person between him and me, and his red-and-blue eyes are filled with fear as he watches me.

I swallow against a sudden overwhelming feeling of guilt. I did break him. I changed him with my magic, and now I can't change him back.

At the thought, a sudden craving, a hunger, stirs inside me. And a small voice whispers there in the darkness. *But the pleasure . . . Remember how good it felt? Do it again.*

Blocking out the disturbing thoughts, I shift my gaze back to the team leader while taking a step back. "Look—"

"No," he snaps. "Shut up. Oleander was a crowd favorite." He casts a glance up at the sky. "I hope they're watching, because now we're going to make you pay for what you did to him."

I raise my hands and take another step back. "You don't need to do this."

They continue advancing on me, malice glittering in their eyes.

"Need?" the leader says with a vicious smirk. "No, we don't need to. But we want to."

My heart patters nervously as I continue retreating, keeping my hands up, while they stalk toward me.

A blond woman on the left narrows her eyes at me. "Where's the rest of your faction?"

"Oh." I take another step back, passing right next to a thick tree trunk. "They're over there, setting up an ambush."

The entire White Faction stops dead in their tracks. Blinking, they stare at me in shock.

"What?" the leader blurts out. "What do you—"

A massive storm wind slams into them from the side. The force of it is so strong, and it catches them so completely off guard, that they only manage to cry out in panic before they're sent flying right into that swirling yellow cloud next to them.

Since I'm standing so close, I'm also in the blast range, but the thick tree I was passing takes the brunt of the hit. Branches rattle and leaves flutter down as the winds crash into the tree. I dig my heels into the ground, staying firmly behind cover.

Then the wind dies down.

A moment later, loud thuds echo through the forest as the White Faction lands somewhere inside the yellow haze.

Straightening, I peek out from behind the tree to find my friends strolling back out of the bushes they were hiding behind.

From inside the cloud, cries of alarm and panic start to rise.

"Where are we?"

"Why are you blue?"

"I can't find my hands!"

"I think my hair is on fire!"

"I can't find my hair!"

I flash my friends a satisfied grin. "Well, that should keep them busy for a while."

Lyra laughs and elbows Galen in the side. He shakes his head but smiles as well. Next to him, Alistair casts a dubious look at the mass of yellow.

"Yeah, except now the cloud is moving," he points out.

Turning my head, I find that the cloud has indeed started to swirl violently, shifting it away from us and moving it more to the sides. I lift my forearm and hold it over my nose and mouth as those countless yellow specks begin spreading dangerously.

While taking a step away from the spreading cloud, Alistair shifts his gaze to Draven and arches an eyebrow. "Couldn't have gone for more of a precision blast?"

Draven gives him a sidelong glance. "Loud and messy."

Alistair snorts.

"Enough yapping," Isera interrupts. "We've bought a head start. Let's use it."

Leaping into action, we spin around and take off in the other direction.

Not the one that the White Faction came from, in case they left some traps or other nasty surprises. That yellow cloud is rippling and swirling after Draven's blast of wind, but we keep a safe distance from the edge while running around it instead. The panicked yells and incoherent mumblings of the White Faction quickly fade as we cover more ground.

But the farther in we get, the thicker the woods become.

Above us, the leaves stop rustling and the canopy grows so thick that the distorted sunlight can barely pierce it. Those curtains of purple moss hang unmoving like death shrouds from the twisted branches, and not a single bird or insect can be heard.

I pull at the collar of my fighting leathers. It feels as if the air isn't moving at all in here.

While wiping sweat from my temple, I scan the area around me.

Alarm shoots up my spine.

I whip my head around, but when my gaze lands fully on the space between two trees, the looming shadow I thought I saw is no longer there. My heart beats furiously in my chest, and I draw in a deep breath to calm myself. I'm just jumpy from that encounter with those strange beings in bronze breastplates.

We continue deeper into the forest.

Those pale blue mushrooms that grow on the tree trunks look unnaturally bright in the gloomy forest, which seems to darken with every step. And the air is getting thicker. I pull at the collar of my clothes again. Why is it getting so freaking hot?

A dark shadow streaks past through the woods.

I snap my gaze toward it.

But yet again, I can't see anything.

My heart pounds. I give my head a firm shake. Mabona's tits, pull yourself together.

"Uhm," Lyra says from a little to my left. "Not to be an alarmist or anything, but is anyone else seeing things?"

We all whip around to stare at her as we blurt out, "Yes!"

Surprise and relief crashes through our group like waves as we glance at one another. Apparently, we were all starting to hallucinate things. But just like me, no one else dared to say anything.

"We should probably get out of here," Galen says, glancing suspiciously at the pink flowers and yellow lichen and pale blue mushrooms that seem to be getting more numerous. "There's so little . . . air."

"Yes," I gasp out.

My heart is still slamming against my ribs, and the air seems to press in on me from all sides. It's so warm and stifling that I can barely breathe. I pull at the collar of my leathers again. Goddess above, I want to take them off.

We pick up speed, trying to get past this section of the woods faster. The yellow cloud is no longer visible next to us, and I'm not sure when we lost sight of it. It's getting increasingly difficult to keep my wits about me. To think at all.

Something is wrong.

The thought echoes through my skull. But I can barely concentrate.

"I'm not actually a descendant of the Seelie Queen," Isera blurts out. "I just made that up."

I snap my gaze to her, my mouth dropping open.

She stops dead in her tracks, staring down at her chest with wide eyes, as if she can't believe the words actually came out of her own mouth. We all stop as well, blinking at her in shock.

But apparently, she isn't the only one who suddenly gets the urge to spill her closely guarded secrets, because Galen blurts out, "I don't know how to trust myself anymore. After I found out the truth about Draven, I don't trust my own instincts anymore."

"I don't actually want to be alone," Alistair says, his eyes as wide and stunned as the rest of us. "I'm just terrified that people will hurt me again."

"I'm worried that I might be a villain." The words are out of my mouth before I can stop them. It's as if every safeguard in my mind is suddenly gone, and my mouth is just blurting out my deepest, darkest secret without my consent. "All my life, I've tried so hard to be good.

But if push ever comes to shove, I'm terrified that I might become a villain."

"I'm so tired of never being allowed to have a bad day," Lyra picks up. Her eyes are wild, slightly unfocused, as she gazes out at the rest of us. "People always expect me to be cheerful, and when I have a bad day, everyone makes such a big deal of it. Everyone else gets to have bad days all the time. But not me. Why do I always have to be the one who has to lighten the mood?"

"If we win this war, I don't want to go straight back to the Western Isles and be responsible for everyone again," Draven says, desperation lacing his voice. "I want to just fly off and take *decades* to actually enjoy my freedom first. To actually be free for once in my life."

Deafening silence settles over our group as we just stare at each other. It hangs in the oppressive air above us like a sword. Goddess above, I can't believe that I actually admitted that. That I actually said that out loud. And based on the way everyone is staring at each other, we're all feeling the same thing.

Something is wrong, my mind yet again pushes. Insistent. Urgent.

"Azaroth's flame," Lyra presses out. "I'm so freaking hungry."

I blink in surprise as she grabs a handful of pale blue mushrooms from the tree next to her and stuffs them into her mouth. For a while, we all just watch her stand there and chew and swallow those strange mushrooms. My mind feels thick. Like it's filled with sludge. I know I should be doing something.

Trying to force a breath of clarity through my thick mind, I ask, "Are you sure you should—"

Lyra stands up straight. Everything about her demeanor changes in a heartbeat. Blinking, she gives her head a quick shake. Then she looks down at the mushrooms. Then back up at us.

"You need to eat this," she says. Her voice is suddenly crisp and clear. No trace of confusion or uncertainty. "Now."

"No, thanks," Alistair says, giving the weird mushrooms a dubious glance.

Turning to the nearest tree, Lyra rips off more mushrooms and holds them out to us. Her orange eyes are more serious than I have ever seen as she says, "Trust me."

The sincerity in her tone strikes something deep inside me. And in the others too, apparently, because we all reach out and take some mushrooms. I pop two of them in my mouth, chewing carefully.

They taste surprisingly fresh. Kind of like a minty herb. But it's not as if it's the most delicious thing I've ever eaten.

I swallow, casting a confused glance at Lyra.

Why did she want us to—

The fog clears from my mind.

That thick haze that has been pressing against my brain and making me feel as if I'm suffocating disappears as if blown away by a crisp mountain breeze. I suck in a deep breath, feeling my lungs expand and finally fill with air.

"What the hell just happened?" Alistair asks, looking stunned but fully present at last.

"I'm not sure." Lyra holds up one of the pale blue mushrooms. "But I think these counter the effects of it."

We all glance down at the mushrooms before meeting each other's gazes again. Tense awkwardness suddenly hangs over our group. None of us clearly meant to share what we blurted out a few minutes ago.

"Have I mentioned how much I hate forests?" Alistair mutters, shattering the tense silence. "If I never have to see another forest again in my entire life, it will be too soon."

We all draw in a small collective breath of relief. Perfect. We're just going to pretend we didn't hear those secrets we just shared.

"Speaking of endless forests, how much time have we spent here?" Galen asks, worry crinkling his brow.

Draven tilts his head back, glancing up toward the sky. Except we still can't see the sky. Only a thick canopy of leaves meets us up there.

"I don't know," he replies at last, sounding troubled. "Can anyone remember when we stopped seeing the yellow cloud?"

We exchange a glance, but no one speaks up. Uneasiness slithers through our group like snakes. Whatever was affecting us earlier clearly messed with our senses. We might have lost a lot more time than we think.

And while we've been stumbling around in here, the other two factions have been getting closer to the portal. The only portal that leads out.

If even one person gets to the portal before us, we will be left behind in these poisonous woods in this foreign land with these dangerous fae-like beings.

My heart starts beating faster, and panic crawls up my spine.

How would we ever find our way back to our own world?

42

A renewed sense of urgency pulses through our group. I cast a worried glance from side to side, but the forest is quiet and still around us. Dread curls in my stomach. There is no telling how close the other teams are to the portal.

"We've lost too much time," Draven declares. Authority rolls off his broad shoulders as he meets each of our gazes in turn. "We're going back to our original plan. We split up and move in teams of two."

"If you fly, those guys in bronze armor will spot you and shoot you out of the sky," Galen points out.

"So we stick to the ground for now." He cuts a glare up at the thick canopy. "I can't even get to the sky from here." Tilting his head back down, he meets our gazes again. "But we need to split up to cover more ground. It doesn't matter how far away the rest of us are, as long as one of us makes it through the portal, we'll all be transported back."

He's right, of course, so no one voices any objections.

Draven nods. "Move fast."

And with that, he turns and jerks his chin at me.

We take off through the trees.

Footsteps thud against the ground behind us as Lyra and Alistair dart away in another direction while Isera and Galen pick a third path and do the same.

Stressful tension courses through my veins like liquid lightning. We need to make it to the portal first. Goddess above, we can't get stuck here. Draven and Lyra and Galen would never see the rest of their clan again. Isera would never get her revenge. I would never get *my* revenge. I would never be able to free the Seelie Court and show them all that they were wrong about me. I would never be able to find out the truth about my parents. Everything I have worked for, everything I desperately want for myself, would be lost.

My pulse thunders in my ears as I sprint through the forest next to Draven.

After weeks of Jocasta's grueling training, I'm in better shape now than I was during the Atonement Trials. But I'm still not a soldier. My breath rasps through my throat as Draven and I hurtle through the woods. I focus on putting one foot in front of the other.

We need to get out of this thick part of the forest. We might not be able to fly straight to the center, but we need to get to an area where we can at least fly up through the canopy so that we can check which direction the center is in. That time we spent lost in a daze messed up everything.

Patches of the sky at last start to become visible between the foliage.

Hope surges inside me. Now, we just need to—

"Down!" Draven yells.

Not hesitating a second, I dive forward and throw myself on the ground right before a blast of water crashes through the air above me. Pain pulses through me as my hip connects with a twisted root, but I roll aside as a lightning bolt cracks into the ground right next to me. Water sloshes as the blast hits the trees to my right.

Battle cries split the forest.

I shoot to my feet right as a mass of Unseelie fae in white fighting leathers pours out through the trees and crashes into us like a flood.

Draven sends a storm wind slamming into them, throwing three of them back. Lightning splits the air as one of the remaining players shoots a white bolt straight at Draven's chest. It forces him to throw himself sideways, which gives the leader of the White Faction time to reach him. Steel rings between the trees as Draven yanks out his massive sword right before the guy can slam his own blade into his side.

The third person still on her feet, which is the blond woman who spoke before we ambushed them earlier, shoots another blast of water magic at me right before she leaps at me. I duck and twist, narrowly evading the water, but that makes it impossible to evade *her*.

She crashes into me, sending us both sprawling on the ground.

Air escapes my lungs as she lands on top of me.

I gasp in a breath and yank out my dagger from my thigh holster.

Somewhere above, the other three members Draven blew away with his wind rush out from the trees again. Lightning crackles and wind howls and steel clashes as Draven fights furiously to take down his two opponents before they can become five.

Steel glints above me.

I yank my head to the side right before Blondie can slam her knife down into my eye.

The blade hits the ground with a thud and sinks into the grass right next to my cheek.

"You ruined him!" she snarls at me, and yanks it back out of the ground.

I ram my dagger toward her side. She throws herself sideways, evading the strike but also taking her weight off me. Scrambling to my feet, I yank my dagger up again to block hers as she thrusts it at my ribs.

"Oleander was *mine*!" she growls, her eyes feral as she jabs the knife at me again. "And he was perfect! He was strong and dominant and ruthless." Shoving my blade aside, she swipes at my throat. "And now he's a trembling mess!"

I throw myself backward, evading the swipe to my throat. She launches herself after me, fury crackling across her entire face as she rams her blade at my chest. I yank up my own dagger to block it. With a flick of my wrist, I shove her knife away and slam my fist toward her jaw. But she's moving too fast. Too frantic. Too angry.

"He was perfect!" she screams at me. "And you ruined him! You ruined everything!"

Her words hit me like a punch to the gut.

They strike at something deep. Something that throws me off guard. Because they are so eerily similar to my mother's words. My mother's parting words before I left the Seelie Court. *We loved each other. And you broke us. You ruined us. You ruined everything.*

My stomach turns and my chest tightens.

Because regardless of whether it happened because I created emotions of hatred in my parents' chests or if they simply started resenting me of their own free will, she is right. I did ruin them. No matter what the answer to that new question is, the fact remains that I ruined their lives with my magic.

Pain slices through my skin.

I suck in a hiss and yank my head back. Fumbling, I try desperately to pull my focus back to the present. Blood slides down my skin from a shallow cut across my cheek. I was so thrown by Blondie's words that I've barely been paying attention to her knife.

Slamming my fist into her wrist, I manage to shove her hand away before she can land another hit.

Those awful words still echo inside my skull. *You ruined everything.* Pain still rips at my heart. I can't breathe. Goddess above, I can't breathe.

So I turn to rage instead.

Lifting that massive lid inside me ever so slightly, I breathe in some of the burning rage and searing hatred in there until that fire fills my soul and smothers the pain. I summon my magic.

"I ruined him for you?" I snarl at her, blocking her next strike. "Well, let me do the same to you, then. Then you can be ruined and perfect together again."

Fear flickers in her eyes for a moment.

And I know, deep down, that I could have latched on to that already existing spark. But I don't. Because I *crave* more.

Summoning a separate bone-white flame of fear, I shove it into her chest.

She gasps.

And pleasure floods my body. Pleasure and *power*.

Holding her gaze, I stare into her yellow-and-red eyes as I increase that flame of fear. And I drink in the sight as terror floods those previously so angry eyes of hers. I breathe in. Deeply. Pleasure and utter satisfaction thrum inside my entire soul as I keep watching that fear grow.

It's intoxicating. For someone like me—someone who has never had any power, not even over my own life—the feeling of having this kind of complete and utter power over someone else is so intoxicating that it's making me delirious. I hold her life in my hands. Her mind, her very soul, is mine to shape as I wish. That knowledge, combined with the addictive pleasure that comes from creating emotions out of nothing, sets my whole soul aflame with ravenous hunger.

More. More. More.

I want *more*.

Cutting off my connection to the blond woman before me, I turn toward the rest of the White Faction. Blondie crumples to the ground, shaking hard and throwing her arms over her head to protect herself. Whimpers spill from her lips as she cowers on the ground at my feet.

I ignore her.

My gaze flits across the forest ahead. Two people are lying dead on the ground a short distance to my right. Wind and rain and lightning crackle between the twisted trees, making the purple moss snap in the harsh gusts, as Draven fights the remaining three. One of them is Oleander.

The Unseelie fae shoots a cluster of shadows at Draven. They snake through the air, aiming for Draven's forearm while he is busy parrying a thrust from someone else.

Fury pulses through me.

Summoning another bone-white flame of fear, I slam it into his chest right next to the first one.

Pleasure floods my soul again, and a soft moan slips from my lips. Oh, Goddess. *More.*

Across the grass, Oleander's shadows evaporate before they can trap Draven's arm. Instead, the fae man reaches up and grabs at the leathers above his heart while choking noises come from his throat. Then his eyes roll back in his head and he collapses on the ground. My magic is cut off abruptly.

I study him. His chest doesn't rise and fall. Either he died of a heart attack caused by too much fear, or he died because it's not possible to shove two identical emotions into someone's chest. Regardless, I can't bring myself to care.

Because I want more. I want to feel that sparkling warm pleasure again.

Turning my gaze to the next Unseelie fae, I summon another flame of fear and shove it into her chest. She gasps, dropping her sword and staggering backward.

Pleasure floods me again. Like a sparkling warm hug. Like the softest of clouds. Like a summer wave rolling over my body. Closing my eyes, I draw in a deep breath, relishing in the feeling.

The pleasure is abruptly cut off. I snap my eyes open again. Blinking, I find that Draven has run his sword through the woman's chest, killing her before I could bathe in more of the pleasure.

Grinding my teeth, I focus back on Blondie instead, since no one can kill her before I'm done. Steel clashes and lightning cracks as Draven focuses on his final opponent.

On the ground before my feet, Blondie is still trembling with her arms over her head.

"Look at me," I snap at her. "I want to see your eyes."

Still shaking, she lifts her head to stare up at me. Fear pulses across her face.

"Please," she begs.

I summon my magic and reach toward that flame of fear in her chest again. Then I start to increase it. But no pleasure follows this time. Anger rips at my chest. I want to feel it. But apparently, it only happens when I first create the emotion, before I disengage it.

Decreasing her fear slightly again, I instead summon another emotion. Panic. The harsh yellow flame of panic burns in my mind's eye. I shove it into Blondie's chest.

Pleasure floods my soul again.

She screams. Scrambling back across the ground, she tries to get away. I stalk after her.

"Please," she presses out again. "Please, I'm begging you."

Power washes over me. Oh Goddess, I could get drunk on that power alone. Because I am her goddess now. Her life is mine. I am finally in control. I finally have the power.

I create another emotion. Uncertainty. It floods her features, mixing with the fear and the panic already there, as I shove that beige flame of uncertainty into her chest.

Pleasure once more lights up my soul.

I do it again. And again. And again.

Shock and anger and jealousy and impatience. I shove them into her chest one after the other. Each time, I'm rewarded by that incredible sense of pleasure. It's so all-consuming that I can barely breathe without it. There is nothing else around us. No forest. No ground. Just me and the woman who is now entirely at my mercy.

Summoning a burning black flame of despair, I slam it right into her already crowded chest.

She cries, tears rolling down her cheeks as she begs on her knees before me. "Please. I submit. I surrender. Please. I'm begging you."

Power and pleasure thrum inside me like a storm.

I shove a violet flame of pain into her chest, and she screams. A moan slips from my lips as I drink in the sensation. More. More. More—

"Selena!"

Strong arms wrap around my chest and wrench me away.

The world snaps back into focus around me as I lose the grip on my magic when I'm yanked away from the desperate woman before me.

I stumble as my feet meet the ground once more. Blinking, I try to locate the woman again. But instead, a pair of worried golden eyes lock on me.

"Hey," Draven says, his voice filled with worry as well. His blood-stained hands cup my cheeks gently while he looks me up and down with those searching eyes of his. "Are you okay?"

For a few moments, my mind can't process what is happening. All I can do is stare back at him in stunned silence. My heart beats so loudly in my chest that I can barely hear anything, and my mind spins.

But then, another sound starts making its way through the pounding of my heart.

Screams. Pleas. Desperate begging. Sobbing. Crying. More screaming.

"Please. Mercy. Please, I'm begging you."

Reality hits me like a slap.

Yanking my face out of Draven's hands, I whirl around toward Blondie. The woman is still on the ground. Her body shakes violently, and her eyes are wide and utterly unhinged. She yanks at her hair and slams her hands against the ground in between bursts of crying and screaming and pleading.

I stare at her, horrified.

Draven seems to be able to feel that horror through the mate bond, because he quickly steps over and slits the woman's throat, putting her out of her misery.

I drag in an unsteady breath. Nausea turns in my stomach and horror crawls up my throat as I stare at the now dead woman before me. My head rings as if someone has hit a gigantic bell inside it.

What the hell did I just do?

43

"This is definitely not just a game anymore," Draven says while sheathing his sword down his spine again. "They came at us with the intent to kill."

A jolt shoots through me. Tearing my gaze from the slaughter around us, I glance up at the canopy and the bits of sky visible above as if I can see the mass of spectators watching this from the stands of the arena.

Oh Goddess, people are watching this. In here, with only the twisted trees and colorful plants around us, I've forgotten that the farseer is projecting everything that is happening in here for the Unseelie Court to see. Dread curls around my spine. What must they think of me? How much could they see? I knew what I was doing to the White Faction since I was making the decisions in my mind, but how much of what happened could someone understand from the outside? Could they tell how much I liked it?

Panic flutters through my stomach.

Even now, I can still remember that intoxicating feeling of power and pleasure that utterly consumed me. Still remember how good it felt to be the one in control. To hold someone else's life in my hands. Can still remember that incredible pleasure that comes from creating emotions from nothing. I already want to feel it again.

Jocasta told me that the addictive effect would likely be stronger for me since my magic is stronger, but I didn't realize just *how* intense it would be. I need to figure out how to handle that side effect of my powers. Because what happened here today can never happen again.

"You sure you're okay?" Draven asks, his golden eyes worried as he looks me up and down.

Another pang of dread hits me right in the chest. Oh, Goddess. Draven. He must have been able to feel it through the mate bond. He must have been able to sense the pleasure I felt when I was torturing that woman. How am I supposed to explain all of this to him?

"Yes, no, sorry." I clear my throat and drag in a breath to compose myself while desperately trying to come up with some kind of explanation that won't make me sound like a raging psycho who is one tiny tether away from losing control. "Whatever was happening before we ate those blue mushrooms messed with my head, and I think it's still affecting me a little."

A knot tightens in my stomach. Goddess above, I really hate lying to him. But it's just until I can get a better handle on my powers. Just until I can better manage the side effects. I don't want to be the weak link in our team. I don't want to be a burden and a failure. I don't want to be the one who drags everyone down just because I can't control my own bloody magic. It's absurd. I'm 167 years old, and I still haven't figured my shit out. I need to get a handle on this. Fast.

Because I don't want to be the weak link.

I *refuse* to be the weak link.

So I keep my mouth shut and let Draven believe the lie.

He lets out a low curse under his breath. Then he straightens and flares his wings. "All right, then let's get the hell out of this insane fucking forest."

Blinking in surprise, I glance between him and the small gaps in the trees above. "But the natives . . . They'll see us."

"It's a risk we're going to have to take."

Worry flits through my chest. I don't want to have to face those strange fae-like beings. But Draven is right. We need to find the portal as soon as possible, and flying is the fastest way to do that.

Sliding my dagger back into my thigh holster, I draw in a bracing breath and then give Draven a nod. He lifts me into his arms and then shoots up toward the canopy. My stomach lurches, and I tighten my arms around his neck. I manage to catch his smirk before I squeeze my eyes shut when we reach the treetops.

But Draven maneuvers effortlessly through the gap, and then we're soaring up into the open sky.

Opening my eyes again, I draw in a long breath to refill my lungs. I'm not sure if it's partly my imagination, but the air tastes better up here. It's lighter. More crisp and clear.

I look down while Draven trails to a halt until he's hovering in place.

The forest spreads out like a green carpet below us. But the center of the dome is not where I expected it to be. Whatever was affecting us earlier must have also messed with our sense of direction, because we've ended up farther to the side than I thought we were. Goddess above, we've lost so much time.

Draven must be thinking the same thing, because he simply tightens his arms around me and then flies straight for the center at full speed. My hair whips in the wind as we streak across the sky. I keep my gaze sweeping back and forth over the trees below, searching for both the portal and any signs of those strange beings in bronze armor.

Shouts rise up from the trees.

I suck in a sharp breath between my teeth as Draven suddenly banks hard.

A lightning bolt shoots through the air a second later.

"Fuck," Draven growls.

Storm clouds gather around us right before a torrent of fire shoots through the sky. I gasp, but Draven slams a blast of wind at it, shoving it off course. The flames roar through the open air beside us.

Whipping my head from side to side, I search desperately for our attackers. Alarm crackles through my veins as I spot glinting bronze armor between the trees below.

"Down to the left," I yell over the rushing winds.

Draven snaps his head in that direction, but a block of stone is already hurtling toward us. Yanking his wings in tight, he drops us down in a headlong plummet. The boulder whooshes past above. My stomach lurches as Draven snaps his wings out again, halting our fall. He beats his wings hard, and we shoot through the sky.

Magic crackles behind us.

Draven swerves and rolls to evade a blast of water aimed straight at his wings.

"Arrows!" I scream.

He snaps his wings back in right before a hail of arrows speeds through the air.

My hair whips above my head as we plummet down like a stone. Flaring his wings again, Draven halts our descent but then has to immediately roll us over in the air as flames roar above us.

I tighten my arms around his neck even more as we spin through the air. My pulse pounds in my ears and my stomach rolls as Draven drops us down again and then manages to speed forward a short distance before he has to swerve hard to the side to evade another rain of arrows and a bolt of lightning.

While hanging on to his tense body, I snap my gaze back and forth across the ground, desperately searching for any signs of a glittering blue portal. If we can just make it there, we can—

Something rises up from the ground halfway between us and the edge of the dome. Something *big*.

Fear courses through me as I stare at that dark blot on the sky. From this distance, it's impossible to tell what it is. But it's long and relatively thin compared to its length. Almost like a snake. A massive snake.

"Draven," I blurt out while he dives to escape another torrent of fire. "Draven, something is coming. Behind us."

Spinning us in the air, he evades a block of stone while casting a glance in the direction I indicated. His eyes widen.

"What the fuck is that?" he presses out.

"Watch out!" I scream.

A blast of water slams into us. I gasp as it hits Draven in the back. The sheer force of it sends us tumbling through the sky while water splashes out across Draven's wings. His arms tighten around me as we spin over and over while we tumble toward the treetops.

Then he snaps his wings out again, drops of water bursting out from them like gleaming gemstones.

Lightning crackles through the air. But Draven meets it with a white bolt of his own. A deafening boom echoes across the forest as the two lightning strikes collide. I squeeze my eyes shut against the blinding light that explodes across the treetops.

"We need to find the portal before whatever the hell that is gets here," Draven says as he takes off again.

More lightning and fire and water roar through the air after us.

"Can't you shift into a dragon?" I call over the rushing of wind and crackling of magic. "A real dragon. And just torch that fucking group in bronze armor?"

"No. I tried when we were first attacked. It doesn't work."

A snarl of frustration rips from my lungs. But it makes sense. Hana has pulled this part of the forest into her reality, which is inside the Unseelie Court. That means that the wards that suppress the dragon shifters' ability to shift inside the Unseelie Court now also cover this part of the forest that is inside Hana's pocket reality.

Lightning cleaves the air again.

Draven throws us to the side and rolls through the air. My stomach turns as the ground and the sky switch places over and over again. Gasping in a breath to steady myself, I redouble my efforts to find that goddess-damned portal.

We're getting closer to the center of the dome now.

But so is that massive thing that is flying toward us from behind.

Arrows speed straight for us. But they clatter down on the treetops behind us as we at last start putting some real distance between us and the group in bronze armor on the ground. I snap my gaze back and forth as Draven hurtles across the trees, his wings booming in the air on either side of us.

My mind churns as I scan the woods ahead.

The portal will likely be hidden so that it can't be seen straightaway from above, since Orion knows about Draven's ability to use the half-shift. But it can't be too hidden, because Yster is probably using that portal as his vantage point to look inside the pocket reality and project it to the crowd. So something that shields it from above but leaves the sides open for maximum visibility.

I snap my gaze from side to side, searching desperately for something that fits that description.

A cluster of boulders. No, too limited visibility.

An open meadow. No, too exposed to the sky.

Nothing seems to fit. And there is no hint of glittering blue.

Fire roars through the air behind us where the group of natives is sprinting after us on foot, but we're now too far away to be within reach. At least for another few minutes until they catch up.

I cast a panicked look over my shoulder.

That thing in the sky is drawing closer at an alarming rate.

Flicking my gaze desperately over the forest, I try to spot any hints of glittering blue.

The domed ceiling of the pocket reality reaches its highest point above us. Anticipation pulses through me. This is it. This is the center. The portal has to be here somewhere.

Winds snatch at my hair and clothes as Draven banks, taking us in a wide circle around the very center. I suck in rapid breaths, straining my eyes as I stare through the mass of leaves and twisted tree trunks and hanging moss and lichen-covered boulders. It has to be here. Please, Mabona, it has to be here.

That creature in the air is now speeding toward us.

A strangled noise of utter desperation escapes me as I scan the landscape before us over and over again while Draven flies us back and forth with rapid turns.

Come on, come on, come on, I beg.

Dread sinks into my stomach as a sudden thought hits me.

What if there is no portal.

What if they never actually opened a portal out.

What if we're stranded here.

Lightning cleaves the air.

I gasp as Draven is forced to throw us sideways so abruptly that we almost crash into a massive tree. Whipping my head around, I stare in the direction the group of natives are coming from. They shouldn't have been able to close the distance this quickly on foot.

Another bolt of lightning shoots toward us.

My stomach flips as Draven flies us up higher instead. The lightning bolt cracks into the tree below us, charring the branches. Panic shoots up my spine, because the lightning didn't come from the ground. It came from the thing that has been hunting us through the sky.

"Azaroth's fucking flame," Draven blurts out while diving to dodge a blast of water, followed quickly by a torrent of fire. "What the fuck *is* that?"

Twisting my head, I stare at the thing, at the *creature,* that speeds through the air toward us.

Shock and alarm crash over me like a cold black wave.

It looks like a massive serpent. With wings. And four legs. And a head that is eerily similar to a dragon's head. Saddles have been placed down the spine of its long body, and an entire squad of those tall and muscular beings in bronze armor are seated there. Flames roar through the air as the person at the front shoots another torrent of fire at us.

The creature roars and snaps its jaws.

"Fuck," I breathe.

Draven dives toward the trees.

I suck in a sharp breath, gripping his neck tighter as we speed over the treetops. The creature roars again, and magic crackles through the air as another lightning bolt cracks into a tree right behind us.

"Find the portal," Draven calls as he swerves and dives before shooting back up again.

The winged serpent speeds after us.

I whip my gaze back and forth as trees and glens and clusters of boulders flash past below us. My heart pounds against my ribs.

Something hidden from above but with open areas around it. There has to be something like it.

Unless I'm wrong.

Unless I'm looking for the wrong thing.

Panic seizes my heart, squeezing it tightly.

Water cuts through the air. My stomach flips as Draven snaps his wings in, sending us plummeting, before snapping them back out again. Storm winds roar through the air as he hurls them at the winged serpent and the squad atop it before shooting a blast of lightning.

Deafening booms echo across the woods, and lights flash. They leave black contours dancing before my eyes, and I blink furiously to clear my vision.

My pulse thrums and my heart slams against my ribs.

Draven twists and rolls through the air as fire streams toward us.

The forest and the sky spin in my vision.

A blast of wind crashes into us.

I scream as we're thrown toward the ground before Draven manages to snap his wings out again. The grass trembles right underneath us as he manages to stop us from slamming into it. My stomach twists and churns as he shoots us back up again.

But right before we make it up into the sky, something catches my eye on the other side of the wide glen.

Hope surges inside me.

Something blue. Something blue was glittering there underneath a thick branch.

"It's here!" I scream. "The portal is here!"

Fire roars toward us. Draven shoves a storm wind straight at it, blowing the flames back at our enemies. They scream, and the winged serpent roars in fury as it's forced to shoot upward in the air to evade.

"The other side of the glen!" I yell over the howling winds.

Draven's wings boom around us as he spins in the air toward the portal.

A blast of water slams into us from above.

I gasp, accidentally sucking cold water into my lungs, as the massive blast hits us so hard that we're thrown straight out of the sky.

Draven wraps his wings around us as we crash down into the trees.

44

Grunts of pain rip from Draven's chest as we slam into the mass of branches so hard, they crack and snap underneath us. His wings block out everything around me as we shoot downward from the force of the hit and then slam into the ground.

I gasp as the air is knocked from my lungs. But Draven's body took the brunt of the hit, and his wings protected us from the sharp branches when we fell. He draws in a strained breath as he unfurls his wings.

Sunlight hits me in the face. It streams down through the hole in the canopy that our bodies created, the light slightly distorted from the half-translucent dome above. I blink and struggle to my feet while Draven does the same next to me.

I turn toward him.

And dread explodes in my chest.

"Draven," I gasp out. "Your wings."

His massive black wings are ripped and torn in several places from the crash through the sharp branches. Blood slides down from the edges of some of the jagged tears.

He clenches his jaw. "I'm fine."

A roar comes from above.

We throw ourselves to the side right before a stream of fire pours down through the hole in the canopy. Heat washes over us and embers sail up in the air. The torrent of fire ends when the winged serpent passes out of view and is forced to turn back to reach the hole in the treetops again.

But the attack did its damage.

The forest floor has caught fire.

My mouth dries out as I jump to my feet again and stare at the fire now spreading across the grass.

The winged serpent with the riders on its back streaks past the hole again, and lightning splits the air.

It cracks into the burning grass with an explosion that makes my ears ring. White light flashes before my eyes as our enemies manage another lightning bolt before their mount has passed the edges of the hole again.

Dark storm clouds start gathering around us.

"Selena!" Draven calls over the roaring flames. "You need to take out that winged serpent!"

My heart jerks. Me? How am *I* supposed to take out—

With a snarl, I cut the thought off before I can finish it.

I am *not* the weak link.

I can do this.

While blinking the flickering black afterimages of the lightning strike from my vision, I tilt my head back and summon my magic. Dark clouds spread out between the trees around us as Draven pours more power into his own magic. I drag in shallow breaths of scorching hot air as the fire rages around us.

Then the rain starts.

A furious rainstorm crashes down over the ground as Draven calls on his elements. Wind and rain whip against my face, soaking my hair and running in rivulets down my black fighting leathers. I block it all out as I stare up at that hole in the canopy above, waiting for the winged serpent to return.

The fire on the ground begins to sputter out, smothered by Draven's violent rain.

I summon a massive flame of bone-white fear, keeping it hovering in front of me.

My heart pounds against my ribs.

I can do this.

I am not the weak link.

I can do this.

The winged serpent streaks past the hole.

Fire streams down toward us as the lead rider hurls a massive torrent at us.

But I don't move a single inch, trusting Draven to handle it.

Instead, I call up every ounce of power from the depths of my soul.

And then I *push*.

The winged serpent screams as I shove the massive flame of fear into its chest. Thrashing in the air, it almost bucks its riders from their saddles.

Pleasure crashes over me when my magic hits. But I'm more prepared for it this time. Clenching my teeth, I try to block out that intoxicating feeling while I continue to increase the creature's fear.

The torrent of fire has almost reached us.

Draven slams a storm wind into the flames.

The fire shoots back up toward the creature and its riders above. They scream, clinging to their saddles with panicked grips.

And the winged serpent bolts.

"Run!" I scream at Draven as the winged serpent takes off across the sky, speeding away in terror.

I cut off my magic, knowing that the damage is already done. The creature will keep fleeing in mindless terror until its riders can manage to put it down. That thought sends a pang of unexpected sadness through me, but it was trying to kill us, and we needed it gone.

Draven lurches into motion as well. Our boots slap against the now soaked grass as we sprint toward the glen and the portal that is waiting on the other side. The dark rain clouds evaporate behind us as Draven releases his magic as well.

Exhaustion rolls over me.

Because the creature was so massive, much bigger than just a single person, I had to use an enormous amount of magic to create that fear in its chest.

I drag in shaky breaths, my legs already trembling, as we hurtle across the ground and toward the portal. The Red Faction is still out there. And there is no way in hell that anyone could have missed our battle in the sky earlier, which means that everyone will be heading right toward this location. We need to get to the portal first.

My boots pound against the grass as I focus on putting one foot in front of the other. Draven's ripped wings are still bleeding, and I'm not sure if he can actually use them properly right now. I gasp air into my lungs as we run. Every part of my body feels like it's filled with iron. Goddess above, I need a rest. Just a minute to let my magical energy build back up a little.

But we don't have a minute. So I keep running.

A jolt shoots through me.

There!

Across the grass is a twisted tree with bright green leaves above and purple moss hanging from the branches. And one of those thick branches has grown out and up before twisting and growing straight down again. It forms something that looks almost like a doorway.

And right inside that doorway of branches is another doorway. A glittering blue portal. Beyond it, the sands of the arena are visible.

I can't stop the whimper of relief that erupts from my chest.

We did it. We found the portal. We—

The Unseelie King steps into view on the sand right on the other side of the portal.

Dread sluices through my veins.

"Oh, how hard you've fought to get here," he calls through the glittering blue doorway. His black-and-silver eyes glint, and there is a vicious smirk on his lips as he watches us sprint toward him. "But are you sure you want to actually step through the portal?" He motions up toward the top of the doorway. "Read the inscription above."

My gaze snaps to the thick branch that runs over the top of the portal. There, someone has carved two sentences with a knife.

All magic comes with a price. The cost to use this portal is the death of the one who loves you.

I screech to a halt.

And so does Draven.

Only five paces separate us from the portal now. But neither of us moves.

On the other side, the Unseelie King flashes us a cruel smile. "Told you I would make this game interesting." His gaze locks on me. "If you step through, Draven will die. And if he steps through, you will die." A hint of angry defiance flickers in his eyes for a moment, as if remembering how Isera forced him into this bargain against his will, and he spreads his arms in a taunting challenge. "How is that for a grand finale?"

Dark storm clouds gather around Draven, and lightning crackles down his arms. But all he can do is stand there on the grass, a few strides away from victory, and flex his hand in frustration and anger.

"You son of a bitch," I snarl at the Unseelie King. "You cheated!"

Something lethal flashes in Orion's eyes, and he lowers his arms again. Drawing himself up to his full height, he locks a sharp stare on me, sounding more insulted than angry as he declares, "No, I did not cheat. I simply stacked the deck in my favor."

"It's the same thing! You—"

"And *this* is why I would never risk my court to help you," he snaps with sudden frustration, cutting me off. Flicking his wrist with an agitated motion, he gestures at both me and Draven while contempt flits across his regal face. "*This* is why you will never win against the Icehearts. You still play by the rules. You play fair. And you expect your enemies to play fair too."

His words, and the frustration in them, stun me so much that I just suck in a sharp breath.

"But they don't," Orion Nightbane continues, his voice hard. "Bane and Jessina Iceheart are some of the most ruthless and cunning people this realm has ever seen. And you still believe in being *good*." He practically spits the word at me, full of utter contempt. His eyes are merciless as he stares me down. "Only a villain can take down another villain. And that is something you will never be."

I stare at him, my heart beating so loudly in my chest that I can hear the blood pounding in my ears.

"So stay here," he presses on, flicking his wrist to indicate the forest around us. "Stay in this new world or continent or wherever the hell Hana has put you, and build a new life. Away from them. Start over. Give up your foolish heroic notions of freeing our continent from the Iceheart Dynasty. For if you go to war against them, you go to your doom. And you are not taking my court down with you."

And with that, he stalks away from the portal and out of view.

I stare at the empty sand, the only thing now visible on the other side of the portal. My heart slams against my ribs and my mind spins.

As much as I want to hate Orion right now, I can't seem to be able to. Because in his own twisted way, I get the distinct feeling that he is actually trying to help us. That he truly believes that we will only die needlessly if we go up against the Icehearts, and that this is his way of offering us another life.

"We can't stay here." Draven says the words carefully, as if worried how I might react. "My clan is still out there. They've been in hiding and on the run for months now. I can't abandon them."

I turn toward him. "I know."

Relief flits across his features, and he nods.

Tense silence falls over us as we both turn to stare at the glittering blue doorway. The unspoken question hangs like an executioner's blade in the air between us. We need to get out, but how the hell do we get through the portal?

My mind churns, and I take Draven by the arm and move us a short distance away from the portal. Just in case the Unseelie King is standing right on the other side, where we can't see, listening in.

"The son of a bitch picked the only emotion that I can't manipulate," I growl softly as Draven and I come to a halt on the grass a little farther away. "Otherwise, I could temporarily decrease your love for me while I step through the portal. Then once you have been transported back as well, I could just release my magic again. But love is the only emotion I can't manipulate."

Draven forces out a long breath and rakes his fingers through his hair. It's still wet from the rainstorm, and he flicks the drops away from his hands when he lets them fall back down. "So how do we get through it, then?"

"I don't know. The one who loves you will die? Everyone has at least one person who loves them."

A jolt goes through Draven's body, and he stands up straighter. "Isera."

I frown, trying to figure out what he means. When I do, my frown deepens even more. "It would've been a good loophole, but I don't think Orion actually loves her. He *wants* her, yes. But I don't think he loves her."

"No, I mean, Isera doesn't have anyone who loves her."

The words hit like a stab through my chest. And for a moment, all I can do is stare at him, my mouth slightly open. But he's right. Isera said it herself. She has been alone her entire life. She has no one. No parents. No partner. No friends. Sure, she has me and Alistair now, but neither of us actually knows her well enough to love her.

A pang hits my heart.

Goddess above, how sad is that?

"She will be able to step through the portal without anyone dying," Draven continues. "And that will transport us all back too. We just need to hold the portal until she gets here and then—"

Fire roars across the glen.

Draven throws out a blast of wind, barely managing to redirect the flames before they can hit. Fire crashes into the trees to our left instead, setting the purple hanging moss aflame.

Whipping around, I gasp as a squad in bronze breastplates charges out of the woods.

Panic rips at my chest. The group of natives who were hunting us from the ground before the winged serpent showed up! I had forgotten about them.

Next to me, Draven flares his wings wide.

And then sucks in a hiss.

Oh, fuck. His wings.

Making a snap decision, I spin to face him and grab him by the collar. "My magic. Take it. Take enough to heal your wings."

He jerks back, horror flashing across his face at the suggestion, and then has to throw another massive gust of wind at our enemies to stop the blast of water their leader directed at us.

"Don't argue!" I snarl. "Just take it. We need to hold the portal!"

Hesitation flickers in his eyes for a second. Then he grabs me by the throat and crushes his lips against mine. I gasp as he inhales sharply, pulling my magic with it.

Strength leaves me in a rush as the magic is sucked out of my body.

Draven's wings immediately begin to heal at an incredible pace while he breaks away from me.

"Go!" I yell, shoving him toward the charging squad.

Thankfully, he sprints toward them straightaway and doesn't see the way I stagger sideways from the sudden exhaustion. I had already used up a lot of energy when I lost my mind and created all those emotions in Blondie's chest, and then again when I made the winged serpent flee, and now there isn't much left.

Steel sings into the air as Draven draws his sword while summoning a lightning storm. His wings are now completely healed.

I yank out my dagger as well while calling up what remains of my magic. Creating emotions from nothing takes much more energy than simply manipulating ones that are already there, so I focus on that instead, since it will make my magic last longer.

Dread curls around my spine as I watch Draven charge straight toward those nine people. Just like the squad who rode the winged serpent, only the leader seems to be able to use magic. But the other eight carry bows. How the hell are we supposed to—

The Red Faction bursts through the trees.

Shock pulses across their faces as they take in the scene before them.

The strange beings in bronze armor halt their attacks on Draven and turn to stare as well. For a single second, that moment seems suspended in time.

Then Draven slams a massive storm wind into the bronze-clad squad.

They scream, half of them flying backward and crashing into the people behind. The leader leaps to his feet, a snarl on his face, and throws a torrent of fire back at Draven, who is countering with another blast of wind. The other squad members lurch to their feet and swing their bows toward the Red Faction.

Panicked orders split the air as the team leader yells at the rest of his faction. Two of them summon fire and water to block the hail of arrows while their fastest runner, a woman with golden hair, breaks off from the group. And sprints toward *me*.

A jolt shoots up my spine, and I cast a panicked glance over my shoulder.

Oh shit. She's heading for the portal. And if she makes it through, her entire team will be transported out with her and the pocket reality will collapse. It won't matter if we can hold off against these strange beings in bronze until Isera gets here. If one person from the Red Faction steps through, the portal will disappear, leaving us trapped here with these furious beings forever.

A snarl of fury rips from my lungs as I spin around and sprint back toward the portal, aiming to cut off the woman's path to it before she can reach it. I have to keep her from reaching it.

She snaps her gaze toward me. Anger crackles across her face, and she picks up speed.

Panic pulses through my entire body like lightning strikes as she hurtles across the grass at an impossible speed. I run with everything I have, but she keeps getting closer.

Ten strides from the portal.

Eight.

Six.

Three.

I slam into her from the side.

She gasps as my body connects with hers so forcefully that we both go crashing down on the grass in a tangle of limbs. I yank my arm out from between her body and the ground, and then I stab my blade straight toward her throat.

No time to hesitate. No room for second thoughts. No chances to knock her out or to make her surrender. She needs to die. Right now. Before she can get through the portal.

Panic flashes across her face, and she yanks her head to the side right in time.

A pulse shoots up my entire forearm as my blade slams into the ground instead, sinking deep into the grass. With a growl, I yank it back out. But that buys her enough time to get her knee up in between us.

I suck in a sharp breath as she kicks hard, forcing my body away from hers. The force of it throws me backward. She pushes herself up from the grass and tries to get to her feet, but I launch myself at her again. A cry rips from her throat as I manage to slash my blade across the back of her hand. Drawing her other fist back, she tries to punch me in the face.

But she doesn't summon any magic, which means that running impossibly fast probably is her magical ability.

I duck her punch, twisting my body sideways as I try to get back on top of her. But she kicks her knee out, forcing me back again. While swiping with my dagger, I reach blindly toward her. Grabbing her collar, I yank her body sideways and throw her to the grass. She gasps, panic bursting in her eyes as she hits the ground hard while I roll on top of her.

The portal glitters only a single stride away now.

She reaches for it, stretching out her hand toward the sand on the other side. Her fingers almost brush the glittering blue frame.

I scream.

And ram my blade down through her throat.

Shock pulses across her whole face, and her hand falters.

With that shock and a sudden flood of fear in her eyes, she stares up at me as I yank the blade back out. Blood wells up from the wound, bubbling as she tries to breathe. Only gurgling sounds make it out.

For a few seconds, all I can do is stare down at her as the light dies in her eyes.

Then she goes still, her dead eyes staring up at me unseeing and her fingers one single inch away from the portal.

Warm blood trickles down her throat from the wound and spills over the hand I still have buried in the collar of her red fighting leathers. The feeling of it snaps me out of my stupor, and I yank my hand back.

Flicking warm blood from my fingers, I stagger to my feet while sucking in a shuddering breath.

I have recovered enough strength that I will be able to use my magic to create one emotion. And I need to use that on the squad leader in bronze so that Draven doesn't have to—

My heart . . . stops.

Time seems to slow to a crawl as I stare out at the glen before me.

The rest of the Red Faction are fighting six of those beings in bronze armor across the charred and bloodstained grass. The other two bow-wielding natives have their weapons pointed at Draven.

And Draven . . . Draven's back hits the ground with a thud loud enough to echo across the glen. As if he was high up in the air just a moment ago. Up above him, the leader of the bronze squad is hovering in the air, wind magic rushing around him.

And a massive boulder is speeding straight toward Draven's head. It's big enough that it will crush his entire torso when it hits.

It's not a question of *if*. It's *when*.

Draven, dazed from the hard landing that knocked the back of his head against the ground, will never have time to summon enough wind to push that massive boulder aside. And I can't use my one remaining burst of magic to create fear in the squad leader's chest, because the attack has already been thrown. It won't matter if I break his entire fucking mind with fear. That boulder is still going to crush Draven's skull.

Each fraction of a second seems to span an eternity as I stare at the inevitable end to the life we were just beginning.

Draven is going to die.

He is going to die.

I scream.

And throw everything I have into one last attack created from pure desperation.

An attack against the person I love more than anything.

Against the person who loves me more than anyone.

My magic shoots across the grass.

A massive wildfire of red-violet hatred slams right into Draven's chest.

And our mate bond *shatters*.

45

Blinding pain slices through my chest as I throw myself through the portal. In a heartbeat, the twisted forest and desperate battle are replaced by warm sand and a cheering crowd. I whip my head around, panic still crackling inside me like lightning.

Isera and Galen have appeared on the arena floor a short distance to my left. Both of them were running, and they stumble and almost fall over when the ground underneath them changes abruptly. A few steps away, Lyra and Alistair have materialized. They're standing back-to-back, crouched into fight stances. Fire burns in Alistair's palm, and sunlight glints off the sword that Lyra is holding. They jerk back and blink in shock at the new environment around them.

Then my gaze finally finds *him*.

Draven.

He's lying on his back on the sand, staring up at the bright blue sky above the arena.

Alive.

The air escapes my lungs in a long whoosh.

He's *alive*. No crushed skull. No shattered torso. No broken bones and rivers of blood. He was transported back before the boulder could hit.

The glittering blue portal winks out beside me, closing the door to the strange forest and the lethal beings in bronze armor and the Red Faction who is still trapped in there with them. A few steps from it, Orion Nightbane gapes at us. His eyes are wide with shock, and his mouth has dropped open as he stares between the six of us.

Isera, having recovered from the abrupt end to her sprint, saunters toward him with a smirk on her face. "So, about that bargain, pretty boy."

With a smile on his face, Galen rushes over to Draven and grabs his forearm, pulling him up from the ground.

"You did it!" Lyra calls, her face beaming as she bounces over to them as well.

Even Alistair smiles as he follows her.

I just stand there, staring at Draven as he brushes sand off his armor.

For a second, the moment seems suspended in time.

Then Draven turns to me.

And my heart stops.

Burning hatred flares up in his eyes as his gaze meets mine.

Pain stabs at my heart, and I suck in a sharp breath. My mind is still trying to block out everything. The pain. The memories. The knowledge of what I've done. The implications of it. A fragile shell of glass is keeping it all back, and I'm afraid that if I breathe too deeply, it's going to shatter and let everything in.

With my mind still a numb void, I summon my magic and reach out toward Draven. Another sharp jab of pain spears through my heart as my magic connects with a red-violet wildfire of hatred. A wildfire that has my distinctive feel to it. Hatred that *my* magic created.

My heart pounds in my ears as I try to smother that flame.

It decreases steadily at first, going from a wildfire down to a flame. But once it reaches a steadily burning flame, I can't lower it any further.

A whimper of pain and desperation slips from my lips as I throw everything I have into trying to extinguish that flame of hatred.

But it doesn't work.

No matter what I do, I can't remove it.

Because I created it.

And now, it's permanent.

A sob rips from deep within my chest, and I have to press my hand against my mouth to stop the sound of it.

All around me, the crowd is cheering and yelling in the stands. The noise of it vibrates through the packed arena like the roar of a storm. Across the sand, Isera is smirking and gloating about our victory to the Unseelie King while Lyra is laughing and telling Galen and Draven about the fight that she and Alistair were in when they were transported back.

All of them are smiling.

None of them know what I had to do to buy us this victory. What I had to sacrifice to save Draven's life.

Because he is alive. The boulder did not crush his skull. And the portal did not kill him. Because he no longer loves me.

He hates me now.

And I can't take it back.

Those fragile glass walls keeping everything at bay start to crack.

I suck in a gasp. Whirling around, I sprint toward the nearest exit. No one stops me. And I'm glad for it. Because if someone had, I think I might have killed them.

My vision starts to blur as I stumble through gloomy hallways until I finally reach a door. Shouldering it open, I stagger out into the deserted street outside the arena.

The sun is shining brightly down from a clear blue sky, and colorful spring flowers bloom in the ceramic pots that dot the windowsills on the other side of the street. Leaves rustle in a tree farther down the road as a gentle breeze sweeps between the houses. Across the city, the rush of the waterfalls fills the air along with birds that chirp merrily as they fly past. Water glitters in the canals. And behind me, the entire arena is still cheering.

Everyone is happy.

Everything is beautiful and bright and colorful.

But all I can see in my mind is a pair of golden eyes staring at me with utter hatred.

The glass walls shatter.

A raw scream tears from my throat.

My knees buckle, and I crash down on the cobblestone street. Slamming my hands into the stones before me, I scream and scream and scream until all I can taste is blood and iron and pain.

Agony carves through my chest like a burning blade. It feels as if someone has ripped my heart out. As if someone has ripped *him* out.

I can still feel Draven faintly through what remains of my mate bond, but his side of it has shattered. It leaves me feeling unmoored. Untethered. As if I'm drifting, lost and alone, through a vast, empty universe.

Tears stream down my face as I slam my hands against the ground and scream my lungs out. Scream for broken bonds and lost love and shattered futures.

I had him. I finally had him. The missing piece of my soul. The other half of my heart. He was all mine. And now, I've lost him.

No. No, I haven't lost him. I have *destroyed* him. I have ruined him. I have taken his love for me and smothered it underneath a mountain of hatred. A burning flame of hatred that doesn't belong to him. A flame of hatred that I can't remove. Even now, even here on this deserted street, I can feel it faintly through my side of the mate bond. Like a death blow echoing from far away.

I've ruined him.

I've ruined us.

Gasping, I try to drag air into my lungs. But I can't breathe. A massive weight is crushing my chest and I can't fucking breathe. Tears stream down my cheeks. I can't move. I can't think. Pain slashes through the torn remains of my bleeding heart.

And all around me, the world keeps on going. The sun keeps on shining. The birds keep on singing.

Rage and pain and utter devastation crash through my broken soul.

Why is the sun still shining? Why are the birds still singing? How can the world possibly keep on going after this?

But the answer comes from deep within the poisonous pits of my darkened mind.

Because I have only done what I always do.

I have ruined everything.

46

Every glance is a knife through my heart. A burst of agony that constricts my lungs and blinds my vision for a second. It's utter torture, and I don't know how I'm going to survive walking the final distance out of the Unseelie Court. Let alone fight the rest of this war together with him. Not when he looks at me like that.

Hatred burns in Draven's eyes as he cuts me a glare. He's angry about everything now. Everything I do is somehow wrong. Everything I say is stupid or annoying or unnecessary. That burning hatred in his chest tries its best to find fault in everything. In my very existence.

And on top of those hate-filled glances are the looks of worry and heartbreak I get from the rest of our friends. They know now. They know what I was forced to do in order to save Draven's life. They pity me now. I can see it in their eyes. And I hate it, because now, just looking at *them* also reminds me of *him*.

"This is never going to work," Orion Nightbane complains, not for the first time, as he strides along with us toward the rippling wards up ahead.

"Your confidence in us is inspiring," Alistair drawls, strolling along next to Lyra.

Isera cuts the Unseelie King a mocking glance. "I didn't take you for a coward."

Lightning flashes in his eyes as he locks them on her. "I am not a coward. I am a realist. Do you actually think you can take down the Iceheart Dynasty? There are six of you, for God's sake!"

"There are seven of us." A smirk tugs on Isera's lips. "Don't forget. You're one of us now."

"Malachi's balls, don't fucking remind me." But he looks grudgingly impressed rather than angry as he shoots her a glare back. "However, my point still stands. We can never win a war against the entire Iceheart Dynasty. Apart from me, you have no allies."

"We have my entire clan," Draven says.

The sound of his voice sends a stab through my chest. Clenching my jaw, I force myself to keep my eyes on the wards ahead instead of glancing at him.

"You have one dragon clan," Orion says, exasperation lacing his words. "They have *eight*."

"So we steal some of them back," Lyra offers in a cheerful voice. "Recruit them to our side."

"Don't forget the dryads," I add. "If we can convince them to help us, they could—"

"No one asked you," Draven growls.

And by instinct, I turn to look at him. Hatred burns in his eyes as he glares at me.

Pain stabs through my chest, and an iron fist grips my heart, squeezing it hard. I try to draw in a breath, but my lungs don't seem to work.

I snap my gaze back to the plains outside as we come to a halt right before the wards.

But I can't get that image of Draven's hate-filled eyes out of my mind. Agony claws at my soul, and I have to suppress a raw sob.

Goddess please, there has to be some way to reverse this. Some way to remove that flame of hatred from Draven's chest. This can't possibly be it. This can't be how we end. Not after everything we have gone through, everything we have done, to get to this point.

To my left, Orion whispers something under his breath and then flicks his wrist in the direction of the wards. "After you."

Isera strides through without hesitation, which makes Orion narrow his eyes at her. The rest of us follow.

Warm winds tasting of spring sweep across the plains before us, making the grass rustle, as we at long last step out through the wards and leave the Unseelie Court behind.

The moment we're through, Draven cuts me another look burning with hatred.

For a few seconds, we just stare at each other. Then black smoke explodes across the grasslands as he abruptly shifts into a dragon and simply flies off without a second look back.

My very soul crumbles.

I drag in an unsteady breath as a wave of world-ending sorrow crashes over me.

"I hope this was worth it," Orion says.

A few strides away, Galen casts me a hesitant glance. "I hope so too."

We gained a lot by going to the Unseelie Court. An outside observer would consider this mission a success.

Haldia saved me from dying from magical ice flames and fixed my severed spine. I found a competent teacher who trained me physically and who taught me how to use my magic in ways that I hadn't even known were possible. I learned that my parents might not actually resent me after all. And we gained an incredibly powerful ally.

I'm stronger and more powerful than I have ever been in my entire life, and Orion and his entire Unseelie Court are now going to help us take down the Iceheart Dynasty.

And all it cost me was . . . *everything*.

Another wave of agony and heartbreak and despair crushes me so thoroughly underneath the sheer force of it that I feel like I'm drowning in a cold black ocean. Lost and desperately clawing against the oppressive water and violent waves without a single hope of ever reaching the surface.

I can't breathe.

Draven's wings boom through the air as he flies off, leaving me behind.

My shattered heart aches with agony, and the pressure on my chest is so massive that I can't get a single breath down.

I can't breathe. Oh, Goddess above, I can't breathe.

And in that moment, I know, without a shadow of a doubt, that this pain is going to kill me. I'm going to die if I have to feel this utter agony for even one more second.

Desperate, I reach for something else.

For the first time in my life, I shatter the walls around that massive pit of burning anger and searing hatred that I have kept buried deep inside me all this time. A gaping pit of world-ending fury roars inside me.

I breathe it in.

I breathe it all in, letting it consume me.

Rage and hatred surge up, filling the void in my heart and burning through my whole soul. It sears through me with a violent, raging fury until it drowns out the sorrow and agony and pain that is trying to strangle me. Burns through me until all I can feel is that furious rage and hatred. Until my whole soul has been consumed by it.

And something inside me *snaps*.

He said that only a villain can take down another villain.

Fine. Then that is exactly what I will become.

Acknowledgments

I know. You probably threw the book across the room just now, didn't you? I wouldn't be surprised. I really am sorry about leaving you on such a brutal cliffhanger. Or am I?? Muahaha.

No, but in all seriousness: Thank you for continuing to accompany Selena on her journey. I hope you enjoyed this book and that you're excited to see Selena enter her villain era in the next one. Thank you for reading!

I would also like to once again thank the absolutely amazing Sarah McCabe for seeing the potential in these books and for opening up a wonderful new future for this series. I'm beyond happy that Flame and Thorns has found a new home at Simon & Schuster, and I'm so thrilled that this series is part of the launch of Scarlett Press.

To the entire wonderful team at Simon & Schuster: Justin Chanda, Anne Zafian, Anum Shafqat, Bridget Madsen, Tatyana Rosalia, Michael McCartney, Chrissy Noh, Caitlin Sweeny, Lisa Quach, Bezi Yohannes, Perla Gil, Remi Moon, Amelia Johnson, Elizabeth Huang, Trey Glickman, Shannon Pender, James Akinaka, Kayah Hodge, Amy Lavigne, Julia Ashley Romero, Lisa Moraleda, Nicole Russo, Antonella Colon, Christina Pecorale and her sales team, and Michelle Leo and her education/library team. Thank you for all your amazing work.

A massive thank-you to K. D. Guthauser at Story Wrappers for the gorgeous cover. I'm so happy and grateful that the new cover for *Court of Lies and Deceit* is illustrated by you.

I would also like to thank all the incredible artists that I have worked with this past year. Keksi (@keksi_bunny), Nophie (@nophie.blue), Ellie (@mageonduty), Mien (@mien.artist), Shayndl (@shayndl_art), Anya (@dannetannet), Nicole (@coleyart), Mori Di (@moridi_art), Eva (@evaroseart), Mary (@marybegletsova), and everyone else I've commissioned: Thank you for all the beautiful character art you have drawn. Seeing Selena and Draven come to life in your art has been a dream. Thank you also to Michal Kváč for the stunning landscape art. I have loved watching the world of Flame and Thorns come alive in your illustrations.

Another huge thank-you to Laura Horowitz, who has brought the Flame and Thorns series to life in a different medium: audio. Thank you for your incredible audiobook narration. I'm so lucky that I get to work with you.

To Jennifer Davis, Laura Bartlett, and Faye Ostryzniuk, who have been there to cheer me on since the very beginning of my author career. Thank you for your kindness. I'm so glad we connected all those years ago. Talking to you always brightens my day.

I would also like to say a massive thank-you to Kaila (@kaila.books) and Miranda (@probablyoffreading) for your early and continuous support of the Flame and Thorns series. I am eternally grateful for the way you have shared your love for these books with other readers. Thank you for your enthusiasm, creativity, and for your incredible kindness.

And of course, an immense thank-you to the most important people in my life: my family and loved ones. To my mom, my dad, and my amazing brother Mark, thank you for always believing in me. Thank you for all the love and support. I truly don't know what I would do without you. Thank you also to my wonderful cousin Karolina. I treasure our friendship immensely. And thank you to Lasse, Ann, and Martina for all your kindness as well. I'm so glad I have all of you. Spending time with you always brings me joy.

I am also very fortunate to have friends both close by and from all around the world. My friends, thank you for everything you've shared with me. Thank you for the laughs, the tears, the deep discussions, and the unforgettable memories. My life is a lot richer with you in it.

Lastly, I would once again like to thank you, the reader, for following Selena on this adventure. Your support means the world.

BONUS SCENE

Do you want to know what Draven was thinking during that final chapter? Scan the QR code to download the exclusive bonus scene and read the ending from Draven's perspective.